The CIRCLE of SODOM

A Gripping New Thriller

By

Pat Mullan

© 2001, 2002 by Pat Mullan. All rights reserved.

No part of this book may be reproduced, stored in a retrieval system, or transmitted by any means, electronic, mechanical, photocopying, recording, or otherwise, without written permission from the author.

ISBN: 0-7596-9222-X

Library of Congress Control Number: 2002090472

This book is printed on acid free paper.

Printed in the United States of America
Bloomington, IN

1stBooks - rev. 03/12/02

THE CIRCLE OF SODOM
A Gripping New Thriller

"A compelling read from start to finish…"
Susan Kelly, New York Literary Agent.

"Congratulations! A huge accomplishment…"
Gary Goss, author of 'Hitler's Daughter' (Lyle Stuart, Inc.)

"You've written a cracking thriller that's a thumping good read…I think it's exceptionally well done…"
Fiona Stewart, Editorial Director, UK.

"Just finished…heartfelt congratulations…*The Circle of Sodom* is a world class thriller that will establish you in the forefront of today's writers…you are riding a winner!"
Doug Nagan, Essex, Connecticut, USA.

"An entertaining read…it certainly has pace!"
Robert Jocelyn, Connemara, Ireland.

...and comments from readers of the work in progress:

April 30, 2001...this novel has the potential to be a great book.

May 1, 2001...first of all, the storyline concept is a good one, easy to market with good potential sale quality. Plot's great. Characters are very good. Dialogue is really quite good. ***This is a marketable novel...as to the possiblility of transforming it into a movie? Yes, definitely.***

May 1, 2001...You give the impression of an encyclopedic knowledge of history. The little details sprinkled throughout added a lot of flavor. Your general writing style is solid.

May 1,2001...I imagine this as a very interesting thriller. I was very impressed with the author's knowledge of medical procedures in the Korean section. He either has some experience in this field or has done some excellent research. That part struck me as very professional.

May 7, 2001...This is very good, and reads well. It kept my attention and left me wanting to know what happens in the big picture. I was impressed by your restraint: you dealt with topics - torture and homosexuality - that could, if taken too far, make the reader uncomfortable; but you were able to keep the anxiety up without crossing the line into an area in which I would no longer have enjoyed the story. As it is, you have created a believable and sympathetic character. **I would like to read more of this**

story, as you will inevitably introduce more well-crafted characters and plot twists!

May 8, 2001…WOA! I wish that's all I could say…WOA! is really the only word I need. This is GREAT! I am really amazed that this hasn't been published yet. It does NOT read like five or six Bond books, but so what if it did? Ian Fleming wrote a great story and had people turning pages. **This was extremely gripping and at times I wanted to turn away, but couldn't. Great work!**

May 11, 2001…this makes me want to read more…this sets up so many questions **the full novel itself must be quite a ride!**

May 11, 2001…this is the most compelling excerpt I've read…the bar scene is dynamic…it sizzles with underlying suspense…the reader is "there," hearing, smelling, seeing, tasting…feeling they're being set up for something…same with the apartment/torture/death scene…

That's it. This is the stuff of blockbusters…on the page and on the screen.

BY PAT MULLAN

Childhood Hills
The Circle of Sodom

and coming very soon

Who Killed Hammarskjold?

For Jean

ACKNOWLEDGEMENT

I always cringe when I watch the Hollywood Academy Awards and see Oscar winners who thank everyone from their parents to their God. Authors sometimes do likewise. So I have had a long debate with myself about whether or not to include these words of thanks. As you can see, I have both won and lost.

Firstly, I am indebted to my wife, Jean; my first reader, my editor, my book doctor. An English teacher, she critiqued and edited my work page by page. I am also indebted to Fiona Stewart for her critique, her insight, and her experience. For factual verification: Dr. Henry Watson advised on medical references, Annemarie Whilton and Maureen Holmes checked the accuracy of some US locations, Todd Whilton added his Gloucester sailing expertise; and an unknown limousine driver in New York informed me that the elevated West Side Highway no longer existed. Others who wrote to me spurred me on: Robert Jocelyn, Susan Kelly, Doug Nagan, to name just a few.

Writing is a solitary occupation that depends on fortitude and endurance. Many of my friends and colleagues read the work in progress and offered encouragement. You all have my gratitude.

Finally, I owe a debt to Gary Goss and Dan Masterson, two writers who gave me the confidence to continue.

Pat Mullan,
Connemara, Ireland,
July, 2001.

1975

PROLOGUE

53rd MASH
Korea
1975

*T*he wind almost blew MacDara off his feet as he grabbed the outer door to the Emergency Room and forced his body inside. A chaotic sight unfolded before his eyes. The two emergency tables were occupied - one by a Korean youth with a deeply lacerated forearm which Captain Green was carefully suturing, the other by a thirtyish looking G.I. who was getting his leg wrapped in a soggy plaster cast. The floor was untidy with bundles of clothing and the disposal cans overflowed with bloody swabs and bandages. Strips of surgical tape were suspended in readiness from I.V. stands and the sides of the medication cabinets. Two G.I.'s lay on litters inside the door waiting their turn for treatment. An I.V. ran into the smaller, semiconscious, one and the other gripped his abdomen and moaned constantly. Medics were rushing back and forth with syringes, plasma and intravenous bottles.

MacDara edged his way through and moved down the corridor to check in with Sergeant Taylor. People who were *injured and people who thought they might be lined the pale green walls of the corridor and sat or slouched on the sagging black vinyl couches in the outpatient area. Empty litters were stacked near the door for return to the ambulances. An old mamasan wailed unceasingly on the floor beside a bedraggled little girl.*

"That's all that's left of her six kids. She lost the other five. Drowned when the monsoon washed their hooch away. She and the little one wouldn't be alive now if they hadn't been rescued by a couple of guys from the 1st Cav."

The information came from Sergeant Taylor. But neither had time to dwell on this tragedy. Another victim had just been brought down from the hill. A young GI - unconscious, no sign of life. MacDara cut the uniform from his body and attached an electrocardiogram machine. There was no response. The needle traced a wobbly and uncertain line on the paper. As MacDara adjusted the IV, Captain Green called for a scalpel and rib-spreader. He made an incision near the heart. There was little blood from the wound. Then he inserted the device to separate the ribs, and exposed the circular pink mass of the heart. MacDara handed him the adrenalin. He injected it into the heart. There was no response. On Captain Green's orders, MacDara cut the electric lead from an old ECG machine, stripped the wire bare at the ends and inserted the plug in the nearest outlet. The captain applied it directly to the heart. The flesh was scorched and the body bounced on the litter each time the electricity was applied. After thirty minutes, they gave up.

MacDara was half asleep, holding his head in his hands at the desk in the outpatient area, when the telephone startled him. It was Major Whiteside.

"Who's the senior medic on duty tonight?"

"I am, Sir".

"OK, MacDara. Get someone to take over for you and meet me in ten minutes at the side entrance to the operating theater."

Major Whiteside was the Commanding Officer of the 53rd MASH and the senior surgeon on the hospital staff. He sounded unusually strained. MacDara didn't stop to inform Sergeant Taylor. Instead he left through the rear door of the emergency room and bounded the couple of hundred yards to the barracks. He knew his friend Murph was in bed at this time of the night.

"Murph, Murph, wake up! Major Whiteside needs you in Emergency now!"

"Shit! Goddam! You were in danger of getting brained" Murph yelled as he sat bolt upright in his bunk. Everybody knew that Murphy Armstrong slept with his shovel under his pillow at night. Murph suffered from an irrational fear of a North Korean invasion.

Murph pulled on his white uniform, grabbed a parka and followed MacDara across the compound to the side entrance to the Emergency Room. Once inside, MacDara briefed Murph on the night's events and casualties, turned over the outpatient desk to him and headed for the operating theater.

Major Whiteside arrived two minutes later and directed MacDara to prepare a private examination room and equip it with a sigmoidoscopy kit. When it was ready, the Major returned with a tall, saturnine colonel. Few words were exchanged. The colonel undressed and Major Whiteside placed him on his side on the bed and asked him to tuck his knees up in a fetal position. What followed was almost a dreamlike sequence in MacDara's mind. As Major Whiteside guided MacDara in providing light, he entered the colonel's rectum with a proctoscope and retrieved several long rubbery cartilage-like objects. They looked like nothing MacDara had ever seen before. The procedure ended as quickly as it had commenced. The colonel dressed and left. MacDara disposed of the objects. Major Whiteside cautioned total confidentiality.

The CIRCLE of SODOM
A Gripping New Thriller

1999

Pat Mullan

The CIRCLE of SODOM
A Gripping New Thriller

ONE

New York, Monday, October 4, 1999

Owen MacDara looked out of the 34th window of GMA headquarters on Park Avenue. It was four pm on the first Monday in October. The sky was gray and threatened snow. Dozens of yellow taxis moved north and south on Park Avenue in a relentless stream. He wondered if he'd be lucky enough to get one at six o'clock.

Global Management Associates was MacDara's alter ego. After the army and Korea he had headed for New York and started in investment banking. In two short years he was a Vice President. One year later he had a plum European assignment, working out of London with relationship management responsibility for high net worth clients in EMEA (Europe, Middle East and Africa). Within a few years MacDara was a Senior Vice President back at headquarters in New York with general management responsibility. And impatient again. He hadn't made that million yet. And he didn't like working for others.

In 1984 he had resigned from the investment bank and formed Global Management Associates with two close

Pat Mullan

colleagues. GMA's mission capitalized on their skills. They provided financial advice to high net worth individuals and management consultation to financial institutions. Their territory was the world. Ten years later GMA had become the advisors of first choice for the global financial marketplace. And MacDara had prospered. He had long ago made that first million.

MacDara was lucky. A cab had just pulled up outside his building to discharge a fare and he beat three other people to the taxi's door. This was New York. Social Darwinism at work. Every month Owen and three close friends, Murphy Armstrong, Angelo Russo and Iggy Cummins, met at their favorite watering hole, Costelloes. They had first met while serving in the army in Korea and had worked at staying in touch over the years. The cab dropped Owen at the corner of 50th Street and Second Avenue. He walked the rest of the way. Costelloes entrance almost begged for anonymity. Carved out of an old brownstone building, the faded canvas awning covered a dimly lit entrance set well in from the street.

Connolly will be standing at the bar as I enter, mused MacDara to himself. He was glad of the certainties of this life.

Murphy Armstrong, in these moments of self-doubt, thought he should see a doctor, a psychiatrist. But the thought passed as quickly as it arrived. He didn't really think that he was going crazy. But he did think that he was being followed. It's just that he never saw anyone following him. Not even their shadow.

It had all started three weeks ago. He had left his law office on the west side of Manhattan and had decided to walk across to Second Avenue. He'd stayed late, preparing a brief on a discrimination case. A triple header. His client was a young black woman. She had a strong case of discrimination on three counts: being a woman, being black and being the victim of sexual harassment. He was on his way to Costelloes, the pub where he met every month with a few of his old army buddies from Korea. It was a Monday night. Few stayed late in town on a

The CIRCLE of SODOM
A Gripping New Thriller

Monday and most Manhattanites were home, glued to the TV, recovering from their weekend in the Big Apple. So the streets were relatively deserted. He'd been walking alone on 53rd between Sixth and Seventh Avenues, heading east, when he felt the sensation for the first time. The hairs standing on the back of his neck, a palpable sense of danger. He stopped and looked back, scanning the street in both directions. There was no one there, but the feeling wouldn't go away. He kept walking and gradually forgot about it, convincing himself that he was overtired, overworked. His body reacting to stress. He didn't really believe that but he wanted to give himself a scientific explanation. A rational man's way out.. He didn't tell his buddies about his fears when he met them at Costelloes. He was afraid that they would ridicule him.

Tonight Murphy Armstrong had that same sensation of being followed. He was walking towards the west side, to the Peppermint Stick, to pick up Iggy Cummins before they headed for their regular session. He stopped at Fifth and 52nd to buy a pretzel from a street vendor. There wasn't a soul in sight, but he still felt that he was being watched. He walked briskly, frequently looking over his shoulder and seeing nothing.

Ernie Miller was good. The best. He imagined he should have been an American Indian or maybe an Indian scout. Kit Carson - that's it. One hundred and fifty years too late. He'd just have to settle for tracking his prey in the urban jungle instead of the lone prairie. Wearing a black leather jacket, black jeans, with a black ski cap covering his white-blonde hair, Miller had merged into the black railings outside the 21 Club. He could see Armstrong stop about a hundred yards away on the other side of the street, look over his shoulder, hesitate and then move on again.

He'd been following Murphy Armstrong periodically for about two weeks. Picking his spot. Somewhere sleazy, where random crime was the norm, the accepted. Don't make it

Pat Mullan

obvious. That's what he'd been told. An accident, a mugging, a random act of violence. And take them out separately. It doesn't matter who goes first, MacDara or Armstrong. But whoever goes first must go in a way that doesn't alert the other. A tall order. But Miller thought he had figured out how to fill it. Four of these old army buddies met to 'shoot the shit' every so often. Armstrong and his three buddies. MacDara, Cummins and Russo. Miller had no interest in Cummins or Russo. But he did have an interest in Cummins's place of business. A topless bar, the Peppermint Stick. Real sleaze, just the place for mayhem and an 'innocent victim'. Murphy Armstrong dropped in there occasionally to chat with Cummins, have a beer and ogle the tits and asses. Miller decided to fill his first order at the Peppermint Stick.

Iggy Cummins saw the police burst through the swinging doors of the Peppermint Stick. He had called them. No way he'd tackle the big lug harassing his topless barmaids. The big guy'd been here a couple of times before. Iggy remembered. The last time was only a week ago. He had come in with another guy. They had stayed an hour. It had been a slow night and the two of them took the booth in the corner. Two things - no, three - stood out to make Iggy Cummins remember. They had tipped Sally a fifty dollar bill. Nobody did that. And they had gotten into a heated argument just before they had left. And, oh yeah, the third thing. Who could forget a six foot three male with white-blonde hair? Almost an albino.

Iggy nodded to the two cops. One was a regular beat guy. He knew him. He pointed out the albino at the end of the bar who, by this time, was lying halfway across the bar flicking his thumb backwards and forwards over Sue's left nipple.

The albino moved fast. Grabbing Sue by the hair, he yanked her around the corner of the bar and held her in front of him with his left arm. His right hand now held a gun. He squeezed four shots in rapid succession at the two cops. People dived for cover

The CIRCLE of SODOM
A Gripping New Thriller

in all directions amid the crash of bar stools and glasses. Two of the shots felled the first cop. He lay face down in a pool of beer mingling with his own blood. The second cop, gun drawn, dived for cover. A shot got Murph right between the eyes as he sat at the bar. Murph never knew what hit him. He was dead before he reached the floor.

The albino backed out onto 7th Avenue, dragged Sue to an illegally parked white Corvette on the corner of 52nd Street and headed west. Sirens blared on 8th Avenue as the surviving cop called in for backup and an ambulance for his partner.

Iggy Cummins pushed himself up from the body of his friend Murph and looked around at the devastation in the Peppermint Stick.

Sue cringed on the passenger seat of the Corvette as the albino ran all the red lights west towards Tenth Avenue. Her lip was bleeding where he had punched her when she'd resisted. He'd used a scarf to tie her hands together behind her back.

At the 54th Street exit ramp from the West Side Highway, the car skidded. The head-on collision with the parked Peterbilt truck finished off the Corvette. Miraculously, the albino emerged, dragging Sue behind him. He then hijacked a taxi that had just left the highway, taking the driver and the male passenger hostage. He ordered the taxi driver to head south towards the Lincoln Tunnel. But they never made it. Four blocks ahead, a police car had set up an emergency road block. The taxi driver deliberately rammed the police car. Two police officers, guns drawn, moved towards the taxi. But the albino, armed now with a pump-action shotgun, killed them both. Angry at the taxi driver, the albino summarily executed him. The passenger lay unconscious in the rear of the taxi, wounded in the melee.

The albino, still dragging Sue, hijacked another car and continued south. He didn't get far. The police had cordoned off the entire west side from the fifties to the lower twenties. The

Pat Mullan

final shootout at the next police roadblock on 34th Street left one more policeman and the albino dead. The driver of the second hijacked car was lucky. He escaped with scrapes and bruises. Sue was not so lucky. They found her in the back seat. Her throat had been cut.

Angelo Russo looked at his watch. It was six pm. Time to wrap it up. He put the finishing touches to the design rendering for a new building in Connecticut. Maybe he'd take another tour of the site this weekend, he thought. Russo Associates had beaten three of the top New York interior design firms in landing the half million dollar project. Taking one hundred and sixty-five thousand square feet of office space from a building shell to move-in condition in just four months was the most aggressive job he'd ever done. And he'd paid a heavy price. For the past eight weeks he'd seen his kids only on weekends. Even then they had to compete with an armful of drawings. Angelo locked his briefcase in the credenza in his office. He wouldn't need it tonight. Leaning across the round table that served as a desk and conference table, he grabbed the phone.

"Jimmy, Angelo here. Tell the guys I'm running a half hour late…Yeah, yeah, I know…I'll be there, swear to God…Jimmy, I swear I'll be there - just tell the guys."

As he hung up the phone, Angelo thought that sometimes Jimmy Connolly sounded just like his mother.

He took a last look around before leaving. The main office space of Russo Associates housed twenty workstations. He had an open-plan corner office. There was one conference room, which was in continual demand. Still, this was good space; Madison Avenue was a step up from the drafty four-dollar-a-square-foot-loft in Tribeca that had been their home for their first five years. Russo Associates was seven years old. They had grown from three associates and one small contract to twelve full-time architects and up to ten temporary professionals at

The CIRCLE of SODOM
A Gripping New Thriller

project peaks. Total project revenue this year should reach three million dollars.

Jimmy Connolly hung up the phone and pushed through the throng at Costelloes bar into the small cosy dining room at the rear. As he approached the round corner table, David, his Chinese chef, materialized from the kitchen in a haze of smoke that floated upwards from a juicy sizzling steak he held in both hands. The succulent sauce permeated the dining room. The sizzler was Costelloes special. Jimmy reached the table just as David placed the sizzler in front of Owen MacDara.

"Owen, that was Angelo on the phone. Running a half hour late, as usual. That means an hour, you know! By the way, where's the rest of your gang?"

"I don't know. Iggy and Murph should have been here before me. It's not like them to be late", said Owen, as he cut eagerly into the sizzler. He was already on his second Bud and didn't seem concerned.

Jimmy Connolly owned Costelloes. He stood at least six feet four, with wide shoulders and a shock of prematurely silver-gray hair. His lionine head housed a broad Irish countenance tinged with ready humor and a mischievous and knowing glint in the eyes.

Out of the corner of his eye, Jimmy could see his bartender, Mike, heading directly towards him. Mike looked agitated.

"Jimmy, it's the phone again. Iggy Cummins. You better take it. Sounds serious."

Jimmy grabbed the extension in the dining room.

"Connolly here."

"Jimmy, it's real bad! We've had a shooting here". The stress in Iggy Cummins's voice vibrated over the phone. "Murph's dead! If Owen and Angelo are there, break this to them and tell them I'll be there some time - after I give a statement to the cops. Tell them not to leave. I'll be there - no matter how late."

Pat Mullan

The phone went dead. Iggy Cummins had hung up without giving Jimmy a chance to utter a word.

Jimmy opened the bottle of Mondavi Cabernet and placed it in the center of the table between Owen and Angelo. He did not pour any into their glasses as he usually did. Not tonight. Angelo had just arrived and he and Owen were still stunned by the news of Murph's killing. It was Connolly who broke the silence.

"Murph was the greatest guy; wouldn't hurt a fly."

"I know. There's no justice in this world. The Good die young."

"Yeah! The bastard who did this will probably get away. Even if they catch him, some clever lawyer will get him off on a technicality."

"It sucks! It just sucks! When are we going to get tough on crime in this country? When are going to make them pay?"

"Oh, we make them pay alright. In prisons like country clubs. Exercise equipment, television, counseling."

"You're right! They come out fat and sassy after doing three out of twenty. Time off for good behavior. No wonder they have no compunction about blowing your head off. If they're caught they do three years in a country club."

MacDara just sat there. He wasn't even tuned in to this exchange between Connolly and Russo. He still hadn't said much when Cummins finally joined them, at about ten thirty. It was going to be a long night. Costelloes didn't close till four am. This was turning into an Irish wake. An Irish wake for a black brother.

Iggy Cummins went back over the shootout between the albino and the cops in the Peppermint Stick. He blamed himself for Murph's death.

"If only I hadn't called the cops."

"But you had no choice," said Owen, "You couldn't let your girls be molested and you wouldn't have been able to tackle the guy yourself."

The CIRCLE of SODOM
A Gripping New Thriller

"How were you to know he had a gun?" said Angelo.

Jimmy Connolly had just arrived at the table again in time to overhear the conversation.

"They're right, Iggy. It wasn't your fault. You can't blame yourself."

But Iggy Cummins was inconsolable. He was on his second Paddy's and getting more maudlin by the minute. *Yes*, thought Connolly, *this will be a long night.*

The late night news persisted on the TV in Costelloes dining room. Sandwiched between a mass murder in a McDonalds in Texas and a murder suicide in upstate New York, the killing in the Peppermint Stick was just one more ingredient in the nightly diet. MacDara was watching in a trance when the regular news was interrupted: the Chairman of the Joint Chiefs of Staff had died from a heart attack he had suffered earlier in the week while on a visit to the Guantanamo Bay base in Cuba. The President announced his replacement, a four-star Pentagon strategist, unknown to the public: General Zachary Walker.

"My God, I know that face!"

The tall saturnine colonel that they had treated in secrecy in Korea was now General Zachary Walker, Chairman of the Joint Chiefs of Staff. MacDara remembered that Murph had been there the night that Major Whiteside had operated on the colonel.

A crazy thought entered his head. Was that why Murph was dead?

Pat Mullan

TWO

...three months previously...

Washington, D.C., Friday, July 9, 1999

General Zachary Walker lived alone. The army was his life. He had little time for anything else. Unless it was his God. At least, that's what he told himself.

Zachary Walker was tired, mentally tired. He took off his jacket and shoes, loosened his tie and collapsed on the bed. His feet protruded from the end, so he tucked up his knees and turned over on his side. It was eleven o'clock at night and he had just arrived home. It was not unusual for him to work a twelve-to-fifteen-hour day. He was in good health: physically fit, with great reserves of energy.

Today had been more stressful than any day he had spent in a long time. It started with a strategy meeting at six thirty am with the President and the National Security Council. His boss was away on a field trip and he was the acting chief. The meeting was called to assist the President in the latest crisis in Europe. This time it was Chechnya. The Russians were at war

The CIRCLE of SODOM
A Gripping New Thriller

with them again. They wanted vengeance for terrorist bombings in Moscow that they blamed on the Chechen rebels. Russia's new president, Vladimir Putin, intended to put his name on the political map. America was opposed to Putin's plans but, as usual, were caught between the need to encourage Russia towards democracy and the need to take a stand against them on this.

The President's approach was thorough. He sought the best advice, political and otherwise, and then made his decision. Often that decision was at odds with the position on Capitol Hill. It seemed that as one crisis ended in Europe another commenced. First Bosnia, then Kosova, now Chechnya. He remembered Bosnia. That war had lumbered from one disaster to another and seemed intractable. The Serbs were advancing again. The President's close political allies on Capitol Hill were advising him to aggressively arm the Bosnians. The Russians were threatening to intervene on the side of the Serbs. NATO was impotent. Their western-European allies refused to act decisively on the matter. The President was damned if he did and damned if he didn't. He couldn't avoid assessing the political damage from either course of action. It was a no-win situation. But the President's primary motivation was a desire to end the fighting and bring the parties to the negotiating table. Even if it took force of arms to achieve it.

Zachary Walker had returned to his office at nine am, when the past came back to haunt him in the voice of Major Henry Whiteside. The major was in Washington and wanted to see him. He agreed. As he hung up the phone he could feel his heart beating faster, and a wave of the claustrophobia he had suffered as a youth swept over him. The past was closing in on him again. He got up from his desk, shut his office door, turned the key in it and then lay down on the black leather couch in the conference area of his office. The claustrophobia made the walls and ceiling move towards him, giving him that old feeling of suffocation he hadn't experienced since his teens. After years of self-control and success, he felt frightened and vulnerable. Like a little boy. He could hear his Mamma's voice: "Zachary! Oh, Zachary!" She always used Zachary, never Zach, when she was angry or stern.

> *Isobel Shepard Walker was a God-fearing woman. He had respected her but he had also feared her. She was a domineering woman who broached no straying from the rules; her rules. She was always in the front pew in church on Sundays. She always sang louder than anyone else.*
>
> *The Shepards and Walkers were Scots-Irish. Their ancestors had left Ulster in the 1750s and worked their way south from Pennsylvania through the Cumberland Gap towards Appalachia. By the 1780s they had established a homestead in the Waxhaws, a settlement northwest of Charleston, South Carolina. When General Walker's great-grandfather, Zachary (all the first born males in the Walker clan were named Zachary) was born in 1832, the family was firmly established in the hardware and livery business in Charleston.*
>
> *The family had a long history of military service. An ancestor had fought with Andrew Jackson in his campaigns against the Creek Indians in 1814. Zachary's great-grandfather had distinguished himself at Appomatox during the Civil War. And his father was one of the first to step ashore on Omaha Beach during the Normandy landings in World War Two.*
>
> *"Zachary! Oh, Zachary!" His mother was waiting for him at the door. He was late coming home from school again, but he couldn't tell her the reason why. He couldn't tell her about Charlie Pettigrew. Mrs. Pettigrew and his mother were very good friends. And Charlie was one of his mother's favorites. Zachary was nine years old and he didn't know what to do.*

The CIRCLE of SODOM
A Gripping New Thriller

He remembered the day it started. He was only seven years old. His mother had been visiting Mrs. Pettigrew one afternoon. Charlie was fifteen years old then. Mrs. Pettigrew told Charlie to take little Zach out to see their new spaniel puppy. The puppy was liver and white, only three months old and very playful. It was lying on its back and Charlie was petting its stomach when he leant over and asked Zach to put his hand in his pocket. He said he had a surprise for him. Zach innocently reached into Charlie Pettigrew's pocket. He still remembered his shock. There was no bottom in Charlie's pocket and Zach's small hand circled Charlie's erect penis. It felt warm and strong. He was both fascinated and repelled. And he knew he was doing something very, very wrong. Charlie warned him not to tell his mother, but Zach would have been too frightened to tell such a thing to his mother. That's when it all began.

The memories flooded in and out with the waves of claustrophobia. And as the claustrophobia subsided, so did the memories. His anxiety attack gradually left him and his breathing became regular again. He used to worry that his past would come to destroy him. The years had passed. He had become more powerful. He had stopped worrying. Until now. He resolved to call Senator Sam. But first things first. His military sense of order took over. He would meet Major Whiteside.

His mind went back to that night in the 53rd MASH in Korea, nearly twenty-five years ago. Only two people knew about that: Major Whiteside and Senator Sam. Henry Whiteside had agreed to keep the matter in absolute confidence for ever. As the years passed, General Walker had accepted that commitment from Henry Whiteside with confidence. Senator Sam also knew. But, as the senator had said, the future of

America and the world was bigger than that and no event in the past should be permitted to undermine the future. The senator would know what to do. *But, first*, he thought, *I must meet Henry Whiteside.*

The Colombia Cafe was just another coffee shop. The customers were mostly blue collar, maybe sixty percent black. It was safe from the Washington elite.

Major Whiteside was already savoring a large mug of their special coffee when General Walker arrived. He had changed quickly into civvies - jeans and a turtleneck - before setting out. He'd had no trouble eluding his security detail.

The men appraised each other and came to the same conclusion. The years had been kind to them.

"Henry, You're looking good."

"I was just about to say the same about you. I never felt better. I think Ruth is enjoying my retirement more than me. And Kate has grown up into a beautiful young lady, Zach."

There was a wistful look in Zachary Walker's eyes as Henry Whiteside moved his newspaper and made room for him to slide into the booth directly opposite. He nodded to the hovering waitress who filled a large mug of coffee, placed it in front of him, reached into the pocket of her apron and handed him three small plastic containers of cream. She left the menu and moved on.

"Thank you for taking time to see me," Henry said.

"I had to come. What's this all about?"

"I'm not sure where to begin. After I took early retirement, Ruth and I went back to our home in Gloucester. I still do some work for the V.A. But I always had an urge to write. And I wanted to put down my memories and experiences; my view of the times and events I lived through."

"But, what can I contribute?"

"I thought you might help. Shed some light. I've always kept my word, but I'm troubled. Seems as though nobody wants

The CIRCLE of SODOM
A Gripping New Thriller

me to write my memoirs. And that bothers me. What is everyone worried about?"

"What do you mean? Who's trying to stop you?"

"Well, nobody's trying to stop me. It's not as obvious as that, But everybody's clammed up. Washington is not at home to me. Most of my old colleagues are either too busy or have previous engagements. People know I'm on my way before I arrive. They've been warned in advance not to talk with me."

"Are you sure you're not imagining these things? You know, you have a lot of time on your hands. Most of us still don't"

"No, I'm sure of it. It's nothing innocent like that. I can smell it. I believe I've turned over a rock and found something rotten under it."

"Henry, that's very melodramatic! What are you saying?"

"OK. I'll put my cards on the table. Let me tell you what I think. Then maybe you'll help."

Henry Whiteside discussed his research. His memoirs covered his entire military career, but focused on Korea, Vietnam and the aftermath. Being a physician he was also viscerally interested in the nation's well-being. And he felt that America's conduct had been damaging to the nation's health. The failure to treat the returned Vietnam veterans with the same respect as the vets of other wars was a symptom of the malaise at the heart of the nation. He wanted to explore that malaise in his memoirs. He had ended his military career disillusioned over the handling of the Vietnam war. Now he was interested in the healing process of those involved, those in command in that conflict. The more research he did, the more people who were willing to talk with him, the more convinced he became that America's soul was sick. Some of these former colleagues were prescribing a treatment for the illness that would surely kill the patient.

"And you know what that treatment will do for us, Zachary? It will destroy our democracy. It will destroy our freedom. And we will enter the millennium under the dictatorship of the Right. We will sow the seeds of our own Armageddon.."

"But your fears are all based on very circumstantial things. You might be magnifying this out of all proportion. Remember, this democracy is very resilient. It can bend without snapping."

"I only wish that I believed you. But I don't. And I'm concerned about you. You're in a most powerful position in this nation. You're vulnerable. I must be frank. I have to talk about it."

"Well, Henry, if you must. But, I assure you, I am not vulnerable."

"I went to see Rev. Andrew Magee. I know all about the Followers. I know about your involvement. Korea was not just the result of your own personal weakness, Zachary. It was a ritual, wasn't it? Who else knows about that?.

"Nobody knows," lied Zachary Walker. "Those things are behind me. They're between me and my God. And I want it kept that way."

"There are powerful forces at work in this country. And many are operating with the authority of God. I cannot walk away from that. I fully intend to keep my pledge of confidence to you. But I want a quid pro quo. I want people to talk with me. You can make that happen, Zachary"

It was three o'clock when General Zachary Walker got back to his office. He picked up the phone and dialed Senator Sumner Hardy's private number. "Sam, I need to see you. It's important."

Uijongbu, Korea, Monday, July 12, 1999

Hajin Kim sat cross-legged on the satin cushion at the head of the table in Madame Ahn's mission house in Uijongbu, thirty miles north of Seoul. He was the guest of honor, as befitted the head of the Church of Solitude and Contemplation, whose followers were commonly referred to as the Costies. They had become as familiar on the streets of western cities as the Hare Krishnas, whose members wore saffron robes and shaved heads. The Costies wore charcoal-gray Nehru-style uniforms adorned only with a large wooden cross hanging from their necks on a heavy leather thong.

Madame Ahn sat to his right and her chief minister, Chae, sat on his left. About twenty-five Church members were dining at the four tables in the central room of the mission house. The meal was the traditional Korean one of bulgogi and kimchi, strips of sauteed beef over rice and fermented vegetables. Small cups held makli, the favorite Korean rice drink. Custom dictated that one should not sip the makli; when raised to the lips one must drink it all. Of course, an attentive host will refill the cup immediately. The wise drank sparingly. Makli was extremely potent.

The meal had just commenced when the telephone was brought to Hajin Kim. He had instructed Seoul that he was always available to his people. He insisted on an open line policy, if not an open door policy. None of this was very practical, given his schedule and itinerary. His life was usually booked six months in advance.

"How can I serve you?" said Hajin Kim in his customary greeting as he picked up the telephone. It was General Zachary Walker. It had been at least two or three years since they had spoken. The general wanted to know if Kim had been contacted by Major Whiteside. The major was writing his memoirs and was unearthing matters that would be best left forgotten. Kim assured General Walker that he had not had any contact from the major.

As he hung up the phone, he felt a sense of wonder. All those years ago. And yet only yesterday. But I've travelled so far, he thought. And so has the general. That was another time. Another place. He remembered again.

Pat Mullan

Hajin Kim's early religious experience had been Buddhism. His early life in Pusan had been marked by frequent attendance at Buddhist retreats, many of them in total silence. At twelve, he rejected his disciplinarian father and his father's religion, too. Until his teens he rejected all religion. Then, one day in Seoul, he was handed some literature by a Follower and invited to spend an hour in a coffee shop. The hour stretched into late evening and Kim joined the Followers.

A new convert to the Followers was always assigned to a mentor for the first year. Hajin Kim's mentor was the person who had recruited him, the Follower with whom he had spent that seminal day in the coffee shop in Seoul: an American, named Charlie Pettigrew.

He had been a member for a year when he met Zachary Walker.

Tennessee, Wednesday, July 21, 1999

High up in the mountains of Tennessee, Lt. Colonel George McNab, Christian, hero and highly decorated Vietnam veteran, was preparing for Armageddon. McNab headed one of the most visible militant elements of the new puritan politics that was spreading throughout the United States. His Millennium Covenant Community was located in two hundred acres. At least fifty homes and a community and worship center were completed. Numerous other houses were under construction. There was no information on how many people comprised the Millennium Covenant.

McNab and his Millennium Covenanters were armed with every conceivable weapon. They had made solemn pledges to defend each other and their neighbors against the ravages of Armageddon, which they believed to be imminent.

Colonel McNab was out of breath when he led the column of twenty-seven men and three women into the compound. *Not as indestructible as I used to be*, he thought. At fifty-six, Colonel McNab was trim, lean and agile. His erect bearing made him seem taller that his five foot eleven inches. He still looked in better shape than the rest. They had just returned from a three-day field trip and the colonel had put them through a gruelling survival game in the local hills. Their jungle fatigues were crumpled and muddy and they slumped under the weight of their backpacks and bed rolls. Disciplinarian to the end, the colonel called them to attention and into formation in the center of the compound. It was ten am. He took their salute and then dismissed them, saying that there would be a debriefing at thirteen hundred hours in the community center.

The official US Government car was parked outside the colonel's front door. He'd recognize that car anywhere. Senator Sumner (Sam) Hardy. *Must be important. Sam wouldn't come here otherwise*, thought McNab.

"George, it's so good to see you", said Senator Sam as the colonel entered, "they told me you'd be back any minute so I hung around for awhile."

"You're a little out of your way, aren't you, Sam?", said the colonel.

"I had to be in Nashville on Senate business and I needed to see you on a matter most urgent. I couldn't entrust this to anyone else, George," he said.

The Senator was a neat man, about five ten, and impeccably tailored. He was the junior senator from Virginia, an attorney and expert on international law by profession. The years he'd spent in London with the family law firm had left him with an unflinching loyalty to English tailoring. His suits were Saville Row and his shirts were tailor-made for him by Turnbull and Asser on Jermyn Street. The Senator could trace his ancestry back to the Daughters of the American Revolution.

He was only forty-five, but his black hair was already thinning on top. His father and grandfather had been bald in their fifties. The senator expected the same. His complexion was sallow and he wore his favorite rimless glasses. People often remarked how much he looked like the photos of Woodrow Wilson. The senator always assured them that there was no family relationship. Not that he didn't have presidential aspirations. Senator Sumner Hardy had more than aspirations. He fully intended to be President by the year two thousand. He had been the independent presidential candidate of the religious right the last time. Testing the water. Building a support base around the country. Biding his time. In the meantime, the senator was building an apparatus of power, one that would make him President, if not by popular election, then by dictate of the chosen, by pledge of the Covenanters.

In 1992, his religious right supporters had won control of a number of school boards in California and Oregon. By the mid-nineties, they were being swept into office throughout the USA. In many cases, they softened their hard-right religious beliefs to gain popular electoral support from the disaffected. They had formed a solid fifth column of power across the nation. Just waiting for Senator Sam to summon them to the defense of the righteous.

"OK, Sam. Let me have it," said the colonel, still in his command voice.

"Zach's got a serious problem. I'll be frank with you. He's being blackmailed over an indiscretion in his past," lied the Senator.

"Hell, if the skeletons came out of any of our closets, we'd all be blackmailed. What's the big deal?"

"It's more than that. The blackmailer is a former colleague. A retired major. He's threatening to expose Zach in some memoirs he says he's writing. Zach's just one heart attack away from becoming Chairman of the Joint Chiefs. And we need him there."

Colonel MacNab needed no further explanation. The present Chairman of the Joint Chiefs had had three heart attacks in two years. Zachary Walker was, in effect, the acting Chairman. "A traitor. A renegade. If there's anything in this world I can't stand, it's one of us turning against our own. A court martial. Then a firing squad. That's what we'd do with a traitor if we were at war."

"But we are at war, George."

"You're damn right, Sam. We sure are."

"Will you take care of it, George?" It was an order, not a question.

"With pleasure. Just give me the details. Our colleague will be returning from London in a couple of week's time. His people are experts at this."

"Make sure they confiscate any memoirs. I want them brought directly to me. No one else sees them. Is that understood, George?"

"You bet. It's as good as done, Sam."

THREE

Gloucester, Massachusetts, Tuesday, August 3, 1999

    Henry Whiteside had been riding at anchor for about two hours. He had shut off *The Whitey's* engine three miles out, far enough away from everything to give him the sense of solitude that he desired. It was a good morning for writing. The memories flowed freely and fully. He wrote with a gold Cross felt-tip, a present from Ruth on his last birthday. Holding it beween his finger and thumb made her seem close to him. The tip was smooth and the ink flowed easily. He liked that too. That was important to him. There seemed to be a synergy between the pen, his hand, his head and the page; a symbiosis that brought forth words and images and memories. Memories and images that weren't consciously there until he made that vital connection: pen to paper. That's why he didn't use the word processor when he was writing. That symbiosis didn't happen when he was sitting at the keyboard. Fingers to keys to Intel chip didn't work. Only pen to paper.

    He had paused in his writing to contemplate all of this and to watch a lone gull that was circling overhead. The water lapped gently against the side of his boat, a soothing sound. Time to get

The CIRCLE of SODOM
A Gripping New Thriller

up and stretch, do some exercise. Maybe go for a swim. It was late morning and getting warmer. He scanned the horizon on all sides, spotting a vessel heading out to sea. His briefcase lay open on the deck beside him, so he gathered up all the pages of his manuscript, put them inside and closed the briefcase. Just in case a page blew away, although there wasn't even a breeze. He didn't lock the briefcase. He'd probably do another hour's writing after his swim and then head home. Ruth would be expecting him. He took off his clothes, stacked them neatly and put on his swim trunks. Then, watching another boat approach in the distance, he started his ten minutes of stretching exercises.

Sal stood looking at the boat's wake, just a ripple disappearing on the smooth surface of the water as soon as it appeared. He was not a seaman. In fact, he'd never learned to swim. Even though the seas were calm and the skies unthreatening he did not feel as safe as he did on dry land. But it was very beautiful out here, in the morning. They were heading out to sea just off the coast of Gloucester, Massachusetts. Nick, his 'brother' on this assignment, had practically grown up at sea. His immigrant forbears had been Greek sponge fishermen in Tarpon Springs in Florida. Nick was at the wheel and they were beginning to pick up speed. They would soon rendezvous with their target.

Their engine had begun to splutter and cut out as they neared the boat anchored up ahead. They could see a man on the deck. He appeared to be doing exercises. The spluttering engine had attracted his attention. He had stopped exercising and was standing watching them approach. As they drew abreast, the engine gave its last splutter and died. Nick appeared to try, in vain, to force life back into it. Finally, he gave up. They were near enough to the other boat to read its name. *The Whitey*. The man was still on deck. Nick yelled across: "We're in trouble. Do you have ship-to-shore?"

The man yelled back: "Yes, I do. Do you need to use it?"

Nick shouted back that he did. The man agreed he should come aboard, and Nick crossed over in the dingy, leaving Sal behind.

Sal watched expectantly as he saw Nick climb on board the other boat. The man met him and they exchanged greetings and words of introduction, it seemed. Nick thrust out his right hand. They shook hands. Then the man turned around, leading the way towards the cabin. That was when it happened. Nick grabbed him from the rear. The man resisted strongly, but Nick had already stuck the disposable syringe deep into his muscular tissue. Within seconds he had lost consciousness and collapsed at Nick's feet.

Nick was barely out of breath from his brief struggle. The old man was fit. But not fit enough for Nick, who prided himself on a Jack LaLanne-built body. Without the drugs the old man still wouldn't have stood a chance. He found a life jacket, put it on the old guy, inflated it and then dumped him overboard alongside the dingy. Looking around, he spotted the briefcase, opened it, took the manuscript and left the briefcase lying open on the deck. Back in the dingy he started up the outboard motor, grabbed the old man and towed him back to the boat, where Sal was waiting to help him winch the old guy aboard. Their engine sparked to life and they sailed back the way they had come, leaving *The Whitey* sitting alone at anchor.

The Senate Office Building, Washington, D.C., Thursday, August 5, 1999

Senator Sam Hardy thought that the Federal Express dispatch rider could easily have been cast as Brando in *The Young Lions*. Blond, Aryan looking, standing at attention outside his office door, motorcycle helmet tucked firmly between his ribcage and his left arm, he waited, motionless, for Nora to return with the senator's signature of receipt. Senator

The CIRCLE of SODOM
A Gripping New Thriller

Sam accepted the square package emblazoned with the Federal Express delivery logos. Easily recognizable. He didn't examine it; just signed for it. He received important papers periodically in this manner. Nothing unusual. Unless you considered Brando. That was unusual.

It was only after Brando had left that the senator picked up the package to open it. He tried to read who had sent it but the words were blurred. He ripped the package open and extracted another one, wrapped in plain brown paper, on which were hand printed the words: *Totally Confidential* and *For your Eyes Only*, in black indelible ink. It was the size of legal paper and the thickness of at least a couple of hundred pages. He made this assessment as he cut through the binding with his scissors.

It was a manuscript, handwritten on yellow legal paper. The cover page answered his unspoken question. It stated simply: *Reminiscences of an Army Physician, by Henry Whiteside.*

"Sam, burning the midnight oil again?," quipped Senator Holden, as he poked his head around the door of Hardy's office on his way out of the building.

"It goes with the territory, Jess. I'm speaking on this latest appropriations bill in a couple of days. It's the most screwed up proposal I've ever seen. I think the Democrats are living on another planet!," replied Hardy.

"Well, you won't get any argument out of me on that one. Gotta go. See you tomorrow. Get outta here before midnight, at least!"

"Thanks, Jess. I know you have my welfare in mind. God! What did I just say? Welfare! Another piece of madness. Night, Jess."

But Senator Jess Holden was already well out of hearing. Which suited Sam Hardy just fine. He got up and turned the key in his office door, sat down behind his desk and selected a small desk key from the bunch that he always kept in his pocket. Reaching down to the right, he opened the large filing drawer in his desk and retrieved a plain brown paper package. He took out the contents and started to read at page one hundred and fifty-three of the reminiscences of Major Henry Whiteside. This was the third night that he'd stayed late to read Whiteside's memoirs and he planned to finish them tonight.

Two hours later, he had finished the manuscript. He tilted his chair into a reclining position and leant back, staring at the ceiling, a favorite position when he was in deep thought. He started to review what he had just read. Especially the chapter and notes that dealt with the surgical procedure Henry Whiteside had performed on Zachary Walker.

Major Whiteside dwelt, at some length, on his personal dilemma. He had promised General Walker confidentiality. And he had exacted the same commitment from the senior medic who had assisted him, Owen MacDara. But Henry Whiteside had clearly been troubled all these years by that strange event. And he had begun to feel that there was some sinister aspect to it. He had convinced himself that Zachary Walker was vulnerable. 'Vulnerable to some growing internal menace.' That's exactly the language he'd used in his notes. During his research, he'd come to believe that there were forces inside America that were fed up with the direction of the nation. He felt that these same forces were preparing themselves to act. *How right you were, Major Whiteside,* thought Senator Sam.

Whiteside's notes implied, on the one hand, a sense of paternalism towards General Walker and, on the other hand, a clear sense of patriotic duty towards America. So it was unclear whether Henry Whiteside would have broken his promise of confidentiality. His notes were quite ambiguous regarding his intent. But extremely clear regarding his fears.

But it was the detailed notes on the incident in question that held Hardy's interest. Henry Whiteside described that evening at the 53rd MASH in graphic detail, including the names of the people involved. There were only four, including the patient. That left Whiteside, the attending paramedic, Owen MacDara, and the medic who had taken over from him, Murphy Armstrong. Major Whiteside noted, parenthetically, that he doubted if Armstrong knew what had happened that evening. *Well, that's just too bad, Mr. Armstrong. You were in the wrong place at the wrong time.*

Senator Hardy decided that these loose ends must be cleaned up. General Walker's past must remain in the past.

Office of The Chairman of the Joint Chiefs, Washington, DC, Wednesday, August 11, 1999

Zachary Walker didn't know what to believe. Senator Sam had assured him that Major Henry Whiteside's disappearance at sea was an unfortunate accident. But "It's an ill wind that blows nobody any good, Zachary," he had said, and then stood back as though he expected to hear an echo of that pronouncement. Sam liked the sound of his own voice.

"Henry Whiteside was a man of blind integrity. We talked. I don't know if we'd have been successful in getting him to lay off. That's the plain God's honest truth, Zach. He was a stubborn man. His death has done us all a favor."

That conversation had happened a week ago and Zachary Walker was still troubled. He couldn't get Henry Whiteside out of his mind. Somehow his past was unraveling, he felt.

He remembered.........

His family and friends thought that he had it made. He was graduating High School at the top of his class and he had been elected to the National Honor Society. It was Prom Night and his date was the most desirable girl in school, Hillary Jarvis. All the guys had invited Hillary. Zach couldn't believe his good fortune when she accepted his invitation. Blonde, bedroomy blue eyes, full sensuous mouth, high cheekbones, dimples, cleavage that tantalized and legs so perfectly formed that both men and women looked back at her as she passed on the street. Hillary knew all this, of course.

Zach had hired a limo for the evening. Big deal for an eighteen year old. He picked Hillary up at her home at eight. She was stunning in a sheer black evening dress, off the shoulders and suspended only by her ample breasts. Her parents greeted Zach like a member of the family. They were also leaving, to attend a business dinner with Mr. Jarvis's law partners.

At the end of the night the limo dropped them off at Hillary's house. It was midnight. Her parents had not come home yet, and Hillary invited Zach inside. She led him into the family room, that cosy unpretentious space with big soft couches, stereo, lots of books on the shelves and the weekend's newspapers on the floor. A plush black sheepskin rug lay on the floor in front of the large red-brick fireplace. She took Zach's jacket and he undid his maroon cummerbund and sank into the couch. Hillary had turned the lights on low and now she picked up the remote control and the voice of Elvis filled the room.

She walked towards him, kicking her shoes off on the way and sank to her knees on the black sheepskin rug. She held out her right hand, inviting him, and, it seemed to Zach, commanding him. He obeyed. Her mouth found his and her tongue darted inside. Her lips yielded and she fell back onto the sheepskin rug as Zach pulled the top of her dress down over her breasts. He nuzzled his face into them and marveled at the size of her nipples with the dark rings and little bumps that surrounded them. *He gently took each nipple between his lips and teased them until they were firm. Hillary had undone his belt and pulled down his black dress pants. She tried to reach him but he pressed harder into the rug, preventing her hand from discovering that he couldn't get it up. Zach was lucky. He was saved the embarrassment. They heard her parents' car approaching on the gravel driveway that led up to the house.*

Zachary Walker had never made it with a girl, even though he'd tried. He felt attracted to them, but he could never consummate anything. The only real sex he had had was with Charlie Pettigrew. But he had become disgusted with that. He stopped seeing Charlie when he was fifteen. He didn't think he was homosexual. He felt he'd been used by Charlie. But in the last three years he didn't know anymore. Sometimes he felt sexually attracted to other boys.

Zachary's confusion about his sexual orientation led him to isolate himself from others. He devoted all his spare time to his affair with the army and by the time he received his appointment to the U.S. Military Academy at Westpoint, Zachary Walker had become a singularly focused, confident young man. He had suppressed his sexual nature.

At least he thought he had. Until he met Joy-San Park that Saturday night in the Officers' Club at Camp Red Cloud in Korea. She had a special Eurasian beauty, the progeny of a liaison between a Korean mother and an American father during the Korean war. Zach would learn this later. That Saturday night he was drawn irresistibly to her like a moth to a bright light.

In those early weeks after they first met they were inseparable. They shared so many of the same interests. She loved literature. Zach had always read voraciously. She introduced him to Korean theater, even taking him to see a Korean production of Shakespeare. It only seemed natural for Zach to be open with her about his sexual ambiguity. They had become so intimate in every way that physical intimacy seemed natural and normal.

But she didn't rush Zach. She would bathe him with warm towels and massage his body with her nimble fingers and oriental expertise. She knew all the acupressure points and every erotic trigger. Gradually, Zach responded. He didn't count the days or the weeks but after about three months he and Joy-San actually achieved intercourse. And that was the beginning of the end for them. Zach's military career had no place in it for a partner, especially one of dubious family origins. His sexual ambiguity also dominated his nature. The success with Joy-San only aroused his sexuality, something he had suppressed for a long time, and he felt himself drawn once more towards members of his own sex.

By the time that Zach had finally convinced Joy-San that there was no future for them, she was pregnant. Intentionally. If she couldn't have him, she wanted his baby. He wanted her to have an abortion and she stayed away from him in the last months of her pregnancy. She went to live with an aunt in Seoul. But she had a difficult pregnancy, which ended in tragedy. Joy-San died giving birth to a beautiful baby daughter at seven and a half months into her term. Despite his sorrow, Zachary Walker knew that he couldn't care for the baby. He also knew that he didn't want the little girl growing up as a mixed-blood child in Korea, where she would be a victim of racial prejudice.

Zachary Walker knew that Ruth Whiteside couldn't have children of her own. He also knew that Ruth wanted a baby. So he called Henry Whiteside. He insisted that neither Ruth nor the little girl should ever know that he was her father. And Henry Whiteside kept that secret.

The CIRCLE of SODOM
A Gripping New Thriller

FOUR

...the present......

New York, Tuesday, October 5, 1999

It was almost three am when MacDara finally left Costelloes. Somehow he found where he had parked his car that previous morning on First Avenue, climbed in, turned the key in the ignition, flipped on the headlights and moved out into the Avenue heading for the midtown tunnel. He never made it. Four or five blocks later the police car, lights flashing, pulled alongside. MacDara glanced across to see an officer pointing his finger and commanding him to pull over and get out of the car.

The policeman shone his flashlight in Owen's face.

"Raise your arms to shoulder height. Now touch your nose with each forefinger."

It didn't work. Owen touched the top of his nose with his right forefinger but his left kept missing. He tried twice more but only made things worse. Now he missed with both fingers! That sealed his fate. The policeman cuffed Owen's hands behind his back and put him in the rear of the police car. There

Pat Mullan

were no handles on the inside of the doors, and he was separated from the driver's seat by a clear plexiglas partition.

At the police station they locked him in the drunk tank. Only a small, square opening in one wall connected him with the desk sergeant. In a few minutes (or so it seemed) they came for him again, two of them. First they fingerprinted him, holding each finger rigid and pressing it first on the ink and then on the paper. Next they made him blow into a tube to record his blood alcohol level. Then they dumped him back in the drunk tank.

Owen MacDara had seldom thought of that strange procedure in the 53rd MASH in Korea in 1975. Until last night in Costelloes, that is. That tall, saturnine colonel was now the Chairman of the Joint Chiefs of Staff. The feeling of unease wouldn't leave him.

MacDara had just woken up to find himself in the drunk tank at the police station. His head was killing him. His mouth felt like a gorilla's armpit. I really tied one on last night, he thought. Haven't been as drunk as that since my army days. That night in San Antonio. Years ago. Three-day hangover. I'm a lot older now, he told himself. This hangover will last for a week.

"MacDara, there's someone here to see you." The desk sergeant's voice seemed to boom through the small window that connected the holding cell to the precinct's front desk. Iggy Cummins was standing at the desk.

"Connolly called me. You left some kind of garbled message on his answering machine at three thirty this morning. You were definitely out of it, Babe!"

"Iggy, it's all very vague to me. I think they told me I could make one phone call. Jimmy's number was the only one I could remember."

"What happened?"

"I knew I should have taken a taxi when I left you guys last night."

"That's what we thought you were going to do."

The CIRCLE of SODOM
A Gripping New Thriller

"Sure...but I remembered that I'd parked my car over on First Avenue. Nobody could have convinced me that I couldn't drive."

"Owen, you should have stayed at my place last night."

"Now you tell me. As I remember, you weren't too sober yourself."

"Listen, I called Ted Billings. He's handling whatever charges they've got against you. Right now we need to get some breakfast into you while I fill you in on the latest."

P.J. Clarke's stood stubbornly surrounded by towering skyscrapers in midtown Manhattan. The old brownstone was an institution. No financial inducement by the developers had succeeded. So it stood incongruously amid the faceless steel and glass structures. P.J's still served the best eggs benedict in town. MacDara wondered where they got their bacon from as he cut through his second egg smothered in the hollandaise sauce that must surely be a secret recipe. He had downed three mugs of their best coffee and was feeling a little more human as Iggy described the carnage and shootout between the cops and the albino.

"Owen, I met with the cops this morning, the CID. The brass in the NYPD are uptight about this one. Since the World Trade Center bombing last year they see terrorists everywhere. They want to meet with you and me at 3 o'clock today."

"Why?"

"I had to tell them about our friendship with Murph and our get-togethers at Costelloes. I'm sure they'll be talking with Angelo too."

"I don't know how I can help them. Murph is gone. Are they gonna bring him back?"

Cummins didn't respond. MacDara had grown morose again. He finished two more cups of coffee in silence before he headed for his apartment to soak out the night's boozing in his tub. He told Cummins he'd meet him at the precinct at three.

Pat Mullan

Captain Duffy was taking a personal interest in this one. There had been a one hundred percent increase in wanton killings and mayhem in his upper Manhattan precinct in the past year and Duffy wanted to know why. None of the so-called experts could tell him. The killing in the Peppermint Stick and the slaughter of the four policemen by the albino was the last straw. He had had to see their widows and young children and write a personal letter of condolence to each family. The public was on the Mayor's neck and the Mayor and the Commissioner were both on his. Duffy had assembled three of the best CID men in Manhattan to investigate the slaughter. The team was headed by Lieutenant George Nichols, a Jamaican who had worked his way up from the beat while taking night classes in criminology at John Jay. Nichols had smashed two of the largest drug rings in the city in the past five years. Murray and Gennaro, the two detectives assisting Nichols, were the most decorated officers in the NYPD.

This was the team that greeted MacDara and Cummins when they arrived at Nichols's office in the 42nd precinct. After the preliminaries, Captain Duffy explained that he was going to sit in on this one. Lieutenant Nichols took over from Captain Duffy.

"Mr. MacDara, we understand that you were a close friend of the deceased, Murphy Armstrong."

"That's right. Murph and I first met in the army. Korea. Twenty years ago", said MacDara, making it sound as though it were yesterday.

"We know that, Mr. MacDara. Four of you, including Armstrong, met regularly. Mr. Cummins told us that. We pulled your service records," said Nichols.

"Why? Murph's death was just another random killing. Isn't that right?" said MacDara.

"Do you really believe that, Mr. MacDara?" said Nichols.

"There's nothing to suggest otherwise," said MacDara. He wasn't about to voice any unsubstantiated claims against the

The CIRCLE of SODOM
A Gripping New Thriller

Chairman of the Joint Chiefs. They'd lock him up and throw the key away.

"We're not so sure. The perpetrator - I believe you call him the albino - has never been known to commit a senseless killing," said Nichols.

"You know who he was?" questioned MacDara.

"Yes, we do. We had no luck with his fingerprints. So we tried Interpol. They had both prints and DNA on him," said Nichols.

MacDara waited as the lieutenant went around his desk and picked up a blue folder. Detectives Gennaro and Murray had not uttered a word since the meeting began. Captain Duffy had retreated to a corner of the office. Lieutenant Nichols opened the folder.

"The albino's real name was Eberhard Mueller. German national - East German, actually. When he was nine years old his father drove him and his fifteen-year-old sister through the Brandenburg Gate into West Berlin. The East German guards fired on them. His sister was killed instantly. His father was seriously wounded but managed to drive into West Berlin. He died a few hours later. The boy was placed in a West German orphanage. At nineteen he joined the Baader Meinhof Gang. In the subsequent five years he became one of the most ruthless members of the gang. The West German security police were on his trail in Bremen three years ago when he simply disappeared. There's been no trace of him since then. Well, not until he killed your friend, Murphy Armstrong."

Nichols paused, poured himself a glass of water from a tall jug on the desk and continued.

"He had a driver's license made out to Ernie Miller and an address in Miami: Costa Del Sol. It's a development of townhouses situated on a golf course just fifteen minutes west of Miami's International Airport."

"The Miami police checked him out for us. Just received their report. Ernie Miller showed up in Miami two years ago.

Pat Mullan

Had an American accent that sounded like Lawrence Welk. Said he was from Wisconsin. They knew little about him. Loner. Kept to himself. Worked as a golf pro at many of the clubs in the Miami area. Apparently, he was good," continued Nichols.

"His neighbors in Costa Del Sol haven't seen him for a month. But they didn't think that was anything unusual. He often went away for days or weeks at a time. Golf tournaments, he said."

The phone rang. Nichols grabbed it.

"It's for you, Captain."

Duffy materialized out of the corner, took the phone and answered in a series of monosyllables. "Yeh, yeh, yeh, yeh," each one a little louder than the previous one. He hung up the phone.

"I have to leave. But I'll be in close touch on this one. I don't want terrorists loose in my city. Lieutenant Nichols has my full authority in this investigation."

The door slammed as he left. It was the only discordant sound since Nichols had started to speak. He continued.

"There's one thing about Eberhard Mueller that not even Interpol knew of. He had a small discreet tattoo on the inner side of his left forearm. An 'S', like a snake, enclosed in a small circle. Interpol's records date back to his days with the Baader Meinhof gang. We must assume that this tattoo is more recent."

Nichols opened the blue folder, picked up a photograph of the tattoo on Mueller's arm and passed it to MacDara and Cummins.

"Have you ever seen this? Do you know what it is?" asked Nichols.

MacDara and Cummins examined the photo. The tattoo had been enlarged so that it was perfectly clear. A red snake in the shape of an 'S' inside a black circle.

"Never seen anything like it before. Sorry, we can't help you on this," MacDara answered for both of them.

The CIRCLE of SODOM
A Gripping New Thriller

"But you do see now why we think your friend's killing might not have been a random murder, Mr. MacDara? Tell us what you know about Murphy Armstrong," said Nichols.

"There's very little to tell. Murph's life is an open book. You have his service record and his family background", said MacDara.

"Did he make any enemies? Who did he associate with? What was he involved in?", asked Nichols.

"Lieutenant, Murph didn't have an enemy in the world, as far as I know. Everybody liked him", said MacDara.

"What about his job? Did he create enemies there? Did he ever talk with you about that?", pursued Nichols.

"Again, Lieutenant, Murph was well known in the Civil Rights Movement. He always worked within the law. He was not confrontational. He never used his position to gain political points", continued MacDara.

"Nevertheless, he may have made enemies, Mr. MacDara. If his death was not an act of random violence, then somebody wanted him dead", argued Nichols.

"I hear you, Lieutenant. But Murph wouldn't hurt a fly. Even the people he defeated in court respected him. I'm afraid you'll have to look elsewhere for a reason", said MacDara.

Lieutenant Nichols glanced over at Gennaro and Murray. He asked them if they had anything to add. Neither of them had. Then he turned to MacDara and Cummins.

"Gentlemen, I want you to let us know where you'll be at all times. Contact us immediately if you think of anything. No matter how trivial it may seem to you."

And, as they both rose to leave, Nichols face broke into a wide smile and he said, almost satirically, "Gentlemen, have a nice day!"

Pat Mullan

Gloucester, Massachusetts, Thursday, October 7, 1999.

Ruth Whiteside had aged. She was fifty-five but looked seventy-five. There were dark circles under her eyes and her skin had an ashen hue. Yet nothing could hide the fact that she had once been a most beautiful woman.

"Please join me on the deck, Mr. MacDara. Henry loved it here"

Ruth Whiteside lived in a comfortable old New England colonial overlooking the bay in the old-town part of Gloucester. All ocean-going traffic passed right in front of them. The deck connected to a wooden pier that stretched out into the water.

MacDara had phoned his contacts in the military and had discovered, to his surprise, that Major Whiteside had retired ten years ago. He had always thought of Major Whiteside as a lifer, a career army professional, even though he was a medical man. He recalled the previous day's phone call.

"Mrs. Whiteside, you won't know me. I served with your husband at the 53rd MASH in Korea. My name is Owen MacDara"

"Oh, Mr.MacDara, so many of Henry's friends have called these last few months"

"Well, Mrs. Whiteside, I'd very much like to meet with your husband. I believe it's important"

There was a long silence over the phone.

"Mrs. Whiteside?"

"Yes, Mr. MacDara, I'm sorry. You took me unawares. I thought you knew. Henry passed away two months ago."

After recovering from this unexpected news, MacDara felt that it would be better to talk with Mrs. Whiteside personally. Maybe her husband had confided in her over the years. Maybe she knew something about that event in the 53rd MASH and the mysterious colonel who was now Chairman of the Joint Chiefs of Staff.

MacDara's reverie was broken by Ruth Whiteside.

The CIRCLE of SODOM
A Gripping New Thriller

"Yes, Mr. MacDara, it's easy to forget the world when you look out there. Henry and I thought that the sea soothed the savage breast. It's a great place for contemplation here"

"Tell me about your husband. How did he pass away?", asked MacDara, using the same euphemism that she had used yesterday over the phone.

Ruth didn't answer him right away. MacDara could see that she was struggling with herself.

"Mrs. Whiteside, I'm sorry. Maybe I'm asking too much. We've only met and you really don't know me."

"No, Mr. MacDara, it's alright. It's just that I've never really talked about it. I miss Henry. I've never really been alone before. It takes a lot of getting used to. And I'm afraid. Afraid to trust anyone."

There was a long silence before she spoke again.

"You knew Henry. And there's something about you. Something that makes me feel I can trust you. And I need to talk about it."

She paused for a while and looked out at Gloucester harbor below. MacDara gave her time to compose herself. Finally she turned to him and said, "Mr. MacDara, in some ways I think that Henry is still with us. I can feel his presence all the time"

She went on to relate how her husband had been given orders to Vietnam at the height of the Tet offensive. Even though he fought for his country, he fought by saving lives. But Vietnam disillusioned him. He knew the body count given to Washington was a lie. He knew about the cover-up of the massacre at My Lai. And other massacres. He lost his loyalty to the army. So he took early retirement at fifty. They moved back here to Gloucester. This was their summer home. They both loved the sea, especially Henry. When he wasn't consulting at the VA Hospital or working on his memoirs, he was out in his boat.

"On his memoirs?" queried MacDara.

"Oh yes, Henry had started to write about a year ago. He was at the center of events in Korea and Vietnam and had personally

Pat Mullan

known many of the household names of the period. It was also therapy for him. He wanted to record the events that he had witnessed. And their participants. Henry had a great sense of history. He felt he owed this to posterity"

Ruth Whiteside went on to describe Henry's very last day. He often went out on his boat alone to write. He had said that the solitude and the sea stimulated his memory. It was a Tuesday in August. Henry had chosen to get up at dawn. He wrote and thought better in the morning. That was the difference between them. His brain worked best in the morning and hers in late evening. She always wanted to talk when he wanted to go to sleep. She had heard him get up that morning as usual. He crept around to avoid waking her. But she was always awake, although he never knew it. He had probably gone down to the end of their pier, untied the dingy and rowed out the short distance to his boat, *The Whitey*. The boat's name was a joke at his own expense. Henry had always known what the troops had called him. As usual he had climbed aboard, tied the dingy to the mooring and prepared to sail. There would have been no one in the bay at that hour, and he would have started the engines and headed out to sea as dawn appeared on the horizon.

Henry had always been back home in time for their afternoon tea. Lapsang Souchong. One of their pleasures. But he didn't come home. By six o'clock that evening Ruth, filled with worry, had contacted the Coast Guard. It took them less than an hour to locate *The Whitey*, anchored about three miles out. There was no one on board. The Coast Guard had conducted a thorough search for the next seventy-two hours and had continued to check the area for the following week. But Henry Whiteside had never turned up. No body was recovered.

"That's the hardest part of it, Mr. MacDara. We never found Henry."

"What do you think happened? Does anyone have a theory?" asked MacDara.

The CIRCLE of SODOM
A Gripping New Thriller

"Not really. Henry sometimes went for a swim if the sea was calm. He may have done that and got into some kind of difficulty. That's the only thing we can surmise", said Ruth. "But the mystery remains."

"By the way, Mr. MacDara, on the phone you said you had something very important to discuss with Henry?" Ruth asked.

MacDara took her back to that night at the 53rd MASH in Korea. Twenty years earlier - it just didn't seem so long ago. He described the events of that monsoon night, especially the final strange surgical procedure that Major Whiteside had performed on the mysterious colonel. He did not tell her that colonel was now the Chairman of the Joint Chiefs. Better that he keep that to himself for the time being.

"Did your husband ever tell you about any of this, Mrs. Whiteside?" asked MacDara.

"No. Henry never brought his job home. And he never discussed the medical problems or history of his patients, not even with me. Henry always felt that was a private matter," responded Ruth.

"You said he was writing his memoirs. What about the manuscript? He might have put something in it," MacDara said.

"We'll never know, Mr. MacDara. The manuscript was lost the day that Henry passed away. Henry wrote in longhand in yellow legal pads. He had everything with him in his briefcase that day", said Ruth.

"What happened to it?" asked MacDara.

"We don't know. The briefcase was lying open on the deck. It was empty. A squall had moved in that afternoon. We can only assume that the loose pages were blown away. I'm afraid we'll never know."

There was a finality in Ruth Whiteside's voice. She went on to describe those last few months of her husband's life. How absorbed he had been in his memoirs. He told her about the trips. For research, he'd explained. Four times to Washington, once to Los Angeles and once to Miami. He said he needed to be scrupulously thorough and accurate. She then said that she had never seen Henry so preoccupied, at times morose. He seemed to be troubled inside. She had tried to get him to talk but he wouldn't. Writing those memoirs had changed him.

MacDara was tired. He looked over at Ruth Whiteside. Two hours had passed since they had started talking. It was nearly noon on a clear fall day. The sun was full in the sky and its steely light glinted across the water in the bay, highlighting the boats anchored there. A painter's paradise. MacDara could see that Ruth Whiteside was drained. He apologized for intruding on her privacy and asked her to call him if she remembered anything at all. She assured him that she would. As he drove away, the last image of Ruth Whiteside was fixed in his mind. She had just sat there and said, barely audibly, "I miss him. I miss him so much."

Dune Road, The Hamptons, New York, Friday, October 8, 1999.

MacDara's gut told him that something was wrong. He always lived to regret it when he went against the advice of this gut. There just had to be a connection. Murph is dead. His killer is dead. Major Whiteside is dead. The mysterious colonel from the 53rd MASH is now Chairman of the Joint Chiefs. Too much of a coincidence. MacDara didn't buy it. *But what will I do*, he thought. *Who can I talk with?* Major Whiteside had been his best chance. He had been the link. If only he could have seen a draft of the major's manuscript. If only he'd used a word processor. If only...*I need to discuss my fears with someone. Someone who can help. Someone who won't accuse me of having a vivid imagination.* MacDara wracked his brain.

He picked up his watch and saw that it was almost ten am. Still in bed. He felt drained, emotionally and physically. The events of the past few days had taken their toll. Grabbing a robe,

The CIRCLE of SODOM
A Gripping New Thriller

he flipped on the coffee machine and slipped his feet into his sheepskin slippers, a gift from Michelle last Christmas. Funny, he had even been getting serious about her, and where was she now? In Australia. Packed up and left with a nomadic German adventurer. The coffee had finished dripping. Filling a hefty mug, MacDara slid the glass doors open and went out on the deck. A couple of catamarans were still anchored out there, and the morning's stillness was broken by the gentle slaps of the waves against them.

He was at his house on Dune Road in the Hamptons, an hour's drive from Manhattan. His weekend summer escape from the Big Apple. He didn't use it much in late fall or winter but it seemed the perfect place to go after leaving Ruth Whiteside yesterday. He had spent ages in the jacuzzi last night, and then the ten hours' sleep and the strong coffee had revived him.

"Who can I talk to?" he said to himself, out loud.

"Just a minute. Shields! Of course!"

Shields had been a lieutenant colonel at Battalion HQ at Camp Red Cloud in Korea. They had both loved photography and often shared the dark room together at the post craft center. He remembered Shields's disappointment when he failed to win the Camp Red Cloud photography competition that final year in Korea. He also remembered the incredulous look on Shields's face after MacDara himself took first place with a photograph of a young Korean boy hanging onto the railings outside the Chosun Palace Hotel in Seoul with a modern skyscraper being erected in the background. MacDara had titled his winning entry *The Threshold of Change*.

After he had returned to the States and finished his army service at Fort Knox, Kentucky, he and Shields had exchanged a couple of brief letters. Usual best wishes for the future. MacDara didn't maintain contact. He was back in civilian life and, besides, he felt that they came from different classes, different worlds. Shields's father was a four-star general whose last command had been the Caribbean theater of operations.

Pat Mullan

Westy, General Westmoreland, used to visit Shields's home when he was a youth.

The latest information he had had regarding Colonel Bartley Shields was a small news item buried in the Sunday papers a couple of years ago. It said that Major General Bartley Shields had been reassigned from the Army War College in Carlisle, Pennsylvania, to the office of the National Security Council to the President.

National Security Council, Washington, DC, Friday, October 8, 1999.

The National Security Council had offices in the west wing of the White House. Unlike any other support function, the NSC often usurped the role of the State Department, the CIA and the Joint Chiefs of Staff. The NSC was responsible for advising the President on action to take at times of crisis, usually crises involving confrontation with hostile nations or adversaries. The Executive Committee of the National Security Council advised President Kennedy during the Cuban missile crisis of 1962 when the United States and the Soviet Union came perilously close to nuclear war. They worked in total isolation, even from their staffs, during that crisis. War Game scenarios are the forte of the NSC.

General Bartley Shields had been a designer of games at the Army War College. His games explored the alternative uses of tactical nuclear weapons. But it was not that expertise that had brought him to the attention of the President. General Shields had been instrumental in creating the current generation of war games, more appropriately called strategic option games. The first generation of war games centered about a fairly simplistic model: the U.S. is hit first by a nuclear attack, is severely wounded, but manages to launch a massive counterstrike and survives. What kind of a planet remains is anyone's conjecture.

The CIRCLE of SODOM
A Gripping New Thriller

Global warming and nuclear winter fears were pushed to the background. General Shields's generation of games were predicated on the world being drawn into a nuclear confrontation by a terrorist attack. But, more relevant to today's terrorist threat, General Shields's model housed a database of all known terrorist groups, confirmed or implied associations with each other, links to governments, legitimate 'front' organizations and reputable or even renowned persons with suspect sympathies. No prior work had pulled together such a comprehensive contemporary database on terrorists and their sympathizers, associations and motivations. The system, using the latest computer technology and communication networking, was known as STOP, for Shields Terrorist Operations Program. STOP was now used in conjunction with JANUS, an adaptation of the earlier generation MTM (McClintic Theater Model), to run the games at the Army War College. STOP, like JANUS, was top secret.

Not long after his appointment to the National Security Council, General Bartley Shields was named as the NSC special advisor to the President in all matters relating to terrorism. In that new capacity, General Shields reported directly to the President.

Lt. General Bartley Shields was alone. He was working late in his Washington office. It was nine thirty pm on a Friday in early October. He was going away for a long weekend. Just over a month until Thanksgiving and then the Christmas season. He and his wife needed a well-earned break before the grandchildren descended on them. But these intelligence reports had only reached him late today and Bart Shields knew that Monday might be too late. Constant vigilance: the only counterpoint to the terrorism that now seemed to be such a part of our lives.

For a long time the people of the United States had had the perception that terrorist acts and outrages were events they read about that happened in other places: the Middle East, Athens, Tel Aviv, Belfast, London. The only time they were conscious of

Pat Mullan

such threats was when they travelled by air. The metal detectors at the airports invaded their privacy and, at the same time, lulled them into a sense of false security. On the twenty-sixth of February, 1993, all of that changed. The World Trade Center in New York was bombed. Six people died and a thousand others were injured. The bomb was made from fertilizer and fuel oil - chemicals available to anyone. Fifteen people, including a Sheikh, were indicted in the plot. They included Palestinians, Jordanians, Sudanese, Iraqis, a Puerto Rican, and a black American from Brooklyn. Some had fought in Afghanistan for the mujaheddin against the Russians. Evidence of a second plot had been discovered. The conspirators had planned to bomb four other New York targets: UN Headquarters, FBI Headquarters, and the Lincoln and Holland tunnels.

The terrorists were now using a new weapon in their arsenal: high technology. The man accused of planning the World Trade Center bombing used a laptop computer to map out his intended bombing campaign against US airlines. He even used an encryption program to protect the data on his hard drive. It would have been a simple matter to connect his laptop to the Internet and download US airline schedules. He also carried a suitcase that contained explosive gel, invisible on airport X-ray machines.

The phone rang for the fifth time before the general picked it up. Must be Millie, he thought. Anxious to get us out of here, no doubt.

"General Shields. This is Owen MacDara. 53rd MASH, Korea. It's been almost twenty years. I persuaded your wife to give me your telephone number. Please don't blame her. I'm a good persuader"

"Owen, is that really you? We often wondered what happened to you after you left the army."

"General, I need to see you. It's very important."

The CIRCLE of SODOM
A Gripping New Thriller

Bart Shields could tell when a voice sounded truthful and MacDara's certainly did. He was sure his phone was secure. His office was swept frequently. But one never knew these days.

"Where are you?"

"In New York."

"Millie and I are travelling through New York tomorrow morning. On our way to our house in Connecticut for a few days. I'll meet you at the Yacht Club for lunch. Let's say twelve hundred hours. I'll phone and make the reservation."

"General Shields, thank you, sir. I'll be there!"

General Bartley Shields hung up the receiver and leant back in the contour leather chair that he favored. He hadn't thought about Korea recently. And MacDara. Yes, he remembered MacDara well. Used to call him the FBI - Foreign Born Irish! Tried to keep him in the service. But MacDara wanted to go back to New York and make a million. I wonder if he did. Highest IQ in testing at Fort Dix during basic training. They, too, had tried to sign him up. For OCS, Officers Candidate School. But MacDara just wanted to do his two-year hitch and get out. Tops at everything. Earned the top marksmanship badge for his accuracy with the M16 rifle. There were three levels: marksman, sharpshooter, and expert. MacDara made expert. Wasn't satisfied in Korea either. Had to be the best medic. Trained in minor surgery with the docs. He was the only medical specialist that the doctors treated as one of their own. Even Dr Johnson, that tall rangy Texan, trusted MacDara. Shields remembered being at the 53rd MASH one afternoon for his routine medical examination when a badly lacerated GI was carried into the emergency room on a litter. He'd just been in an accident on field duty with the 1st Cav. and had been flown into Chopper Hill. MacDara was on duty in the Emergency Room. Doc Johnson examined the wounds, looked at MacDara and said: "Go ahead. Two percent xylocaine. You know what sutures to use. I'll check it over when you're finished."

Pat Mullan

And then there was the Karate. MacDara wanted to understand the people, the Koreans. So he started taking lessons in the Korean language. When Karate classes started, he was one of the first to sign up. Many dropped out, but not MacDara. In a few months he had a brown belt and was well on his way to a black belt, Shields reminisced. Suddenly, Bart Shields started laughing out loud. He had just remembered his anger at losing the photography contest. *Photography was my domain*, remembered Shields, *but MacDara won there too. Yes, I really tried to get him to re-up and go to OCS. He'd have made a fine officer, a fine commander. Yeah, I'm looking forward to seeing him again tomorrow. I wonder what can be so important after all these years.*

The New York Yacht Club, Saturday October 9, 1999.

The New York Yacht Club, organized in 1844 and incorporated in 1865, was a firmament of the American East Coast establishment.

General Shields raised his glass. "Cheers, Owen. It's good to see you again."

"General, the pleasure is mine. I am indebted to you for taking time out to see me."

"Not at all. Wouldn't have missed it. No inconvenience. We were coming up this way. And, besides, I was curious to find out about you."

"My life can't be as dramatic as working for the President, Sir."

"Let me be the judge of that. Remember, I wanted you to make a career with us but you chose not to. Tell me, did you make that million?"

"Yes, I did make that million. On paper, at least. I'm in consulting. GMA, Global Management Associates."

"What does GMA do?"

The CIRCLE of SODOM
A Gripping New Thriller

"We specialize in a number of niche areas. General management and strategic planning. We also do financial planning for corporate and private clients. Recently, we've been advising governments on everything from defense planning to fiscal policy."

"Impressive! I do remember seeing GMA involved in some projects a couple of years back in our General Accounting Office. Never realized that you and GMA were one and the same."

"I try to let the company protect my privacy. Only my own clients meet me personally. I like it that way."

Lunch had arrived. It had been a couple of years since Owen had dined at the Yacht Club. Bit too stuffy for him. But he remembered that the food had been good. Looked good this time too. His scallops were the best. As Mario refilled their glasses from the Chablis cooling on ice beside their table, Bart Shields nodded his approval of his blackened Cajun-style salmon. No one talked for a while. They had spent this first twenty minutes getting comfortable. They were well into lunch when Shields broached the subject.

"What is of such great importance that you needed to see me?"

"Sir, I need to take you back twenty years, to Korea."

"Owen, I don't understand. I had a feeling over the phone that you were talking about the present."

"Yes, I am. But, to understand my concerns about the present, I need to start at the 53rd MASH in 1975."

As Shields sipped an after-lunch espresso, MacDara took him back to that night of the terrible monsoon and the medical procedure performed by Major Whiteside on the mysterious colonel. He also described how that thirteen month tour of duty had established a close bond between himself and three others: Murphy Armstrong, Iggy Cummins and Angelo Russo. He talked a little about each of them. He told how Murphy had finished law school after Korea and had become a civil rights lawyer; a good one. Most recently, he had been working with the New York office of the NAACP, the National Association for the Advancement of Colored People. Since Korea, all four had maintained contact. In the last five years they'd been fortunate to find themselves in New York and they had grown accustomed to meeting regularly in their favorite Manhattan pub, Costelloes.

MacDara could see that General Shields still liked his Macanudos. As Bart Shields rolled the tip of the cigar clockwise in his mouth, Owen brought events current. He described Murph's killing, the albino's violent end and, finally, his visit to Ruth Whiteside to learn of another tragedy, the death of her husband. Shields finally spoke: "Henry's death saddened me. We were good friends."

"I didn't know. I'm sorry."

"That's all right, Owen. Henry and I had two loves: the army and the sea. I would say that Henry left his first love with a broken heart, but never his other love, the sea. He and I continued to meet occasionally. We were both members of this club."

"Did you know that he was writing his memoirs?"

"Not until nearly the end. It must have been July. The month before he died. He called to see me in Washington on his way to Virginia. Told me about the memoirs. Said he was doing research. Meeting various people to confirm his understanding of some of the history he'd been part of."

"Did he tell you anything in particular?"

"No, Owen, he didn't. He did seem very preoccupied. But I attributed that to the writing. Henry was always a perfectionist. I felt that the memoirs had taken control of him."

They both paused while Mario refilled their espresso. General Shields crushed the stub of his Macanudo in the ashtray and looked directly at MacDara. Owen had deliberately not discussed the identity of the colonel that Henry Whiteside had treated in Korea. Now he felt that it was time to do so.

The CIRCLE of SODOM
A Gripping New Thriller

"General Shields, that colonel that Major Whiteside treated in Korea. I saw him again the night that Murph was killed."

"Where?"

"On TV. The 11 o'clock news. He is Zachary Walker, the new Chairman of the Joint Chiefs."

Bart Shields had just raised the espresso cup to his lips and now he choked, face red, and splattered the coffee over the white tablecloth, almost hitting MacDara. Mortified, he stood up, grabbed a couple of napkins and mopped up the damage. As serious as the matter was, MacDara still found it difficult to suppress a good laugh at the general's expense.

Having composed himself, Shields sat down again and, looking directly at MacDara, said: "Zach is a colleague and a fine soldier. We meet regularly with the President. You must be mistaken."

"No, General, I'm not! And that mysterious medical procedure still bothers me. If it had been innocuous, would Whiteside have sworn me to secrecy?"

"Do you really think there is something sinister in all of this?"

"Sir, I don't know. The only people, other than myself, who knew about it are both dead. And both under tragic circumstances."

"But that could be a complete coincidence. What about you? Why are you still alive?"

"I've thought about that myself. That's the weak link in my premise. Maybe I'm on their list, and they're just waiting for the right event. An event that can blend into the daily tragedies. Just like Murphy and Henry Whiteside."

"But who are 'they', Owen? Are you saying that all this is part of a conspiracy? Look what happened to Big Jim Garrison. He tried to prove that Kennedy's assassination had been a conspiracy."

"I'm not so sure that Garrison was wrong, General. If my gut is right, something really bad is going down. And the Chairman of the Joint Chiefs could be involved. If I'm wrong, then all that's happened is that we've lost a couple of close friends and I've had some sleepless nights."

"All right, I'll help. But this is strictly between you and me. If you're right, you could be in danger."

"I've got to take that risk. If I am right I've got to get to them before they get to me."

General Shields was highly skeptical of all conspiracy theories. Most of them turned out to the creation of charlatans who preyed on the fears of the public. Still MacDara was no charlatan. His fears deserved to be laid to rest.

"Owen, I'll need some more information, some more evidence to support your fears, before I can be of any use."

"General, you're already of great help to me. Now I have someone to talk to about this. How can I contact you?"

"I'll be in touch with you early next week. Don't call me at my Washington office."

Two and a half hours had passed. A long lunch, thought MacDara as he looked at his watch. He was indebted to Bart Shields.

The general was anxious to leave. He was cutting into their Connecticut weekend. Millie wouldn't complain. She never did. But Bart Shields felt guilty anyway.

They had already said their good-byes when MacDara spoke once more.

"General, I almost forgot. One last thing. It may not be important, but you never know."

MacDara described to Bart Shields the tattoo that had been found on the albino's forearm. The red serpentine 'S' enclosed in the black circle. A discreet tattoo, almost hidden.

GMA Headquarters, New York, Friday October 15, 1999

The package was delivered by special courier, and MacDara had to sign for it personally. It was from General Shields and

The CIRCLE of SODOM
A Gripping New Thriller

contained an internal modem and encryption card for a personal computer. There was a letter from the general and procedures to follow to connect to Shields's private electronic mail system and procedures for password control. And instructions for installing the card in the computer's 16-bit expansion slot. It was a specially designed modem using top-secret encryption and detection technology guaranteed to protect the contents of any messages travelling to or from Shields over his private email system network. The most widely used encoding system is the Data Encryption Standard (DES). It was designed by IBM and approved for use by the National Institute of Standards and Technology in 1976.

DES is built around a number of encrypting procedures that are then repeated several times. The US military's Advanced Research Project Agency Network (ARPANET) is broken up into smaller subsystems for security purposes. But these small subsystems remain vulnerable. Vulnerable to international spying and sabotage. And sabotage can be accomplished by 'viruses' that can progressively destroy software and databases. It was precisely this vulnerability that the Shields's encryption card defended.

As instructed, MacDara installed the card in his PC, dialed up General Shields's email network and followed the procedures for logging on and establishing passwords. When he had finished, MacDara committed the passwords to memory and destroyed Shields's memo and procedures.

FIVE

**National Security Council, Washington, DC,
Wednesday October 27, 1999**

Larry Sanderson paced nervously back and forth in front of General Bartley Shields's desk. But he was not nervous. Larry Sanderson could not sit still. When he had a problem to solve he paced the floor even faster. He was thirty-five years old, slight of build, with reddish hair that seemed to be glued to his head in tufts. His eyes were sensitive to the light and he wore tinted glasses to protect them. He stopped briefly, lifted his head and looked directly at General Shields.

"Boss, I tried every key and cross-referenced every data element. I spent the last four hours accessing our new relational database. Nothing! Absolutely nothing!"

Sanderson was the Senior Software Designer and expert on STOP. Shields had brought him to Washington when he left the Army War College. He had worked on STOP since the feasibility and specifications stage. He was unstructured and unorthodox. Many people said he was unmanageable. Certainly he could not function as a member of a team. But everyone

The CIRCLE of SODOM
A Gripping New Thriller

conceded that he was brilliant, a genius. And he was totally loyal to Bart Shields.

"Larry, I didn't expect this one to be easy. The tattoo is the only information I have at this time."

"Boss, I pulled every reference to tattoos and special markings and insignia. There's nothing on a snake inside a circle."

"Any other ideas?"

"Well, I tried everything we have on reptiles. Every snake imaginable from adders to rattlesnakes."

"Nothing?"

"Not a thing! No reference to any known or suspected people or groups. And I believe we have the most current database in STOP on terrorists and their friends and sympathizers."

"Maybe we're taking this too literally, Larry?"

"What do you mean, Boss?"

"Let's think outside the paradigm. Suppose we look where we wouldn't. Can we do something like that?"

"We could try. We've got that Artificial Intelligence System we've been building. Especially the fuzzy logic modules. But they're only in the acceptance testing stage. Lots of bugs. May not be reliable."

"Larry, what have we got to lose. Remember, this is only between you and me. Nobody else knows. And I want it kept that way."

"Boss, this is top secret. There's no audit trail or record of any access I've made to STOP for this purpose. I disabled all monitoring and logging. After all, I built the software."

"Sorry, Larry. I should have known. When can you get me the output from your Artificial Intelligence system runs?"

"In about four days, sir. Will that be all?"

"Yes, Larry, and thank you. You know how to arrange our next meeting on this matter. When you're ready. And, remember, it's important."

But Sanderson was gone, mentally that is. He was already working the problem. Eyes on the floor, he stopped pacing and moved sideways through the door of Shields's office, bumping into Colonel Robert Travers, aide-de-camp to General Zachary Walker. Sanderson backed off and kept going without any apology.

"Strange guy! I'll never understand how you put up with him, sir."

"Hi, Bob. Come on in. Yeah, Sanderson is an eccentric all right. But it's his mind that matters to me, not his bearing or social graces."

Colonel Robert Travers was everything that Larry Sanderson was not. Six foot tall, erect and square jawed, his penetrating blue eyes looked directly ahead. He still wore his hair in the same crew cut style he was given on the day he joined the army twenty-five years ago. An enlisted man, he rose from private to sergeant in one year. In Vietnam he earned a field commission to officer and, at twenty years old, was the youngest company commander in the war. He went back to war in the Gulf. His battalion spearheaded the rout of Saddam Hussein's army. Colonel Travers was the most decorated soldier in the US Army. He was a true patriot. 'For God and Country' was not a slogan from less complex times to the colonel. It was the way he led his life. To Colonel Travers, America was God's promised land, and in defending his country he also believed he was on God's side in defending the righteous.

"That may be so, sir. But he still wouldn't last a minute in my command."

"That would be a mistake, Bob. Larry Sanderson is probably one of the most important weapons we have in our defense. He is expanding the capability of STOP. And you know how important STOP has been to the tactical planning and deployment of the Delta Force."

Shields went on to discuss Sanderson's development work with the Artificial Intelligence Subsystem of STOP. The current generation of the STOP system relied mostly on expert subsystems for its analytical work. Expert systems are based on pre-established rules against which data is processed. They are used in medicine by analysing a patient's symptoms, medical history and lab tests and then suggesting possible diagnoses to the doctor. But this is a long way from Artificial Intelligence - the ability of a system to perform the same kind of functions that characterise human thought. The way the human mind works is still not understood. The design of Artificial Intelligence must enable the computer to analogously duplicate these complex and still-mysterious processes. Sanderson had been working for some time on the concept of parallel processing - interlinked and concurrent computer operations. He was now working on the creation of networks of experimental computer chips, called silicon neurons. These chips mimic the data processing functions of brain cells. The transistors in these chips emulate nerve cell membranes to operate at the speed of neurons. Integrated with fuzzy logic software, computers could deal with the area of probability. Fuzzy logic could assign degrees of truthfulness or falsehood to variables derived from the information processed by Artificial Intelligence systems.

Shields could see the far away look in Travers's eyes.

"Aw, I'm sorry, Bob. Every time I get into this subject, I get carried away. It's inconsiderate of me."

"No, sir. It's fascinating. But I'm afraid my mind gets turned on by more tangible subjects. Speaking of which, General Walker asked me to drop in and invite you to our next RAT Force exercise. Two weeks from now. Friday, the 12th. Twelve hundred hours."

"I'd be happy to, Bob. Where?"

"At the Company, in Langley. We're using Dick's special facility."

The Company was the CIA, headquartered in Langley, Virginia. The present Director was Richard Smallwood, a career intelligence officer, well respected within the administration.

Pat Mullan

As Travers left, Shields got up and walked over to his office credenza. He pulled out a drawer that contained a phone connected to a specially secure line.

"Rose, it's Bart Shields. Please put me through to the President, if he's available."

"Good morning, General Shields. Please hold for a moment".

"Bart, how are you? What are you up to?" the familiar voice of the President came on the line.

"I'm just fine, Mr. President. I'd like to see you for a half-hour some time today, if that's possible."

"Sure, Bart. Come on over around five thirty."

"Thank you, Mr. President."

As he hung up the phone, Bart Shields reflected on how relaxed and sure of himself the President always sounded. It was comforting to work for a leader who was intelligent and knowledgeable and who didn't scream at the nearest person when he was under pressure.

The President looked tired and rested, both at the same time. A rare phenomenon. His ruddy face, bright eyes, easy smile and agile movement contrasted with the dark circles and bags under the eyes. It was precisely five thirty. The President kept rigorously to his schedule. He had to. His days often ran beyond midnight.

The President greeted Bart Shields with his usual warm handshake and with an arm around his shoulder guided him to a corner of the office where they both sat together. The President had another appointment at six. Shields reckoned that half an hour was more than adequate.

"Well Bart, what's on your mind?" said the President in a manner he used to make it easier for people to bring problems to his desk.

The CIRCLE of SODOM
A Gripping New Thriller

Briefly, Bart Shields outlined the discussion with Owen MacDara. He defended MacDara's integrity and filled the President in on MacDara's background.

"Bart, there are many things that Zach Walker and I disagree about. But there's one thing I'm sure of. Zach's an honorable man."

"Mr. President, I believe that too. But I can't ignore this."

"Bart, you have my full authority to pursue the matter. But it's strictly between you and me at this point. Be discreet."

"Thank you, Mr. President. I'll keep you informed."

"Do that, Bart. Thank you."

The meeting took only twenty minutes. As Bart left he knew that the President had enough to worry about without adding this, but he also knew that he had done the right thing. The spectre of Watergate, Irangate and other cover-ups was a sickness that he wanted no part of. He would handle this matter in total secrecy. But it would be open to the President from the outset. Bart Shields trusted this President implicitly.

Pat Mullan

SIX

Langley, Virginia, Friday November 12, 1999.

The Rapid Anti-Terrorist (RAT) Force, known to themselves as the Rat Busters, was the newest and most elite force assembled to fight terrorism. Comprising former members of the Navy Seals and the US Delta Force anti-terrorist unit, the RAT Force also included people skilled in everything from hostage negotiation to assassination. This was a proactive force as well as a reactive one. They didn't operate like fire-fighters, waiting to assemble and slide down that pole when the next fire erupted; they maintained a hit list of known terrorists and had already successfully assassinated two of them in the past six months. Counter-terrorism was also high on their list of tactical weapons. Infiltrating terrorist groups and compromising terrorist sympathizers by sexual entrapment were important tactics. Captain Ward Dobson, the RAT Force Commander, reported directly to the Chairman of the Joint Chiefs. The Force served at the pleasure of the President. The Langley exercise started promptly at twelve noon. General Shields arrived at eleven in time to join General Zachary Walker for morning coffee.
"Glad you could make it, Bart."

The CIRCLE of SODOM
A Gripping New Thriller

"Wouldn't have missed it, Zach. This is my reason for existing. Ask the President!"

"Oh, yes. This President has certainly elevated the fight against terrorism to the top of our country's priorities."

"Not just our country. He has encouraged our allies to move this fight high up on their agenda as well. Given all the priorities that these governments are facing, that's a major accomplishment."

"I agree. And he has taken the constraints away. We can now fight fire with fire."

"It's an entirely new ball-game. The terrorists are now into high technology. Sophisticated timing devices. Computers. Communications networks. Electromagnetic transmitters."

"You're right. We're in a catch-up mode. Our game playing needs an update."

"I'm looking forward to this afternoon's exercise, Zach."

"Travers tells me that your man, Sanderson, is pushing the limits in his development work on STOP. I'd like to see some simulation runs. When you're ready, of course."

This was Bart Shields first meeting with Zachary Walker since the lunch with Owen MacDara at the New York Yacht Club. It only served to reinforce his feelings about Zachary. A good colleague and a fine soldier. There had to be a simple, innocuous explanation for the Korean incident. Bart Shields dismissed these fleeting thoughts as the invited guests assembled for the afternoon's exercise. Experts on terrorism from the United Kingdom, France, Germany and Israel were among those invited.

This game was designed for maximum complexity. The players were assembled into a cast comprising a negotiating team, land-based and amphibious assault teams, hijacking specialists, terrorist teams, terrorist cause sympathizers and control teams. It played out over three days on two continents and four countries. Co-ordinated terrorist actions commenced at eleven am, London time on day one of the game. TWA Flight

17 from Paris to New York had been hijacked by five terrorists, three men and two women, identifying themselves as the Patriots, who ordered the flight diverted to Baghdad. Almost simultaneously, at six in the morning in New York, a massive explosion ripped through the 42nd Street subway station killing eight people and injuring seventeen others. A couple of hours later the casualties would have been much higher.

As these events were taking place, a message was received by all television, radio and newspaper offices in Europe and America. It demanded the release of prisoners in France, Israel and the United States and 100 million dollars in reparations for the 'exploitation of our oppressed people.' It demanded a further ten million to support 'the liberation struggle of our Patriot volunteers.' The message set out a timetable for the demands to be met, with a schedule of executions of the airline hostages, commencing with the first two at eighteen thirty hours on day one, if the demands had not been met by eighteen hundred hours.

The team, control groups and players received their assignments. The game commenced.

At eighteen thirty hours on day one, the first two hostages are executed and thrown from the plane at Baghdad airport. Saddam Hussein's government, given the aftermath of the Gulf War, refused to cooperate with the Western governments. At nineteen hundred hours the United States had agreed to pay the ten million dollars to the Patriots and France had agreed to release, to a neutral country, the two people awaiting trial in Paris. The terrorists had also agreed to suspend any further actions until ten am the next day and to meet with a delegation from sympathetic mediators. In the meantime, all diplomatic efforts were underway to exert pressure on every nation and organization that would be supportive of the Patriots. At twenty-one hundred hours on day one, working behind the scenes, the RAT Busters, using intelligence gathered on the passengers of TWA Flight 17, had identified two of the hijackers. Feeding the data to STOP they were able to ascertain the Patriots' command

The CIRCLE of SODOM
A Gripping New Thriller

structure, their training sites and the probable domicile of their leaders.

At 0800 hours on day two the negotiating team met the hijackers in Baghdad. In a sealed envelope they carried the ring finger of the second-in-command of the Patriots, who had been executed by the RAT Force in Tripoli the previous evening. It also contained a statement from the Patriots' commander stating that he was being held captive and would be executed if any further hostages were killed.

By day three, the game had ended. All remaining passengers were set free. The Saddam Hussein administration guaranteed safe passage to the hijackers and they were secreted away. The remaining bomb in the Port Authority terminal in New York had been disclosed by the terrorists. It was rendered safe. The disbursal of the ten million dollars from the designated Swiss account was blocked. And the RAT Force surrendered the Patriot's commander for trial before an international court at the Hague. The game ended.

This game had differed from prior games in one significant aspect. The RAT Force had mounted a successful counteroffensive. The last real offensive had ended in failure. The Delta Force had suffered eight dead and five wounded on April 24, 1980 in the unsuccessful attempt to rescue the hostages being held at the American Embassy in Teheran. It was obvious that gaming strategies against terrorism had changed. Had events in the real world also changed? Shields looked forward to Sanderson's Artificial Intelligence system. He'd feed all the variables of this game into it and see if STOP arrived at a similar resolution.

Pat Mullan

SEVEN

Miami, Florida, Saturday December 4, 1999.

Every December Liz Russo took the kids down to their condo in Florida. Angelo always promised to join them. A promise seldom kept. These days the excuse was the Connecticut contract. Even when he did join them he'd rather spend his time golfing at the Doral. She was fed up listening to war stories about the Blue Course.

Naked, Liz caught a glimpse of herself in the floor to ceiling doors that opened on to the patio and thought that, at thirty-three, she could still pass for her mid-twenties. The workouts at the health club kept her body trim, her legs looked like Angie Dickinson's used to and her breasts were still firm with big, prominent nipples. She was conscious that her nipples jutted out through the sheer bras that she wore. But Liz believed that her face was the best part of her. Fair skinned, almost milky, gray-green mysterious eyes, with a sensuous mouth, Liz's face invited. Invited friends, enemies and trouble.

Angelo had called that morning. Problems with the fabrication of crucial kitchen equipment. Had to straighten the matter out. Couldn't be down for two more days. She didn't

The CIRCLE of SODOM
A Gripping New Thriller

believe him anymore. Clemencia, her Colombian baby-sitter, was due to stay with the kids that weekend. Well, Liz reckoned, she was going out anyway.

She saw him sitting there. At the bar in JohnMartins. He didn't fit. It wasn't just the navy Brooks Brothers suit. It was the sense of certitude that he exuded.

JohnMartins was an upmarket Irish pub on Miracle Mile in Coral Gables. It was beyond lace curtain. A good place for a draught Guinness. Or just to hang out. Or have a cocktail before or after. Even dinner in their Waterford Crystal dining room, with the ever-so-proper harpist in attendance, could be excellent. Miami didn't have a pub culture like New York or Chicago and JohnMartins was one of the few to fill that void. Liz felt comfortable there.

"The next drink is on him, Liz." It was the voice of the proprietor. Liz hadn't noticed him amble up beside her. He pointed to the bar and the Brooks Brothers suit raised his glass in acknowledgement.

They got the corner table in the dining room and they both chose the Irish smoked salmon with crumbling slices of freshly baked Irish soda bread. Liz was hungry. It hadn't taken much persuasion to join him for dinner. His eyes were the most compelling blue she had ever seen. She felt hypnotized by them. As he spoke, she couldn't help thinking how much his voice reminded her of Richard Burton. English with Welsh undertones. A voice that was cultivated, theatrical. And earthy. Sensuous. That's what she felt. Sensuous. He was talking: "I'd like to see more of you, Liz."

"But, Tony - we've just met. And I don't even know your last name."

"All my best decisions have been made on impulse...and it's Thackeray, Tony Thackeray."

"What brings you to Miami, Tony?"

Pat Mullan

"I'll be in the States for about two months this time. We have a number of important clients on both the East and West Coasts. I like to see each of them personally when I'm here. Good business."

"What's your business?"

"The Thackeray Institute. We're what you'd call in the States, a "think tank". We help you think about the future. Right now everybody wants to know what the millennium will bring. Everybody's excited and apprehensive about the twenty-first century. That's good for us. We're needed."

"Where's your home, Tony?"

"I don't know anymore, Liz. I divide my time between Europe, the States, and Asia. I suppose Europe is home base, but I'm seldom there."

"You're a nomad, a gypsy," said Liz, who was more interested in Tony's body than his mind tonight. The gin and tonics and the Chateauneuf du Pape had given her a feeling of wellbeing. She had kicked off her shoes and stretched her right leg under the table to meet his. Her toes had ventured under his pants and were gently caressing his leg. The harpist played on……

They didn't linger over coffee.

He was staying at the Fontainbleau Hilton on Miami Beach. The taxi swung off Collins Avenue and dropped them at the steps to the main entrance. It didn't take them long to cross the crowded foyer, grab an elevator and reach the twenty-ninth floor. Liz was in his arms as the door closed behind them. He carried her into the room, kicking his shoes off on the way. She moved her tongue around the inside of his mouth as her hands removed his belt. It was hot and she wore a backless dress with no bra. Her breasts were in his hands. Gently fondling each, he sank his face into them. Her nipples were hard under his tongue and she slowly eased them out of his mouth as she slipped to her knees in front of him.

The CIRCLE of SODOM
A Gripping New Thriller

It was eleven a.m. and they were lounging by the pool with the Fontainbleau Hilton tower forming a semicircle behind them and the boardwalk separating them from Miami Beach and the blue-green Atlantic. Liz's strawberry daiquiri was both delicious and decadent.

"So, why don't you leave him?" ventured Tony.

"I've often wanted to do just that. But Angelo would charge me with abandonment. I wouldn't get a penny. And he could make a serious claim for custody of the children," said Liz.

"What about all his liaisons and affairs? Don't you have grounds for suing him for divorce?"

"Yes, that's true. But we'd be splashed all over the front pages. And I don't want the kids to be subjected to that."

"So, if you won't sue for divorce and you won't leave him, what do you do, Liz?"

"Go on living separate lives, I guess. God, I just hate Angelo now. I wish he were dead. That would solve everything."

"You're serious. I believe you mean that."

"Yeah, there's nothing any more. Even the kids are growing up without him. A heart attack would save us. God, there were days when I wished that something would fall on him on that construction site. But he's so bloody careful. Always wears his hard hat on the site."

Tony raised his glass and told Liz she deserved a run of good luck. He looked into her eyes and said that he wished he could make her dreams come true. Liz would be back in New York in a couple of days. Tony said that he'd be there the following week. Staying at the Plaza. Liked to be close to Central Park. Enjoyed jogging there in the morning. He promised to call her when he arrived.

Liz watched him as he strode purposefully to the diving board, stood on the edge for maybe ten seconds, stretched out his arms and dived. Almost theatrical. But something else, thought

Pat Mullan

Liz. Power. That's it. She'd never met anyone who personified power like Tony Thackeray.

EIGHT

Gloucester, Massachussetts, Friday December 10, 1999.

The phone rang repeatedly on MacDara's desk but he didn't pick up the receiver. He had asked Nena, his secretary, not to be disturbed. Then the buzzer sounded to signal that Nena needed to speak to him.

"Yes, Nena, what is it?"

"It's a lady called Ruth Whiteside. Wouldn't leave a message. Sounds urgent. Insists on speaking directly to you. I'm sorry, Owen."

"That's alright, Nena. I'll talk with her."

"Mrs. Whiteside, good morning."

"Oh, Mr. MacDara, I had to reach you. It's something that may be important. I was going through everything in Henry's office and I found a journal he'd been keeping."

"That is important, Mrs. Whiteside. I'd very much like to see it."

The call was brief. Owen thanked Ruth Whiteside and immediately buzzed Nena.

"Nena, please cancel my appointments this afternoon and call a taxi. I want it in ten minutes."

"Where shall I tell them you're going?"

"To La Guardia. I'm taking the shuttle to Boston. Should be back tonight. If not, I'll let you know where you can reach me."

There was a hourly shuttle service between New York and the East Coast cities of Boston and Washington. Traffic was building at mid-morning in the city and he just missed the eleven o'clock shuttle. He had to settle for the noon flight, arriving at Logan airport in Boston about forty-five minutes later. Nena had called ahead and reserved a car for him at the airport. By one fifteen, MacDara was negotiating his way out of Logan and heading north for Gloucester.

Ruth Whiteside was expecting him. Nena had called to tell her. She met him at the door.

"Just in time for afternoon tea, Mr. MacDara. I do hope you like Lapsang Souchong."

As she ushered him into the living room, the strains of a Bach concerto played softly in the background and a most striking young woman rose to be introduced.

"Mr. MacDara, this is Kate, our daughter."

"Pleased to meet you, Mr. MacDara."

"Ms. Whiteside, the pleasure is all mine."

"Please call me Kate."

Kate Whiteside must have been five nine. She had a dark complexion and almond-shaped eyes. Almost looked Eurasian. Her shining black hair looked as though it had been styled by a top Parisian hairdresser. It was cut short at the back, in layers, and angled at the sides to frame a face more Asian than European. Her mouth was exquisite, perfectly formed and completely sensuous. The blue jeans she wore accentuated her long shapely legs. A casual loose-fitting red shirt, open at the neck, could not conceal her figure. But it was the eyes that captured MacDara. Brown and yet not brown. Other colors reflected the light too: green, yellow and gray.

The CIRCLE of SODOM
A Gripping New Thriller

A gentle cough from Ruth Whiteside brought them back. They both realized that they'd been standing there unselfconsciously absorbed in each other's presence.

"Tea, Mr. MacDara," Ruth insisted on addressing him formally.

"Thank you, Mrs. Whiteside, just the remedy after a shuttle flight."

Two comfortable easy chairs and a couch surrounded a driftwood coffee table on which Ruth Whiteside had arranged her best Lennox china. She served tea the way his mother used to when he was a child back in Ireland. Heat the pot first. Then add boiling water directly onto the required amount of tea. Let stand for a few minutes only, and serve. It had been a while since he'd had Lapsang Souchong.

His thoughts were interrupted by Ruth as she reached under the coffee table and produced a dark brown leather-bound book.

"Henry always kept a diary as a scheduler and time manager. Part of his army discipline. When he started his memoirs he began to keep a journal," said Ruth.

"Why do you think it is important?" asked Owen.

"Take a look. It starts last year, just after Henry began his memoirs. Not every day has an entry. Only those of importance," Ruth answered. She was animated. She still hadn't let Henry go, and the discovery of the journal only reinforced his presence.

Owen paged through the journal. It was thorough. Some entries carried notes on research needed, people to see, recollections to confirm and follow-up assignments. One section contained a travel log of dates and destinations. Sometimes the person or place to be visited was noted, sometimes not. Other journal entries memorialized the highlights of a visit or research conducted on a particular day or on one of the planned trips. Some of these entries were a few pages long.

"You're right. This is important. It might help me find the answers I need," said Owen.

Pat Mullan

"What answers are those, Mr. MacDara.?" said Kate.

"Please call me Owen," said MacDara.

"I have not told Kate much about your last visit, or your concerns, Mr. MacDara. I felt that our conversation was privileged and I didn't want to burden her," said Ruth.

"If it's anything to do with my father, I want to know. My dad was in good health and totally at home on the ocean. I'm not satisfied with any of the explanations given for his disappearance," said Kate.

MacDara decided that Kate should know. He described again the events of twenty years ago at the 53rd MASH in Korea, including the strange surgical procedure on the colonel.

"Owen, what's so important about all of this? And what's it got to do with my father? You talk about it as though it might be something sinister," said Kate.

"Yes, Kate. It might be sinister. Why did your father swear me to secrecy?" said Owen.

"Maybe he wanted to protect the patient's privacy," responded Kate.

MacDara assured her that that had been his assessment at the time, even though he had been mystified himself. He decided to tell her why he now needed to know. He described the role that Murph had played that night at the 53rd and his senseless killing in the Peppermint Stick. Finally he told her that the mysterious patient of her father's was no longer mysterious. He knew he was breaking a confidence to her dad, but he felt she and her mother should know why he was concerned. So he told them that General Zachary Walker, the new Chairman of the Joint Chiefs of Staff, had been that patient.

"Owen, that's crazy. Do you think that the Chairman of the Joint Chiefs is trying to eliminate anyone remotely involved with his treatment twenty years ago at the 53rd?" said Kate.

"I know it sounds crazy. Maybe it is. Maybe I'm paranoid. That's why I was reluctant to tell you," said Owen.

The CIRCLE of SODOM
A Gripping New Thriller

He got up and walked over to the sliding glass doors that opened onto the redwood deck at the rear of the house. Kate and Ruth followed him. Out on the deck, MacDara turned to face them.

"Suppose, just suppose, that you father uncovered something when he was writing his memoirs. I don't know what. Something dangerous. Something evil," said MacDara. "And, just suppose that General Walker was part of that evil. And that your father discovered something sinister behind the procedure he carried out on the general twenty years ago," Owen continued.

"Are you saying that my father's death, disappearance, was murder?" said Kate.

"I'm sorry, Kate. I know this is hard on you and your mother. But, if I'm not paranoid, then your father's disappearance and Murph's murder are connected," said Owen.

"Then you must be in great danger yourself, Mr. MacDara," said Ruth Whiteside.

"Yes, I'm sure I am. But, if my theory is right, they want these deaths to look normal. Just another statistic. But I'm not waiting to be taken out like a sitting duck. I'm going after them," said Owen.

Kate saw the determination in his face. The danger and his resolve to fight only intensified her attraction to him. Maybe it's because I haven't been with a man for a while, she thought. But she immediately dismissed that thought. She had always acted on impulse. She was an Aries. And her impulse told her that she wanted MacDara.

Kate Whiteside was married. Separated. The divorce would be final any day now. Even while married she had kept her own name. She had not become Mrs. Fuller. They had met at grad school at Harvard. She was in the fine arts program and he was completing a doctorate in nuclear physics. The attraction was cerebral and physical. They both shared a love of classical music. And he was good in bed. The marriage lasted five years.

Pat Mullan

They never became good friends. Instead of growing closer together, they grew further apart. By the second year of marriage, she wanted a baby. He didn't. By their fourth year, he wanted a baby. She didn't. She wanted out.

"Kate, Kate," her mother broke in, "are you daydreaming again?"

"Sorry, Mom, must have been," said Kate.

"Mr. MacDara says he's going back to New York this evening. You're going too. Maybe you'd like to keep each other company," said Ruth.

"I'm taking the shuttle back in about an hour from Logan. If you're packed, I'd be happy to have you accompany me," said Owen.

"Nothing to pack. Travelling light. Most of my stuff's in New York. Yes, I'd love to," said Kate.

"Good, that's settled. Mr. MacDara, would you like to borrow Henry's journal? You can always return it to me when you no longer need it. It's no use to me. I've got so much to remind me of Henry," said Ruth.

"Yes, Mrs. Whiteside. I was going to ask you for the journal. I'll keep it safely for you," promised Owen.

Ruth Whiteside watched Kate and Owen close the front gate, climb into their car and wave to her as they departed; she remembered again……

She was the tiniest, prettiest baby I had ever laid eyes upon. A China doll. Except that she wasn't Chinese; three-quarters American and one-quarter Korean. And she's all mine, all ours. All those years that Henry and I tried. I couldn't love her anymore if we had created her ourselves. She was only two weeks old and less than five pounds in weight. A premature baby but perfect in every way. I had brought her home just two hours earlier and I hadn't taken my eyes off her since. She was still asleep and I couldn't see her

The CIRCLE of SODOM
A Gripping New Thriller

breathing. She was motionless. But she had the longest eyelashes and the most perfect heart-shaped mouth. That's what I remember. And Henry was happy to see me so happy. He had doted on that child. And she on him. Oh, yes, Henry, we were very privileged to have Kate; but will she be strong enough without you?

At six pm Owen and Kate were lifting off the runway at Logan headed for La Guardia in New York. Nena had a limousine waiting for them at la Guardia. Owen had no appointments the next day, Friday. He had told Nena he'd be in his house in the Hamptons if anything urgent was needed. She could be the judge of that. That was one of Nena's strengths. His clients often accused her of protecting him. On the way to La Guardia, Owen had already persuaded Kate to spend the weekend at his house on Dune Road. There was no-one waiting for her at her apartment on Madison and 92nd and she was between jobs. Her assistant curator's position at the Metropolitan Museum of Modern Art had ceased to be funded so she only had the art appreciation class that she taught at the New School. And the next class was not until Tuesday evening. So she was free. The way Owen put it was difficult to refuse.

"I could use the company. Since Michelle left I watch sunsets alone. It's not the same."

He had already told Kate about Michelle and the nomadic German she had followed to Australia.

"This is not a proposition. You have your own bedroom, your own bathroom. There's no obligation to share anything but the scenery. It'll be good for the artist in your soul."

"OK, I agree. You know you're an excellent salesman. I'm sure you've been told that before," laughed Kate, deep down in her throat in the kind of husky way that reminded him of Lauren Bacall.

Pat Mullan

On Friday night they shared a bottle of Chateau Meaume 1990 and watched the sunset. On Saturday night Kate went to Owen's bedroom. They made love and missed the sunset.

Before the weekend was over Owen called Ken Baker. Baker Security had offices in New York, Boston and Chicago. They were one of the top five security companies in the northeast. By the age of forty Ken Baker had made Assistant Chief Inspector in the New York City Police Department. But he had been unhappy that he earned much less than his friends in business and other professions. So he had retired early and founded Baker Security with one contract and five employees, all retired NYPD police officers. That was ten years ago.

MacDara had chosen Baker Security a number of times to fill contracts with GMA's clients. He had liked Ken Baker the very first time they met. Over the years they had become good friends. So Ken thought nothing unusual of it when he got a call from Owen at ten o'clock on Sunday evening at home.

"Ken, hate to bother you at this time, but I need a favor," said Owen.

"Owen, no trouble at all. What can I do for you?" answered Ken.

"There's a lady, a friend not a client, that I think may be in some danger. It's not something that I can take to the police. I have no specific evidence to back up my fears," explained Owen.

"So you want to keep her under surveillance, is that it?" asked Ken.

"Precisely. But be discreet. No need to alarm her unduly. She's a fiercely independent woman and she might feel badly about someone watching her, even if it was for her own protection," said Owen.

"Tell me a little about her," said Ken.

So Owen talked about Ruth Whiteside, the mysterious loss of her husband, where she lived, and his suspicions that she might be in danger if her husband's disappearance had been the result of foul play. He told Ken no more than that. Ken didn't probe the matter any deeper with Owen. They trusted each other.

"I've got just the man for the job," said Ken, "Frank Nagle. Frank was one of my first five employees. I think of them as the founding fathers. Frank always had a summer home up on Cape Cod. With the children gone, he and Sally wanted to spend more time on the Cape. So, three years ago, he moved to our Boston office."

"Sounds good to me, Ken," said Owen.

"Frank's not on any contract at present. And he's not working on any proposals. So I can make him available right away," said Ken.

"I want twenty-four hour, seven days a week protection for Ruth Whiteside, Ken. I'll pay for it. Just send the bills to me personally, not GMA," said Owen.

"If that's what you want, Owen. I'll let Frank decide who he wants to support him. I'll call you in a week's time with a security report. Usual corporate procedure," said Ken.

"Thanks, Ken. I owe you one. Are you keeping score?" said Owen.

"I think we're even. Don't worry about it," laughed Ken.

Owen hung up the phone and explained to Kate the arrangements he had made. She was relieved but still worried. Kate was convinced that her father's disappearance was not an accident.

NINE

University Club, Manhattan, New York, Friday December 17, 1999.

GMA's Connecticut project was ahead of schedule and under budget, a performance that called for recognition. Owen MacDara reserved the University Club in Manhattan for a function to acknowledge this outstanding progress.

An array of lucite blocks, tombstones to banking people, sat on the table near the dais. They displayed project milestones and warm words of praise for those whose accomplishment had been truly exemplary. Fat bonus checks, in discreet envelopes, also awaited those whose performance had far exceeded expectations. It was one of those necessary morale-building events that MacDara used to maintain esprit de corps on all of GMA's very visible and high-risk projects.

MacDara added his own touch to the evening, handing out 'gag gifts' specially selected to match the idiosyncracy of the recipient or to commemorate a well-remembered and, preferably, embarrassing snafu. This was the 'roast' of the evening. Thick skins were expected.

The CIRCLE of SODOM
A Gripping New Thriller

Later, they headed for Costelloes. MacDara had set up an open tab at the bar for two hours. Everyone was welcome. Project members, GMA managers, suppliers, construction managers, interior designers, jacks-of-all-trades and invited guests. Within an hour Costelloes was packed to the rafters. Not even breathing space. Owen never ceased to be amazed at the drawing power of free drinks. Angelo Russo couldn't make the event. He was in Atlanta presenting an interior design proposal for a new municipal office building. Liz Russo had come instead. Owen could see her squeezing her way through the throng with a tall dark stranger in tow. Another liaison. Angelo and Liz's 'open' marriage had become common knowledge. They didn't try to hide it any more. Especially Liz.

"Owen, I've got someone who'd like to meet you."

Liz Russo moved aside and MacDara came face to face with Tony Thackeray.

"Mr. MacDara, Tony Thackeray. Glad to meet you." The handshake was firm and not prolonged. But it was Thackeray's eyes that held Owen. Marbled blue, the bluest eyes he'd ever seen. Intelligent, sparkling, yet cold. The eyes were level with MacDara's, making Thackeray about the same height, nudging six feet. Dark complexioned, blue pinstriped suit, Cambridge tie, expensive Italian shoes all combined to define power, confidence, ability and a distinctly European aura.

"Call me Owen. Tony, I take it you're not one of Russo's stable of architects. They keep springing someone new on me all the time."

"Hardly", responded Tony Thackeray. Owen could detect a thinly veiled tone of indignation. Liz jumped in to salvage things: "Tony heads a think tank called The Thackeray Institute. He's in the States giving lectures to a number of groups around the country."

"Yes. The Thackeray Institute. I have heard of you but I'm afraid that's all I know. What are your lectures about?", asked Owen.

Pat Mullan

"The Future. My favorite topic at the Institute. We're all interested in the future, aren't we? I'm sure GMA would benefit strategically if it really knew what the marketplace were to look like in, let's say, five, ten years' time."

"Maybe we can get you to talk to us, if your schedule permits"

"I'd be happy to."

The crush of the crowd, now completely uninhibited thanks to Guinness, Jameson, Dewar's, Budweiser and other household names, prevented any further conversation. MacDara had been intrigued by the meeting with Thackeray and asked his Executive Vice President, Dick Massey, to follow through and prepare a briefing for him on Tony Thackeray and The Thackeray Institute.

GMA Headquarters, New York, Tuesday December 21, 1999

Three days later Owen MacDara received a confidential briefing document on Tony Thackeray. Tony Thackeray was in reality the Honorable David Anthony Llewellyn Thackeray, son and heir of Lord Haverford and scion of that great Anglo-Welsh family. The Thackeray fortune was one of the legacies of Empire, derived from South African mines, Australian sheep ranching and Hong Kong financial institutions. As well as an Imperialist, Lord Haverford had been considered a Fascist in his prime. It was rumored that he had funded Oswald Mosley and his Blackshirts in Britain during the war years. But that had never been proven.

He had founded The Thackeray Institute in the late fifties around the time Anthony Eden was withdrawing from Suez, another loss to the power and influence of Great Britain. Lord Haverford had written a controversial book at the time, *The Decline of the Realm*, postulating that Britain was suffering from a malaise that would lead to the destruction of the nation and

The CIRCLE of SODOM
A Gripping New Thriller

infect the body social, politic and economic of Western civilization. His thesis centered on the diminution of order, patriotism and solidarity and their corrosive effects on the economic and political life of the nation. He foresaw a bleak future for Britain at the millennium: devolution of the United Kingdom, absence of value systems and national ethos, endemic corruption, moral depravity, anarchy in the inner cities, chaos and thuggery masquerading as patriotism, and finally economic collapse. The book's publication started a furore at the time. Lord Haverford was accused of scaremongering and he was vilified in the media. But Lord Haverford was thick skinned. He took it all in his stride, firm in his beliefs and convictions. He founded The Thackeray Institute to reverse the trend he had forecast, to build up a cadre of people schooled in his values, a cadre of people who would inherit the leadership of Britain and steer it away from its own destruction. A number of well-placed people in Britain and the West today are graduates of Oxford, Cambridge, Harvard, Trinity, Princeton, Yale - and the Thackeray Institute.

Young Tony Thackeray got the proper education: Eton and Cambridge, followed by two years of postgraduate work in Zurich at the Malocco Centre for Strategic Studies, under the guidance of Nobel Laureate, Dr. Johann Malocco, winner for his economic theories in the twenties and again for his genetic research in the forties. Dr. Malocco was the *eminence grise* of the conservative right. Tony had then completed a year of advanced work at the Thackeray Institute before joining the management of the Institute. It was always understood that he would succeed his father as head of the Institute. And he did. But not before he had redefined its mission for the nineties and into the twenty-first century. He had split the Institute in two: the traditional role would continue under a Chancellor serving at his pleasure, and a new mission would commence: the mission of examining and thinking about the future. Tony would actively direct this new 'think tank'.

Pat Mullan

Lord Haverford was ninety-three years old. Upon his death, Tony Thackeray would become the next Lord Haverford.

It was an understatement to say that MacDara found all this information about Tony Thackeray intriguing. He extended an invitation to him to be keynote speaker at the annual GMA dinner. Tony Thackeray accepted.

The CIRCLE of SODOM
A Gripping New Thriller

2000

Pat Mullan

TEN

**GMA Dinner, Helmsley Palace Hotel, New York,
Friday January 7, 2000.**

Every January GMA hosted its annual extravaganza for clients, prospective clients, management, friends, associates and anyone that it might make good business sense to invite. The festivities always commenced with a sumptuous reception, usually in the Helmsley Palace Hotel, followed by dinner and presentations of gifts to those who had excelled at GMA's business during the past year. Each year MacDara chose a keynote speaker for the dinner. Sometimes it was someone of the caliber of a Tom Peters or an Alvin Toffler. At other times the speaker was chosen not so much for the message but, rather, for the massage, as Marshall McLuhan might have said. Tonight's keynote speaker would be Tony Thackeray.

GMA's dinners were noted for their food, drink and fun. Wine connoisseurs were always sated by evening's end. MacDara never failed to select the best. Tonight he walked into the reception promptly at six pm, bypassed the trays of exotic hors d'oeuvres, and went straight for the oysters on the half shell. An attentive waiter brought him a glass of Corton

Pat Mullan

Charlemagne, Grand Cru 1988, one of the great white Burgundies. Almost everyone had arrived, and there was a buzz of excitement in the air. MacDara was soon surrounded by GMA staff who seldom encountered him in the normal course of business and by clients who wanted to get his attention on pet issues or proposals. And surrounded, too, as his old English professor at St. Columb's used to say, by the usual number of 'sycophants and obsequious poltroons'.

"Are you afraid or are you excited tonight?"

Thackeray's voice carried strongly and clearly to even those who sat at the tables on the perimeter of the dining room. A trained voice, well able to command an audience. The tinkle of glasses stopped, the conversation ceased and everyone turned to look at the figure standing at the podium.

"About the future, I mean. Are you afraid of the millennium? Afraid of the new century? Afraid of technological tyranny, genetic manipulation, war, environmental disaster, destruction of the social order? Or are you excited? Excited about the twenty-first century? Does the information superhighway turn you on? Do you believe that our advances in genetics will make you live longer and healthier? Do you believe that your life will be richer because you won't be stuck in a job? Do you believe that retirement is a nonsense? When someone predicts revolution, do you think information? Or are you terrified? Terrified of an Orwellian Society threatened by an ignorant, deprived and violent underclass? Terrified of the destruction of the social order? Ask yourself now? Are you afraid or are you excited? Or are you a little of both? And where is God in your future? Or does that matter? Are you a Christian, a Buddhist, a Hindu, A Moslem, a Jew? Or are you an Atheist? Will your belief, your conviction, your certainty about life be undermined or strengthened in the twenty-first century? What do you want it to be? Can you influence the future? Or is it too late? Do you feel you are not in control?"

The CIRCLE of SODOM
A Gripping New Thriller

"Ladies and Gentlemen, welcome to 'The Future'."

By now, Tony Thackeray had hooked his audience and, like the expert angler that he was, he never let that fish off his hook for the rest of the evening. His theme was the future, his thesis was Vision. He took his audience back to the nineteenth century. Back to the confident ruling classes of Europe. Confident in technology. Confident in Capitalism. Confident in economic advance in the coming twentieth century. A vision that failed. The first half of the twentieth century was a disaster. He asked if this was going to be repeated. Are today's ruling classes just as confident of the twenty-first century? Is their vision flawed? If the millennium holds disaster, can it be avoided? If it can't be avoided, how do we survive it? And what is happening among those who are reacting to the destruction of the social order, the destruction of traditional beliefs and values? What is their common denominator? Is it their fundamental Christian beliefs? What is their vision? Is it of a coming Armageddon? Is this exciting or is it terrifying?

He foresaw a period of change like none in recent history. He saw a new world growing underneath the old, like a new fingernail emerging to replace a damaged one. The challenge: to survive and grow in the new world and not get discarded when the old one self-destructs. His premise: we can shape that new world and protect ourselves from annihilation when the old one dies. And Tony Thackeray was there to sell the excitement of that prospect to his captive audience. His admonition: ignore official forecasts, treat the planners with skepticism, beware of the gospel of the management gurus, be loyal to yourself firstly, understand that we're in a meritocracy; above all, see don't look.

Is Charles Murray correct in *The Bell Curve* when he predicts a future where the intelligent will marry the intelligent and the rest will sink into a genetic underclass? Is Charles Handy correct in *The Empty Raincoat* when he predicts 'lots of customers and not lots of jobs' and the emergence of 'portfolio' workers who will carry their skills around with them, a kind of

Pat Mullan

'have gun, will travel' career? Or perhaps you see a bleaker future; perhaps you agree with Professor Ian Angell of The London School of Economics. He sees the world dividing into 'intellectual hot spots' and vast regions of outlaw territory. Just like your own Wild West! Existing social structures will be destroyed, the sanctity of human life will end, the death sentence will be routine for petty crimes, nations as we know them will cease to exist, the chief executives of multi-national companies will take their seats in the United Nations! Do you believe that that is our future?

How will you finance your life when governments can no longer afford to pay Social Security to a population that has a far greater proportion of elderly people? We have eight billion people on this planet. Do you think our supply of people far exceeds the demand?

And don't forget genetics. We'll soon be able to tell the genetic characteristics of every individual. How will we use that? Screen and eliminate? Weed out the undesirables? Create a super race? Who will be given the power and the right to make such decisions? Will you be eliminated or will you survive? How can you assure your survival in this brave new world?

Tony Thackeray's voice invaded MacDara's consciousness again.

"I'll ask you again. When someone predicts revolution, do you think information? Or do you think social? That's right! We're now in the midst of the greatest social revolution in history! Will anyone get married in the twenty-first century? Will most children be born out of wedlock? How will your children be educated? Are we throwing out our moral baggage? Are you a pendulum theorist? Do you believe that the pendulum of history swings between permissiveness and puritanism? Are we reaching the apex of permissiveness? Do you believe, with the fundamentalists of the right, that the pendulum is swinging back toward them? Are they purposely tilting it toward themselves by controlling the power that moves it? How are

The CIRCLE of SODOM
A Gripping New Thriller

they gaining that power? Are they going to save us or destroy us? What do you think? Will they bring about the Armageddon they've been predicting? Do you need to know how to survive if that Armageddon comes to pass? Am I scaring you?"

They were already rising to give him a standing ovation as he concluded his remarks the way he had begun: "Are you afraid or are you excited tonight? Ladies and Gentlemen, welcome to 'the Future'!"

Liz Russo and Tony Thackeray went straight to his suite at the Plaza Hotel after the GMA dinner. Speeches were nothing new to Thackeray but he felt especially good about this one. There was something about MacDara that made him want to impress him. That was an unaccustomed feeling for Tony Thackeray. Few people made such an impression on him.

Liz Russo felt good for entirely different reasons. Tony Thackeray had awakened her body, making her feel more sensuous than she ever been. As they entered his suite she could see that it had been prepared for them. Candlelight bathed the room from a tall wrought iron stand, a new addition to the furnishings. Beethoven's *Moonlight Sonata* played softly, and a bottle of Montrachet, newly opened, sat in a silver wine cooler on the bedside table. Rivulets of condensation trickled down the ouside of the bottle.

Liz tastes the Montrachet on his lips as they kiss. He undresses first and now she feels the warmth of his hand as he slowly unbuttons her blouse, and the slide of the silk against her flesh. She pulls his head towards her, the strands of his hair arousing her as they caress the soft skin between her fingers. They seem to fall as one, in slow motion onto the black satin sheets.

Pat Mullan

Manhattan, Madison Avenue and 92nd St, Saturday January 8, 2000.

It was the night after the GMA dinner, and Owen MacDara was still coaxing his body into recovery. Too much wine, too much of everything. Experience told him that only time and his liver would get rid of the poison. He was in Kate's apartment at Madison and 92nd, a fourth floor walk-up in an old sturdy stone building, built to last. Kate had asked him to stay over last night, and it seemed the sensible thing to do at three in the morning. Kate had left to teach her weekend art class at the New School, and Owen found himself, still in pajamas and still unshaven, lapsing in and out of consciousness on the living room couch. It was a comfortable room, with an old unused fireplace set in the gable wall. Books were piled high on shelves in the alcoves at each side of the fireplace. A hi-fi system sat where the fire used to be and CDs and cassette tapes were stacked around the hearth. A few of Kate's own pastels and charcoal sketches crowded each other in a corner of one wall and a large Claude Monet print, *Sur La Plage a Trouville*, in a bluish wooden frame, took center stage on the opposite wall. Owen realized that this was the first time that he had been alone in Kate's apartment and, as he looked around, he felt a sense of voyeurism.

He forced himself to get up, went to the bathroom and splashed cold water on his face. Then he went to the kitchen and brewed himself a large pot of tea. It was the drink he still preferred to coffee at times like this. He checked his watch. Eight o'clock. Kate would be home about ten thirty. That gave him two hours. Two hours with Henry Whiteside's journal. He had had the journal for three weeks and had delved into it, as time permitted, to read and peruse the notes and entries. Some of it was in a 'shorthand' that only the major would have been able to decipher. Owen reflected that it reminded him of the unintelligible scribbles on most doctors' prescriptions. Other entries were quite descriptive and legible, written in a flowing hand. He moved the tea into the living room, located the journal and positioned himself in a chair in the corner under the big reading lamp. He opened the journal where he had last placed the bookmark and looked at the entry for the day:

April 23rd, 1999

Spent the day in Charleston with Rev. Andrew Magee of the Free Universal Church. He was Colonel (now General!) Zachary Walker's family pastor. Knew that Zach had joined a religious sept, The Followers of God, in his late teens. Stopped attending Sunday services after that. Within next five years two ministers of The Followers of God were charged with pedophilia. It was a big scandal at the time. One got ten years. Rev. Magee never heard of The Followers of God again. Well, nearly never. Until his fellow minister, Rev. Roy Sinclair, started to get senile prematurely. He said that Roy had a mission of his own: to convert every soul he could away from these cults. Roy felt that these religious cults were the Devil's instrument. Anyway, during his last six months in South Carolina, Rev Sinclair suffered many episodes of total memory loss. Rev Sinclair was a pastor in the Free Universal Church in Ulster (Northern Ireland). He had been on a five-year ministry in the U.S.
<u>*Follow-up note to myself: visit Roy Sinclair in Ireland.*</u>

Major Whiteside never lived to make that visit. Owen MacDara decided that he would make it for him. But, first, he needed to talk with the Reverend Andrew Magee.

Pat Mullan

Charleston, South Carolina, Monday January 10, 2000.

From the airport in Charleston it was only a twenty-minute drive to Reverend Andrew Magee's Cape Cod ranch-style home. MacDara had called ahead and Magee was expecting him. Andrew Magee was a large-framed man with a big open face. He had a shock of white hair and the most soothing Southern accent that MacDara had ever heard. He didn't waste time. His handshake was firm and sincere. He ushered MacDara into his sitting room. His wife, an inconspicuous woman, appeared and disappeared just as quickly, leaving a pot of coffee and a plate of home-made cookies behind.

MacDara explained that he was retracing Major Whiteside's movements in the months before his disappearance and presumed death. Just to see if he could shed any light on the major's disappearance. MacDara described Ruth Whiteside, her faith and her sense that her husband was still with her.

"Mr. MacDara, I only met Major Whiteside once, but I liked him."

"Yes, Henry Whiteside was well liked. He visited you last April. Let me show you an entry he made in his journal for that day."

They sat in silence for a moment while the Reverend glanced through the entry. "That's a good summary. He told me about his memoirs. He wanted to find out about young Zach Walker. Well, he's not 'young Zach' anymore, is he? He told me that General Walker had played an important role in Korea while he was there. And he wanted to learn more about the early influences on his life."

"That's how you got on to the Followers of God?"

"True. But, not directly. Zach came from a fine family, was active in the scouts, and volunteered for a lot of charitable work in our church. I feel that we had failed him when he left us and joined that cult. I knew Major Whiteside would probably find this out anyway and I'd rather he got it from me."

"And Reverend Sinclair?"

"Oh, yes. Roy. He had a vengeance against all cults. Roy felt they were agents of the Devil, cloaked in the trappings of Christendom. He believed they were a mockery of God. Just like the Black Mass."

"He knew about Zachary Walker?"

"Oh, yes. I told him. Roy is an Ulsterman. He was on an exchange ministry with us. And he spent all his spare time advising our youth on the inherent evils of these cults. I believe he tried to contact Zachary Walker. I don't know if he ever did. You see, his mind had begun to deteriorate. He had Alzheimer's disease. He went back to Ireland again."

"When did he return?"

"Oh, about seven years ago. But his mind must be gone entirely."

"Did he ever discuss what he knew about these cults with you?"

"Rarely. I had the feeling that Roy thought that what I didn't know wouldn't hurt me. You know the old joke: 'I can tell you. But, if I do, then I'll have to kill you'.'"

"Did he ever seem to be afraid?"

"Not Roy! He was about the Lord's work. And he had great faith that the Lord would protect him. But I had a feeling towards the end that he was in danger."

"How do you know?"

"Well, I don't really know. Not exactly. It was just a feeling I had. A sense that something was wrong. Maybe I was misreading the signs."

"What was happening?'"

"It was during Roy's last year with us. He used to disappear for three or four days at a time. He would never tell us where he'd been. We didn't pry, of course. But we were worried about him. Each time he returned he seemed to be in a state of deep depression."

"Did you try to find out what was troubling him?"

Pat Mullan

"Many times. But he wouldn't say anything. Just said he was doing the Lord's work. Fighting the Devil. We knew he'd been out there fighting those cults, but we never figured out what he was actually doing. Was he trying to convert them or was he out there trying to destroy them, like the Lord destroyed Sodom & Gomorrah? Wait a minute. That reminds me. In those last days, when his mind began to go, I'd frequently hear him praying for the destruction of Sodom. I never knew if it meant anything, or if it was just the ravings of the disease. You know, it's crazy of me to say this, but maybe that disease has been his salvation."

Owen MacDara knew he would learn nothing further from Andrew Magee. He had to go and see Reverend Sinclair. It was the only link he might have with the cult of General Walker's past. He certainly couldn't walk up to the general and put the question to him. He was the general's past and, if he was right, the general was trying to bury that past. So he thanked Reverend Magee for his time, said a courteous goodbye to Mrs. Magee, and caught the next flight back to New York. At the Aer Lingus desk he booked two round-trip tickets to Shannon.

ELEVEN

**Connemara, Ireland,
Friday, January 14, 2000.**

It was an unusually mild evening as Owen MacDara picked up his glass of Paddy's and walked over to the large picture windows of Ardree House to look at the sunset. Sunsets in Connemara should be listed as the eighth wonder of the world, he thought. The mountains, the Twelve Bens, were transformed. As the sun set further into the lough, the marbled grays, greens and ochres on the hillside turned into shades of bronze and gold, very soon changing again to gentle mauves. The clouds had also changed into soft pink, warming the cold turquoise sky. MacDara never tired of it.

He and Kate had arrived in Ireland that morning on an Aer Lingus flight from New York to Shannon. They made the two-hour drive to Ardree House in record time. Ardree House was MacDara's sanctuary, his retreat from the world. It was country Georgian, standing on over twenty-three acres verging the lough. The house itself stood amid an acre of gardens. Eucalyptus trees fronted a stand of Chilean fire trees and yucca plants dwarfed the

Pat Mullan

Japanese maples that grew close to their base. There were even rhododendrons that blossomed in January.

They had come to Ireland to see Reverend Roy Sinclair. He lived alone in the old rectory in the village of Eglinton. The village was in Northern Ireland, about seven miles outside the city of Derry.

"If the Reverend Sinclair has Alzheimer's, isn't this going to be a wasted trip?" asked Kate, wanting to be persuaded otherwise.

"Well, Alzheimer's sufferers have been known to retain long-term memory but not short-term. That's our only hope," answered Owen.

"What do we know about Alzheimer's?"

"Not much. Very little is still known about the way our memory works. We only remember what we have stored in the first place. Even then we seem to store bits of memory in different locations in the brain. To retrieve the memory, we have to reconstruct it from these different locations."

"Aren't there drugs that can help?"

"Believe me, researchers have been working all over the world trying to develop a neuro-protective drug to fight disorders such as Alzheimer's disease. No luck so far."

At eight the next morning, Owen and Kate drove through the gates of Ardree House and headed north. It was a six hour drive to Derry, their first destination. Derry is Northern Ireland's second city. The city lies just north of the border that separates the British-governed Northern Ireland from the Independent Republic of Ireland. They planned to drive north through counties Sligo and Donegal. No rain was forecast. This was Kate's first time in Ireland and she looked forward to the journey.

Owen lapsed into silence as they got closer to Derry - Londonderry to those who consider themselves British. But it was always Derry to MacDara. He had a love-hate relationship with the place. He'd won a scholarship to St. Columb's College when he was eleven and spent four years there as a boarding student. St. Columb's was run by priests although half the teachers were laymen. It was there that MacDara's reverence for priests and awe for the institution they represented had ended. Maybe it was there that the seeds of agnosticism, or even atheism, had been sown. MacDara preferred to think of himself as a secular humanist these days. Eccentric priests had dominated the classrooms. Father Toner, who taught mathematics, would often pick up the heavy bound Hall's algebra and whack an unsuspecting student across the side of the head. MacDara remembered one of many incidents.

"MacDara, where's Doolan today?"

Father Toner purposely mispronounced Dolan's name. Dolan was not a boarder. He was a dayboy and lived at home in the city.

"He's sick, Father."

"How do you know that, MacDara?"

"Well, he said he wasn't feeling well in class yesterday, Father. So I assumed he was sick today."

"You assumed, MacDara! You have no proof!"

"No, Father."

"Q.E.D., quod erat demonstrandum. Proof, MacDara! In other words, you don't know and you lied to me. Isn't that correct, MacDara?"

"No, Father!"

"I said, isn't that correct, MacDara?"

"Yes, Father."

"Come up here!"

MacDara could still feel the sting in the palm of his hands from the six slaps that he received for lying from the leather strap that always hung threateningly just inside the side pocket of Father Toner's long dark soutane. St. Columb's was Catholic to the core. Its original role had been to prepare boys for the priesthood, and that was still a principal mission.

The Church controlled the education system. Newspapers and radios were banned at the college. Outside influences and distractions were to be avoided at all costs. All evidence of civil authority was absent. The authority of the Church was paramount. Small rebellions preserved the sanity of the few who refused to become brainwashed by the system. MacDara was one of those few. They used to draw lots to choose a volunteer who would risk scaling the high walls that surrounded the grounds and making it to Wee Johnny's in Bishop Street to buy a packet of Woodbine cigarettes, the cheapest available. They had a special hideout behind the walls, where they smoked while someone kept a lookout for the prefects. They also made radio receivers; crystal sets, they called them, MacDara recalled. He remembered the night that the Dean had entered his dormitory after lights out and tripped over a crystal set earthing wire he had tied to the metal leg of the adjoining bed. That got him twelve, six on each hand with a leather strap, outside the Dean's office the next morning. His hands had swollen to double their size after that; couldn't hold a pencil in class that day.

His reverie was broken by Kate.

"Where are we now"?

Looking around, MacDara could see that they had entered the Strand Road and were heading uptown towards the Guildhall and Shipquay Street, a very steep street that led up to the Diamond, the center of Derry's shopping district. A British war memorial dominated the center of the Diamond. The Bogside lay on the low flatland beyond the Diamond, land outside the walls of the City; land where the poor and the powerless lived. The Bogside was fertile breeding ground for militant Irish republicans. It was the center of Civil Rights rebellion and protest against the British authorities in the sixties and seventies. One of the most photographed gables of a house in the Bogside still proclaimed 'YOU ARE NOW ENTERING FREE DERRY.'

Once again, Kate's voice intruded upon his thoughts..

"Owen, where are you? What are you thinking about?"

The CIRCLE of SODOM
A Gripping New Thriller

"Oh, nothing deep, believe me", MacDara lied, "just an old tongue twister; say this quickly: 'Shipquay Street's a slippy street to slide upon.'"

"I think you've regressed to your childhood. Is that what this place does to you?"

MacDara didn't respond. Kate's question was rhetorical.

They weren't staying in Derry. They were only passing through on their way to Eglinton; but MacDara couldn't resist giving the old city a lookover. Circling the Diamond he headed back down Shipquay Street, around the Guildhall and towards Craigavon Bridge. They crossed Lough Foyle and took the road to Eglinton.

Eglinton is a small village easily accessible from the main road. It wasn't difficult to find the former Church of Ireland rectory that was now the home of the Reverend Roy Sinclair. Mostly red-brick Tudor, with ivy clambering everywhere, it stood in the midst of a grove of ancient oak trees. MacDara lifted the black cast-iron knocker on the weather-beaten front door and knocked twice. It sounded very loud. At least three or four minutes passed, and they were beginning to wonder if anyone was home, when they heard the sound of a key in the lock. As they turned to face the door it opened and they were greeted by a prim-looking woman. She wore a simple navy dress, sensible shoes and her dark hair, streaked with gray, was combed severely back from her forehead into a bun.

"Good afternoon. I'm Jean Smythe. I'm Reverend Sinclair's nurse. You must be Mr. MacDara and Ms. Whiteside."

"Good afternoon, Nurse Smythe," responded MacDara, "we're so grateful that you could arrange our visit with Reverend Sinclair."

"Not at all, Mr. MacDara. But, as we told you on the telephone, Reverend Sinclair will not be able to appreciate your visit. He has moments of lucidity, but they are very rare."

Pat Mullan

"We understand that, Nurse Smythe, and we realize that our visit may be a futile one. But we felt compelled to see him in any case."

"Very well, then. Do come in. Please wait in the drawing room and I'll bring Reverend Sinclair to see you. Would you like tea?"

"Thank you, Nurse Smythe. That would be perfect."

Nurse Smythe opened the paneled teak door to the right of the entrance hallway and ushered them into the drawing room. A turf fire was blazing in the grate and a large gray cat lay purring on a rug in front of the fire. The drawing-room furniture was old with a patina earned from years of use. It was the kind of furniture that antique dealers scoured the country to find. Owen and Kate chose two high-backed chairs by the fireplace. Looking around they observed a drawing room that had been lived in, one that reflected the interests and personality of the inhabitants. A chaise longue, overshadowed by a tall brass reading lamp, nestled under a big bay window. On either side of the window a variety of books of all sizes bulged from the shelves of two floor-to-ceiling bookcases. A piano sat, unobtrusive, and they imagined unused, in the farthest corner. Renoir's *Dance at Bougival* hung in a gilt frame on the opposite wall near a mahogany sideboard that served as a pedestal for family photographs; ancient tintypes in metal frames on one side and modern portraits in carved wooden frames on the other side.

Roy Sinclair was a small neat man in his early sixties. He followed Nurse Smythe as she carried the tea into the drawing room. He was holding a barmbrack, an Irish raisin bread, on a round wooden carving tray. He didn't speak. Just stood there with a beatific smile as Nurse Smythe made the introductions. She relieved him of the barmbrack and guided him to a comfortable high-backed rocking chair. He perched on it and began to rock gently back and forth.

The CIRCLE of SODOM
A Gripping New Thriller

"Half an hour only," Nurse Smythe admonished. "He tires easily."

As the Nurse departed, Owen opened his briefcase and placed a number of documents on the small table between the Reverend and himself and started to talk directly to him. He talked about America, about Charleston and about the Free Universal Church, showing Reverend Sinclair photos of the church, the neighborhood in Charleston, even a gathering of church elders with whom he had worked. But he met with no reaction. Reverend Sinclair just continued to smile in a trance-like way, gently rocking back and forth in his chair. Owen persisted. He started with the photographs again. He had a number of photographs of Reverend Andrew Magee mixed in among all the others; some taken in groups, some head and shoulders, some closeups, even one of Reverend Magee in the pulpit.

It happened quite unexpectedly. The rocking chair stopped and Reverend Sinclair picked up the photo of Andrew Magee in the pulpit, held it out in front of him, and simply said "Andrew!". But, just as quickly, his eyes lost their focus and the rocking started again. Still afraid to hope, Owen continued to talk. He talked about Zachary Walker, about the general's appointment as Chairman of the Joint Chiefs, about the Followers of God, about religious cults. He was still talking to Roy Sinclair when Nurse Smythe returned.

"It's time, Mr. MacDara. This is enough stress for him."

"Thank you, Nurse Smythe. I just wish we could try a little more. He almost remembered for one brief moment."

"Mr. MacDara, it's most frustrating. We all love him. Those brief moments are so elusive. They raise our hopes and then dash them again."

As Owen prepared to gather up his documents and photographs he accidentally overturned his briefcase. Everything scattered on the floor at Reverend Sinclair's feet. Kate and Nurse Smythe dropped to their knees to help pick things up, as MacDara berated himself for being a klutz. The grip on his wrist was strong and firm and unexpected. He looked up. Reverend Sinclair had stopped rocking. He held a photograph in his hand that he had taken from Owen. It was a close-up of the tattoo found on the inner arm of the albino.

"Sodom." Distinct and strong. Reverend Sinclair stood up as he uttered the word. He just stood there staring at the photograph. "The Circle of Sodom," he said, again, in a voice one could imagine he used when preaching a sermon.

Just as suddenly, he let his grip relax on the photograph and it floated to the floor.

They left the bottle of Black Bush they had picked up in Shannon. Reverend Magee had told them that Roy was fond of a night-cap. He was still smiling and rocking away as they thanked Nurse Smythe for their visit.

MacDara climbed the stairs at Ardree House to his office on the second floor. The large window over his desk looked directly west over the lough. Smoke was rising from the chimneys of a few widely scattered cottages in this sparsely populated land. Four yucca plants thrived behind the natural dry stone wall that bordered the front gardens, nourished by the warming influence of the Gulf Stream. MacDara reckoned if he could see over those low hills the next land to the west was America. It somehow made it seem as if New York was next door.

He stepped over piles of newspapers, books and magazines that still lay on the wooden floor from his last time in the office. At the desk, he opened his sturdy blue Lands End traveling bag and took out his laptop. In a few seconds he was on-line. Following the instructions that he had committed to memory, he accessed General Shields's email system and entered his passwords. Cleared to transmit he sent the following message:

The CIRCLE of SODOM
A Gripping New Thriller

At Ardree House. Saw the Reverend. New information on the tattoo. Check out 'The Circle of Sodom'. Arrive New York, Kennedy, at 2:30 pm on Thursday, 27th. Will make contact then.

Pat Mullan

TWELVE

The National Security Council, Washington, D.C., Tuesday, January 18, 2000.

Shields had never seen Sanderson so agitated. The words were tumbling from his lips in bursts as he paced the general's office. He was unintelligible. Shields waited until Sanderson shifted to a lower gear.

"Larry, you've been here for almost ten minutes and I haven't understood a single thing you've said. Slow down and get a grip on yourself."

"Sorry, Boss. The AI system has just blown my mind. It's thinking! Literally thinking!"

"What have you got for me?"

"I fed it the data on your tattoo as well as the description of the albino. I also gave it scenarios on the killings in New York. And I input the Circle of Sodom data and the religious variables."

"Did it produce anything?"

"Boss, you bet it did! The possibilities! You're hardwired to STOP. Let me connect my laptop. I've got the AI screens loaded and I'll walk you through what we've got. I'll bring up the Preliminary Thoughts screen, PT1, for you. Look at that."

Page one of the PT1 screen appeared on Sanderson's laptop, and Bart Shields began to read:

> *Preliminary Thoughts:* *After looking at all the data I believe that the snake in a circle is more than just the logo of a club or a gang. I'm searching for a deeper meaning. There is definite religious and supernatural significance. Adam was tempted in the Garden of Eden by the Devil who appeared in the form of a snake. The Hopi Indians of Arizona believe that snakes are their brothers. They believe they are the children of their ancestors, the Snake Maid and the Snake Hero, who were changed into snakes. They hold a snake dance ceremony every two years. Look at the religious dimension in James Dickey's poetry. Dickey believes in reincarnation and hopes that the soul passes from one kind of creature to another. In his poetry he reincarnates man as a rattlesnake. Dickey sees the rattlesnake as a symbol of justice and, in a definite biblical reference to the Garden of Eden, he has said: "The justice of the Lord, in its most striking case, depended on the intervention of the snake."*
>
> *Preliminary Probability:* *The snake in the circle tattoo probably identifies a member of an organization. The organization might be secret. It might also be religious. Its mission might be to exact justice.*
>
> *I must do more research. I'm searching.*

Shields was on his feet, pacing back and forth just like Sanderson. Except that Sanderson was still seated at his laptop.

"That's astounding, Larry. Do you mean to tell me that the STOP AI system produced that screen from the input you gave it?"

"That's right, Boss. You are looking at a true Artificial Intelligence. This has never been done before."

"Well, you're right, Larry. It is mind blowing. When will we get more?"

"It's a matter of total system availability. I suck up every resource in the configuration. I'll have to wait until the weekend to initiate AI again. Let's say Monday. If I get the run time, I should have more for you then."

"Excellent! Great stuff!"

Sanderson logged out, disconnected his laptop from the hardwired line in Shields's office, and left. Shields sat down at his desk, turned to his PC and entered an encrypted message to be retrieved by MacDara the next time he accessed the email system. The text of his message read:

> *Owen, STOP's first results on your tattoo. Thinks you should be looking for a secret religious organization. I think you might be dealing with some kind of cult. I'll know more by Monday. Contact me soon.*

Task Four Systems, Cambridge, Massachusetts, Friday, January 21, 2000.

Doug Holder was nervous. Security was tight at Task Four Systems. Their defense contracts were highly sensitive and their software top secret. Everyone, visitors and employees alike, had to present authorization to the guard at the main entrance before they were permitted into the building. All briefcases had to be opened for inspection by the guard. Every item leaving the building, other than personal possessions, had to be accompanied by a permit authorized and signed by the respective department head. Computer and software items got special attention. Even program diagnostic listings had to have authorized approval to

The CIRCLE of SODOM
A Gripping New Thriller

be taken out of the building. Floppy disks, CD Roms, and any other storage media were not permitted to enter or leave the building under any circumstance. Employees wore photo ID badges. The badges were also the keys that facilitated access throughout the company. There were three levels of access: operational and clerical areas only; high risk areas, which included the data processing and communications center as well as programming and systems development; finally, complete access, including the executive offices on the fifth floor. Few people, other than the President and his top executives, had this highest security level. As a Senior Programmer in the Software Development Division, Doug Holder had the next level of clearance.

That gave him little comfort on this particular day. He had closeted himself in the men's room, taken off his shirt and T-shirt and taped two three and a half inch diskettes to his body. The disks contained the latest release of communications software scheduled for installation at a number of strategic military sites in North America and Europe in exactly thirty days. He never left the building at the five o'clock rush hour but today would be an exception. He wanted the guards to be well occupied as he left.

But he didn't have to worry. It was a Friday evening, everyone's mind was on the weekend, and Doug had a vacation day on Monday. The guard was processing people out the door as fast as he could. He gave Doug's briefcase a quick once-over and wished him a good weekend.

**The Millennium Covenant, Tennessee,
Saturday, January 22, 2000.**

Within the hour Doug Holder was at Logan, boarding a flight for Atlanta. He changed planes there, travelled on to Memphis and booked into an inn near the airport. At nine the

Pat Mullan

next morning he was sitting in his favorite place, the Cracker Barrel, enjoying his favorite breakfast. Eggs over easy, sausage patties, biscuits with white milk gravy and a generous helping of baked apple slices simmering in their special cinnamon sauce. He was halfway through when Will Baxter joined him.

"Any problems?", asked Will, seeking confirmation that all had gone well.

"No. Not a thing".

"Have you got it?"

"Yes. Are you all set?"

"We're ready. We've completed coding and tested it on your current software release. Works every time".

"What's the game plan?"

"We'll put the code into your new release. Then we'll do regression and acceptance testing on each of the modules to make sure everything works as intended".

"How long will that take?"

"All weekend. We've got it scheduled hour by hour. You'll just about make your return flight on Monday. The data center is on hot stand-by waiting for us to begin".

"OK, let's do it!".

One hour later Doug Holder was sitting in Will Baxter's jeep climbing into the mountains. Mountains that he and Will grew up in, went to school in, chased girls in. He'd lost his virginity in these hills. And his innocence too. At sixteen he'd lost his father and his faith in American justice. He was named after his father. Douglas. The Reverend Douglas Holder, pastor of the local Baptist Church.

His father had been alone in his church the night he died. When he wasn't home by midnight, his mother called the Sheriff and asked him to check and see if everything was alright. The Sheriff found his father lying in a pool of his own blood. He'd been bludgeoned to death and the church ransacked and looted. Everybody knew who'd done it. They arrested the three of them the next day. Black trash that his father went out of his way to

The CIRCLE of SODOM
A Gripping New Thriller

help. There was a trial, if you could call it that. They went scot-free in three weeks. Circumstantial evidence. Insufficient to prove that they were guilty beyond a shadow of a doubt. The American Civil Liberties Union brought in one of their big guns, one of Kunstler's fellow travellers, to defend them. Turned it into a race issue. Will Baxter's father was angry. Everybody knew that he was in the Klan. So it was no surprise when burning crosses appeared outside the houses of this trash. And even less surprise when one of them was found hanging from a tree near the church.

Doug Holder blamed America, the American government, the American justice system for freeing his father's murderers. He also blamed America for his father's murder. It hadn't been difficult for Will to recruit him, to give him a chance for revenge. And there was a sweetener. Colonel McNab was paying him well. A third payment of fifty thousand dollars would be deposited in his account in Switzerland when this release was successfully implemented.

The present abruptly erased the past as Will Baxter rounded a bend and came to a full stop at the entrance to the Millennium Covenant. Doug Holder had been here before and he had always been impressed by the drill. Two guards, armed with machine pistols, manned the guard post that straddled the chain-link fence. They knew Will but they still asked for his ID and his visitor's authorization for Doug Holder. Then one of them made a phone call announcing their presence and requesting authority to let them enter. Task Four Systems could learn a few things about security from these people, he reflected.

Once inside the compound they made a beeline for the data center, the only building with satellite dishes on the roof. More security, even tighter this time. Guard at the entrance, card-key access through the outer door, and then Holder was taken to the security office for processing. This room, bristling with electronic gear and TV monitors, was where his fingerprints, palm prints, voice prints and photograph were taken and compared to those still on file from his last visit. Then he was issued a temporary access badge that would facilitate his access for the next two days; at midnight on Monday it would expire. That accomplished, he followed Will Baxter along the hallway until they reached a floor-to-ceiling steel turnstile. Putting his access key in the lock, Will entered the turnstile to be trapped in a six foot by six foot enclosure where he faced a door with a two-way mirror and was observed by a camera mounted close to the ceiling. Standing directly in front of the camera, he placed the palm of his right hand on the square glass top of a free-standing verification module. At the same time, he spoke into a wall-mounted microphone, giving his name, occupation and his own personal identification code. That done, the door clicked open and he was free to enter the data center. Doug followed, but it took him twice as long. He felt especially vulnerable when he was trapped between the steel turnstile and the inner locked door. He breathed a sigh of relief as the door clicked open. Will was waiting for him inside and echoed the thoughts in his own mind.

"Yeah, I know. It's a bitch, man. I don't like it either. But we have no choice. Can you imagine how many people would give their right arm to get in here?"

Bypassing the machine room with its impressive arrays of disk drives and consoles, they continued past the printer pool where all the printers and other input-output devices were pooled for more effective resource management. Next they circled the true nerve center, the communications room, with state-of-the-art consoles arrayed in a semi-circle, monitoring every terrestrial line and satellite transponder node in their global network. Finally they reached their destination, the project acceptance test site, a very modern utilitarian room filled with terminals, flipcharts, chalkboards, whiteboards, wall-to-wall bubble and gantt charts showing critical-path timelines, milestones, contingency plans, restart-recovery plans and 'drop-dead' objectives.

The CIRCLE of SODOM
A Gripping New Thriller

Five people, three men and two women, were standing in a circle around one of the project milestone charts. They opened up the circle to greet Doug and Will. Introductions were unnecessary. Doug knew them all from the last intensive four days he had spent here. Doug handed over his two diskettes to be copied and backed-up for recovery. A detailed testing plan for the day illustrated one wall. According to the timing it should have commenced a half-hour ago. Each of them knew their assignments. They conferred briefly and then manned their respective terminals. It was going to be a very long weekend.

The ringing of the phone startled them. It hadn't rung since Doug had arrived. He looked at his watch. It was one pm on Sunday afternoon. Been here a whole day already. Felt like a week. Worked right through the night. Kipped out for a couple of hours on the couch in Will's office. He felt grungy but satisfied. The testing had gone well so far. He picked up the receiver after the fourth ring. It was the colonel.
"Holder, I want to see you before you leave. Twenty minutes time. My office, OK." It was a command, not a request.
"Yes, sir. I'll be there".
Doug Holder was surprised. He hadn't expected to meet Colonel McNab on this visit. When he entered his office the colonel was playing with his favorite pacifier, an iron railroad spike. He was tapping the corner of his desk with it, just like a drumstick. Finally, he returned it to the desk drawer, cleared his throat, looked at Holder and commenced to talk: "I wanted to thank you for the work you've done. I know we're paying you well for the risk, but I also know that you want to avenge your father. We can't bring him back. But we can bring back the values we believe in. Turn this country around. Make it a real God-fearing place again. With liberty and justice for the people who are entitled to it. And hell and damnation for everybody else!"

Pat Mullan

The colonel got up, drew himself to his full erect bearing and looked out of the window.

"Your hills. My hills, too. And they'll be our children's hills and their children's hills. Even if we have to fight for them tree by tree." Turning around, he walked over and looked down at Holder, who hadn't moved a muscle since he had started to talk.

"Our people are fed up with the liberal mollycoddling of criminals and the destruction of the morals of this nation. They will turn out those bastards in Washington and their 'intellectual' friends, who are destroying our institutions. But we don't expect them to give up without a fight. That's why we need to be prepared. The work you are doing is part of that preparation. If the time ever comes when we have to use it, we will. It's better to cripple our own forces than risk another civil war in this nation. That would make Sherman's march on Atlanta look like a boy scout outing. No, we don't want that. Nobody would win. And we must not lose this one. So, I look on this as an insurance policy. And you're carrying that policy for us".

Doug Holder wasn't prepared for what happened next. The colonel reached down and actually lifted him out of the chair, holding him in a vice-like grip about two inches away from his face: "Son, this will be our very last meeting. I will not see you again. But if you are ever discovered you give them nothing, I repeat, nothing, but your 'name, rank and serial number'. You do not mention this outfit under any circumstances!".

He released Holder but continued to back him into the wall, all the time looking him directly in the eye and drilling his forefinger into his chest, while he repeated, over and over again, "Do you understand that? Do you understand that?"

The acceptance test ended successfully at noon on the Monday. Doug Holder made his return flight with ease. He carried back with him the two diskettes containing the new release of communications software that would be installed at all strategic military installations in thirty days time. The software now contained the instructions that would disable those installations upon a single command from the colonel's communication center. Doug Holder was well pleased.

THIRTEEN

**Gloucester, Massachussetts,
Thursday, January 27, 2000.**

The kid was dead. He'd been garrotted with piano wire. The wire had been twisted so tightly that his jugular had been severed. Blood had spurted all over the windshield and the dashboard. A sandwich with one bite taken lay sodden at his feet, and potato chips were everywhere, scattered from the bag in his left hand.

Baker Security monitored all stakeouts. The kid was supposed to call in every two hours. He called at midnight. He was due to call again at two am. When they didn't receive his call and couldn't raise him on the mobile they sent another security officer to investigate. Marty King had seen violent death before but he wasn't prepared to see the kid like that. And he wasn't prepared for the destruction he encountered when he entered the Whiteside home.

Frank Nagle's phone woke him at two forty-five am. That never happened to him anymore, he thought.

The CIRCLE of SODOM
A Gripping New Thriller

"Frank, it's Marty King. I'm over at the Whiteside house. I'm afraid I've got bad news. The place has been hit...and, Frank, I'm real sorry. The kid is dead. I think you'd better get over here right away."

Frank Nagle was devastated. Benny Cafolla, they all called him the kid, was Frank's protegee. He was a North End kid. A smart, streetsmart, Italian kid. Hardest worker. Frank would have trusted him with anything. Wanted to grow up and join the FBI. Worked for Baker Security evenings and weekends to help pay his way through Boston College.

Frank Nagle arrived at the Whiteside home just as the ambulance was leaving. The street had been cordoned off and at least four police cars were standing outside Ruth Whiteside's front door. Police banner tape marked the perimeter of the property. The police knew Frank, and let him through. Marty was waiting for him in the family room, or what was left of it.

"She's still alive. Barely. Unconscious. In a coma. They really did a job on her. Both arms are broken and her body is beaten and bruised beyond belief," Marty answered the question in Frank's eyes.

"What animal did this?" asked Frank.

"That's what we'd all like to know. The police are combing the house and the area for any shred of evidence they can find. These people must be crazy. Or on drugs. Or something. Look at this," he said.

Paintings were ripped, furniture was slashed, tables overturned, vases broken, everything wantonly destroyed. Henry Whiteside's den had been totally ripped apart. Books lay in heaps on the floor, bookcases had been toppled over and his desk ransacked. Could the destruction in the rest of the house be a cover for the ransacking of Major Whiteside's office? If that was the case, what were these people looking for? All of these thoughts tumbled through Frank's head.

Lieutenant Malone, in charge of the investigation at the scene of the crime, wanted to know too. He questioned Frank and Marty, but neither could contribute anything of value. Frank had thought it was just another routine assignment. Vulnerable lady, living alone. Family worried about crime. Money no object. Wanted her protected. But it was obviously more than that.

Frank told Lieutenant Malone that he had been asked to personally look after Mrs. Whiteside by Ken Baker. The Lieutenant assured them that he would be in touch with Mr. Baker some time that day. He had allowed them to briefly visit the crime scene, even though he had sealed it off; they were veteran cops and well known to Lieutenant Malone, but he still admonished them not to touch anything and insisted that they wear booties and gloves before entering the crime scene.

It was nearly five am by the time Frank left the house. As he made his way to his car, he could see that all the shrubs on either side of the front pathway had been ripped out.

"The bastards!" he snarled, to no one in particular.

Dr Bill Watson and the two best paramedics at Addison Gilbert Hospital in Gloucester were on board the helicopter with Ruth Whiteside. She was in a coma. They had treated the trauma, set both of her broken arms, and stabilized her vital signs. But she needed the kind of care that Addison Gilbert was not equipped to provide. So they had taken the decision to move her immediately to Massachusetts General Hospital, MGH, in Boston.

Ken Baker had been involved from the moment Ruth Whiteside entered the emergency room at Addison Gilbert. He had made her the most important patient in New England and he now had the entire trauma facility at MGH waiting to receive her. Ruth Whiteside's vital signs were being fed into an on-board computer on the helicopter and transmitted, in real time, to the main monitoring system at MGH. Every breath she took was being monitored.

The CIRCLE of SODOM
A Gripping New Thriller

It was seven am on a bright clear morning and Bill Watson could see the brick townhouses of Beacon Hill as the helicopter meandered over the Charles River, following Storrow Drive towards MGH. He had seen MGH from the air a couple of times before, so he had no trouble recognizing the mix of old and new buildings that comprised the hospital complex. In minutes they had landed on the roof where a medical team was waiting to receive Ruth Whiteside.

The flight from Shannon to New York had been uneventful. MacDara had even managed to catch a couple of hours' sleep. They landed at JFK on schedule at two thirty in the afternoon and their baggage was among the first to appear on the carousel. Customs waved them through, a redcap loaded their baggage on his trolley, and within twenty minutes they were running the gauntlet of anxious faces waiting in the International Arrivals area. They soon saw the white cardboard sign held aloft, with *MacDara* in bold black letters. But it wasn't held, as expected, by the waiting limo driver. It was Ken Baker. He welcomed them with a tight little forced smile on his lips. He looked wan and tired. Owen and Kate knew instantly that something was wrong. Ken took them away from the throng of people and told them about the attack on Kate's mother and the murder of the kid.

Kate looked stunned. She didn't speak. Owen reached for her and she sank her face into his chest and started sobbing uncontrollably.

Ken waited until her sobs had subsided and then spoke again: "She's in Massachusetts General Hospital in Boston. We had her airlifted out from the Addison Gilbert Hospital in Gloucester. She's getting the best medical care we can find. We'll take the next shuttle flight to Logan. My car is waiting outside. I'll take you over to La Guardia now."

Dr. Stan Hoffman was the best trauma specialist in the northeast. He met them as soon as they arrived at MGH and took them to a private room.

"How's my mother? Is she going to be all right?"

"Ms. Whiteside, your mother is a very strong woman for her age, but she has suffered severe injuries. Both her arms were broken, but they're simple fractures, not compound. Multiple contusions elsewhere but no further broken bones and no damage to any internal organs. Now, she does not have a fracture to her skull but she is still in a coma. This kind of a coma is the most difficult to make a prognosis about. We simply do not know when she may regain consciousness. But all her vital signs are stable and she is breathing without assistance. So that's a good sign and we're hopeful. Your mother is very lucky to be alive, Ms. Whiteside, and she is getting the very best care."

"Thank you, Doctor, May I see her?"

"Yes, of course. Your presence may be therapeutic. If you like, you can stay in the hospital. We'll have a bed provided for you."

"Yes, I would like to stay with her."

"Very well, then, I'll bring you and Mr. MacDara to see Nurse McDermott. She will take you to your mother."

After reassuring himself that all was being done that could be done, Owen MacDara left Kate at her mother's bedside, called Ken Baker and told him to put twenty-four-hour protection on Ruth and Kate Whiteside at MGH. And this time, to make it fail-safe. Then he caught an evening flight back to New York.

The CIRCLE of SODOM
A Gripping New Thriller

FOURTEEN

**GMA Headquarters, New York,
Tuesday, February 1, 2000.**

They were waiting for MacDara when he reached the office on Tuesday morning.

His three senior associates looked somber and shaken. It was Dick Massey who broke the silence.

"Owen, I don't know how to tell you this." Dick's usual contented look was gone. There was no mirth in the eyes and his face appeared ashen, even through his full Viking beard. "Angelo's dead. He was killed on Central Park West yesterday."

MacDara said nothing. This is a dream, he thought. It's not happening. He had a ten am with Angelo that morning to finalize the contract on the telephone switch for the new building in Connecticut. GMA had a consultancy contract to provide project co-ordination and expertise on the job.

Owen sat down in disbelief. But he knew this was no dream. His financial controller, Al Bernstein, just stood there, lifeless. Al had worked closely with Angelo on this project. They had become good friends. And Al, loquacious Al, had never been

Pat Mullan

known to stand silent for a minute. Janet Duffy, his MIS Director, stood beside Al, looking distraught.

Grasping for comprehension, he asked, "How did he die?"

"Angelo was murdered. Shot!" said Dick.

"But, why? How?" Owen said, almost inaudibly, still trying to comprehend.

It was Al who spoke this time. Everything pent up inside was unleashed. "We don't know what happened. Nobody knows a damned thing. Liz was with him. She's in a catatonic state. Total shock. Nobody can get anything out of her. They were visiting friends on Central Park West. One of the kids' birthdays or something. Jesus, this fucking city. Bastards! If I ever find out who did this to Angelo, I'll tear them apart!"

Al just choked up and the tears began to flow. Owen grabbed him around the shoulders and held him.

Owen called the NYPD and asked to speak with Detective Gennaro, who was assigned to Murph's investigation. After his call had been forwarded five or six times he finally connected. He briefed Gennaro, who informed him that Angelo's murder had been committed within their jurisdiction and the investigation had already been assigned to Lieutenant Nichols.

The Southern District Court Building in Lower Manhattan is a large, gray, cold, uninviting stone edifice. Its corridors are cheerless. The pale-green paint is chipped and scuff-marked.

Assistant District Attorney William Stern's office was equally cheerless and spartan. He was on the phone when MacDara entered, and nodded for him to take a seat. Detective Gennaro was already there, notebook in hand. He greeted MacDara with a thin-lipped smile. MacDara sat on one of the three heavy wooden chairs that lined the back wall. Gennaro sat on his left. A wooden bench, like a church pew, lined the wall to the right. Assistant DA Stern sat behind a large ugly wooden desk under a window with dirty panes, which covered most of the end wall of the office.

Stern hung up the phone and looked at MacDara. He was young, late-twenties, early-thirties, with a high forehead, receding hairline and a thin, ascetic-looking face. Large bifocals bisected his face.

"Mr MacDara, I understand you were a close friend of Angelo Russo," Stern opened in a surprisingly deep voice.

"That's right," said Owen.

"You met regularly at Costelloes pub, I understand," said Stern.

"About once a month. We were old army buddies and liked to keep our friendship alive", said Owen matter-of-factly.

"Do you know of anyone who might have wanted to kill Mr. Russo?" continued Stern.

"No, I don't. As far as I know, Angelo didn't have an enemy in the world", responded MacDara.

"Isn't it true that he had marital problems?" asked Stern, as he got up and walked around in front of his desk.

"I don't know anything about that", said MacDara, with irritation.

"Oh, come on Mr. MacDara. Don't be coy!" Stern's voice was loud and impatient.

MacDara didn't respond. He'd known that Angelo and Liz had an open marriage. But he had no intention of discussing that with Stern. The way he saw it, it was none of Stern's business. Besides, what had all this got to do with Angelo's murder?

"Let me remind you that I can call you as a witness when this case goes to trial. And I needn't remind you that you will then have to answer under oath!", said Stern, when Owen failed to answer his question.

"Angelo's private life was his own. I knew little about it", reiterated MacDara.

"Mr. MacDara, I find that hard to believe", said Stern.

Pat Mullan

As MacDara stared poker-faced at him, Stern went around behind his desk and flipped over a page of an open notebook in the center of the desk.

"Isn't it true, Mr. MacDara, that on the night of June fifteenth last year you drove Liz Russo home after her husband had thrown her out of their car?" questioned Stern, as though he had MacDara in the witness box.

"Well, many couples have big fights once in a while. As far as I know, they kissed and made up a few days later", Owen said dismissively. "Why are you asking me all of this?" he asked, feeling himself getting angry and knowing that he shouldn't lose control here.

"I'll tell you why, Mr. MacDara. Mrs Russo sat on that bench yesterday with her attorney beside her. She claimed that she and her husband had a good marriage and a loving relationship. She lied, Mr. MacDara", said Stern, as he came around the desk again, "I don't want you to sit there and try to protect your friend's reputation. I want the truth", Stern almost yelled as he ran his hand over his balding forehead.

MacDara just sat, impassive. He decided that, in this case, silence was golden. He didn't like this Assistant DA. Ambitious. Out to make a name for himself, thought MacDara.

"You can go now, Mr. MacDara. But I want you to stay in touch with Detective Gennaro and his team," said Stern.

As Owen got up to leave, Stern still hadn't finished his monologue.

"His wife is a cold fish, Mr MacDara. If she had her husband killed I intend to prove it. And, if necessary, I'll put you on the stand!"

MacDara had no time to grieve. That same afternoon the message that appeared on his PC was cryptic:

The CIRCLE of SODOM
A Gripping New Thriller

Subj: ***Command Performance***
Owen: Meet me in my office at 3 p.m. tomorrow. The President wants to see us. Be there.
Bart.

Well, MacDara mused, there was no mistaking what was meant by a 'Command Performance'.

He packed an overnight bag and planned to spend an hour in the office in the morning before taking the shuttle to Washington from La Guardia. Next he phoned Kate at MGH. There was no change. Ruth Whiteside was still in a coma.

FIFTEEN

**National Security Council, Washington, DC,
Wednesday, February 2, 2000**

Owen MacDara was punctual. His watch read two minutes to three as he entered General Bartley Shields's office. Shields was on the phone, crouched behind a cloud of cigar smoke. A minute later he hung up the phone and waved his hand vigorously through the air in a vain attempt to get rid of the smoke.

"Owen, you look like shit!" said Shields.

"I didn't sleep much last night," said Owen, and then went on to tell about the murder of Angelo Russo.

"The NYPD must be hot on your case. Two murders and you're connected to both victims. But I don't see any connection between Murphy Armstrong and Angelo Russo. Unless someone with a grudge against Costelloes is intent on eliminating you and your drinking buddies. Even that's too far fetched for New York!"

"I don't think there's any connection. If my theory about Murph's killing is right, Angelo's death is totally unrelated. No, I don't know why Angelo was killed. Maybe Stern is on the right track. Maybe Angelo's murder is personal. But I can't believe Liz Russo had anything to do with it."

"I think I'll make a call to the police commissioner up there. I know him well and it's time to brief him on our interest in the Murphy murder. I won't tell him everything. I can't. Besides, we don't know the hell what everything is anyway. But I'll encourage him to take the heat off you. And maybe get him to give you a hand if you happen to need it. I can't do much about Stern. I don't have the same influence at Justice. And the President doesn't want me to raise any alerts just now. Which brings us to why you are here."

Shields had been walking around the office as he talked. Now he went back behind his desk, sat down, retrieved the cigar that had died in the ashtray, knocked the ashes off the tip, stuck it in his mouth and lit a match. Satisfied that he had succeeded, he blew a ring of smoke into the air and began to talk.

"The President is worried. There's something happening in Washington that scares him. He sees a convergence of radical right-wing groups, from the militant militias to the religious right. He believes that they have strong friends and supporters right here in the government. There seems to be a threat in the air these days. It's not something tangible, something he can take action on. But he's worried. He's worried for our democracy. And he's not sure who to trust anymore. Even in his own cabinet. This President is feeling isolated. And vulnerable. I've never seen him like this before. And we've been close friends for years."

Shields put the cigar in the ashtray and got up from behind the desk again. He walked over to Owen. "That's why he wants to see you. He trusts me and I trust you. The President wants you to help him on this one. I think he hopes that you'll find evidence that proves his fears are unfounded. But I'm sure he'll tell you in his own words. And remember this - he has complete faith in Zachary Walker."

Pat Mullan

The White House, Washington, DC

The President met General Bartley Shields and Owen MacDara at the door of the Oval Office. He was entirely like the image he projected in the media: friendly and engaging. He greeted MacDara warmly, held his hand in a firm clasp, then transferred his hand to Owen's shoulder and guided him to a chair.

"I'm glad you could come. Bart has told me a lot about you. I've asked you here because I need your help. Bart, please proceed."

"Thank you, Mr. President. Before I commence I'd like to say that the seriousness of what I am about to cover has just been underscored by the events of recent days. We got through Y2K without any terrorist attacks. But only because we were vigilant. As you know the Jordanians arrested thirteen suspects and uncovered a plot to attack Americans at hotels and tourist sites. We arrested people who had come in through the Canadian border. We believe that they were planning to bomb right here in Washington. Some of these people may be working with Osama bin Laden. There may already be foreign terrorist cells in this country, just biding their time. And we've got to find them and stop them. Bombs aren't the only weapons in their arsenal. It's the chemicals that worry me the most. Look at what happened in Japan not too long ago. Eleven people were killed and more than five thousand injured when Sarin nerve gas was released in the Tokyo subway system. The Japanese found a chemical plant for the large-scale production of Sarin. Even worse, they discovered the ingredients needed to produce biological weapons."

General Shields had set up his laptop computer so that the President and MacDara could easily view the screen, still talking as he did so.

The CIRCLE of SODOM
A Gripping New Thriller

"Mr. President, the deadly thing about Sarin is that it is a simple compound that any amateur chemist could put together. As you know, it was first developed by Germany in World War Two but they never used it. Saddam Hussein did. He used it against Iran."

"What does it do, exactly?" asked the President.

"It's totally colorless and odorless. It's absorbed through the skin or lungs and affects the nervous system. Your lungs become congested, you sweat and you vomit. Then you go into convulsions and you can die in about fifteen minutes. It's twenty times more lethal than potassium cyanide. It's also heavier than air, so it stays close to the ground and can kill a lot more people."

"That's exactly why I put top priority on this. We're vulnerable and the World Trade Center bombing brought that home to us. We need to be able to cope effectively if we suffer casualties like the ones in Japan. That doesn't mean that I don't expect us to prevent something like this from happening here. We've got to stop it before it happens."

"I know, Mr. President. All our agencies are ready and well trained to limit casualties from just such an attack. But we're way behind in detection. We're on top of the movement of material that might be used for nuclear weapons and we've got the best hi-tech sensors to help us detect conventional stuff, but we're nowhere on this chemical thing."

General Shields's laptop was linked to STOP and he briefed the President on Sanderson's most recent AI breakthrough. His briefing was succinct and took only a few minutes.

"But, Mr. President," he concluded, "our own home grown terrorists may be the biggest threat we face. The Oklahoma bombing proved that. And only a few weeks ago in California we arrested two members of a militia group who were planning to bomb a propane storage tank. They hoped that martial law would be imposed and that that would inspire a revolution against the U.S. government. About the very same time, we arrested another militia leader in Florida. He was plotting to steal explosives to blow up transmission towers and power lines."

When General Shields had finished the President put down the glass of water he had been sipping and looked directly at Owen MacDara, calling him familiarly by his first name, as though he had been an old school buddy.

"Owen, this is where you come in. I called you here because I need you. Bart, bring us up to date on the matter we discussed."

Bart Shields was rolling one of his favorite cigars between his right thumb and forefinger. He'd never light up in the Oval Office. Occasionally, he'd put the end in his mouth and roll it around his tongue, just like a pacifier. He put down the cigar and looked directly at MacDara. "The President knows everything we've discussed. I've briefed him on the murder of Murphy Armstrong, the disappearance of Major Whiteside and the assault on Ruth Whiteside."

MacDara remained silent. Even though he had convinced General Shields to listen to his theories and fears, he had never expected to be sitting in the Oval Office with the President. Shields continued.

"I've also informed the President about your suspicions regarding General Walker—"

The President interrupted. "And I feel exactly the same as Bart about Zach Walker. He's an outstanding American and a great patriot. Your suspicions must be unfounded."

MacDara didn't respond to the President. He held his own counsel as Bart Shields started to speak again.

"There's always been extreme groups in this country: the Ku Klux Klan, the Aryan Nation, the Symbionese Liberation Army, the SDS, the Black Panthers and many others. But something's changed out there. The movement to the Right is not just another case of the pendulum swinging again. We're not talking about fiscal and religious conservatism. This movement is more

The CIRCLE of SODOM
A Gripping New Thriller

sinister. Out in the West, the Midwest and the South we see more and more anti-government movements. Some have acted to roll back taxes, others, the more sinister ones, are training in combat fatigues with assault weapons. These are the people we arrested in California and Florida. And let's not forget the Liberal East. Some of the intelligentsia of these movements can be found in our prominent Eastern universities and think tanks. We have evidence that leads us to believe that many of these groups have established a network of relationships. That's new and that's a threat to our democracy." Shields paused, reached for the Macanudo and stuck it in his mouth again. The President cut in.

"We're certain that there are people belonging to this movement right here on Capitol Hill. In our own Government. Maybe even in my Cabinet." The President was grim. His usual affable demeanor had disappeared. "That's where you come in, Owen. I need to know the extent of the threat to this nation. I can't use the CIA, the FBI, the Secret Service or anyone in the NSC. We could have a mole or a fifth column anywhere. Bart Shields would trust you with his life and I would trust Bart with mine. I want you to find out who's behind all of this."

Even though Shields had prepared him for this MacDara still felt overwhelmed.

"Yes, Mr. President. I only hope that I can do the job."

"Owen, I've looked at your record and your accomplishments. You're well qualified. And I believe you have a score to settle with somebody. You'll report directly to General Shields but you'll have my full authority. Can you turn your business over to someone for a while?"

"Yes, Mr. President, I can. My business is run by my senior managers. They all own a piece of GMA. Dick Massey, my Executive Vice President, already handles the daily operating affairs. He's often been in full charge in my absence."

The President rose from his chair. The meeting was over. As he ushered General Shields and Owen MacDara from the

Oval Office, he once again put his hand on Owen's shoulder and said, "I know you'll succeed. And when you do I won't be able to recognize your accomplishment. Remember, Owen, this meeting never happened. The people of America must never learn of this evil. It would destroy us."

Back in his office General Shields finally lit his Macanudo. Small nimbus clouds of smoke circled his head, giving him a surreal appearance. Taking the cigar out of his mouth he looked across at Owen MacDara and his face broke into a mischievous grin.

"I wanted you to join us years ago, Owen. It's a shame I've had to resort to such extreme methods to get you on board!"

Owen MacDara had fully regained his composure. He laughed heartily with Bart Shields at his own expense. Then they got down to business.

"How long will it take to turn over the reins at GMA?"

"Couple of days. That's all. I'll put Massey in charge and brief my seniors."

"OK. Let's say we meet here in three days. I'll brief you in more detail then. I also want you to look at the latest output from the STOP system. And, we'll decide on a plan of action for you."

MacDara took the next available shuttle to New York and headed straight for Dune Road. He called Dick Massey at home and asked him to arrange two meetings at GMA Headquarters from eight in the morning: first hour with Dick and then another hour with his senior managers, starting at nine am.

Dune Road, The Hamptons, New York, Wednesday, February 9, 2000

Ruth Whiteside was awake. Out of the coma. Owen MacDara found himself infected by the euphoria in Kate's voice.

The CIRCLE of SODOM
A Gripping New Thriller

"I know it's four am. I know I woke you up. But I couldn't wait."

"How is she, Kate?"

"She's great. She's alert. Knew me right away. The only thing she seems to have lost is time. She can't believe she's been in a coma."

"Is Dr Hoffman with you?"

"Yes. He left instructions to be notified anytime, anywhere, if she regained consciousness. He got here about an hour ago. Says he'll keep her for at least a week for further examination. Then, if she seems all right, he'll send her home to convalesce. But she'll need daily physical therapy. Even though her fractures have healed, her confinement hasn't helped. She probably won't be able to walk right away. But that's the least of my worries now that she's back with us."

"Does she remember what happened to her?"

"Yes. Just as though it happened yesterday. Which, to her, it did. Owen, she's asking for you. Wants to see you as soon as possible, but I think it's best that you don't see her till she gets home. I don't want her to relive what happened for a while."

"You're right, Kate. As much as I'd like to see you both. I have to go to Washington and Miami for a few days. I'll fly up when I get back. Hopefully, your mother will be at home by then."

It was four thirty am and MacDara was too wired to sleep anymore. So he quickly donned a sweatsuit and sneakers and walked the few yards from his front door to Dune Road. Turning left he started jogging, heading west towards Captain Norm's, remembering the last time that he and Kate had treated themselves to the Captain's fresh seafood and a carafe of the best house white in the Hamptons. There had been a moon out that night. He remembered Kate afterwards, profiled against the yachts moored there, hair blowing in the wind and an ebony glow on her cheekbones in the dusk of the evening.

Pat Mullan

A couple of other joggers were out and an occasional vehicle moved in and out of his vision. Even at five am life was stirring on Dune Road. So he didn't pay much attention to the two men in the late-model Ford that pulled out of the side road on his right as he passed. When he jogged he liked to get his heart rate up, so he usually maintained a good pace. He was completely unaware that the Ford was following a couple of hundred yards behind him.

About a mile from his house he hit an area of open ground on his left with only a couple of houses sited on the distant dunes on his right. He was startled by the noise of rapid acceleration and glanced over his shoulder just in time to see the Ford bearing down on him, doing at least eighty. He had barely time to jump free, landing in the dunes on his left. Sprayed by sand, he could not make out a license plate, but noticed a patrol car pull out with lights flashing and give chase to the Ford. People on Dune Road paid well for their police protection.

MacDara picked himself up and turned back. Time to cut short his run. The near miss bothered him. What if it hadn't been just a random encounter with some joyrider, some nutcase? What if it had been intentional? He made a mental note to brief Shields.

The National Security Council, Washington DC, Thursday, February 10, 2000

Sanderson was livid. He was pacing up and down in front of Shields's desk. MacDara had only heard about Sanderson, never met him. He sat transfixed. Sanderson started to talk, his words running together as fast as his feet: "We're under attack, sir. We're really under attack!"

"Tell me again, Larry."

"It's like I said. I was in the middle of the next AI run. Surfing the Internet and every other network. AI starts to warn me that our command computers are being hit on up to a thousand times a day. Sir, that's an invasion!"

"What do you mean by 'hit on'?"

"Hackers! People trying to crack our network security. Beat our encryption systems."

"You mean computer nerds playing games?"

"No, sir. Some of them, maybe. But not this many. This is an organized attack. AI thinks so too!"

General Shields told Larry to sit down. His order was not obeyed. Larry continued to pace the floor restlessly. Shields swung his chair around and picked up the phone. "Sally, get me Colonel Tomkins at our Intelligence and Security Command."

Bart Shields sucked on his unlit Macanudo as he waited. MacDara tried to speak to Sanderson but he was ignored. Larry had retreated into his own head again.

"Dick, Bart Shields. I have Larry Sanderson here. He's telling me that hackers are trying to get into our command computers at the Pentagon. Do you know anything about this?"

"Yes, I know about that. We've always detected twenty-five or thirty a day. There's more?"

"How would a thousand a day sound like? No, I'm not kidding, Dick. Larry Sanderson says that STOP's AI system detected them. Larry, would you pick up the phone and talk to Dick Tomkins."

That was the first time that Sanderson stopped his restless pacing. He crossed to Shields's desk and took the receiver.

"Yes, sir, Colonel Tomkins. AI detected and logged them. About thirty percent of them originated outside the country. Seventy percent right here. Yes, sir. I'll do that, sir."

Sanderson handed the telephone back to Shields.

"Dick, I'll be down there to see you. I want to get to the bottom of this right away." He hung up the telephone and lit his Macanudo. Somehow, Sanderson was standing rooted in the same place.

"Larry, are you able to identify any of them?"

"AI tagged two of them. One came from a computer in a cybercafe in London. You know, one of those places where nerds and yuppies drink coffee and surf the net. Number two started out here in the U.S.!"

"Where?"

"Tennessee. It came from a computer up in the hills. Beyond Nashville. Someplace called the Millennium Covenant."

"Millennium Covenant. Isn't that the crazy bunch that were preparing for Armageddon. McNab? Right? Colonel George McNab. Vietnam hero. Patriot. God save us from ourselves." General Shields threw his hands in the air, as though imploring the Almighty and told Sanderson, "Check those messages out again. See if AI can tag any more of them. This Millennium one is probably an isolated instance. But we can't assume anything. I want everything you can put together on Colonel McNab and his merry bunch."

As Sanderson left, Bart Shields looked at Owen MacDara: "What do you think, Owen?"

"I don't like it. One thousand attempts to break into our command computers is not just the work of individual hackers. Sounds like somebody's preparing to launch an infowar against us. I believe you should take this seriously. Vietnam hero or not, McNab sounds like a regular nut. And a dangerous one. I'd assume he's guilty until proven innocent."

The CIRCLE of SODOM
A Gripping New Thriller

SIXTEEN

Florida,
Tuesday, February 15, 2000

"**B**ushmills, please. Straight up, no ice."

They had taken off from La Guardia about twenty minutes earlier and were now cruising at thirty-one thousand feet. MacDara had a window seat in business class. The sky was a clear blue but the ground below was screened from view by a thick quilt of white cotton clouds.

"Your Bushmills, sir."

The steward handed him a glass and two small bottles of Irish whiskey. He adjusted the table attached to the seat in front of him, opened and poured one of the whiskies, and savored the smooth peatiness of the Bushmills. One of the indulgences of flying, he told himself. He didn't normally have a Bushmills at eleven o'clock in the morning.

The flight wasn't full and no-one had taken the seat next to him. He pulled his briefcase from under the seat in front of him and took out Major Whiteside's journal. He wanted to read that entry again, the one that described the Miami trip.

Pat Mullan

> *March 12, 1999………flew down from Washington, D.C. to Miami. Drove to Key West and stayed overnight with Dr Dan Pepper. I needed his views and opinions of a lifetime in medicine. He was my role model at Walter Reade. He's 91 and sharp as a whip. Still does push-ups every day till it hurts. He's got a half-dozen projects going at once. Great two days…the best memories…could have stayed longer. Must go back when I've finished these memoirs. Maybe I'll take Ruth next time…liked Key West.*

It was eerie. As MacDara made his way through the airport the air was filled with the buzz of conversation. But it wasn't in English. The buzz was Spanish. Nothing had a *Norte Americano* ambience.

There was no line waiting for taxis and he got one right away. In minutes he was taking the airport exit south to Le Jeune. He didn't notice the gray Corvette that pulled out after him.

The taxi dropped him five minutes later outside the rental agency that GMA always used. He was a VIP customer and the late-model Jaguar he had requested was gassed up and ready.

He took the 836, commonly known as the Dolphin Expressway, west to the turnpike and headed south towards Homestead and the Keys. Traffic was sparse on the turnpike and MacDara cruised at about fifty-five. Passing through the western outskirts of Miami he could see the newer housing developments on his left. Single family homes, crowded close together. Spanish style, cream walls, cinnamon roof tiles. Further on he noticed older developments; some houses still being repaired from the hurricane of two years ago. On his right shopping malls and warehouses flashed by, broken by open land used for growing shrubs, plants and the ubiquitous palm trees that dotted and clustered the Miami landscape. Further south, towards Homestead, he couldn't help noticing the deterioration. The homes were gray box-like flat-roofed shacks; an occasional one adorned with a white picket fence or a well-maintained flower garden, which only tended to emphasize the shabbiness.

The turnpike ended and the Last Chance Saloon stood as an outpost to the twenty miles of everglades and mangrove swampland that had to be crossed before reaching the Keys. MacDara was now on US1, a two-lane roadway punctuated by signs advising that there were passing lanes ahead. Periodically the road did expand to four lanes, changing back to two almost right away, it seemed. MacDara was in no hurry. He was enjoying the pleasant contrast of water and plant-life on each side of the road; a wilderness again. He was attracted to the extremities of the planet, he thought: the Florida Keys, Connemara. His pleasant reverie was broken by the sounds of the traffic that had built up behind him in his rear view mirror, itching to drive through him. A gray Corvette was riding up his tail. Well, MacDara decided, they could all wait until they reached the next passing lanes. He wasn't going to speed up today for anyone. The passing lanes came and went and a rush of traffic moved out to the fast lane and whizzed past, free at last. It was only when the single lane traffic resumed that MacDara noticed the gray Corvette still riding close on his rear bumper. It had not passed. He began to feel irritated, but his state of mind refused to permit it. He could see two people in the Corvette. *Pricks*, he thought. *Another time I'd teach the bastards a lesson; but I refuse to get annoyed today.*

About a half hour after leaving the Last Chance Saloon, the mangrove swamps ended and MacDara reached Key Largo, the first of the communities on that necklace of islands that reached out into the Gulf of Mexico and ended at Key West. He began to feel even mellower and the refrains of an old song took over his mind: *Bogey and Bacall in Key Largo; oh yeah, two of my favorite people*, he thought, *Humphrey Bogart and Lauren Bacall.*

He had had it. Enough was enough. He could still see the Corvette dogging him in his rearview mirror and he was sick of it. *Avoidance, not confrontation today,* he advised himself. Should be close to the Greek's place by this time. The Greek on the Creek. Just the right place for a beer and some fresh fish. A couple of hundred yards ahead. He swung off the road to the right, past the tall battleship-gray buildings that housed the boatyard, and nosed the Jaguar into the parking area behind the Greek's. Just a diner sitting on the boardwalk at the side of the channel that bisected the Keys. But the food was good, he remembered. A forty-five minute break, he reasoned, would let that Corvette tailgate someone else.

An hour and a half later the strains of a reggae band greeted his ears as the Holiday Isle resort at Islamorada approached. Teeming with cars, noise and lithe young bronzed bodies. He slowed to a crawl, feasting his eyes on the spectacle as he passed. It was the screeching of tires that jarred his spine. The gray Corvette was back. It had just swung out of the jungle of cars at Holiday Isle and was once again riding his rear bumper.

MacDara finally got the message. He put his foot to the floor and shifted up into overdrive. The Jag responded instantly. In seconds the needle was hovering around eighty, but the Corvette was closing the distance. Traffic was light and MacDara easily swung out to overtake and pass the vehicles ahead. No sirens. That meant there were no patrol cars in the vicinity. That was good and bad. Good because he didn't want the local cops involved. Bad because this contest would go down to the wire. A winner and a loser. MacDara didn't intend to end up as shark bait off the Florida Keys.

The crack of the rifle was unmistakable. MacDara ducked instinctively as the bullet shattered his rear window. Glancing in his mirror he could see one of his pursuers standing up in the open sunroof with a weapon raised to his shoulder. Immediately MacDara started to weave the Jaguar zigzag across the road, startling a driver in the oncoming lane. They were trapped on this road, the hunter and its quarry. Nowhere to go unless you chose the Gulf of Mexico on the right or the Atlantic Ocean on the left.

Two more shots in quick succession. *But they couldn't hit a barn door if it was moving the way I am*, thought MacDara. He knew he had a forty-five in the glove compartment. But it was useless in this contest, and he wanted to pick his own place to take a stand. With the Corvette in hot pursuit, MacDara literally flew through Long Key and Duck Key. It was only when he glimpsed the small airport to the right that he realized that he had reached Marathon. The seven-mile bridge lay just ahead. A gleaming span that rose and arched high in the air and flowed down to the last quarter of the Keys. He felt that the Jag had enough under the hood to stretch the distance between himself and the Corvette - enough to get to Ramrod Key, where he planned to make a stand. But the Corvette was fast. He was nudging a hundred and twenty miles an hour as they reached the high point of the bridge, and he hadn't shaken the Corvette.

MacDara wove in and out of half a dozen vehicles ahead of him, narrowly missing more surprised drivers heading towards him. But his plan was foiled. As they neared the end of the bridge the Corvette had managed to block his zigzag and had almost drawn alongside. The guy riding 'shotgun' in the sunroof had opened fire again, the bullets breaking the side rear window and narrowly missing MacDara.

They were just off the bridge and reaching Spanish Harbor Key when the good ol' boy materialized out of nowhere speeding towards them in a souped-up Ford pickup. The Corvette had nowhere to go. The driver tried to veer left at the last minute but the good ol' boy just kept coming at him, giving him a glancing blow on the side as they collided. The Corvette crashed through the low barrier and seemed to take flight, then dropped straight down into the blue-green Atlantic, the gunman screaming as he hung out of the sunroof. It sank immediately. Shark bait. MacDara didn't wait around for explanations. He

Pat Mullan

kept moving. It was only when he reached Duval Street in Key West that his heart-rate resumed its normal sixty beats a minute.

MacDara checked into the Reach Hotel, his favorite place, as soon as he arrived. Still shaken from his harrowing ordeal, he took a long shower, changed and then called Shields on his private line. He was lucky. Shields answered on the second ring. Owen briefed him on the attempt on his life.

"Somebody's trying to stop me. They don't want me to find out what Whiteside uncovered. They seem to know my every move."

"Well, I've got another lead for you, Owen. It's about Murph's killer. You already know that he worked as a golf pro around the Miami area. The Miami police checked him out for the NYPD. He was well known at the Doral course. As you know, I had started my own background check on Miller. It happens that Javier Uribe, the head of security at the Doral, works for me from time to time. I just had a call from him. It seems he's found a sports bag that belonged to Miller. I asked him to hold it for you. See him before you leave."

The phone call to Shields had been therapeutic, but not enough. He had an urge for a margarita and Sloppy Joe's served the best in town. A big open busy place with a very long bar and a good band on stage, Sloppy's was just the kind of therapy that Owen MacDara needed. Hemingway's favorite drinking place, it was owned in the thirties by Joe Russell, charter boat captain, rum-runner, and the author's fishing companion for twelve years. It must have been three am when MacDara's therapy session ended and he tumbled into bed in his room at the Reach.

He had set the combination alarm clock coffee machine for ten am and awakened to the sound of the coffee beans in the grinder. Filling a large mug he opened the sliding glass doors and went out on the patio, feeling the cooling breezes coming in from the Atlantic. His head was still fuzzy from the Margaritas he had consumed in Sloppy Joe's the night before. His room, with its cool Mexican tiled floor and warm Indian dhurrie rugs would be hard to leave this morning.

Dr Dan Pepper lived on the east side of Key West, close to Simonton and Duval Streets and only a stone's throw away from the Reach Hotel. MacDara had no difficulty finding him. He lived in a distinctive two-story Conch house, constructed by ship's carpenters in the late nineteenth century. It was adorned by an ornamental balcony and deck that fronted the entire house. A scarlet flowered Cordia Sebestina tree, commonly known as a Geiger tree, dominated the garden.

Dan Pepper had been expecting him. He was sitting in a wicker chair on the porch immersed in the daily papers. He stood up and grasped Owen's hand with the energy of a man at least twenty years younger. He took him into his study and left to bring back some refreshments. When he returned he found Owen glancing through a copy of Hemingway's *The Old Man and the Sea* that he'd extracted from a shelf where medical books like *Gray's Anatomy* and *Harrison's Principles of Internal Medicine* were intermingled with works by Hemingway, Turgenev, Joyce and Tom Clancy.

"You know, Owen. I think Hemingway had it right after all."

"What do you mean?"

"When he killed himself. He knew that life was only worthwhile if he could still write. He couldn't write anymore."

"But what about his family? Didn't he also have a responsibility to them?"

"He did. But what have you got to offer them if your own life has lost its dignity?"

"This doesn't sound like you at all. Not the man I've read about...and certainly not the man I'm looking at."

"Oh, I've been lucky, Owen. I'm as fit as a fiddle and the old mind still works. I wonder sometimes what I'd have done if it had all started to fail, the body, the mind, the whole shebang.

Pat Mullan

Don't dismiss Hemingway's option as the act of a crazy and selfish person."

"You'll never go like Hemingway. What did MacArthur say: 'Old soldiers never die, they simply fade away'. And I don't see anything fading about you. You'll probably live to be a hundred and fifty!"

"Owen, I don't have time to think about it. I'm too busy. Henry was too busy as well. He had no time to die. I still don't believe it."

"You're not alone. We all don't believe it. That's why I'm here. Tell me about Henry's visit with you in March last year."

"That was odd, you know. Hadn't heard from him in years. Then, suddenly, he just shows up. Calls me the day before from Washington. Writing his memoirs, he says."

Dr. Pepper walked over to a wall of his study that was covered with photographs, degrees, memberships and awards and took down a group photograph in an antique pine frame.

"There we are, the seven of us at Walter Reade. That's me, my two colleagues, and the four interns that worked closely with us. Henry was my favorite. There he is, to my right. Such dedication and competence. If you wanted a surgical procedure executed to perfection, you'd ask Henry to do it."

Owen could swear he saw Dan's eyes moisten as he spoke.

"Henry and I kept in touch regularly after his internship at Walter Reade. He often consulted me when I was at the New York Hospital and later at Johns Hopkins. Even during his Korean tour. He encountered cases of sickle cell anemia in one or two of his black troops. And, once he had a patient with a virus that he couldn't identify. But after Korea our contacts stopped. I hadn't heard from him since he retired. But that wasn't unusual. Our work no longer dealt with the life and death problems of our patients."

Dan Pepper paused and stared out the window at the scarlet flowers on his Geiger tree. He had lapsed into a world of his own. Owen didn't break the silence. A minute or two later he willed himself back to the present and spoke again: "Henry was troubled. Something in Korea. Such a long time ago. He wanted my advice again."

"Did it have anything to do with a colonel who is now in a very important job?"

"How did you know that?"

"I was there."

Dan Pepper studied Owen's face for a while and decided to continue. "Well then, you know. Henry talked to me back then. Thought there might be a question of ethics if he was asked to disclose what happened. On the other hand he felt this particular colonel might be vulnerable. An easy target for the Soviets. Remember, we were still in the Cold War in those days."

He was still holding the group photograph he had taken down from the wall and he had been unconsciously wiping the glass with the cuff of his sleeve. Now he went over and put it back on the wall again.

"We talked it over, but I'm afraid it was a matter that only Henry could make a judgement on. He felt strongly about this particular colonel and he had given him his promise. So he kept quiet. And as the years passed he forgot about it. Until he started writing his damn memoirs."

The change in tone in Dan's voice showed a harshness Owen had not expected. Owen did not say anything. He waited for him to pick up where he had left off.

"Henry had found out something. I don't know what it was. But he was certain that General Walker was an easy target. And not for the Soviets."

"Did he know who?"

"Yes. I believe he suspected who was behind it, but he had no proof. One thing he was sure of. He was certain that the enemy was right here in this country. Do you know what I'm saying?"

"Yeah, I believe I do."

Pat Mullan

"Henry was afraid. He was sure he was in danger. But he didn't know if anyone would listen to him."

"He was right. Nobody would."

Dan Pepper stopped talking again. He had a faraway look in his eyes. It was almost as though he were replaying an old reel of the past in his head. "Henry didn't think he'd live through this. I thought he was being melodramatic at the time. He told me if he disappeared or was murdered that he wanted me to share a secret that he'd kept for years. He didn't want to take it to the grave with him. He told me to use my best judgement. I think that Henry would have trusted you with his secret. I'm too old to protect anyone."

MacDara hadn't expected any surprises so he had no time to prepare himself for what Dr. Pepper had just said.

"Dr Dan, we only met an hour ago."

"Oh, I checked you out as soon as you called to make this appointment to see me. Everyone who's ever known you would trust you with their life. That's good enough for me. Henry has a daughter, doesn't he?"

"Yes, he does. Kate. A beautiful young woman. I'm very fond of her."

"Then it's doubly important that you know. Kate is adopted. Henry and Ruth couldn't have any children."

"Is that the secret?"

"That's part of it. Henry always knew her real father. But he swore an oath of secrecy. Ruth doesn't even know. Henry never told a soul. I think he was afraid for Kate's safety if he were no longer around. When I tell you the rest of the secret, I think you'll understand."

Dan Pepper paused, not for effect, but to regain his composure. Owen could see that this was very stressful for him. Finally, he looked at Owen directly. "General Zachary Walker is Kate's father."

When unexpected news is received, good or bad, people react in either one of two ways. They either show their emotion by babbling incoherently or instead they shut down like a clam, incapable even of speech. Owen MacDara reacted in the latter way. He couldn't say a thing. Dan went to the drinks cabinet and poured double scotches for both of them.

Back at the Reach, Owen MacDara poured himself a Glenlivet straight up and tried to deal with the revelation he'd just received about Kate.

Kate knew she had been adopted. It was obvious by her early teens that her complexion and facial structure were racially different from both her parents. So they told her. They always knew they'd have to. They told her that she'd been adopted as an abandoned baby in Seoul. She had accepted that and felt very privileged. Henry and Ruth Whiteside may not have been her biological parents but they were her real parents in every other way. She loved them dearly. Kate had told Owen all of this one evening at Ardree House.

It was the revelation that General Zachary Walker was her father that he must come to terms with. He decided that the secret would remain with him unless he had to use the knowledge to protect Kate. From what Dan Pepper had told him, he was sure that that was what Henry Whiteside wanted.

Owen MacDara called the Doral Country Club and booked a room for the night. He checked out of the Reach and was in the Jag heading back up the Keys by three thirty. The sun was shining and the sky was a deep blue with no clouds, only the aerial artistry of an airforce jet as it took off from the nearby airbase. The tranquility made yesterday's contest with the Corvette seem like a dream.

A little over three hours later, MacDara was turning the Jag over to the valet at the Doral. He checked in and was given a suite in one of the executive lodges overlooking the golf course. It was too late to see Javier Uribe so he showered, changed and relaxed over a superb steak dinner in the Club dining room. The DJ in Rousseau's nightclub had an affinity for Sinatra. MacDara had one nightcap, a Courvoisier, at the bar. Ol' Blue Eyes was singing 'I Did it my Way' as he left.

Javier Uribe was a small, dark, compact Chilean. Ex-Special Forces, he remained in the Reserves and spent his weekends skydiving. He was a security consultant to powerful individuals and corporations. A Latin G. Gordon Liddy. He consulted on security matters for the Doral and their wealthy and important clients, many of whom frequented the Doral Saturnia, their adjacent health spa. On occasion he accepted special assignments from the National Security Agency. He was expecting MacDara. After the obligatory handshake he got right to the matter.

"Yeah, man. The right thing would have been to turn this over to the NYPD team investigating the murders. But this thing stunk to me. So when I found this locker of Miller's and the bag he had stashed, I thought it might be important. I've worked for General Bart before, so I asked his advice. You know the rest."

He took a key from the ring at his waist, opened his desk and pulled out the large bottom drawer on the right. Reaching down he brought out a black imitation- leather sports bag with the zipper attached to a small combination lock.

"No-one knows about this discovery but myself. And General Bart. I'll turn this over to you. I don't want to know about it."

The meeting was over. No pleasantries. Javier, the Efficient. That's how MacDara thought of him as he took the bag back to his suite.

It wasn't difficult prising the lock away from the zipper and sliding it open. Nothing much inside at first glance: a golfing glove, some golf balls stamped with various clubs and tournaments, a plastic bag of Doral Country Club tees, a small dog-eared notebook on a wire spine, a Publix supermarket shopping bag - probably contained some dirty laundry, guessed

The CIRCLE of SODOM
A Gripping New Thriller

MacDara as he peered inside. His guess was wrong. It contained a long white robe of a simple monastic style.

He picked up the notebook and leafed through it. Scattered notes on various pages, some handwritten in pencil, some in ballpoint, mostly notes on golf dates, a shopping list, some flight times from Miami International and Fort Lauderdale, and one curious entry: an address in Dania of the El Habesh Mosque.

MacDara found the place just as dusk was falling. Which suited him fine. It was an odd, circular building, almost like an upturned chamber pot. The building was about two hundred yards off Sheridan in Dania, just south of Fort Lauderdale. It was difficult to spot from Sheridan because it lay in a run-down part of the neighborhood. Abandoned warehouses and piles of rusting cars sitting among hills of used tires camouflaged it from the road. He would never have found it if Miller's notebook hadn't mentioned the steakhouse nearby. Old ranch-style building with weather-beaten red shingles. Unmistakable.

He pulled into the steakhouse parking lot, already full - the steaks must be good here. He found one of the last parking places and squeezed in. As he got out of the car the aroma of grilling steak wafted out of the kitchen. He suddenly felt pangs of hunger and realized that he hadn't eaten since breakfast. Anyway he never could resist a good steak, and he thought he might run into somebody who knew something about this mosque. After all, they were practically neighbors.

The Ponderosa Steakhouse had stolen its name from a popular TV western. Inside it acted out its role. Country and Western music greeted MacDara at the saloon-style swinging doors, and a buckskin-clad waitress wearing a white cowboy hat welcomed him with a cheery 'Howdy'. It was a big noisy sprawling place, with rough-hewn wooden tables filled with diners. A horseshoe bar that also doubled as an eating counter dominated one corner.

Pat Mullan

There was plenty of room at the bar and MacDara let the waitress guide him there. The bartender was a good-looking dark-haired buxom lady, probably in her late forties, who could easily pass for her late thirties. MacDara ordered a draft Coors and she brought him the menu. He ordered the T-bone, medium rare, with an order of ranch-house fries. While he waited for his order he found out that the bartender's name was Clara, that she was originally from Georgia and had moved south to Florida years ago. There was a story there but he certainly wasn't about to learn it on one visit. Just then his steak arrived, sizzling and hot. He sliced into it, perfect medium rare, and it melted in his mouth.

"Clara, I'm in heaven. I think this is the best steak I've ever had!"

"Yessir, I never get tired of people telling me that."

"Name's Owen, Clara. Just curious, but where do all your customers come from? You're way out here in the boondocks. Nothing around but those old empty warehouses and that odd-looking mosque place."

"We're known by reputation, Owen. People drive for miles to eat here. And we get a fair amount of folks who wander in, just like yourself. Never take the book by its cover. You might be surprised to know that we get good business from that old mosque as well."

"That old mosque! It looked abandoned to me."

"No, siree, it sure ain't. As a matter of fact they're having one of their meetings there tonight."

"What kind of people are they, Clara?"

"Ah, that's the surprise. They're clean-cut all-American boys. See that table over there. Be leaving soon."

MacDara looked over his shoulder at the table that Clara had nodded towards. Five neat, well-groomed young men were just finishing and settling the check with their waitress. They could easily have passed for a group of Westpoint cadets. MacDara made a quick decision. He would join their meeting.

The CIRCLE of SODOM
A Gripping New Thriller

"Clara, thanks, I'll sure be back. By the way, do you have a phone?"

"Sure. Back there, through that door, alcove beyond the men's room."

There were two phones in the alcove, both unoccupied. MacDara dialled Shields's private line. There was no answer, so he left a message. He knew that Shields checked his messages with regularity. He told Shields where he was, what he was about to do, and that he would call again in two hours. If Shields hadn't heard from him by then, he could send in a rescue party.

He went out to his car and took the plastic shopping bag containing Miller's white robe out of the trunk. There were few lights on this stretch of roadway and the traffic was sparse, so he had no trouble dashing across and disappearing among the piles of old tires on the opposite side of the road. The mosque stood alone on an empty lot about a hundred yards beyond the last abandoned warehouse. MacDara could see robed figures, in twos and threes, approaching the mosque door. He hid behind the warehouse and donned the robe. It reached his ankles and the sleeves were too long. He rolled the sleeves up into cuffs at his wrist and hoped no one would notice. Blend and belong, he told himself.

He mingled with three or four others as he entered the mosque. No one challenged him. They seemed certain of their own isolation.

The inner doors opened into a panelled hallway that ran around the circumference. The lighting was subdued. People seemed to know exactly where they were going. MacDara tossed a mental coin and went left. Doors led off the hallway to rooms situated around the periphery of the mosque. He passed two large double doors on his right that gave access to the center of the building. He imagined that he heard voices, a faint chanting sound, as he passed those doors. He walked slowly, unsure of his next move. Robed young men passed him and entered doors on his left.

Pat Mullan

There were few older men like himself, and there were certainly no females. Some rooms had large single-pane picture windows looking out onto the hallway and MacDara could easily see into these rooms. He halted at one window to watch some kind of an initiation ceremony. A casually dressed young man, blindfolded, was walking the gauntlet between two rows of robed brothers while an elder brother read from a looseleaf booklet. The ceremony seemed to be ending. His blindfold was removed and each of the brothers embraced him. The elder brother then presented him with a white robe. He was putting on the robe when a gong sounded from somewhere deep in the heart of the mosque. Robed brothers exited the rooms and rushed towards the sound of the gong. Momentarily unbalanced, MacDara stumbled into someone and fell over. He felt a hand grabbing his arm from behind, then two arms helping him back to his feet. He turned, apologized to the brother and thanked him for his help. The young man, still holding his arm, looked at him earnestly, as though pondering what to say. Then he just smiled, relinquished Owen's arm and moved on. Everyone was going through the two double doors into the center of the building. Owen followed.

Incense rose in bursts from burners swung by a white-robed person at each corner of the central chamber. A round black carpet covered the entire floor, accentuating the white circle, twelve foot in diameter, at its center. A cylindrical red altar stood in the middle of the white circle. A red snake coiled around the base of the altar and climbed up into the air. From its head, an arc of ambient light shone directly on to the circle. About one hundred hooded white-robed figures stood motionless in circles around the altar. MacDara entered and merged into the outer circle. In his white robe he was indistinguishable from the others.

All eyes were focused on a black-robed figure kneeling at the altar. Minutes passed in total silence. The chamber filled with the heady aroma of incense. The black robe rose and turned

The CIRCLE of SODOM
A Gripping New Thriller

to face MacDara's sector of the chamber. He was hooded, with his face cloaked in shadow, and MacDara had a sense that he was lithe and agile. A white circle enclosing a red snake emblazoned the front of his robe. He raised his arms and stretched them towards his audience and his voice carried with the depth and timbre of a Shakespearean actor.

"Brothers! The Day of Judgement is here! Your day of judgement. Our world has been flailed by Communism and decadence. Scourged by the spineless. Their own Bible says 'the Lord would be more severe on the Day of Judgement than he had been with Sodom and Gomorrah'. You were born to exact judgement on those who have brought us to the brink of destruction. Those who have violated our good earth. Those who are too weak to govern. Those who have not had the backbone to purge our societies of their impurities."

Silence dominated. The only sounds came from the swinging of the incense burners, almost keeping cadence with the sermon.

MacDara looked right and left. Everyone was standing to attention, transfixed, almost drugged in their hypnotic stance. MacDara felt hypnotized himself. The incense, the ambience, the voice...The voice. It reached inside him again, and he came out of his trance as he listened to the closing exhortation.

"Brothers, the infidels will fulfil their own prophesy. Read their Book of Revelations: *'gather them to the battle of that great day into a place called Armageddon.'*"

His voice reverberated from the rafters of the cathedral ceiling and the brothers all raised their right arms with clenched fists and responded in unison. "You are Truth. You are Justice."

"Brothers, the time is near. We have reached the millennium. Before this year has ended our world will be engulfed in a Holy War. The infidels will fulfil their prophesy. The signs are here."

"You are Truth. You are Justice."

"Brothers, you are the Chosen. You are the New Life. You will not perish. You will inherit the Earth."

"You are Truth. You are Justice."

"Brothers, your Chosen One is going to be persecuted. The infidels will attack you. But you will not perish. You will inherit the Earth."

"You are Truth. You are Justice."

Six robed figures, with distinctive red armbands, moved into the white circle and surrounded the Chosen One.

"Brothers, the disciples of the Inner Circle will protect the Chosen One."

"You are Truth. You are Justice."

"Brothers, be prepared to give your lives for your Inheritance. Have no regrets. If called, do it willingly. You are the New Life. You will be reincarnated. You will not perish. You will inherit the Earth."

"You are Truth. You are Justice."

MacDara had seen and heard enough. That voice was unmistakable. The very same voice that gave the keynote speech at his own GMA dinner in January. *It was Tony Thackeray!*

The Chosen One was now kneeling at the altar again. The Inner Circle stood around him. The Brothers had begun to move clockwise, within their respective circles, around the altar. The incense burners were swung even more frantically and the air had become thick and smoky. MacDara had seen enough. He slipped from the chamber and left the mosque.

It's Tony Thackeray! As he crossed behind the pile of used tires back to the steak house parking lot, MacDara's head was on fire. *I have found The Circle of Sodom!* He went straight to the Ponderosa. His heart was thumping and he felt like heading straight for the bar and asking Clara to fix a double scotch and keep them coming. Yes, this is a night to get drunk, he felt. But that would have to wait. Right now he needed to get to Shields. So he bypassed the bar and headed for the phone.

The CIRCLE of SODOM
A Gripping New Thriller

Washington, DC,
Friday, February 18, 2000

When the flight arrived from Miami General Shields was there to meet him. They didn't talk until Shields had closed the soundproof barrier that separated them from the driver. Then he reached over to the bar and poured two glasses of Dewars.

"What happened in Florida?"

"I know who heads the Circle of Sodom."

General Shields sat upright. You could almost imagine him coming to attention as MacDara spoke those words.

"Owen, this is too serious for levity. I have no sense of humor these days."

"It's no joke, sir. I'm certain that I know who it is."

MacDara went on to describe his uninvited attendance at the service in the El Habesh Mosque.

"That voice was unmistakable, sir. I didn't see the face but there's only one voice like that. His name is Tony Thackeray."

MacDara went on to describe the Honorable David Anthony Llewellyn Thackeray, his family pedigree and his keynote speech at the GMA dinner.

"But you didn't see this person. You still can't be certain it's Thackeray."

"I am certain. Tony Thackeray has a messianic presence. There's only one voice like that. And the Thackeray Institute, the perfect cover. It gives him a legitimate reason for the lifestyle that he leads."

"OK, just suppose that you're right. What about this cult that he heads?"

"They're new. Or they must have been well hidden. They have an inner circle that acts like bodyguards. He calls them his disciples and says that they'll protect the Chosen One. And he is the Chosen One."

"This circle of theirs, that's your Circle of Sodom?"

"I'm certain of it. That snake in a circle on the Chosen One's robe was exactly the same as the tattoos. I'm sure if I'd been able to get to any of those six disciples that I'd have found the same tattoo on their arms."

"None of this makes any sense to me. Why would Thackeray want to use his Circle to eliminate Murph and yourself? And what about the attack on Ruth Whiteside and the murder of Baker's security man? Was he involved in that? And don't forget the killing of Angelo Russo. Where does that fit into any of this? I think it's stretching things a bit to connect all of this to Thackeray. And what, in heaven's name, would be his motive. He has everything. This does not make any sense."

Owen couldn't argue with Bart Shields's logic. He only knew that all of these events were connected. Shields hadn't finished.

"Tell me something else. What link could there possibly be between Zach Walker and this man Thackeray? They're from totally different worlds. And you've always maintained that the killing of Murphy Armstrong and the attempts on your life are connected to that incident in Korea with General Walker. Now you're telling me that Thackeray is responsible. If both of these assumptions are correct, then you're really saying that Zach Walker and Tony Thackeray are in this thing together. I find that difficult to buy."

Owen finally cut in. "You're right, sir. It all sounds illogical. But I'm convinced there's a connection. Maybe not in the case of Angelo. I've been thinking a lot about that. The Assistant DA, Stern, told me that he was convinced that Liz had bumped off Angelo. Well, suppose he was right. Look at it this way. She and Angelo were in trouble. Angelo was screwing around. She has the odd fling herself. Meets Thackeray. They looked pretty thick to me. Suppose he does her a favor and eliminates Angelo? She may not have asked him to do it. But, if Thackeray's Circle is responsible for these killings, what's one more to him?"

The CIRCLE of SODOM
A Gripping New Thriller

"Now, that is plausible. Maybe too plausible. This all hinges on your belief that Thackeray is involved in these killings. We do not have one shred of evidence for that. Even if you do establish that Miller was a member of this cult and that Thackeray is indeed the head of it, that does not prove a thing. Besides, what is his motive? I have to come back to that. I see no possible motive."

He had to admit that Shields was right. It all seemed a bit too far fetched. But so were the deaths of Murph and Angelo and the kid.

Owen did not tell Shields about Kate Whiteside's real father. As far as he was concerned, that would remain a secret with him forever unless he had to reveal it to protect Kate.

"Sir, I have to find the motive. And the connection between all of these events. I know only one place to begin. At the beginning. Korea, 1975."

SEVENTEEN

**Gloucester, Massachussetts,
Saturday February 19, 2000**

What a spirited lady, thought Owen MacDara, as he looked at Ruth Whiteside. Ignoring the therapist's advice, she had discarded her crutches and was coming towards him using the furniture as props to propel herself yard by yard across the room. Gripping him by the right wrist with the firmness of a much younger person she leveraged him into a seat on the couch beside her.

"I hope I didn't drag you away from something. But I haven't seen you in two months, or so they tell me. I still find that hard to accept."

"So do I," said Kate cheekily, as she appeared with two gin and tonics and gave one to Owen.

She brought a ginger ale for her mother, who said, "The days of G&Ts are over for me. But I do like a glass of white wine with dinner. Sometimes two these days."

"Cheers!" saluted Owen, "I'm glad to see you on the mend."

"Oh, they're mollycoddling me. Therapist every morning. Nurse every afternoon. Even wanted to send me daily hot meals.

You know. That meals-on-wheels business. Well, I gave them what for. I'm not an invalid, you know."

"You'll outlive all of us," said Owen, "you're indestructible!"

"Well, somebody didn't think so," said Ruth Whiteside, changing the atmosphere of levity in the room.

This was a cue for Kate, who said, "I'm off to prepare dinner. You two have a lot to discuss. I've heard it before."

"What do you remember about that day?" asked Owen, as Kate headed for the kitchen.

"Everything. That is, until I blacked out. I was out on the deck when the doorbell rang. It rang again just as I opened the door." She paused to take a sip of her ginger ale and then continued. "They seemed such nice young men. Two of them. Early twenties I'd say. Just the kind of boys that the Mormons send out. They had a religious tract in their hands. You know, something that looked just like that magazine of the Jehovah's Witnesses. What is it called? *The Watchtower*, I think. Well, they started to talk about God and about faith and asked, very politely, if they could come in and talk with me. Normally, I would just say 'no thanks, I'm not interested', to people like that. But that evening I was feeling a little lonely. So I invited them in. Thought I might find it entertaining."

She looked at Owen with a wry smile, "Turned out to be too much entertainment for me!"

"If this is too painful for you -"

"No, no. I must tell you. You need to know. And I need to talk about it. Help me out to the deck."

Owen helped her onto her feet and then let her use him to support herself as they made their way out to the deck. As they sat down Kate arrived with two glasses of Chardonnay and just as quickly retreated again.

"To fortify me," Ruth commented as she raised the glass of wine to her lips. Then she continued, "It was just like day turning into night after they came into the house. Except that it was already night outside. One of them bolted the outer door and the other pulled the drapes across the doors leading out to the deck. I like to keep those drapes open to watch the moonlight on the water. I asked them what they thought they were doing and one of them told me to shut up. Shut up! In my own house! I was shocked. Told them to get out. But one of them grabbed my arm and twisted it behind my back and threw me on the couch. The other one came around behind me, grabbed my hair and held me in a choke hold. I was terrified. I asked them what they wanted. Told them I didn't have very much money. Said they could take my jewellery. One of them said, 'We don't want your money or your jewellery. That's all you people think of. Money.' And he said it with such venom. Then he said, "Where're your husband's papers? Where're his research notes. We know he was writing his memoirs. We want those notes.'"

Ruth stopped and drank some more of the Chardonnay. It did seem to fortify her and she almost looked as though she'd got a second wind as she continued. "I told them I didn't know anything about any research notes of Henry's. Said that Henry never told me anything about his writing. That was the truth. Almost. If you leave out the journal I gave you. They didn't believe me. One of them took down an oar that Henry had mounted on the wall. He started to beat me with it. In a frenzy. I was in agony. I couldn't lift my arms. The pain was unbearable. I was lying on the floor. Gasping for air. I was too hurt to even scream. Then the beating stopped and I seemed to lapse in and out of consciousness. I could hear them tearing the house apart."

Ruth stopped again, finished the Chardonnay, and looked over at Owen. "The next thing I remember was waking up in the hospital."

Just then Kate appeared and announced that dinner was ready. Owen thought that propitious. Despite Ruth Whiteside's considerable inner strength, the memory of the events of that evening had taken their toll.

After dinner Ruth retired for the evening, and Owen and Kate were sitting on the deck enjoying coffee and Drambuie and watching the moonlight throw silver bands across the water.

"It's so peaceful here", said Kate, then corrected herself. "It *was* so peaceful here."

"I won't be able to see you for a while, Kate."

"What's going on, Owen? I'm so worried."

"I just can't tell you now. But I promise you that you and your mother are getting the best protection. Ken Baker won't let anything happen to either of you again. He's one very angry man."

"My father was murdered, wasn't he?"

"Yes, I believe he was. We have no body and no proof, but he had stumbled into something evil when he was researching his memoirs. The attack on your mother proves that. They were trying to find out what he knew."

"They? Who are 'they', Owen? Is General Walker one of them?"

"I don't know who 'they' are and I don't know *what* they are. And I'm not sure where General Walker fits in all of this. Did you ever meet the general?"

"No, I don't think so. Why do you ask?"

"Just curious. Obviously he and your father knew each other well. Thought you might have met him at some social event or something."

"Is there something you're not telling me, Owen? Was there something between my father and General Walker that I should know about?"

"No, no, Kate! Nothing that I'm aware of. I'm just searching for anything, nothing."

"What happened in Miami?"

"I just met with an old colleague and mentor of your dad's. Dr Dan Pepper. Your dad went to see him when he was

Pat Mullan

researching his memoirs. But he couldn't help. Only a great old man who thought the world of your dad."

"Yes, I know. My father loved him. Often spoke with us about him."

Owen MacDara kept his new concern well hidden. Now that he knew Kate was General Zachary Walker's daughter he felt a growing trepidation about her future. There was one thing he did tell himself. She would never learn that from him. He spent the night in Gloucester. In the guestroom. He had barely dropped off to sleep when he felt the warmth of Kate's body and her arm encircling his waist.

EIGHTEEN

**Seoul, Korea,
Sunday February 20, 2000**

Hajin Kim should not have been surprised. That was what he told himself when he took the telephone call. It was nine o'clock in the evening and he was exhorting himself to call Zachary Walker in Washington. It would be seven in the morning there and he'd probably catch the general before he left for his office. He was right. He caught Zachary Walker as he was about to walk out the door.

"General Walker, it's Hajin Kim. I have something very important to tell you," said Kim, without any greetings or preliminaries.

"What is it?" answered Zachary Walker just as directly.

"You called me a year ago to see if Major Whiteside had been in touch with me. He hadn't. But someone else has. I had a call from a gentleman in New York who gave his name as William Edwards. He was inquiring about Charlie Pettigrew. Said there was an inheritance due him from a reclusive uncle. I told him that Charlie Pettigrew was no longer in Korea, that he had left here ten or twelve years ago. I don't feel right about this call. Somehow I feel that this gentleman is not who he said he is. Even if I knew where Charlie Pettigrew had gone I wouldn't have told him. But, of course, I have no idea where Charlie is. Do you think this might be important?"

General Walker already knew it was important. The Pettigrews were always eking out a living when he was a boy. There were no rich aunts or uncles in the Pettigrew clan.

"Yes, it is. You were right to call, Hajin. I believe someone is trying to finish Major Whiteside's memoirs posthumously," he replied. He thanked Hajin Kim for going to the trouble of calling.

Hajin wished him well, and found himself in meditation after the call had ended. But he couldn't clear his mind of Zachary Walker and Charlie Pettigrew. Try as he might to suppress it, that evening over twenty years ago kept intruding from his subconscious. *Maybe if I let all return to me I can exorcise it forever*, hoped Hajin Kim.

And so that evening returned to him as he sat in deep contemplation...

It was the summer of 1975 and the Followers had given his life new meaning. But his soul was troubled too. Preaching the Bible daily on the streets of Seoul had added purpose to his existence. But the Bible was gradually being supplanted by the writings of Arnold Blum, the founder of the Followers. Metaphysical healing was practised in preference to contemporary medical therapy; the Followers believed that they should rely on God to heal them. But it was the sexual ethos of the Followers that had started to trouble Hajin Kim. Women Followers were expected to use sex as a means of attracting converts. Gay men were expected to do likewise. Women, even those with partners, were expected to provide sexual favors to younger members who had no partners. This sexual ethos was beginning

The CIRCLE of SODOM
A Gripping New Thriller

to dominate the philosophy of the Followers. By the summer of 1975 spiritual retreats often employed orgiastic sexual rituals as some kind of sacramental rite.

This was the world that Zachary Walker had been lured into by Charlie Pettigrew. Charlie had invited Hajin to meet his friend, who was an important officer in the US Army. The three of them met for dinner in a neighborhood restaurant not far from the Followers' residence in Seoul. That was the very first time that Hajin Kim had laid eyes on Zachary Walker. He almost felt that he was an interloper as the evening progressed. Too much makli had been consumed and no-one was entirely coherent when they arrived back at the residence late in the evening.

A retreat had commenced the day before and had now reached its spiritual zenith: the sacramental rite of the orgy. The sweet distinctive aroma of hashish perfumed the air and a number of Followers were smoking opium in the chamber known as the Grotto. The floor surrounding the altar in the central worship chamber was covered with mattresses, and the smoke from incense burners clouded the air. Naked bodies in twos, threes and fours cavorted and copulated on every mattress. A Follower stood at the central altar uttering incantations and pleading for the sacramental rite of the orgy to be accepted as a humble sacrificial offering. Hajin knew that they had all joined the rite, but he didn't remember when or how they had decided to do so. That was only one of the blackouts he suffered that evening. He attributed it all to too much makli. The next thing he remembered was waking up in one of the residency chambers about noon on the following day.

Something changed for him that night. His troubled soul could not find peace and he left the Followers by Christmas of that same year. He only saw Zachary

Pat Mullan

> *Walker once or twice in those months, but he seemed to have changed utterly. Somber and unsociable, he never met with Charlie Pettigrew again. The US Army seemed to be his only life.*

MacDara was sure that Hajin Kim hadn't bought his story about Charlie Pettigrew's inheritance. He had found Kim's name and phone number in Major Whiteside's journal with a follow-up reminder to call about Charlie Pettigrew. He suspected that the major had not lived to make that call. Elsewhere in the journal, Pettigrew was mentioned as having had a formative influence on Zachary Walker in his youth. Owen reckoned that Pettigrew must be in his sixties if he was still alive. That would mean he was receiving Social Security. If so, the monthly payments would probably be deposited in some financial institution near where he lived.

A call to General Shields provided the information Owen needed. Charlie Pettigrew was indeed receiving Social Security; he was sixty-five years old. The monthly payments were being deposited in his name at the Royal Bank of Canada in Cheticamp, Novia Scotia.

Nova Scotia, Canada,
Wednesday February 23, 2000

At the rental agency at Halifax International Airport MacDara settled for a Jeep Cherokee. The short Air Canada flight from Boston landed at six pm and he was out of the airport and heading north on 102 by six thirty.

MacDara had been in Canada numerous times on GMA business, mostly to Toronto. He had been to Novia Scotia only once, for a business conference, which had been held at Pictou Lodge. The lodge commanded a vantage point on the north coast above Pictou Harbour and Northumberland Strait, which

The CIRCLE of SODOM
A Gripping New Thriller

separated Nova Scotia from Prince Edward Island. Just the place to spend the night, he figured. Two hours later he had left the Trans Canada Highway and was meandering up the long approach road to the Lodge. He had reserved one of the original log cabins with its large stone fireplace. Even though he wouldn't need a fire on a May evening, it still gave him the feeling of hearth and home. MacDara detested hotel rooms.

By ten o'clock he had showered, changed and dined and was ensconced in a comfortable wooden rocking chair by the fireplace. Time to brief himself in preparation for tomorrow. He took out the Novia Scotia map he had picked up at the airport and pulled out the briefing sheet that Shields had emailed to him just before Owen left New York. He read the text of the message again.

> *Done a little background checking on your Mr Charles Pettigrew. Seems his mother was one Carmel Deveau, an Acadian from Cheticamp, Nova Scotia. She and his father, Charles Pettigrew Sr were wed in New Orleans. Good luck!*

By nine thirty the next morning MacDara was two hours west of Pictou and crossing into Cape Breton over the Canso Causeway, which billed itself, at two hundred and seventeen feet, as the deepest causeway in the world. Traffic was light on the Trans Canada Highway as he pushed deeper into Cape Breton. He reached the junction of the Cabot Trail and headed inland, emerging about an hour later on the coast at Margaree Harbour. He was only a half-hour away from Cheticamp and the vista that surrounded him made the trip worthwhile. Flat undulating coastline, carpeted in green, adorned by distinctive homes and villages, old world and French in character and construction, verged the blue waters of the Northumberland Strait. For a minute he considered Charlie Pettigrew to be a lucky man.

Pat Mullan

It was exactly twelve noon, four and a half hours after checking out of Pictou Lodge, when Owen MacDara swung the Jeep Cherokee into the customer parking area in front of the Royal Bank of Canada branch in Cheticamp. The sun was high in the sky but the breeze from the ocean made the day seem cool. A small branch, two teller windows but only one teller, it didn't take MacDara long to find the manager. A big friendly fellow in his mid-forties, Jean Paul Lavigne loved to talk.

"Ah, yes. Of course, I know Monsieur Pettigrew. Private man, keeps to himself, a recluse almost. But the Deveaus. Ah, so sad. None of them left, I'm afraid. When Grandmama passed away ten years ago the line ended. Except for Monsieur Pettigrew, of course. I believe he was the only living relative. So sad, Monsieur MacNamara, did you say your name was? Oh, MacDara. So sorry. You see, and I'm supposed to be good at names! It's my business. How can I take a person's money if I don't know them? Scottish? No! Irish! Ah, cousins."

When MacDara managed to squeeze in a word he asked Monsieur Lavigne to give him directions to Charlie Pettigrew's house.

"Ah, you see, *mon ami*, it is not so simple. Ah no, not so simple. No one sees Monsieur Pettigrew. He has no automobile, no telephone. Never comes to town. He does not want to see anyone, Monsieur MacDara. Believe me. *Certainement!* He has only one contact with the outside world. Georgie Collet, Little Georgie. A bit innocent, dear Georgie. Twenty-two but a child really, a mind of a twelve-year-old. He's the only one that Monsieur Pettigrew trusts to see him. But, of course, no one has really asked to see him. Before you, I mean, Monsieur MacDara. Georgie takes him some milk and groceries every week. Ah, I think Monsieur Pettigrew pays Georgie well. Nobody knows. But Georgie is never short of money. He may be innocent but he knows the value of a dollar, our Little Georgie. Ah, yes, he knows the value of a dollar."

The CIRCLE of SODOM
A Gripping New Thriller

"Can you tell me where to find Georgie. I've got nothing to lose. I'll ask him to take me", blurted out MacDara, as though he were playing musical chairs, with the banker's voice being the music.

"That's easy, Monsieur MacDara. It's just past twelve thirty. Georgie's always playing hopscotch or something with the schoolchildren in the playground at this time. The teachers are very tolerant of him. So are the children. You'll find him there. It's two streets up and one street over on your left. I wish you luck, Monsieur MacDara."

True to his word, that's where Owen MacDara found Georgie Collet. He was kicking a ball with some of the six- and seven-year-olds. Tall, gangly and a bit toothy, with unkempt black hair, his movements almost mimicked the young Jerry Lewis in those movies with Dean Martin. MacDara stood watching for a while and his opportunity came when Georgie kicked the ball too hard. Owen caught it and carried it back to him while he just stood there with an innocent grin on his face.

"Hello, Georgie. My name is Owen. I want to ask you something very important," MacDara said, and paused long enough to let that sink in.

"I'd like you to take me to see Charlie Pettigrew."

Georgie stopped smiling. He shuffled on one foot and answered without looking MacDara in the eye. "I don't think I can do that. Monsieur Charles would not like that."

MacDara had already considered that response.

"Will you take a letter to him from me?" and, when he saw Georgie hesitate, followed it with, "I'll pay you well. Twenty dollars."

That seemed to convince Little Georgie. He agreed to take the letter. *Ah yes*, thought MacDara to himself, *Little Georgie knows the value of a dollar.*

Little Georgie Collet returned an hour and half later and found MacDara snoozing in his jeep.

"Monsieur Charles says yes. I can take you to see him."

"Hop in, Georgie. Just give me the directions", said MacDara, knowing that his note to Charlie Pettigrew telling him that Zachary Walker was in grave danger had had the desired effect.

They left Cheticamp, heading south again, and then turned west on to Cheticamp Island. Twenty minutes later MacDara parked the jeep on the remotest part of the island and he and Georgie walked the last half mile over a track more suitable for bike riding, until they reached a small ranch-style cabin perched on an incline overlooking the ocean. As they approached, a man rose from a bench on the wooden deck that skirted the house on two sides.

Owen MacDara had never seen a photograph of Charlie Pettigrew and had no fixed image in his mind. Nevertheless, he was unprepared for the person that rose to greet him. A tall angular figure, leaning precariously sideways from the hips, wearing what looked like a dark brown cloak thrown over his shoulders, tied at the waist and reaching his ankles in folds and corners. His hair was long, white and straggly, hanging in wisps around his shoulders. His right hand reached out to greet MacDara while his left supported his leaning frame on a hefty looking blackthorn stick; the fingers were long and skeletal, covered in an almost gossamer layer of skin with tributaries of large prominent veins showing the bluish-red hue of the blood that coursed through them. His countenance glowed with an expression that seemed luminous. A prominent forehead, smooth skin that belied his years, eyes that were very moist and emotional and a wide soft-lipped mouth that slashed his face from ear to ear. His voice was low, cavernous, as he greeted Owen MacDara.

"God bless. Come inside."

Little Georgie stayed on the deck and MacDara followed Charlie Pettigrew into his cabin. It was simple, one bedroom with a large living room and kitchen combined. A lumpy couch

The CIRCLE of SODOM
A Gripping New Thriller

furnished one wall and an old pine table and chairs the opposite wall. A sink and stove huddled, almost incongruously, in one corner.

He offered MacDara a chipped mug of water from a crockery jug that sat on the table but Owen declined and decided to plunge right in.

"Thank you for letting me come to see you."

"Don't thank me. I'd prefer that you weren't here. But I couldn't ignore anything that might hurt Zachary."

"You were very close, Mr. Pettigrew."

"I loved Zach. I'm not sure he returned my love. But that was years ago when we were young. I haven't spoken to him in over twenty years. Oh, yes, I know how important he is these days. I may be a recluse, as you would say, Mr. MacDara, but that doesn't mean I don't know what's going on. I've been leaving what you call the civilized world for years, a world that had no space in it for me. This beach house belonged to my grandmother. My mother brought me up here once or twice when I was little. When Grandmother passed away she left this to me and I moved here about five years ago. It's my last move from your civilized world, Mr. MacDara. I'll die here."

They were both seated at the table. Charlie Pettigrew had pushed his chair away from it and he sat almost astride it, the blackthorn stick between his legs, both hands clasping its bulbous end for support. He had stopped talking and was breathing rapidly and deeply. MacDara sensed that his exhaustion came more from the novelty of talking to someone than from any physical frailty. He regained his composure and looked directly at MacDara. "What kind of danger is Zach in?"

"We believe that he's being blackmailed over some incident that occurred in Korea years ago. It's seriously affecting him. General Walker is a very private man, a very proud man, and, I believe, a very lonely man. He doesn't know that we are aware of the blackmailing and the danger he may be in. The President is also afraid that the nation could be at risk. Zachary Walker holds a very powerful position. We didn't approach him on this matter because we felt that he wouldn't cooperate with us."

"How do I know this is true, Mr. MacDara?"

Owen had anticipated this. When he had conjured up the threat to Zachary Walker as a ploy to prize open the past, he didn't know if it would work or not. He knew that he would need some way to pass the litmus test. The President had given him identification carrying the Presidential seal of authority. Owen handed it to Charlie Pettigrew. After holding it for what seemed to be an interminably long time but was, in reality, only a couple of minutes, he gave it back to MacDara.

"I do not know who might be threatening Zachary but I can tell you and the President about Korea. It's so long ago and it shouldn't be something that's held over Zachary's head like a sword of Damocles. We will all be asked by God to account for our stewardship very soon."

He commenced talking, a far away look in his eyes. He talked about the Followers and about the sacramental rite of the orgy. He described an endless night of makli and hashish at the Followers' residence in Seoul. He remembered the sacrificial offering made by himself and Zachary Walker. He would never forget. It was the central rite of the sacrament.

"I can never forget," he repeated over and over. "That's the last time we were together. We were never close again."

A single tear freed itself from the corner of his right eye and slowly meandered down the smooth glacial surface of his face.

He told how Zachary Walker had lain prostrate on the central altar and how he had entered him again and again with a dildo that looked like a riding crop. "You see, it was a sacrificial instrument."

He went on to tell how the Followers stood behind the altar chanting and offering up this sacrifice. "But that's when it went wrong. I heard a sound, like a rifle shot. I watched the sacrificial dildo splinter into small pieces. It all seemed like it was happening in slow motion."

The CIRCLE of SODOM
A Gripping New Thriller

He wiped the tear from his cheek with the back of his right hand.

"They took Zach to the hospital that night to get the pieces removed. He never came back to the Followers. I never saw him again. I tried many times but he never answered me. He made the army his life. I've watched him ever since. But I never tried to contact him again." He looked directly at Owen, the moist eyes softening the faraway look, and said simply, "I still love him, you know."

MacDara thought that he should feel shock at what he'd just heard. But he felt humbled by it instead. He had learned Zachary Walker's secret and solved the mystery of that strange surgical procedure Major Whiteside had conducted in the 53rd MASH. But he had also heard a story of love. If the civilized world that Charlie Pettigrew was running away from ever learned about Walker's secret he would be destroyed. Whoever eliminated Murph and tried to get him knew that too well. MacDara was now convinced of the connection. Somebody knew about General Walker's past and was trying to bury it forever.

As Owen MacDara was boarding his plane at Halifax, another man, on a different mission, was arriving in Cheticamp. He, too, had arrived to see Charlie Pettigrew. A couple of discreet inquiries were enough to give him the directions to Pettigrew's home. He spent the long afternoon and early evening becoming familiar with the terrain that surrounded Charlie Pettigrew's house on Cheticamp Island. Then he waited for nightfall.

He moved carefully, putting his feet down gingerly before trusting the ground with his full weight. He had been here in daylight and he knew where he was going. But it was different at night. He couldn't risk using his flashlight. It was three in the morning now, and he must have gone a mile already. Another mile to go. Overconfident, he stepped forward firmly and there was nothing there. Unbalanced, he tumbled into empty black space, landing hard. His hands grabbed at grassy tufts but, rooted in sand, they did not hold. He tumbled further, head over heels, until he felt the hard glancing blow against the side of his head and he lapsed into unconsciousness.

His head was killing him. It took him a while to remember where he was. He could feel his hair sticky with congealed blood. Reaching out with his left hand he felt the large boulder that had broken his fall. Rising on one knee he pushed himself to a crouching position and used the boulder to leverage himself back on to his feet. He didn't seem to have broken anything and he was sure that his head wound was superficial. Looking at the luminous hands of his watch he could see that it was almost six am. He had lost the better part of an hour. He couldn't afford to make any more mistakes. He had used up his extra time. And he still had a mile to go.

He could see the house darkly silhouetted against the night sky. The ground was solid and flat and he crossed the final two hundred yards with long loping strides. He pulled back the screen door gently, enough to make a low squeak. He waited. Silence. The door was unlocked and he opened it, sliding his body inside. Then he waited for his eyes to adjust to the darkness. Dawn had stirred in the sky and shapes were taking form. He could see that he was standing in a large room, a table on his left and what appeared to be a couch huddled against the opposite wall. A dark rectangle in the far-left corner must be a door. He crept across the room, noticing that the floor was solid, concrete. No creaking floorboards to concern him. The doorknob turned smoothly in his hand and the door opened silently. He could see the angular contour on the bed in the corner and he listened to the deep, regular breathing. Anxious to get it over with, he strode to the bed, gripped the sleeping body in a firm armlock and placed the chloroformed cloth over the nose and mouth. There wasn't even a struggle. Just a tension in that angular body, then a limp slackness.

The CIRCLE of SODOM
A Gripping New Thriller

Fifteen minutes had elapsed since he entered the house, and dawn was approaching. Picking up the limp body, he tossed it over his shoulder like a rolled-up carpet. Then he left the house and crossed the short distance to the rusted wire fence overlooking the water and the rocks below. He didn't hesitate. One strong heave and he had launched the body over the fence and into the air. He watched it twist once, then fall awkwardly onto the rocks. The water lapped up against it in a macabre ritual of welcome.

He turned without a further glance and left by the same way he had arrived.

Washington, D.C.
Thursday February 24, 2000.

MacDara went to see General Shields as soon as he returned from his visit to Charlie Pettigrew. Shields was expecting him.

He had barely sat down when Sally arrived with two large mugs of General Shields's special rich blend of Colombian coffee. An old army addiction of his.

Owen briefed Shields on his visit to Pettigrew and got right to the point. "The incident in the 53rd MASH is no longer a mystery. Pettigrew told me everything."

He told the story about General Walker exactly as Charlie Pettigrew had told him. Down to the very details of the orgiastic ritual in the Followers' residence in Seoul. As Owen spoke, Bart Shields seemed to sink further into his chair, cupping the mug of coffee in both hands like a comforter. He had forgotten his Macanudo that was now smoldering away in the large black ashtray.

"You realize, sir, if this information had ever been disclosed, General Walker's career would have been finished."

"I know that, Owen. Are you suggesting that Zach Walker has killed to protect himself?"

"What do you think, sir?"

"Never! Not the Zach Walker that I know. But I don't know that other Zach Walker. The one that Pettigrew talks about. It's hard for me to believe that they're both the same man."

"Well, let's face it. They are the same. General Walker is gay."

Bart Shields just stared out the window in deep thought.

"Did you hear me, sir? General Walker is gay!"

"I heard you. It's difficult for me to swallow, that's all. A gay general! A gay Chairman of the Joint Chiefs! Jesus, if the papers ever got wind of that, we'd have hell to pay! General Walker would have to resign!."

"You're right. If you think a guy in the ranks gets fucked - pardon the expression - by his peers when they find out he's gay, what do you think will happen to Walker?"

"I know. I know. But you're not seriously suggesting that General Walker is killing people to save himself. I don't believe that for a minute! Do you?"

"No, I don't. But I believe somebody else wants to save him. I've been thinking long and hard since Pettigrew told me what happened in Korea. Very few people knew that General Walker was gay. Even fewer people knew about the orgy that went wrong that night in Seoul. Major Whiteside knew. He removed the broken dildo that same night in the 53rd Mash. I helped him. Murph filled in for me that night. I never told Murph, but whoever ordered his murder didn't know that. Or couldn't take the chance. It was easier to eliminate him. That's why I'm on their hit list. I know it!"

"But who are 'they'?"

"I don't know for sure but I've got a damn good idea. Thackeray and his thugs did do the killings. I'm sure of that. There's no way that we can prove that Thackeray gave the orders. Not yet anyway. And even if we did, I believe he's only part of it. I believe there's a right-wing conspiracy going on.

The CIRCLE of SODOM
A Gripping New Thriller

And I have to believe that General Walker is involved in some way or other."

"Never! Not Zach Walker!"

"Let me explain. When Major Whiteside started to write his memoirs he found something 'rotten in the state of Denmark'. That's the note he made in his journal. He went to see General Walker. He was troubled by his meeting. He told Dr Pepper. In the doctor's own words he said that Henry Whiteside thought that 'the enemy was right here in this country' and 'he was certain that General Walker was an easy target' The doctor also said that Whiteside was sure that his life was in danger."

"Owen, we know all this"

"But the pieces are beginning to fall in place. I know we've gone over this ground before, but let's look at it again. What do we know so far? Major Whiteside was killed because he was going to say too much in his memoirs. Ruth Whiteside was almost killed when they ransacked her home. Probably looking for the journal and notes that I have. Murph was killed because they wanted to eliminate anyone who knew about the general's secret. That includes me. I've been lucky so far. That's all. At first I couldn't figure out why Angelo was killed. But it does make sense - like I said before, the albino who killed Murph was a member of Thackeray's cult. Thackeray was having an affair with Liz Russo. What's one more to him? Maybe he thought he was doing Liz a favor."

"I know you believe Thackeray was behind these killings? But I still don't see his motive. And I sure see no evidence that Major Whiteside knew that Thackeray even existed. Do you?"

"Ah, but there's a connection. The Thackeray Institute. I did a little research on that organization. It's a place where the conservative elite like to send their kids. A sort of finishing school of the Right. You'd be surprised to know who some of the alumni are!"

"But you're going to tell me, aren't you, Owen."

"How about Senator Sumner Hardy for a start? He was a Rhodes scholar at Oxford. Stayed an extra year in England so that he could attend The Thackeray Institute. He now sits on the Advisory Council of the Institute"

"Owen, there's nothing sinister about any of that. We all know the senator is the leader of the Right in this country. You're not seriously suggesting that he is involved in this. Why, hell, he ran for President last time. His family founded this nation!"

"Well, I think the good senator is involved in this up to his neck! Did you know that the senator served in Korea? He was a second lieutenant, assigned as aide to Colonel Zachary Walker. He was in Seoul the night we operated on the colonel at the 53rd Mash. My bet is that he knows all about General Zachary Walker. I bet he knows exactly what happened that night. So, if that's the case, why isn't someone trying to kill the senator? I think he's got General Walker right in his pocket. Right where he needs him. Now, why do you think it's so important to keep Zachary Walker in his job as head of the Joint Chiefs? Do you think that the senator wants to make sure his back is covered when he makes his move?"

"Owen, that's all wild speculation. You sound like you're talking about the kind of shenanigans that go on in some South American countries! For Christ's sake, man, this is the US of A you're talking about. Not some two-bit dictatorship!"

"If I'm right it explains all these murders. Why would anyone go to such an extent to prevent the world from finding out that someone is gay? Even if that someone is Chairman of the Joint Chiefs? Makes no sense, you say. And you'd be right. It does make no sense. Until you look at it from another angle entirely. They're not killing to stop the world from finding out that General Walker is gay. They're killing to keep him in his job. They want to make sure that their man is in control of the military in this nation. Why would anyone want that so badly? Only if they needed to ensure that they controlled the military.

Or that the military would be ordered not to move against them. That's the way I read it, sir."

Owen could see General Shields wavering. He had picked up his unlit Macanudo and was now sucking it to comfort himself. Owen hadn't finished.

"And what about this mad Colonel McNab and his militia? I ran a check on him after Sanderson traced one of those hackers to his computer. Did you know that the colonel is a card carrying member of the good senator's political party? And that he has given money to every one of the senator's campaigns? We all know that Senator Hardy isn't very happy about the direction this country is taking. He makes no secret about that. All you have to do is listen to him on *Meet The Press* on a Sunday. And he's obviously well known to the Honorable David Anthony Llewellyn Thackeray. From what I know of Thackeray's vision of the future, it fits very nicely with the senator's. And, for that matter, so does McNab's. Strange bedfellows? But maybe not so strange when you think about it."

"Jesus, Owen. I hope that this is all just as crazy as it sounds! But, if it isn't.."

"If it isn't, your General Walker is in one hell of a lot of trouble. And so is our country!"

"You're right, Owen. It's time to get to the bottom of all of this. I'll see General Walker immediately. I'll also see the President."

Sally had left the pot and General Shields refilled their mugs. Owen declined. One mug of Bart Shields's special blend would hold him all day.

"I've got an appointment to see Tony Thackeray."

"When?"

"Couple of days from now. In LA. At the Thackeray Institute."

"How will you handle that?"

"Totally business. A follow-up to his keynote speech at our GMA dinner. I'll invite him to conduct a seminar for our senior

Pat Mullan

associates on the challenges facing us. It should'nt raise any suspicions on his part. If he is behind the attempts on my life there is no evidence to show that I suspect him. As far as he's concerned, his other life is safe from me. So he shouldn't be on his guard. I want to meet him again. I need to know more about him. Not the kind of stuff I'll find in his biographies. I need to get my own feel for him. The GMA dinner was too impersonal for that. Besides, he was on display. The second time I believe I saw him, in his other role as the Chosen One, he was also on display. I want to see him when he's not on display."

"Be careful, Owen. If this Thackeray is all that you say he is, he's a dangerous man."

**Cheticamp, Nova Scotia,
Friday February 25, 2000.**

The boy tossed the driftwood as far as he could and his golden retriever brought it back to him every time. His dad was far behind, enjoying the invigorating feel of the early-morning sea. He watched his son toss the driftwood again and watched the dog chase it. But the dog didn't return this time. He just stood there at the edge of the rocks and the sea, barking furiously. The boy stood where he was and waited for his father.

At first glance, the object at the dog's feet looked like a sack of something that had been washed up on the rocks. It was only when they got closer that it took the form of a man's body.

There was an autopsy. Charlie Pettigrew's cause of death was obvious: fractured skull, severed spine and multiple internal injuries, consistent with a fall onto the rocks from the promontory above. Accidental death, suicide, foul play: each was possible but there was no evidence to help make a determination. Charlie Pettigrew had left a will. His body was cremated, according to his wishes, and the ashes scattered on the sea near his Cheticamp home. He left that home and the couple of thousand dollars in his bank account to little Georgie Collet.

Finally, he had left a sealed package with his attorneys that was to be sent, unopened, to General Zachary Walker, in the event of his death. There was no need to wait for the autopsy and will reading to accede to this wish. His attorneys forwarded the package as soon as they were informed of his death.

Pat Mullan

NINETEEN

**Los Angeles, California,
Monday February 28, 2000.**

Wilshire Boulevard seemed to go on for ever. Even though MacDara had the address, it still took him half an hour to find the West Coast office of the Thackeray Institute. He finally found it on the tenth floor of one of those high rise buildings built recently, almost in open defiance of the San Andreas Fault. Double glass doors with black and gold lettering ushered him into a reception foyer that might have been more suitable for the Dorchester Hotel on Park Lane.

The receptionist was blonde, good-looking and well-tailored. She had a mid-Atlantic accent and MacDara couldn't tell whether she was a Europeanized American or an Americanized European. He introduced himself: "Owen MacDara. I have a ten am appointment with Mr. Thackeray."

She pulled up a screen on her computer and confirmed his appointment. "Yes, Mr. MacDara. Won't you please have a seat and I'll inform Mr. Thackeray that you're here."

Owen thanked her and chose instead to walk over and examine the art on the adjacent wall. He was absorbed in a

The CIRCLE of SODOM
A Gripping New Thriller

limited edition Alexander Calder stonecut lithograph when the timbre of that Anglo-Welsh voice broke in. "Good morning, Owen. So glad you could come."

Owen MacDara turned around and grasped Tony Thackeray's outstretched hand. "It's my pleasure. Besides, I never got a chance to thank you in person for your entertaining and provocative talk at our dinner."

"If I provoked you, then I succeeded. If you found it entertaining then I was doubly successful. Would you like some coffee? Good. Rebecca, coffee for Mr. MacDara and myself in my office. Follow me, Owen."

Tony Thackeray's office reflected his pedigree, his interests and his travels. The desk used to belong to the Lord of the Admiralty, Lord Louis Mountbatten. Primitive African carvings seemed at home beside Mayan and Aztec sculpted busts from Central America. This sense of the past contrasted strongly with a modernist sense of the present. Tall and elegant high-backed chairs by Charles Rennie Mackintosh surrounded an oval table of spalted beech in the adjoining conference room whose walls displayed works by Miro, de Kooning and Hockney.

A young girl arrived with a thermos pot of freshly brewed coffee and blueberry muffins just as they were sitting down in the conference room.

"I'm afraid these are an American product that I've acquired a taste for," said Tony Thackeray as he picked up a blueberry muffin. "Can't find anything quite like them in Europe."

He demolished his second muffin, pressed the intercom on the phone and told his secretary to see that he wasn't interrupted.

"Tell me about the Thackeray Institute. I'd like to know more," said Owen.

"As I'm sure you know, my father founded the Institute to prepare people to manage and to govern. I believe that the contribution made by the Institute is only now being realized. Our alumni sit on the board of most Fortune 500 companies. They're also in politics, law and public service - and not just in our Western society. We're beginning to play a vital role in the new world emerging out of the collapse of the Soviet Union. You'll also find us in Japan, Korea and even in China."

"But you chose to split the Institute and concentrate on that great unknown, the future. Why?"

"Precisely because of what you just said. I don't believe that it is the great unknown. You see, I believe my father was right when he forecasted chaos, anarchy, and economic collapse for the UK. And I believe his forecast applies to our entire world, not just the UK."

Tony Thackeray pressed a button. A section of the conference table slid back and a computer emerged as the large de Kooning print on the end wall retracted to reveal a floor to ceiling audio visual display screen. He hit the enter key and a map of the world appeared, color coded by country and region into degrees of stability based on ethnic, religious, racial, economic, social, territorial, and political conflict. Only a small fraction of the planet was colored with the dark blue of stability.

"Some of this is obvious. Areas like the former Yugoslavia have always been unstable. Look at the bastions of democracy: the UK, the US, France. In the UK the Scots will soon follow the Irish. That will leave an England divided sharply between the haves and the have-nots, with inner cities populated by unwanted Pakistanis, Africans, Asians and West Indians."

He hit a few keys and the Western Hemisphere dominated the screen and then narrowed to bring the US into focus.

"Let's take the US. What do you see? Some areas of blue, lots of red and much gradation in between. Pretty unstable, don't you think? Now, let's overlay that with stability analyses of the US taken every twenty-five years starting in the middle of the nineteenth century. Even in the beginning of this period, when the US had just emerged from the Civil War and the Indian Wars and lawlessness continued in the western states, there was still a dominant blue for stability. You see, the pioneer and puritan ethos had complete solidarity, and those people were

The CIRCLE of SODOM
A Gripping New Thriller

ruling and building. Let's overlay the screen every twenty-five years until we reach the present."

The overlays created their own motion picture for Owen MacDara. More and more stable blues fragmented into shades of instability, eventually ending with the current unstable map of the US.

"That ethos and solidarity that gave this land its stability a century ago are gone. Despite Johnson's great society, blacks are no better off. Racial hatred is stronger than ever. The Godless left and the Religious Right are going to settle their differences at the point of a gun. Abortion doctors are being murdered. The Right have taken out contracts on America."

"You're painting a pretty bleak, one-sided picture. Couldn't you just as readily mount a defense for the side of stability and reason?", interjected MacDara.

"No! Not this time. I believe that mankind, womankind, have reached a watershed in their existence. They are fully bent on a battle to the bitter end."

"If you're right, what can we do to avert it?"

"Nothing! Our only hope is to accelerate it and ensure that our planet is not destroyed in the process."

"That's a truly bleak future you're presenting."

"No, it's not. The truly bleak future is here now. The future I see is one of renewal for the earth. The cutting away of decayed and rotting growth. And the emergence of a new and stronger seed. Our seed. We must survive to govern and rule beyond the millennium."

"And you are that new seed?"

"Yes. I've been nurtured by my father and by the Institute that he founded. I have been well prepared."

"Why are you telling me all of this?"

"Because I have made a judgement about you, Owen. You have the steel to be one of us. I want you to join our movement."

Pat Mullan

This turn of events had taken Owen MacDara entirely unawares. He stood up, walked over to the window and looked out at the sprawl of Los Angeles. *Should I play him along and pretend that I'm interested*, he thought. *No, Thackeray would see through it. Better to play it straight.* He turned around and faced Tony Thackeray who had, by this time, logged out of his system. The de Kooning print once again dominated the wall. The choice of de Kooning was perverse, mused MacDara to himself. He knew that the CIA had used American modern artists like Willem de Kooning as a propaganda weapon in the Cold War. De Kooning never knew about it. The CIA secretly funded exhibitions around the world to show that abstract art was proof of the artistic and cultural freedom that existed outside of the Soviet's rigid system. *But Thackeray knows all that and that's exactly why he has the de Kooning playing such a prominent role in this conference room*, MacDara reasoned.

"Tony, I'm honored that you're inviting me to join you. Truthfully, though, I've never seen the world the same way that you do. Maybe you're right and maybe I'm blind. I don't know. I'll have to think about all of this."

"That's what I specialize in, Owen. Helping you to think. Don't take too long. I'll be in the US for at least another month. The Institute will always know where I can be reached. Remember, we need strong people to govern and lead us after the chaos."

And with that, Tony Thackeray ushered Owen MacDara to the door of his office and thanked him once again for coming. Still in thought, Owen didn't hear the receptionist bidding him goodbye and he didn't see the young man sitting in the reception area until he accidentally knocked over his briefcase. Stooping to pick it up, he apologized to a face that he knew he'd seen somewhere before. It was only after he'd taken the elevator to the ground floor and emerged into the sunlight of Wilshire Boulevard that he remembered. That face was the face of the Brother who bumped into him and then helped him get up from

The CIRCLE of SODOM
A Gripping New Thriller

the floor in the El Habesh Mosque in Florida. *I wonder if he recognized me*, thought MacDara. His face had showed no sign of recognition. But Owen couldn't rely on that. He had to assume that the man had recognized him. And he had to assume that he'd tell Thackeray. *And then,* Owen thought, *Thackeray will know that I know.*

"You're certain it was him, David?"
"Absolutely. I was going to challenge him that night in the mosque because I'd never seen him before. But I decided that he must be a new convert. I never thought about that until today. I knew I had to tell you right away."
"David, you did the right thing. Thank you."
Tony Thackeray realized that he had underestimated Owen MacDara. It was now obvious that MacDara knew that he headed the Circle and must suspect that he was involved in the killing of his friend Murph and the attempts on his own life. But he couldn't prove a thing, despite his suspicions. How much did MacDara really know? He'd been working with Shields at the NSC; that much he already knew. If MacDara knew about the Circle and about him, what else did he know? No more surprises, Thackeray promised himself. That was the last time he'd ever underestimate Owen MacDara.

After David had left, Tony Thackeray reflected on the laws of probability. What was the probability of MacDara's chance encounter with David? How did MacDara find his way to the mosque in Florida? Luck or the laws of probability? Only a couple of trusted Brothers in his Inner Circle knew that he, the Chosen One, was also the Honorable David Anthony Llewellyn Thackeray, head of the Thackeray Institute.

Tony Thackeray picked up the phone, asked his secretary to see that he wasn't disturbed for any reason, locked his office door, removed his jacket, tie and shoes and assumed the yoga posture he used for meditation in his continual search for perfect self-knowledge.

He allowed the past to return, let his mother back in again. He consciously conjured her up in a spiritual exercise that induced a hypnotic state. In that state he would achieve profound contemplation, samadhi, the perfect absorption of his thought with the object of his thought, his mother. She was here again, smiling at him and beckoning him to follow her..................

..........Branwen Hughes was tall, willowy and beautiful, with a fine china complexion. A commoner by English definition, Welsh royalty by her own, she exuded the air of a true aristocrat. The perfect wife, the perfect match for the life she must lead as Lady Haverford.

Daughter of David, who taught history at the local secondary school, and his wife, Dilys, who ran the village post office, outwardly it seemed that Branwen, their only child, led a very protected and privileged life. But Branwen Hughes led another life, a life connected to a mystical and mythical Celtic past. Her very name, Branwen, was taken from the four branches of the Mabinogi, part of the eleven tales comprising the Mabinogion, the repository of the oral storytelling of Celtic Wales. Branwen, of the 'white breast', was one of the three great queens of Britain, and the most beautiful girl in the Celtic world.

In that secret other world of theirs, David and Dilys Hughes were Druids.

They lived in two worlds: the real world of twentieth-century Britain and their other, Druidic, world, with its aversion to time and place and the practicalities of modern daily life. Symbolized best by Peredur's vision in the Mabinogion - 'On the bank of the river he saw a tall tree: from roots to crown one half was aflame and the other green with leaves' - these were the two worlds within which Branwen lived: the green verdant world of daily village life and the flaming,

The CIRCLE of SODOM
A Gripping New Thriller

flickering, emotional and passionate otherworld of her parents.........

.........The boy was only five years old. He sat on a heavy blanket, wrapped well and swaddled in the clothes of his mother and her friends. The moon cast a silvery, eerie light on the sand around him and illuminated the white froth of the sea as it broke on the rocks at the outer edge of the beach. He could see his mother, her golden hair flowing behind her, as she and her friends ran, naked, in a circle that seemed to extend halfway into the water. A fire glowed in their midst and its flames leapt and sparked into the midnight air. As the boy watched he saw two of them lead an animal, a pig, toward the center of their gathering. While the others danced and frolicked, one of them hit the pig between its two eyes with a sledgehammer stunning it and toppling it to its knees and the other stuck a knife in its throat spewing its blood into the sand as its screams filled the night air.........

.........It was his ninth birthday. The party had ended, his friends had gone home and his father had left for London again. His mother had explained that the time had come; he had come of age. He would be initiated into the clan, the family, that evening. The room had been in darkness as they entered, only the nervous coughs and shuffling of feet betrayed the people hidden there. He'd been blindfolded right away. He couldn't imagine why, because he hadn't been able to see anything at all. The Chief Druid intoned the laws of the clan in the Welsh language, a language in which he was as fluent as English, ending with the order 'Let the ceremony begin'. The boy was guided forward, one person at each side, until he bumped into something

hard. Reaching out with his right hand he felt the wood of a table, wood with a curved edge, a round table. As he reached out, his hand was grasped firmly and he felt the sting of the pinprick on his middle finger. Then that finger was held and squeezed and he knew they were taking his blood. Once again he was guided around the table, until he reached the other side. He could clearly hear the rasp of steel as the blade was withdrawn from the scabbard. Pressed cold and hard against his lips he was exhorted to kiss it firmly. Just as quickly the steel was replaced with skin, so soft and warm. The nipple edged its way between his small lips. The voice of the Druid was now the voice of the Druidess, telling him to suck at the breasts of the clan, at the nourishment of the spirit. He did, and he could taste the warm milk.........

.........He had seen his mother naked often but this time was different. She lay prostate on the altar, trance-like. He had watched her drink the potion from the chalice offered by the celebrant, then watched as she reclined, first on her side and then flat on her back, her last movement relaxing her knees and letting her legs stretch out so that her feet dangled over the end of the altar. The celebrant draped his outer vestment over her while those assembled chanted in unison. Just as rapidly, he removed the vestment with a flourish that displayed the intricate Celtic animal, a hybrid of a goat and an eagle, whose foot-like talons entwined around the shoulders and encircled the celebrant's neck the moment he donned it and swung around to pick up the gleaming blade. The boy held the silver and gold chalice under the arm of each person as the celebrant made an incision with the blade and let the blood mingle freely. Then, helping the boy hold the chalice aloft over his mother, they solemnly poured the blood offering over her

The CIRCLE of SODOM
A Gripping New Thriller

breasts, watching it run in a river, forming a pond where her navel was and overflowing to darken the patch of blonde hair framing the entrance to her thighs..........

..........It was his first summer home from boarding school. He was eleven years old and he had come home to a house in mourning, to a funeral. His grandfather, David Hughes, had died. A stroke, they said. He was only sixty-three. The boy was taken into the bedroom where his grandfather lay, white and waxen-still, with his hands clasped over his chest, bony and lifeless. They made him lay his hands over those cold, cold hands of death..........

..........It was his second summer home from boarding school and he came home to a house in mourning again. His mother was dead. Too young, too pretty, too full of life, too much to live for, they said. Drugs, sleeping pills, a whole bottle. There was no suicide note. They said that she had been despondent since her father's death a year ago. He didn't believe it. She would never have left without saying goodbye to him. At the graveside he thought she would suffocate. He thought they were burying her alive..........

..........and so the boy grew into adolescence, nurtured by his father in his future vocation, educated in the hallowed halls of the elite and sustained emotionally by his mother's legacy,
until...
..........in his twenty-third year he was sent by his father to study under Dr. Johann Malocco at the Malocco Center for Strategic Studies in Zurich. It was there that he grew to understand his father's mission and to take it as his own. It was also there that he found

a way to use his mother's legacy to fulfill his ambitions. It was there that he began to meet with a select few who believed as he did, believed there was another way between the failure of Communism and the decadence of the West. The meetings became more frequent, other believers joined, and his natural charisma and authority gave him absolute mind control over all. Before he left Zurich, he had recruited his first disciples and formed his Inner Circle. They would mete out the justice that must be dispensed. Their tattoo, the snake in the circle, symbolized their role and branded them like a Mau Mau blood oath. They chose their name from one of the great Biblical events, the destruction of Sodom and Gomorrah, to remind themselves that the Lord had said He would be 'more severe on the Day of Judgement than he had been with Sodom and Gomorrah'. The justice they must dispense would be most severe…………

Slowly Tony Thackeray returned to the present. He always felt refreshed and reinvigorated by his meditation. Putting on his jacket, he walked over to the window and looked out at the sprawl of Los Angeles. City of Angels. Appropriately named, in a perverse way. He felt a kinship with the Archangel Gabriel. The yoga had focused his mind. If MacDara knew about The Circle of Sodom, then General Bartley Shields and the NSC knew. If they knew, then the President knew. They would have to act now. They could no longer wait for the right political climate on the ground. He decided to call Senator Hardy. Then he would convene a meeting of the Advisory Council of the Thackeray Institute.

But more immediate action was needed. MacDara must be stopped. He picked up the phone and asked his secretary to contact David and tell him that he needed him right away.

The CIRCLE of SODOM
A Gripping New Thriller

Palm Springs, California,
Tuesday February 29, 2000.

Owen and Kate fled Los Angeles without even packing their bags or checking out of their suite at the Century Plaza Hotel.

Dinner in the Vineyard had been Dover sole and rainbow trout. The sommelier had found a superb 1981 Robert Ampeau Montrachet. The young lady harpist had commenced a rendition of 'Danny Boy' as he and Kate were languishing over a final sambucca and cognac. MacDara had seen him as soon as he entered the restaurant and started talking intently to the maitre d'. There could be no mistake. It was the Brother he had seen this morning at the Thackeray Institute; the same one he had talked with that night in the El Habesh Mosque in Dania.

The valet had had their car ready in a couple of minutes and they had sped out of LA, driving east into the desert. Two hours later they had arrived in Palm Springs. They picked the first motel they saw, the Biltmore. MacDara had risked a call to the Assistant Manager at the Century Plaza. An exceedingly generous tip had ensured that their bags were packed discreetly and sent by next available transport to Palm Springs.

They had a private chalet at the Biltmore. There was something sensuous about the smell of the orange blossoms in the warm dry desert air. The door of the chalet was glazed, letting just enough evening light through to softly bathe the room. On impulse, Owen picked Kate up and carried her into the room. Kicking the door closed behind him, he gently eased her feet to the floor, still holding her in his arms. Kate traced her index finger across Owen's lips igniting a fire in him. He gently kissed her eyes, her ears, her face, her hair before merging his lips with hers.

Later, as they sat in the Jacuzzi sipping Armagnac, with the perfume of the orange blossoms wafting through the window, they made a decision. They would disappear here in Palm Springs for a few days. Nobody knew they were here. MacDara

Pat Mullan

could call his office in the morning and reschedule his business appointments. There was nothing that couldn't wait. At least, they convinced each other of that.

It was no place for someone with acrophobia.

MacDara was in a cable car halfway between the Californian desert floor and the summit of Mount San Jacinto. Palm Springs lay five minutes below him. It's a fifteen minute ride, he kept telling himself. Kate was a romantic. He could feel her entire body imprinted against him as he clung to her. Each time the cable car passed a pylon, it seemed to swing wildly. MacDara hung on even more tightly. He didn't look out of the windows and tried instead to focus on the passengers. The car was crowded. One sixtyish, ordinary looking lady stood and swayed in the center of the car. Totally unperturbed. This only made him feel even more vulnerable.

The lights of Palm Springs dotted the desert floor like scattered diamonds. Dusk had descended but people were still skiing on the adjacent slopes. It had been eighty-seven degrees when they left Palm Springs. Here, on the summit of Mount San Jacinto, it was only forty-three. Owen and Kate stood alone on the terrace outside the hilltop restaurant. The restaurant was nearly empty. Most of the day trippers had already left the mountain top and gone back down. It was peaceful and serene. One could almost be forgiven for feeling impervious to the world up here.

Kate slipped her arm through his and kissed him tenderly. The spell was broken. It was time to abandon their hilltop haven and catch the next cable car going down. It was dark now and MacDara knew that he wouldn't suffer from acrophobia this time. The darkness would prevent him from seeing how high up he was.

As he and Kate prepared to leave, two men in ski masks stepped on to the terrace. They moved with stealth. One of them took something from the pocket of his ski jacket. As he did so he was silhouetted against the light from the french windows. The outline was unmistakable. An automatic pistol with a silencer. MacDara moved fast. Pushing Kate to the ground he turned and aimed a karate kick directly at the man's outstretched arm. His foot split the assailant's ulna two inches above the wrist. One shot lodged harmlessly in the wooden deck as the pistol clattered to the ground. The second assailant didn't even try. He turned and fled through the french windows. MacDara picked up the pistol. The first assailant, in agony, holding his useless arm, was halfway to the windows when MacDara pounced on him, knocking him flat to the ground. Holding his head in an armlock, MacDara put the pistol behind his right ear.

"All right! Who sent you to get me?"

"Fuck you!" the man wheezed and struggled against MacDara's stranglehold.

"You have an attitude problem," said MacDara, releasing his stranglehold, stomping hard and breaking all the fingers of the man's good left hand. "I'll only ask you one more time. Who sent you?"

"The Circle found you guilty, man. That's all I know."

As MacDara relaxed his hold his assailant got up from his knees and made his escape. The wrong way. The low parapet of the balcony, shrouded in darkness, caught him sharply in mid-thigh knocking him off balance. He staggered wildly and pitched over the parapet, tumbling down the side of the mountain. The night air carried the sound of his body smashing into the rocks and trees.

Kate was now standing near the window; as Owen hugged her, he could feel her legs shaking against him. She was still in shock as they headed towards the ramp leading to the cable car station. They had only five minutes to make the next one off the mountain.

They retrieved the body from the mountain the next day.

MacDara met the local pathologist, Dr Newbury, at the morgue to identify the man.

"You understand, Doctor, I didn't get a good look at him."

"I do understand, Mr. MacDara. But anything may be helpful, both to you and to us."

"OK. He was well built. Around five foot ten inches and one hundred and eighty pounds or thereabouts. Didn't get a good look at his face. His ski mask came off in the struggle. His head was shaven close. I could feel the stubble. What does your examination reveal, Dr Newbury?"

"As I understand it, some of this information should be no surprise to you, Mr. MacDara." As he talked, Dr Newbury removed the sheet covering the body. "Healthy white male. One hundred and seventy-two pounds, five foot nine inches. I'd put the age between twenty-five and thirty. Fair hair, shaven close on head. Small scar above lip - old wound. Extent of injuries: compound fracture of lower right ulna; four fractured metacarpals on left hand; several broken ribs; multiple contusions and a hairline fracture of the skull."

"But none of these caused his death. That was the result of, in layman's terms, a broken neck. His spinal cord was severed. He was probably unconscious before that happened."

"Who was he, Doctor?"

"We don't know. He had no identification. No wallet, credit cards, driving license, passport - nothing. Just some money in his pockets. All tags had been removed from his clothing. Obviously, he was intent on remaining anonymous. We've sent his fingerprints to the Bureau in Washington. Just in case he's on file somewhere."

"There's just one curious item, Mr. MacDara. He has a small tattoo on the inside of his left forearm. Let me show you."

MacDara moved closer for a better look. A small black circle enclosing a red, serpentine 'S'. The very same tattoo, in the very same place, as the albino.

TWENTY

Office of the Chairman of the Joint Chiefs, Washington, DC, Wednesday March 1, 2000

The package was delivered personally to General Zachary Walker by a young attorney in the Washington law firm of Katz and Bernstein acting on behalf of colleagues in Cheticamp, Nova Scotia. The covering letter informed him of the death of Charlie Pettigrew, the cause of death, and that no conclusion had been reached by the coroner. It then went on to state that they were executing the last wishes of the deceased by ensuring that the enclosed sealed package was delivered, as instructed.

Zachary Walker looked at that package for a long time. He turned it over and tried to feel its contents. He didn't open it right away. He locked it up in his safe for a day while he teased his brain trying to guess what it might contain. Finally, curiosity got the better of him and he opened it. It was a ring, a very beautiful ring. Gold, fine filigree mounting and the most perfect amethyst he'd ever seen. Joy-San's favorite stone. He remembered the day he had bought it for her in Seoul. The memory was as vivid as if it had occurred yesterday. That's what he had been trying to exorcise. The past. The memories. The pain. When Joy-San had died giving birth to Kate the ring had been returned to him. But every time he looked at it it seared the memory of his loss into his heart. Finally, after Charlie Pettigrew had entered his life again, he had thrown away the ring at the end of a night of depression. It was too painful to keep. If he could give away their baby, how could he keep their ring? But Charlie must have picked it up that night. And he'd been holding on to it all these years. Zach marvelled at that. And at Charlie's sense of things. No, Charlie, you're right. Throwing away the ring didn't exorcise the memories. Or the pain. Or the joy. And giving away our baby only left me empty inside all these years. Watching her grow from afar. In the early years, resisting the desire to go to her, to claim her back again. There's an omen in this, he felt. It's Joy-San speaking to me. Telling me what to do. Yes, I must put things right again. Yes, Joy-San, I know what to do.

General Walker had arrived at The Colombia Cafe at precisely three pm; General Shields a couple of minutes later. They had evaded their bodyguards and were dressed casually. Their faces were not well known publically; in fact, Shields was not a public figure. There were few people in the coffee shop at that time: a middle-aged lady sitting alone, absorbed in a Danielle Steele novel as she sipped her coffee and a young couple eating a very late breakfast. General Walker had taken the booth in the rear and had already ordered coffee when General Shields arrived. Zachary Walker got right to the point.

"What's this all about, Bart?"

"Let me start at the beginning, Zach."

And while Zachary Walker sat impassively, Bart Shields commenced with the lunch with Owen MacDara at the New York Yacht Club and brought him up to date with MacDara's visit to Charlie Pettigrew.

"Zach, Charlie Pettigrew told us what happened all those years ago. It's hard for me to understand. So, don't even try to explain."

The CIRCLE of SODOM
A Gripping New Thriller

Zachary Walker's eyes were moist and the mug of coffee trembled in his right hand. He steadied it with his left and said, "Bart, you must believe me. I had nothing to do with these killings. I never heard of Murphy Armstrong until tonight. What happened happened. It was many years ago and I've been living in its shadow ever since."

"You must know, Zach, that if this had been made public, you would have been destroyed."

"Yes, I know. I know. But you have to believe me. I would never have killed to prevent that. Especially not Henry Whiteside."

"Do you know Tony Thackeray?"

"No, I've never heard of him. And I'm afraid I'm not familiar with the Thackeray Institute. If MacDara is convinced Thackeray is involved in these killings maybe you're barking up the wrong tree."

"We don't believe so. Either Thackeray is being used or he, himself, is the user. Are you sure you've never met him?"

"Never! I would remember. And I only heard MacDara's name for the first time a couple of days ago." Zachary Walker knew he had said too much. Bart Shields pounced on it right away.

"Who told you? Who talked to you about Owen MacDara?"

"Bart, it's not important who told me."

"Well, if it's not important Zach, then you can tell me. What are you covering up?"

"Bart, there's no cover-up. All right, I'll tell you. It was Senator Sam. Apparently your MacDara was snooping around asking questions about Henry Whiteside and the senator didn't take too kindly to it."

"Senator Sam? You mean Senator Sumner Hardy?"

"That's right. Sam and I go way back. And we believe in the same things."

"Did you know that the senator is an alumnus of The Thackeray Institute? As a matter of fact, he sits on their

Pat Mullan

Advisory Council. That means he knows Tony Thackeray, the man MacDara believes is responsible for these killings."

Zachary Walker didn't answer. He had nothing to say.

"Does the President know, Zach? He and the senator aren't exactly bosom buddies, you know."

"Listen, Bart. I'm not disloyal to the President. I don't happen to share some of his views about this country. That's all."

"Well, some people would say that Senator Sam is a fascist. That he'd become the first American dictator if we let him. Now, I know that's scaremongering. And I know you're a conservative, Zach, but I'd never have placed you in the senator's camp."

"I'm not in his camp!"

"Well, you must be important to somebody. If our guess is right, they've gone out of their way to protect you. How much does the senator know about all of this?"

"The senator's been a good friend, that's all. I value his advice."

"But somebody has been killing to protect you. And the attempts on MacDara's life. It's all linked together."

"You're surely not suspecting Senator Sam. That's ludicrous. I'd never have expected you to resort to McCarthyism, Bart."

"Hold it, Zach. I never said I suspected the senator. But I want to get to the bottom of this. Don't you?"

"I want it all to go away. What happened to me occurred a long time ago. To a different person."

"Well, it won't go away, Zach. Henry Whiteside kept a journal. Did you know that?"

"No, I didn't."

"He had an entry in it for March of last year. Said he met with you in Washington. Did he?"

"Yes, he did. He was doing his memoirs."

The CIRCLE of SODOM
A Gripping New Thriller

"Didn't he bring up that surgical procedure that he did on you back in Korea?"

"He did. But let me explain. Henry treated that event like a priest would treat a sin that he heard in the confessional. With total confidence."

"But something new was giving him concern, isn't that true, Zach?"

"He was imagining things, I'm sure. Thought that he had 'turned over a rock and found something rotten under it'. He was becoming paranoid. I think retirement had affected Henry's mind."

"But he thought you would become a victim of whatever he found under this rock. Isn't that true, Zach?"

"Yes, it's true. I tried to dissuade him. But I could see it was no use."

"Did you talk with anyone about this at the time?"

"Only Senator Sam. I often sought his advice. I told you that. I thought maybe he could be more successful if he talked to Henry. I didn't want Henry to make a fool out of himself."

"Did the senator talk to Henry?"

"He said he did. But he said he failed. Henry was a stubborn man. But just about then he disappeared and the matter ended."

"Didn't you ever think his disappearance seemed convenient at the time?"

"Just for a minute. It troubled me when I heard it. But my common sense told me there was no connection. Just another tragedy. After all, Henry didn't seem as sure and steady as he used to be. Who knows what difficulty he might have gotten himself into? At least, that was how I rationalized it at the time."

"And how do you rationalize it now?"

"Bart, I don't know anymore," said a very weary Zachary Walker. He was still gripping the coffee mug between his hands. To steady them. The mug had been empty for ages. Now he

Pat Mullan

looked directly at Bart Shields and said simply: "Charlie Pettigrew is dead."

"What? He was OK when Owen MacDara saw him!"

"Well, he's dead. Fractured skull. Broken neck. They don't know if it was accidental or not. Got a note from his lawyer. He left me something. Oh, not money! Charlie didn't have any. Just an item of sentimental value. That's all I know."

"Zach, can't you see. They've killed him to protect your secret. To protect you. But they were too late this time."

"Bart, you don't know that. Maybe Charlie was tired of living."

"You don't really believe that, do you? Stop kidding yourself."

"Bart, I don't know. I just don't know."

"Listen, Zach. I need your help. We've got to stop these people. I believe you are the key."

"But what can I do?"

"Go and see the President. He's in your corner. I haven't told him what MacDara learned from Charlie Pettigrew. But he must be told. I'd rather you did it yourself, Zach. We have to stop this thing."

"This is hard for me, Bart. Really hard. But you're right. I have to let the President know."

There was nothing more to say. They both lapsed into silence for a while, finishing the last of too many coffees, and left.

TWENTY-ONE

**Washington, DC,
Friday March 3, 2000**

The DJ at Xanadu wore a red beehive hairdo, false eyelashes, press-on fingernails and a big, fluffy boa draped around 'her' neck. 'She' had always fancied Larry Sanderson but he had never been interested. It was Saturday and she spotted him at the bar.

"Larry, Honey, where have you been lately?" she gushed.

"Working, Sydney. Just working. Nothing more exotic," said Larry.

"You know what they say about that, honey. All work and no play makes Larry a dull boy. Just let me know when you want to play. I can promise you a good time."

"Sydney, love, thanks. I think I just want to be alone tonight."

"Honey, you don't know what you're missing," said Sydney in a huff as she glided back to play some more selections before the show began.

Xanadu was an upscale gay entertainment place with a bar, restaurant and club. Larry Sanderson seldom went there. It was a bit too yuppie for him. But he enjoyed the shows. Larry managed to keep his private and public personas apart. No one at the NSC knew he was gay. If they thought about him at all, they'd probably conclude that he was asexual, just like his computers. That suited Sanderson. The NSC was a macho heterosexual place. Coming out of the closet could only lead to trouble. There was still lingering resentment over the President's 'gays in the military' policy.

Most people were dancing. The floor was packed and there was a party atmosphere in the place. As Larry watched, spotlights shone on the three circular tables in the center of the floor, illuminating the table dancers, the stars of the evening. They were all good-looking, well-built young men wearing only the skimpiest of red silk underwear. The choreography was professional, their dancing excellent: always provocative but never lewd. Larry had seen the trio before but he never tired watching them. As he sipped his gin and tonic he couldn't help noticing the fair-haired young man looking at him intently from the other side of the bar. When he caught his eye the young man smiled. Larry looked away again. He wasn't out to pick up or be picked up.

Tonight, the bartender seemed to be auditioning. Between serving his customers he was dancing on the bar and tucking his tips suggestively down his pants. On one of his gyrations around the bar he deposited another gin and tonic in front of Larry and whispered in his ear: "Sweetheart, this one's on Joseph," pointing to the fair-haired young man on the other side of the bar, who smiled and lifted his glass in a toast to Larry.

It must have been the numerous gin and tonics, thought Larry as he fumbled to get the key into the lock on the door of his apartment. Joseph had insisted on helping him home after he had slipped off the stool at the bar in Xanadu and dazed himself when he cracked his head against the brass footrail. Now Joseph gently took the key from him and turned it in the lock. Inside

The CIRCLE of SODOM
A Gripping New Thriller

Larry groped for the light switch. Again Joseph helped, and as the lights came on he guided Larry over to the couch in the living room and propped him up on it with pillows.

It seemed ages later but Larry imagined he heard the door opening again, imagined he heard voices and thought he must be dreaming. He was sure he wasn't asleep but he knew he wasn't awake either. He dreamed that hands were lifting him up in the air and carrying him. Funny how the mind can make dreams and imaginings seem so real, he thought.

He wanted to scratch the tickle on his nose but his right hand wouldn't move. He tried his left hand and it wouldn't move either. He felt panic, and his struggle, as well as the smelling salts he'd just been administered, awakened him. As his eyes adjusted to the light, he could see that he was lying on his back on the bed and his wrists and ankles were tied to the bedposts. He was naked.

"Wake up, sweetheart. Are you ready for some fun?" He knew it was Joseph. His eyes focused on the voice and he could see him standing at the foot of the bed. But there were two of him. He must be seeing double. He closed and opened his eyes but the double image didn't go away. There were two of them.

"This is my best friend, dear Larry. He wants to join in. You don't mind, do you? Two's fun but three's an orgy. Isn't that right, sweetheart?"

Larry's panic increased. He could feel his heart thumping loudly in his chest.

"Joseph, please stop. I'm not into bondage and pain. Don't do this. Let me up," he pleaded. But that just aroused chuckles in Joseph and his best friend, who had now emerged from the shadows with a lighted cigarillo between the fingers of his right hand.

"But my best friend here is into bondage and pain in a big way. Especially pain. He just loves to give it, don't you, darling?"

Pat Mullan

Best friend said nothing. Instead he blew on the end of his cigarillo till it glowed red and then, without any warning, he stuck it into the sole of Sanderson's right foot. Sanderson's body bucked in agony on the bed, but the ties held. He started to scream, but Joseph stuck a facecloth in his mouth and gagged him. Best friend pulled away the cigarillo from Sanderson's foot and his body stopped fighting. Gradually Joseph removed the gag and Larry could smell his own burnt flesh.

"That's just an appetizer, sweetheart. Are you ready for the main course?"

"What do you want from me?" Larry wheezed. His throat hurt from the screams that were never heard.

"I'll tell you what we want, sweetheart. We want you to tell us what you're working on. We want to know what programs you're running for General Shields."

Sanderson felt as though the fire from his foot had suddenly hit his brain. They knew. Somebody had found out what he was working on. Or found out enough and had leaked it. Just as quickly he suddenly felt cold, as he realized that Joseph and the other man were terrorists. Maybe even the people that MacDara was looking for.

"That's not a secret. I'm working on the next version of our simulator on anti-terrorism. Everybody knows General Shields's special job in the NSC," said Larry in as controlled a voice as he could muster, still trying to talk his way out of this.

"Wrong answer, sweetheart! Best friend doesn't like wrong answers, do you, darling?"

Knowing what was about to happen didn't help. It only made it worse. Joseph gagged him again and best friend stuck the glowing end of his cigarillo into Sanderson's left foot. He seemed to do it twice as long this time, and when Joseph removed the gag it looked as though Sanderson was semi-conscious. Joseph stuck the smelling salts under his nose and slapped him on the cheeks till he was satisfied that Sanderson was fully alert again.

The CIRCLE of SODOM
A Gripping New Thriller

Larry Sanderson had never thought of himself as a brave person. But he'd never been tested. Until now. Now he knew he wasn't brave. He didn't want to be tortured any more. He broke down and pleaded to be set free, promised them anything if they'd spare his life. Joseph gave him some water and Larry Sanderson talked. Told them everything. Everything that he knew. About the AI system, about Shields, about MacDara, about the Circle of Sodom. He couldn't tell them about General Walker or Tony Thackeray because he didn't know about them. But he did tell them about the investigation into Colonel McNab and the Millennium Covenant. Joseph knew when Larry had finished that he had told them everything. He could recognize a broken man.

"Sweetheart, you did good. You should get a prize. Don't you think so, best friend? Sweetheart deserves a prize, doesn't he?"

Before Sanderson knew what was happening, Joseph had gagged him again and best friend moved towards him from the foot of the bed. He could see the light glinting on the blade and he knew he was going to die. Somehow he didn't fight it. In those split seconds a serene calm descended on him. When his jugular was sliced open he didn't feel it. He only felt the burning in the soles of his feet. And the wetness that gushed from his throat, warming his cold naked body.

The box was sitting on the floor beside his secretary's desk when General Shields returned from lunch at two pm. It was unusual for computer equipment to be delivered directly to his office. He only used a PC, a printer and a modem, and all of those were delivered and installed personally by Larry Sanderson.

"What's this, Sally?" asked Shields.

"I don't know, sir. The label says it's an HP Deskjet printer. A UPS delivery man arrived with it half an hour ago. Did you order a new printer?"

Pat Mullan

"No, I did not. Get me Sanderson on the phone."

"I tried to get him already, sir. But nobody knows where he is. He didn't show up today."

"That's not like Sanderson. Did you try his home number?"

"Yes, sir. But he's not there. Only his answering machine. I left a message."

"OK, Sally. Please call Operations and have them send someone up here to check this out. I'll be in my office. Keep trying to contact Sanderson. Let me know when you get him. I want to talk with him."

Half an hour later the intercom buzzer rang on General Shields's phone. It was Sally.

"Still can't find Sanderson. But Ops are here to open your package. Maybe you'd like to see what's in it."

"Thanks, Sally. I believe I will take a look."

As General Shields opened his office door the young man from Operations had just finished opening the box. He looked distressed and was backing away from the box as Sally reached it. Bart Shields was just in time to catch her as she fainted into his arms. He looked down into the box, to be met by the fixed stare from Larry Sanderson's severed head, sitting on a bed of ice cubes.

"We have to assume that Larry talked. We have to assume that he told them everything he knew."

MacDara had hopped on the shuttle as soon as he received the message about Sanderson. It was early afternoon and he was sitting in Shields's office. Bart Shields looked twenty years older today, he thought.

"You're right, sir. We have to assume that. Where was he killed?"

"In his apartment. They didn't even attempt to clean up. Sanderson's body was still naked, tied to his bed. Blood everywhere. He'd been tortured. Third degree burns on the soles of both feet. Our boys went over the place with a fine toothcomb. But I don't expect we'll find anything. They removed the body and scrubbed the place. We want to keep the lid on this."

"What about Sanderson's relatives?"

"We're fortunate there. He was pretty much a loner and he had no brothers or sisters. Only an elderly widowed mother. She's in a nursing home in Detroit. We checked. She hasn't heard from him in five years."

"What about his work?"

"That's where it's really going to hurt. They say that no one in this world is indispensable. But Larry Sanderson was the exception."

"They also know what we know. I'm sure they suspected we knew something. But now they have the advantage. Or think they do. Luckily, Sanderson didn't know everything."

"But there's two things that he would have told them about. The Circle of Sodom and the Millennium Covenant. I think it's time you paid that visit to Colonel McNab."

"If he's involved in any of this, won't he know that we're investigating him?"

"Of course he will. But investigating him and proving something are two different things. He knows that too."

"So you think he'll see me."

"I'm sure he will. He's as curious about us as we are about him. He wasn't a successful field commander without gathering the best intelligence about the enemy. And we are his enemy."

Owen knew that Bart Shields was right. He had already decided that the good Colonel McNab needed to be checked out. There was no evidence, circumstantial or otherwise, to connect McNab to Thackeray. McNab may be operating his own agenda, one that happened to coincide with Thackeray's. Besides, they would be the strangest bedfellows of all. Then again, maybe not; an old Irish saying came to mind: 'Aithionn ciarog ciarog eile.' Literally, 'One cockroach recognizes another.'

Pat Mullan

Shields spoke again. "Arrange the meeting. You'll have to go in alone, but I can't imagine McNab making a move against you while you're his guest. Still, I'll have backup in position just in case you need to call in the cavalry."

"I agree. If McNab is involved in this, the last thing he'd do is call in the artillery on his own head."

The CIRCLE of SODOM
A Gripping New Thriller

TWENTY-TWO

The White House, Washington, DC,
Saturday March 4, 2000

When General Zachary Walker requested a meeting with the President, he had not expected to be invited to the White House private quarters. Yet here he was. Standing on the Truman Balcony looking out over the South Lawn to the Washington Monument and the Jefferson Memorial. He had mixed emotions. A feeling of ease and an equal feeling of awe. He also felt shame. He had confessed to the President, told him about Korea, asked for his understanding and swore his allegiance. The President was speaking again.

"Zach, I can appreciate how painful this was for you. But, as far as I'm concerned, Korea is in the past. You're a fine officer. A fine American. I trust you. I want you to know that."

"Mr. President, I don't know what to say."

"Zach, don't say anything. But you know you'd be crucified in the media and on the Hill if they found out about this. You'd have to resign."

"I know that, Mr. President."

"And somebody else knows that too, don't they? Somebody who wants you to keep your job. Somebody who wants you to stay in power. I want you to tell me who that is."

"I don't know, Mr. President."

"But you can make a damn good guess, can't you? I know you don't share the same political philosophy as me. That never mattered. I saw no merit in surrounding myself only with people who thought like me. I wanted the best. You are one of the best." The President paused for a while and both of them stood there looking out over the South Lawn.

"Look out there. Don't you feel it? You're at the center of power. That's an awesome responsibility," the President continued as though he were talking to himself. Then he looked back at Zachary Walker. "I know you're not going to vote for me next year. If the person you vote for wins, will you trust them with the power of this office?"

General Walker was still staring out over the South Lawn. Now he turned around abruptly and said, "It's Senator Hardy, Mr. President. That's who wants me to keep my job."

"I think Senator Hardy is a dangerous man. He and his fanatical right are a threat to this democracy. But would he kill to get here?"

"I can't believe he'd do that, Mr. President."

"But you're not sure, are you?"

General Walker didn't answer. He didn't really know what answer to give. It was the President who spoke again.

"Zachary, I want you to continue as though nothing has changed. When the time comes I want you on my side. Will you promise that to me tonight?"

Without a moment's hesitation, General Zachary Walker looked directly at his President and said, "You have my word of honor, Mr. President."

TWENTY-THREE

**Baton Rouge, Louisiana,
Thursday March 9, 2000**

The Henderson House in Baton Rouge was chosen as the venue for a war conference of the generals of the religious right. There were about one hundred of them. They'd been arriving in ones, twos and threes over the past few days, slipping in quietly to this sleepy, remote suburb of Baton Rouge, Louisiana. They commanded an army of two million members, controlled the dominant political party machinery in twenty states and had assembled more political strength than any other organization. They had declared war against the radical left, a movement they blamed for the disintegration of the American way of life. A few invited guests were in attendance. Colonel George McNab had been one of the first to arrive, two days ago. The Honorable David Anthony Llewellyn Thackeray had arrived just in time for breakfast on the opening day of the conference. It was his phone call to Senator Hardy after Owen MacDara's visit in Los Angeles that had caused this conference to be convened. They often used the Harrison House for their conferences and, as it was not peak season, it was easy to get the reservation at short notice. The commander of this army of the right had arrived the evening before; Senator Sumner Hardy had travelled incognito in a rented car. He had used an assumed name and had covered his departure from Washington. The media were the last people he wanted in attendance at this conference.

The Henderson House was a conference center situated in the suburban bedroom community of Baton Rouge. The kind of place chosen by organizations who valued their privacy and whose members didn't need to be entertained in the evening. The Henderson House provided comfortable rooms and chalets, excellent food, and conference facilities that were equipped with leading edge technology. Privacy and confidentiality were their trademark. They were the Swiss bankers of conference centers. This conference had been registered at the Henderson House under a particularly innocuous title: ICA, International Communication Associates. It was scheduled to run for four days.

But there was already an uninvited guest at the conference. After the President had had his meeting with General Zachary Walker he had asked Bart Shields and Owen MacDara to watch every move that Senator Hardy made. Shields had immediately placed Hardy under close surveillance. They wired every place that Senator Hardy used, even his own bathroom. And that's how they discovered him arranging this conference.

Owen MacDara had arrived in Baton Rouge a few hours earlier. He knew that it was impossible for him to get into the conference and there had been no opportunity to wire the place. Even had they managed to do so, it probably wouldn't have worked. Hardy's 'army' had surrounded themselves with experts at the security and surveillance game. They swept the conference center thoroughly. But MacDara knew that being able to see who attended this 'war conference' was justification enough. He needed to identify the conspirators. And he had positioned himself so that he could watch, through his binoculars, the people who arrived at the Henderson House.

The CIRCLE of SODOM
A Gripping New Thriller

The one concession that the Henderson House had made to the leisure pursuits of its clients was golf. It boasted a PGA championship-quality eighteen-hole course, and the ICA Conference had left the afternoon of the third day free for its members to enjoy the course.

Four of them would not play golf that afternoon, though. Instead, they met in the chalet of one of the four: their commander-in-chief, Senator Sam Sumner Hardy.

The four men were seated at the round table in the dining area of Senator Sam's chalet. Colonel George NcNab sat to the senator's right and Tony Thackeray faced him directly across the table. The fourth person sat on the senator's left. He was Colonel Robert Travers.

No pleasantries were exchanged. Only a jug of iced water and four glasses alleviated the plainness of the table's surface. The senator began.

"Gentlemen, you all know why we're here. Our timetable is being dictated by events beyond our control." He looked at Tony Thackeray, then continued.

"Each of you knows how those events began. New York was the first screw-up. When four cops are killed they never get off the damn thing," the senator said matter-of-factly. He took a sip from his glass of water. "We also underestimated MacDara. You made him an offer to join us, Tony?"

"Yes, I did. I felt we had nothing to lose. And MacDara impressed me. He would have made an outstanding Institute alumnus. We seldom find leaders of his ability."

"But you didn't succeed." The senator stated the obvious.

"I had failed even before I started. But I didn't know that until after the meeting. One of my Circle recognized MacDara. He'd found his way into our evening vespers in Florida. He had already tied the Circle to the killing of his friend, Murphy Armstrong. I gave the keynote speech at his GMA dinner this year, so it wouldn't have been a big stretch for him to recognize my voice."

"And, gentlemen, we have verification of all of this. The confession of that excuse for a human being. What was his name? Sanderson? You knew him, didn't you, Bob?"

"Yes, sir. No loss, I can assure you. I found him to be disrespectful and scruffy. A good six months in boot camp would have cured him or killed him. Shields knew what I thought of Sanderson. Good riddance."

"Despite that, it's obvious that he was a genius with computers. MacDara got to Shields and this fellow, Sanderson. Gentlemen, a lot of damage has already been done." Looking at Travers, the senator continued. "As you know, Bob, if Whiteside had continued with his memoirs he would have made your boss's position untenable. We couldn't let that happen. Zachary Walker commands a lot of respect at the Pentagon. We need a player on our team with credentials like that."

"You don't need to worry about General Walker, sir. He's a true believer. I never saw anyone with such faith in God and America. He often says that America was founded on a belief in God and he thinks that this nation is the last best hope for the human race."

"I know, Bob. I've known Zach since I served as his aide in Seoul twenty years ago. And I was only a wet-behind-the-ears second lieutenant in those days."

The tee-off for the seventh green was exactly two hundred yards from the senator's patio. He watched a ball arc into the air and two golfers drive their cart on to the fairway. For a fleeting moment his mind drifted to another golf course: Walker Hill in Seoul, and those times when he and Zach and the "Two Percent Club" talked and planned the future. Until it almost came crashing down on that fateful night in seventy-five.

"Senator Sam," intruded George McNab, "we are ready when you need us. Just say the word."

"George, I know. I wish this nation had a thousand patriots like you. Keep your people on full alert. We may need you sooner than we thought."

The CIRCLE of SODOM
A Gripping New Thriller

The senator got up, went over to the bar and poured himself a Royal Crown cola. RC coke had become an addiction of his. He turned to face the others. The senator was not long-winded. He had never been known to engage in a single filibuster on the Hill.

"Gentlemen, let's take stock. We committed ourselves to govern this nation and lead it out of its decline. We had the last five years, I say 'had', to ensure that the people of these fifty states voted us in at the millennium. These past two days have proven to me that we have built that support. This year we'd have tested that. The White House would have been ours."

The senator paused to ensure that his audience understood the full implication of what he was saying.

"Well, we've run out of time. The President may already be planning to move against us. We never expected this to happen. But we're prepared. I have ensured that the leadership here understands the gravity of the situation. We will need them to marshal support around the nation for any action we are forced to take. George, I want you to confer immediately with the heads of the other militias and ask them to stand by for my orders. Bob, stick to General Walker like glue. I will see the President personally. He must be made aware of the cost of any actions he might be contemplating."

"Thank you, gentlemen. We will not meet again during this conference. Just make sure that I can reach you twenty-four hours a day."

After Travers and McNab had left, the senator went over to the bar and poured himself another RC coke. Tony Thackeray accepted a Heineken, in the bottle. The senator made the observation to himself that he'd never seen Thackeray use a glass for his beer. Always drank it directly from the bottle. An ingratiating affectation from the aristocracy, thought Senator Hardy.

"Are these the days that your Institute prepared me for, Tony?" asked the senator.

Pat Mullan

"You know they are, Sam. When you were at Oxford, you saw the conspiracy of the left. Some of our best intellectuals were involved. You remember that last year you spent at the Thackeray Institute. My father took to you. Surely the many evenings that he and you spent together in debate prepared you well for this day," confirmed Tony Thackeray. "My father is very proud of you," he added.

"Your father would not be proud of the way we handled MacDara. We can't terminate him and he won't join us. By this time the damage is done. Shields knows whatever MacDara knows. And you can be sure that Shields has briefed the President."

Senator Sam crushed the empty RC can with his right hand and threw it accurately into the open trash can in the corner. A direct hit. Every move had to be a direct hit, he told himself. They couldn't afford another failure.

Tony Thackeray reasserted himself. "Sam, my father is convening the Advisory Council of the Institute. We will need to keep the lid on Europe and Asia if we have to move on Washington."

As soon as Thackeray left, the senator started to pack. A repetitive exercise. His mind wandered back to beginnings, to the Two Percent Club in Seoul. How did Zach Walker put it at the time? "Sam, believe me, you wouldn't want to spend any time with ninety-eight percent of the people in this world. We're the two percenters."

That's how the Two Percent Club started with only three members. The colonel, himself and Captain Joe Dodd. The captain died in Vietnam. He remembered again that night the colonel called him for help, the phone calls to Major Whiteside and his drive north with the colonel to the 53rd MASH. It was in the middle of a monsoon and he thought they'd never make it.

The CIRCLE of SODOM
A Gripping New Thriller

The conference of the International Communication Associates ended a day later without incident or controversy. They left as they had arrived, in ones, twos and threes.

Senator Sumner Hardy left early in the evening of the third day. He went directly to Washington.

Owen MacDara had watched them leave: The senator; Tony Thackeray; Colonel McNab and one other person accompanying the colonel. He recognized Colonel Robert Travers, aide-de-camp to General Zachary Walker. It had been no surprise to see Senator Hardy, Colonel McNab and Tony Thackeray in each other's company. It only confirmed the suspicions that had troubled MacDara since that night in Costelloes, the night that Murph had died. But Colonel Travers was the real surprise. *There's our mole,* thought MacDara.

TWENTY-FOUR

**Washington, DC,
Sunday March 12, 2000**

Colonel Robert Travers left his military uniform behind on Sundays. Instead, he donned the uniform of the Reverend Robert Travers of the New Christian Communion. His was not a conventional church or a traditional parish. His congregation numbered about fifty. They were all dropouts from the fundamentalist faiths of Christianity, disaffected because they felt that these faiths had strayed from the Bible and from the strict interpretation and practice of the Word of God. Their church was not made of bricks and mortar. They held their prayer meetings in rented halls and in each other's homes.

The Sunday after he returned from Baton Rouge, Bob Travers was leading twenty-seven of his congregation in prayer at the home of his nearest parishioner. At that same time, Owen MacDara was breaking into the colonel's apartment. Flashes of Nixon and the Watergate 'plumbers' entered his head. He imagined himself getting caught and being put on trial. It would be a show trial. Of himself. Of General Shields. Of the President. One of Bart Shields's operatives had disabled the alarm system

The CIRCLE of SODOM
A Gripping New Thriller

and picked the locks of the french windows that opened onto Travers's first floor balcony. It was ten am and, at this time on a Sunday MacDara had the neighborhood to himself. Most people were still in bed. There were no dead bolts or bars and he entered the apartment with ease. He knew what he was looking for. Evidence. Anything that would tie Travers to those responsible for the murder of Murph' and Major Whiteside.

The balcony opened into the master bedroom. Minimalist, observed MacDara. Wooden floor, scatter rugs, large bed, no headboard, simple pine chest of drawers, old style military campaign chest at foot of the bed, walk-in closet, a Larry Rivers print of the dying confederate and a Remington bronze sitting beside an exercise bicycle in the corner. MacDara searched the chest of drawers and found socks and underwear. Nothing but blankets in the campaign chest, and the walk-in closet revealed only clothes and uniforms. The living room was minimalist too, and the furniture looked uncomfortable and unused. There was a stereo but no sign of a television.

A door leading off the entrance hallway was closed but unlocked. MacDara opened it. The room was small. Maybe ten feet by ten. But lived in, unlike the rest of the apartment. Nothing minimalist here. A plain pine-topped table desk and a gray filing cabinet sat in one corner. A PC, an IBM clone, filled the adjacent corner. Bookshelves, stuffed to the ceiling, cushioned one wall, while directly opposite a few photographs and awards hung almost as an afterthought. A single bed, made up army style, lined the remaining wall. Bedspread drawn taut, like his days in basic training at Fort Dix. MacDara was tempted to drop a coin on it just to see it bounce. Korea had been different. His houseboy did all that. Even prepared his foot locker for field inspections. MacDara realized that his mind had wandered. He needed to focus. He had to assume that Travers could return at any time. He wanted to be long gone when that happened.

His eyes scanned the photos and awards, mostly military. Nothing unusual, until he looked again at one of the photos. There was something familiar about it. He moved closer till he was only a few inches away. He had been right. Two men in combat fatigues and parkas standing in the snow outside a large army field tent. One of the men was Colonel Robert Travers and the other was Colonel George McNab.

The filing cabinet was unlocked and, after a ten-minute perusal of the contents, it was easy to see why. It held nothing more sinister than phone bills, electrical bills, medical records, insurance claims, and normal housekeeping items. The colonel was certainly a meticulous record keeper. The book shelves yielded nothing either. MacDara decided that it would not be his choice of literature if he were stranded on a desert island. That only left the computer. He sat down in front of it, taking note that it was a 486 model with floppy disk and CD-ROM drives and an HP inkjet printer. The system was plugged into a surge protector and looked ready to use. He blew on his fingertips, feeling as though he were about to crack a safe. So far so good, he thought, as the system booted, the printer came online and the Windows screens appeared. He clicked through various accessory and utilities screens and then accessed Word. Half an hour later he had thoroughly convinced himself that Travers only used his computer to type letters and reports, all of them filed with the same meticulousness that he had evidenced earlier in the filing cabinet. He had skimmed through all of the files, finding nothing of any significance. The letters were administrative formalities, and the military reports, dealing with everything from procurement and logistics to military and civilian preparedness, weren't classified or secret. Most of the same information could be acquired by reading the local papers.

MacDara was about to give up when he decided to give the files one last scan. That's when he found it. It had been staring him in the face all along; couldn't see the forest for the trees. At first it just looked like another political memorandum on behalf

The CIRCLE of SODOM
A Gripping New Thriller

of the Committee to Elect Senator Sumner Hardy for President. Except that it was marked '*confidential*'. He had only scanned it the first time. Now he read all four pages, and it was the second last paragraph on the fourth and final page that aroused his interest: '*In the unlikely event that the contingency plan must be executed in the interest of self-preservation and the defense of our manifest destiny all of those on the 'strategic list' will assemble at the chosen location.*' An awkward statement, almost fundamentalist polemic in its undertone. MacDara had seen various lists of people throughout the files, but had attached no particular significance to them. Now he went searching for a 'strategic list'. It wasn't filed under any of the obvious categories. But persistence paid off and he finally found what he was looking for. The memorandum was entitled 'National Preparedness in a Crisis - Contingency Plan: the strategic list.' He started to read the names. Names of great power and authority in Congress, FBI, CIA, the military and even the Supreme Court.

Owen MacDara recollected the President's words. "We're certain that there are people belonging to the movement right here on Capitol Hill. In our own government. Maybe even in my cabinet. We could have a mole or fifth column anywhere."

Owen wondered if he had found the President's *'fifth column'*.

TWENTY-FIVE

**Atlanta, Georgia,
Monday March 13, 2000**

Hans Vertonen's stomach muscles tightened as the wheels of the KLM plane touched the runway. It had been an uneventful flight across the Atlantic. He opened his seat belt, reached forward and grabbed his Toshiba laptop from under the seat in front. As the plane taxied down the runway he took out his passport and visa for one last look. The photograph looked stern, unsmiling, but it was definitely a good likeness. And the visa was authentic. He was Willy Van Meter, IBM Systems Engineer, on a one month visit to the States to attend a computer conference and meet with professional colleagues. Reassured, he returned the documents to his inside jacket pocket and moved towards the exit at the front of the plane. He grabbed his carry-on bag from the rack near the door, smiled a 'thank you' to the stewardess and walked smartly up the ramp into the airport. He had no bags to claim, and his confident stride was rewarded with a brief look at his papers, a perfunctory entry stamp and an equally perfunctory 'enjoy your visit'.

The CIRCLE of SODOM
A Gripping New Thriller

Hans Vertonen was in a hurry. His easy entry into the US had given him a boost of adrenalin. Through the window he could see a lone taxi and he rushed to get it. Propelled by the revolving door he raised his right arm to signal the taxi driver and dashed around a waiting bus. He never saw the other taxi bearing down on him until he heard the screech of brakes.

"I swear, officer. I didn't see him. He stepped straight out from behind the bus."
Beads of perspiration rolled down the ebony temples of Johnny Jackson. He hopped from one foot to the other and his stomach seemed to float on his two hundred and fifty pound frame.
"OK, Jackson. You can move your cab around the corner. We've finished taking measurements. But don't leave. I'll need you to sign a formal statement."
"Yes, officer. Thank you, officer."
The paramedics were loading the body of the young man into the ambulance for the journey to the morgue. The police officer had already stowed the victim's luggage in the patrol car: one carry-on bag and a slim black case containing a laptop computer.

TWENTY-SIX

**The Millennium Covenant, Tennessee,
Tuesday March 14, 2000**

Tight security greeted Owen MacDara when he reached the gate to the compound of the Millennium Covenant. He had driven at least three miles on a one-track dusty road in the Tennessee hills, and was almost convinced that he'd taken a wrong turn, when he saw him. Dressed in camouflage fatigues with a forty-five strapped low on his hip, he held a semi-automatic rifle at the ready across his chest. As MacDara drew closer he could see that there were two of them manning a wooden guard post standing in the center of a chain-link fence, blocking the entrance to the compound. MacDara pulled up, identified himself, and one of them spoke for a few minutes into a hand-held phone. Then he nodded to his buddy, saying, "I'll take him up," and pulled out a US Army-issue jeep, repainted in the blue and red colors of the Covenant. MacDara pulled in behind the jeep and followed for about half a mile through dense trees till they reached a clearing that breasted onto a hill commanding a view of the land that stretched out into the near distance.

The CIRCLE of SODOM
A Gripping New Thriller

Buildings stood in a semicircle around a parade ground and assembly area. The stars and stripes fluttered from the top of a flag pole in the middle. A few jeeps and other four-wheel drive vehicles stood nearby. The guard pulled his jeep in beside them and directed MacDara to do likewise. Jumping out, he approached MacDara and said, "Colonel George is on the firing range. He wants you to wait here. We will come and get you when he's ready to see you."

He directed Owen to a small sparsely furnished hut adjacent to the parking area. They left. Owen decided to use the time well. They didn't leave anyone around to keep an eye on him, so he went out and began to reconnoiter. The buildings in the semicircle were built of sturdy log-cabin colonial construction, a rustic look that gave the place the feel of a holiday camp. But it was the fourth buiding that was different. It was built from concrete. MacDara walked towards it, unhurried, trying to make it look like he was enjoying a casual stroll. A couple of men dressed in combat fatiques came out of one of the log-cabin buildings and walked off in the opposite direction. They didn't seem to notice him. He moved right up to the fourth building for a closer look.

It was built like a bunker from the Third Reich. The windows were barred and an armed guard manned the front entrance. Two satellite dishes distinguished the roof. *Only one thing it could be*, thought MacDara. *Their top secret computer center.*

Just then he heard a shout behind him. "This area is off limits."

He looked back and saw the guard who had left him only fifteen minutes earlier.

"Colonel McNab wants to see you now. On the firing range."

The guard entered the last building in the semicircle, and MacDara followed him through a series of doors leading to a connecting corridor that joined on to another much larger

Pat Mullan

building to the rear. The guard led him through two sets of double doors, accessed only by a security card.

MacDara could see that they had entered an indoor firing range. At least twenty firing positions stretched to his left and another twenty to his right. The guard asked him to wait and went to the end position on the right. Owen could see him talking to someone. Then he returned. "Colonel George is right there. He's expecting you." The guard did an about-face and left.

MacDara observed that all twenty positions on his left seemed to be occupied by contestants armed with handguns, the nearest using .45 caliber automatic pistols. They were firing at target silhouettes about twenty-five yards away. An instructor stood to the rear, armed only with a hand-held mike. The firing had ceased just as MacDara entered and they were counting their scores. The instructor's voice sounded loud and clear. "Shoot 'em in the head! Shoot 'em in the head! Don't forget, these people are wearing vests."

"Owen MacDara," the voice had parade ground strength, "George McNab."

The colonel was dressed like everyone else, in combat fatigues. He wasn't wearing any insignia to distinguish his rank but there was no mistake about his identity. He exuded an aura of command. His gray crew cut hair and the weather-beaten face gave him the stamp of the professional soldier.

"Glad you could see me, Colonel."

"You may change your mind about that. I'm only seeing you, MacDara, because I'm curious. I wanted to look at you. Wanted to see what makes you tick."

MacDara said nothing. He followed the colonel to a cubicle-like office in the corner, which was completely soundproof and had a clear plexiglass front wall that allowed the occupants to observe everything that took place on the firing range. The colonel continued to speak.

The CIRCLE of SODOM
A Gripping New Thriller

"I'll put my cards on the table. I know that you and Shields are on a witch hunt. My people are defending this nation. Meddlers like you are undermining it. You are the real enemy."

"And was Major Henry Whiteside your enemy too?" MacDara asked, incensed at the colonel's intimidating belligerence.

"He was a traitor. Ready to inform on his own kind."

"And you and your fellow patriots killed him. Isn't that right, Colonel?"

"No! We executed him. Justice, MacDara."

"Vigilante justice, Colonel. Who are the enemy you're teaching your people to shoot at out there? An enemy wearing bullet-proof vests? Your own Federal Officers? You're no patriot, McNab. You're just another terrorist!"

Their raised voices reverberated around the cubicle. MacDara knew he was alone in enemy territory. But in the heat of the exchange he had little time to take an assessment of his own safety. He pressed ahead. "Tell me, McNab, is General Zachary Walker 'one of your own kind'?"

"The general is a true patriot, MacDara. He shares our values. He's a fine soldier and an honorable man. That traitor Whiteside was going to smear him. We couldn't permit that."

"Who are 'we', Colonel? Who are the other 'patriots' who share your twisted values?"

"You meddlers will find that out soon enough. I know that you've been snooping. But anything you learned about us won't do you any good. I'm afraid you won't be around, MacDara," said Colonel McNab as he levelled a .45 automatic at MacDara and pushed a button on the side of his desk summoning two armed guards to the room.

"Take him. Lock him up."

"You won't get away with this, McNab." Owen struggled as the guards spreadeagled him against the wall, searched him and cuffed his hands behind his back. They took the small mobile phone that he had in his jacket pocket. He wouldn't be able to call Shields. He was on his own.

"But I already have, MacDara," said the colonel dismissively, as the guards grabbed Owen and pulled him from the room. It was obvious that McNab and his Millennium Covenanters saw themselves as beyond the law. They administered their own justice.

He was in a six-by-six-foot cell, pitch black, no windows, only an air vent embedded in the concrete walls near the ceiling. An iron bed with a lumpy thin mattress and an aluminum pot in which to urinate were the only furnishings. The guards had removed the handcuffs when they threw him in and drew the bolts across on the iron door. Occasionally he could hear someone shuffle or cough outside the door, so he knew that they had left at least one guard behind. They had taken away his watch and he had lost track of the time. He was aware of its passing and knew that it must have been about three in the afternoon when they had locked him up. At least an hour must have passed. There was no way to escape and he forced himself to take stock of his position.

He was certain that they planned to kill him. They would kill him to silence him. To protect General Walker. Just like they'd killed Murph and Henry Whiteside. But he just couldn't figure it. Why hadn't McNab taken him out behind a tree? Why had he been locked up here? Maybe they wanted to hold him as a bargaining chip. No - these people don't bargain! Owen was sure that McNab meant every word when he said 'I'm afraid you won't be around, MacDara!' Maybe they didn't want his body anywhere in the Millennium Covenant. But that was no reason to lock him up. They could have bumped him off when he arrived and taken his body and dumped it far away from here. That would have been much easier than taking him for a ride and risking an escape. No, it just didn't figure. No matter how much he teased his mind, locking him up didn't make sense. He

The CIRCLE of SODOM
A Gripping New Thriller

stopped torturing himself about it. He was certain of two things. They planned to kill him. And he was still alive. He was also certain of a third thing. If he died, he'd go down fighting. He wasn't about to kneel down and let them put a bullet in his brain. He didn't know how long they'd keep him here, but he was going to keep his body and mind alert. He reasoned that his mental and physical condition could make the difference between life and death.

The size of his cell limited his movement but it was big enough for exercise. Somewhere in the recesses of his mind he remembered a forties movie where a prisoner had played imaginary chess on the square ceiling tiles of his cell to preserve his sanity. MacDara's favorite mental exercise was solving crosswords. He frequently did the *New York Times* crossword in ink, boldly filling in each answer with total confidence. When he used to do this on his railroad commute into Manhattan, he'd often observe the riveted stare of a fellow commuter waiting for him to make a mistake. But he never did. So he decided to imagine a crossword on the ceiling. In effect, he created one in his mind, constructing it as he solved it; sometimes providing the answer first and then constructing the clue.

An hour and a half into his imprisonment MacDara was already busy with his exercise and his crossword.

TWENTY-SEVEN

**Washington, DC,
Tuesday March 14, 2000.**

FBI Director Tom Redington was a burly six-footer. He had been appointed to the office after a long successful career heading the police departments of New York, Chicago and Detroit. Bart Shields got up out of his chair to greet him. Redington plunged right in.

"Bart, I've had a number of talks with the President lately. I know what's going on. That's why I'm here. I just hope the President is wrong."

He handed over a sealed folder. General Shields went back to his desk and sat down. Inside the folder were the details of the death of a young man who had stepped in front of a taxi at the airport in Atlanta. He had been travelling on a false passport. Interpol had identified him as a Dutch national, Hans Vertonen.

"Why are you bringing this to me, Tom?", asked Bart Shields.

"Five years ago he served time in prison for attempting to illegally transfer thousands of dollars out of SWIFT into a bank in Sierra Leone"

The CIRCLE of SODOM
A Gripping New Thriller

"SWIFT?"

"That's one of the electronic networks that banks use to transmit their customers' money. Stands for the Society of Worldwide Interbank Financial Transactions."

"Sounds like something out of James Bond."

"No fiction, Bart. It's real. And I don't believe this Dutchman was a lone hacker on his way to rob Wells Fargo. There have been too many attempts to crack our command computers. Your man, Sanderson, discovered that. The guys in Intelligence and Security have been trying to cage one of these critters," he said, employing the word for hacker code, "but they haven't been very successful."

"You're right. They haven't come up with a thing."

"You asked me to tell you if I found out anything about this McNab and his Covenanters." Redington paused for effect before he delivered the punch line. "The Dutchman was carrying an electronic organizer. We got into his secret memo file. One of the items was Colonel George McNab and his phone number. We thought that was curious so we did some more checking."

Director Redington had General Shields full attention at this point. About to light a Macanudo he put it in his mouth and started to roll it around with his lips. Tom Redington continued.

"Our friend, Hans, was one of a group of Dutch hackers who tried to make a deal with Saddam Hussein during the Gulf War. They offered to screw up our military deployment. For one million big ones! Saddam didn't bite."

"I did hear about that at the time, Tom. But where's the connection?"

"Three of the Dutchmen entered the U.S. in the past year. One at New York, one at Chicago and one at Atlanta. Same as our friend, Hans. All on temporary visas. And they've disappeared. No trace of them since. Neither here nor in Europe. Strange, don't you think?"

"Are you trying to say these people are some kind of computer mercenaries?"

Pat Mullan

"That's exactly what I'm saying. No, I'd even call them terrorists. Right in your camp, Bart!"

General Shields threw his Macanudo in the ashtray. He had chewed about a quarter of it. Tom Redington was standing again. Bart Shields got up too and walked around the desk to join him.

"I'm concerned, Tom. I have a man at the Millennium Covenant right now."

"Who?"

"Owen MacDara. He agreed to call if he needed help. I haven't heard from him. Of course, that is not unusual. I don't expect him to check in with me every hour. We didn't believe he'd be in any danger. We were sure that McNab wouldn't be foolish enough to do anything. Let's hope we were right. I can't suddenly send in a battalion of troops to rescue someone who doesn't need to be rescued. It would give them just the ammunition they're looking for. We'd make the headlines in every paper in the country. The government would look like assholes. It would make it seem that we're paranoid, that we're out to persecute these people. Our political enemies would be clamouring for our heads. No, I hope MacDara is not in any trouble. If he is, he'll have to find a way out of it on his own."

The CIRCLE of SODOM
A Gripping New Thriller

TWENTY-EIGHT

**The Millennium Covenant, Tennessee,
Tuesday March 14, 2000**

The light woke Owen MacDara. Its naked glare shone directly in his face. He turned over on the lumpy mattress, feeling the ache in his shoulder and neck muscles.

"Let's go. Colonel George wants to see you."

It was the same two who had brought him here. One of them was holding a flashlight. As MacDara swung his legs over the side of the bed and stood up, the other one returned his watch. He focused his eyes and was surprised to see that it was eleven pm. He'd been locked up for eight hours.

Once out of the building that housed his cell, MacDara could feel his feet crunching on the gravel that covered the parade ground. The guard with the flashlight led the way and MacDara followed while the second guard brought up the rear. They had not handcuffed him this time and, for a fleeting moment, he was tempted to make a run for it. But they had already reached their destination. The guard in front knocked on a door, opened it and ushered him into a building that looked just like a one-room schoolhouse. He assumed it was a briefing and orientation room for the colonel's followers. Colonel George McNab stood almost at attention, still in camoflaged battle gear, flanked by two lean, tough-looking troopers.

"MacDara, I hope you enjoyed your stay with us. I've looked at your military record. You were a good soldier. Expert rifleman. Black belt in karate. I respect that. So I've decided to give you a sporting chance. You'll get a ten-minute head start. My people have been given orders to shoot to kill." Addressing the two guards who brought MacDara to him, he said, "Get him out of here. Take him to the drop-off point."

As they bundled MacDara out of the 'schoolroom' he could hear Colonel George McNab yell after him, "Give my regards to Bart Shields!" and then burst into guffaws of almost maniacal laughter.

Five minutes later the two guards tossed MacDara out of the jeep. They must have travelled a couple of miles over twisting, meandering dirt tracks that had forked at least three or four times. They had given him a canteen of water. Nothing else. As he watched the rear lights of the jeep disappear he tried to get his bearings. His watch was luminous and it incorporated a compass. One of those hi-tech gimmicky things that he'd been given by a client for bringing a job in on time. He knew that the entrance to the Millennium Covenant lay south of the assembly area where he'd been detained. But he didn't know exactly where he was in relation to that. He had tried to get a sense of direction in the jeep but the dirt track had meandered all over the place. Looking at the compass he could see that the jeep was heading west when it left him. South would take him directly into the dense forest that covered much of these hills. He figuratively tossed a coin on it and headed back along the dirt track. Maybe it'll lead me out of here, he thought, without conviction. Two minutes had already passed. He didn't doubt the colonel's word. In eight minutes they'd be after him. The colonel was playing with him. And giving his people some practise in night fighting at the same time. As far as the colonel was concerned he was a dead man.

The CIRCLE of SODOM
A Gripping New Thriller

The dirt track was ridged in the middle, jeep rutted on either side and pockmarked with water-filled potholes from the heavy rains of recent days. It was pitch black. Whatever light peeked out from the cloudy skies failed to get through the treetops and into this track. MacDara stepped calf-deep into a pothole, tripped and fell forward, scratching his right arm on the stony ground. His left foot was soaking wet but he reckoned it would have to stay that way. He tried to navigate the center ridge but found that tricky. A good five minutes had passed and he wasn't making much progress. They'd be coming after him soon and he had no plan. His whole life was driven to plan. Just to complicate matters, he hit a fork in the track. It split into three and he didn't know which to take. He went from one to the other but they were equally rutted. The jeep that brought him here could have driven up any of them. This was a crap shoot. He picked the one in the middle and stumbled on.

Twenty minutes later he had stopped to pee up against a tree when the bullet struck right above his head just about the same time that he heard the crack of the rifle. He hit the ground, peeing his pants in the process. They must be using infra-red scopes, he reckoned. His adrenalin was pumping, getting him ready to fight or flee. He couldn't fight so he had to flee. He swung his body over a ditch and rolled into deep undergrowth carpeted with leaves and broken twigs. Picking himself up he ran and stumbled, directionless, banging into trees in his path. Driven by putting distance between himself and that rifle. But it was futile. Bullets sprayed the trees all around him and he hit the ground again. He began to crawl, motivated by a primal urge to keep moving as the bullets traversed the air above him. For a moment he thought he was back in basic combat training in Fort Dix, New Jersey; right in the middle of the infiltration course - except that he wasn't crawling on his back under barbed wire with his M14 rifle and there weren't any tracer bullets to give him a sense of the trajectory of fire. The firing ceased again and he rose to his haunches and started running. The trees were larger here, with thicker trunks. They must have me on a scope, so I've got to try and elude them, he thought. His eyes had adjusted to the darkness by this time, and the moon was sending slivers of eerie light here and there through openings in the foliage. He stopped and planted himself behind a large tree trunk, focused on the next one directly ahead of him and then ran and planted himself behind it. He kept doing this for at least five hundred yards, hoping that his pursuers were behind him. He didn't know where he was going. But his aim was survival. He wished that he had that M14 he had used in basic. He'd been great at night firing on the range. The infra-red scope had intrigued him. He only hoped his tree hopping had blocked it now. The undergrowth was deeper and thicker here. More fallen leaves and more dead branches and twigs. He'd change strategy. Maybe let them get ahead of him. Maybe see how many of them there were. On impulse, he chose a place and burrowed himself deep into the undergrowth, leaving just enough opening between the dead branches to keep a tunnel of vision. Then he lay totally still. Even suppressed his breathing. It seemed interminable.

Only two minutes had passed when the rustle of tramping feet vibrated the ground around him. They passed, three of them, within five feet of him. His ear to the ground acted almost like a tuning fork, telling him exactly how many and the cadence of their movement. His eyes confirmed his ears. He waited till the sounds receded and then he got up and followed them, again moving rapidly from tree to tree. The third man was a straggler and it didn't take MacDara long to close the distance. An arm lock on his adam's apple and a karate chop disabled him. Surely and silently. MacDara relieved him of the Uzi that he carried, as well as the six-inch hunting knife. He covered the body with undergrowth and moved on. The other two were ahead of him. They apparently hadn't missed their buddy. MacDara checked his compass again and saw that he was travelling due east. Which didn't help him at all. But he no longer felt naked. He started to track the two ahead of him. Stealthily. Suddenly he

The CIRCLE of SODOM
A Gripping New Thriller

heard voices and he moved closer. Now he could see four of them. Two others had joined. Getting even closer he picked up what they were saying.

"How the hell could you lose him?"

"Shit, man, we don't know. He was on the scope and then he wasn't. We haven't seen him since."

"Where's Simms?"

"I don't fucking know! He was there a minute ago. Maybe he stopped to take a shit!"

"Don't get fucking wise on me! Colonel George ain't gonna be too happy if we lose this prick."

"OK, let's fan out. Back the way you came."

MacDara didn't hang around when he heard that. He moved fast. Too fast. His feet landed on a branch that snapped loud enough to give him away. He kept running. The bullets started coming again. He knew he couldn't outrun them so he stood his ground at the next tree. The first of his pursuers caught the full burst of fire from MacDara's Uzi square in the chest. His scream ended in gurgles as he crumpled where he stood. The second one kept advancing, carried forward by his own momentum. He seemed to be firing from the hip, a steady stream of bullets in MacDara's direction but well wide of their mark. MacDara waited till he was abreast of him and shot him in the belly. The other two must have taken cover. Everything had turned silent. But MacDara had the advantage now. He wasn't going to wait there like a sitting duck. He moved out, circled wide, checked his compass, and went on a bearing directly south. Something about his instinct. It never failed him. A couple of hundred yards later he hit the dirt track again. It was running southwest and he followed it in the underbrush. He was lucky. Two jeeps roared past in the direction he had come from. More of them. He had eluded the two following him for the moment. That wouldn't last long. He had to keep on the move. If they were reinforced by the two jeeploads that had just passed, the deck would be stacked against him. Hell, maybe it already was. *But I don't know that*, MacDara told himself. *Gotta keep going.*

Again, his instinct was right. Rounding the next bend he realized that he had come full circle and was about to emerge in the compound's motor pool. Jeeps and two-and-a-half-ton trucks were parked side by side. He waited and watched. Two guards covered the perimeter. They met in the middle and then turned and retraced their steps. As soon as they turned MacDara slipped through and picked the first jeep. He reckoned it'd be gassed up. Standard practise. Using the hunting knife he jump-started the jeep and reversed into the compound. He could hear the guards yelling and shots being fired. But they didn't even come close. The jeep spun on the gravel beneath him as he turned on the high beams just in time to see five or six figures dash from doors in the buildings near the motor pool. Slamming his foot down on the accelerator he hit the road leading out to the main gate. He seemed to fly that last half-mile. The element of surprise was with him. He could see the guard jump aside and drop the phone he was on as he crashed the jeep through the chain-link fence and took the last three miles to the main highway. After a while he could see headlights following in the far distance but once he reached the highway they disappeared. The colonel had never really expected him to make it. For the first time he realized that his left leg was hurting like hell.

Raindrop bubbles stayed fixed on the window panes and the slender shoots of new branches wafted drunkenly in the mid-March wind. Small waves simmered on the watery gray surface of Long Island sound. MacDara had slept for twelve hours. A sleep punctuated by a recurrent nightmarish dream. This was one dream he still remembered upon waking. He had fallen down a chute, a vortex, into a cavern deep in the center of the earth. No light, no windows, no sky, no grass, no flowers and no other human life unless he counted the grotesque hunchback who alternately threatened him, guarded him and fed him some inedible watery grits.

"How does your leg feel this morning?"

Kate had just entered his bedroom, looking radiant.

"OK, until I try to move it. Still painful."

"Doc says you're to rest it for a few days. You know it's not broken but it won't get better if you don't take care of it. And I'm here to see that you do."

"*Jawohl* Frau Nurse!" saluted Owen as Kate picked up a pillow from the chair and caught him directly on the chest. As she tried to retrieve it, he grabbed her and dragged her into the bed.

"Did the doctor prescribe any special therapy to help me recover, Nurse?"

"As a matter of fact he did. But you must lie perfectly still," she said as she slid under the covers and began to unbutton his pajamas slowly, one button at a time.

MacDara had ditched the jeep in Nashville, called Shields, and then caught a flight to New York. The therapy was Shields's prescription. He had called Kate. She was waiting for Owen when he stepped off the plane. Took him directly to Doc Levin at Long Island Jewish for a complete check-up and then home to Dune Road for a soaking hot bath and sleep. And therapy. Two Federal agents were posted outside, courtesy of Shields.

Everyone was now on a war footing.

Pat Mullan

TWENTY-NINE

The Advisory Council, the Thackeray Institute, Wednesday March 15, 2000

Lord Haverford had acted with urgency. The call from his son had been brief but succinct. He knew he was about to see his prophecy fulfilled. He was going to be around after all to watch the work of the Institute bear fruit, to see the people they had trained assume control and avert the world from its own self-destructive binge. *Oh, I warned them. But they wouldn't listen. Well, they left me no choice.* He sent messages to each member of the Advisory Council to come to London immediately.

Hong Kong

The rest of the board members of Taipan Holdings of Hong Kong had been taken unawares. It was entirely out of character for the Chairman to excuse himself and leave in the middle of a board meeting. But that's exactly what James Scott Tsu had done. His executive secretary had entered with a message; no one recalled her ever interrupting a board meeting before.

The CIRCLE of SODOM
A Gripping New Thriller

Chairman Tsu had read the message, remained perfectly still for a minute, then risen and said, "Gentlemen, I must leave. A personal matter of some urgency. Please continue the meeting. Our Vice Chairman will be acting until I return."

One hour later, James Scott Tsu was in his Mercedes limousine on his way to the airport.

Dusseldorf

Karl-Heinz Schell had had a most satisfying lunch. Every Thursday he had lunch with Heidi. There was something exhilarating about an illicit relationship, he thought as he pushed open the double doors leading to his executive offices.

"Any messages, Geisa?"

"Just one. I left it on your desk."

The sense of exhilaration felt by the President of Dusseldorf Industries disappeared as soon as he read the message. He pressed the intercom that connected him to his secretary.

"Geisa."

"Yes, sir."

"Cancel all my appointments next week. Call a taxi. And get Albert for me, please."

London

The RAC Club was a little run down these days. The membership had changed. Too many noveaux riches with no family pedigree. Not the place of my youth, thought Sir Geoffrey Clutterbuck as the waiter refilled his wineglass. Two tables away, an absolutely abhorrent man, expensively tailored, with a gold watch chain braided across his ample girth, was laughing loudly and holding forth in a most grating Liverpool

Pat Mullan

street accent. Just at that moment the waiter returned, carrying a telephone.

"Phone call for you, Sir Geoffrey. I took the liberty of bringing the telephone to your table."

"Thank you, David."

The call lasted no more than half a minute. Sir Geoffrey didn't speak; only responded with polite affirmations and a courteous goodbye. He was lunching alone so it wouldn't be necessary for him to find excuses for leaving just before they brought his main entree to the table.

Brussels

It was late, almost midnight, when Peter Sorensen entered the lobby of the Palace Hotel in Brussels. The EU Minister for Regional Development was very tired. He had sat through eight hours of technical discussions on cross-border transactions, one of the national impediments to free trade within the European Union. He took his room key and had turned to go when the desk clerk stopped him.

"One moment, Mr. Sorensen. I believe there's a message for you." He reached back into the pigeonholes behind his desk and retrieved a white slip of paper. Peter Sorensen opened it. Just a phone number with a request to call immediately. When he reached his room he did just that. He was on a flight out of Bussels at eight am the following morning.

Zurich

Claude Fymat didn't like to be interrupted during dinner. He had arrivd in Zurich from Paris at eight pm and had had a successful day. The contract was signed. As managing partner of Fymat and Fymat he had a right to feel satisfied. Their fee was one million dollars. And the escargots were succulent with just the correct amount of garlic. He didn't like it when he had to leave half a bottle of superb Bordeaux.

Claude Fymat checked out of the Doldergrand at precisely seven thirty the next morning and took a taxi directly to the airport.

London

Number 7 Digby Lane in Belgravia was a mews house. In fact, it was two, converted originally to provide spacious accommodation in an inauspicious location. It was the inner-London retreat of Lord Haverford. A discreet address in a discreet neighborhood where privacy was paramount. So no one paid any attention when five gentlemen arrived, each by taxi, at various times throughout the Wednesday morning and early afternoon.

Still sprightly for his ninety-three years, Lord Haverford welcomed each of them with brandy and a blazing fire in the drawing room. At exactly seven pm, the first formal meeting in three years of the Advisory Committee of the Thackeray Institute met in the conference room at Number 7 Digby Lane. They were connected audio-visually with Senator Sumner Hardy and Tony Thackeray at the senator's home in Virginia. It was Tony Thackeray who spoke after Lord Haverford had opened the meeting.

"You have all been briefed, gentlemen." Assuming that silence was confirmation, he continued. "Senator Hardy will address any issues or concerns."

The senator reinforced the urgency. "As you know, events have moved ahead of us. We cannot wait for the outcome of elections next year. I believe that our cause is in jeopardy. That leaves us no alternative but to implement the contingency plan we agreed at our meeting three years ago."

"Precisely how much time do we have?" asked Sir Geoffrey.

"A month. No more than three," answered the senator.

"*Verdammt knapp!* It'll take at least a month to put everything in place in Bonn," snapped Karl-Heinz Schell.

"Hong Kong won't be a problem. We'll manage any run on the banks, and our people are already in charge at the exchanges. But I must go to Beijing right away. We cannot afford any misunderstandings," said James Scott Tsu.

"Peter, I'm concerned about the EU," said Tony Thackeray.

"Don't be. The EU today is Germany and France, with apologies to you, Sir Geoffrey. Karl-Heinz will take care of Bonn and Claude will handle events at the Elysee Palace. Isn't that right, Claude?" answered Peter Sorensen.

"Correct. France is not particularly friendly with the present US Administration. Our President can always be made to see that America's difficulty is France's opportunity. I do need the full month, senator. If you move next week, we will not be prepared," responded Claude Fymat.

Sir Geoffrey cut in, "This is all fine, gentlemen. But Britain is different. We don't like it when it's perceived that we're being directed by the Americans. On the other hand, we value our special relationship with Washington. Isn't that right, senator?"

"Yes, Sir Geoffrey. I believe that Britain may very well be the biggest problem. How do you plan to deal with that?" asked the senator.

"There will be two positions in Britain. The public one of outcry and defense mobilization, and the private one, which will be more sober. Our alumni hold sway at the Exchequer, the War Office and the Foreign Office. The Prime Minister will be made painfully aware of that. I will see to it. If absolutely necessary, we can demonstrate to Cabinet our technical ability to cripple Britain's communication network and deplete the Bank of England. But I doubt if we'll need to go that far. No, I can assure you that, apart from the public rumblings, life will proceed as usual. Is that not so, Lord Haverford?"

"Quite so, quite so, Sir Geoffrey. And I will keep those blighters in the Lords fully stocked with their finest brandies," he responded, adding an almost senile touch of levity to the proceedings.

"I will be meeting with the President by the weekend. If he chooses to back off, your assistance will not be necessary. But this President is not easily advised. Or threatened," said Senator Hardy.

"Gentlemen, I expect each of you to implement the contingency starting tomorrow", said Tony Thackeray as the conference concluded.

Claude Fymat, Karl-Heinz Schell and Peter Sorensen left that evening. James Scott Tsu stayed over till morning. Sir Geoffrey Clutterbuck also spent the night at Number 7. He had an affinity for Lord Haverford's brandy.

THIRTY

**The White House, Washington, DC,
8:00 pm, Thursday March 16, 2000**

They met in the Oval Office. It was eight pm and the President was tired. It had been a long day. Senator Sumner Hardy got right to the point.

"Mr. President, I'm sure you know why I'm here."

"No, I don't, Sam. Why don't you tell me."

"Don't be coy, Mr. President. You know damn well why I'm here. I'm asking you - no, I'm telling you - to reconsider. You can't win."

"Sam, I think you're a dangerous man! I intend to stop you."

"Mr. President, I came here to warn you. Don't try to stop us."

"Are you threatening the President, Sam?"

"No threat. You can only govern with our consent. I was hoping to let this year take care of that at the ballot box. If you think you can launch an offensive against us, think again. We will not be defeated."

The CIRCLE of SODOM
A Gripping New Thriller

"You are threatening this democracy, Senator. You would lead this nation into another civil war. Do you really want to see brother against brother?"

"Mr. President, this nation is not divided. We are united, north and south, east and west. Our enemies are well known! They're the liberals, socialists, anarchists and atheists who have almost destroyed this country. Get down from your ivory tower! Look at what's happening out there!"

"Don't lecture me, Senator! What you're seeing out there is change, not chaos. You're looking at a society examining its values, changing what it believes in. And you're afraid of that. You want to stay frozen in your privileged, bigoted past. Well, this democracy gives you the right to do that. And it gives you the freedom to persuade others. Persuade, not force, Senator. You will not end two hundred years of democracy while I am President! Do you understand that, Sam?"

"Mr. President, I did not come here to debate your liberal views. I came here to advise you of the consequences if you move against us. Our citizens are well able to defend themselves. We have strong support right here in Washington. And we hold key positions in our defense forces. Are you going to ask us to attack ourselves? If this comes down to a contest between you and me, who do you think is going to win? Did you see your standing in the latest opinion polls? Only thirty-five percent think you're doing a good job!"

The President had been sitting at his desk during the entire discourse. But now he was visibly angry. His face was red and his eyes were fiery with rage. He jumped out of his chair, his voice loud and final. "Senator, this meeting just ended. Get out of my office! Now!"

The senator was not intimidated. His lips arched in a sardonic smile. Then he turned and left.

Pat Mullan

The Hardy mansion, Blacksburg, Virginia, Sunday March 19, 2000.

It was late afternoon. General Zachary Walker drove along the tree-lined avenue that meandered its way to the front entrance of the Hardy mansion. It had been two years since he'd been here. He remembered that it had been in the fall and the bronze, gold and yellow of fallen leaves that painted his path had impressed him with the beauty of the place. The sense of history was still pervasive. When the senator's ancestor built the original mansion in 1773 it had stood at the beginning of the frontier. A stockade surrounded it then to protect it against marauding Indians. Zachary Walker could almost imagine warpainted warriors running towards him through the tall trees. Yet everything seemed so safe and peaceful now. Far away from the frontiers of conflict. Unless he contemplated the events of recent days. The meeting with the President was still fresh in his mind when he received the invitation from Senator Hardy to meet on a 'matter of national importance'. He recalled the conversation in his office.

"I believe that the President is mentally unstable."

"Senator! You can't mean that!"

"Oh, but I do mean it, Zach. You haven't seen and heard him like I have lately. He has developed a siege mentality, a persecution complex. Thinks there's a plot against him. He actually believes that there's a 'fifth column' in Washington trying to sabotage the country. And who does he think is behind it? Me! He blames me! Our successes have spooked him. He's scared. He's afraid of losing. So his mind has contrived this elaborate threat. He's even convinced himself that we're planning a coup. Can you imagine that? Planning a coup! That's lunacy if I ever heard it. And that scares me, Zach. In his state of mind he might do anything. Even launch an attack against his imagined enemies. He would destroy this country. Destroy this

The CIRCLE of SODOM
A Gripping New Thriller

democracy. Two hundred years of independence and freedom up in flames! We can't let that happen!"

The drive down from Washington had given General Walker plenty of time to think. There was no doubt that the President considered the senator to be a dangerous man. But that didn't mean that the President was becoming paranoid. Did it? The President did feel threatened by the move to the right. And what about Henry Whiteside and Charlie Pettigrew? Where does that all fit? Did Henry start all this paranoia when he began his memoirs? And what about this fellow Thackeray? It was still difficult to accept that Henry might have been killed to keep his mouth shut. To protect him. Zachary Walker was confused. Thinking about things didn't help at all. He felt as though he was on a treadmill and that he was incapable of getting off. He'd have to ride it to the end. The End. A shudder passed through him and he fixed his resolve on two things. He had given the President his word of honor and he would keep it. He also decided that this would not be the time to confront the senator.

A number of vehicles were parked in the forecourt. General Walker pulled in beside them. Admiral Donnelly's official car was already there. The senator greeted him warmly in the hallway: "Zach, it's a pity it takes a crisis to get you to visit."

He seemed genuinely cheerful. Odd, thought Zachary Walker, given the reason for this meeting.

"Garret Donnelly, Duke Walter and Hank McKinney are all here. We're still waiting for Phil Mannion and Sheila Gregory. Bob Maxwell might join us too, if he can get away."

The room was large, filled with big stuffed comfortable furniture that softened the unsmiling ancestral portraits on the wall. Everyone greeted General Walker as he entered.

"Don't get up", he said to the three men, and accepted a Scotch on the rocks from the senator.

There was a relaxed atmosphere in the room. Partly because everyone was at least one drink ahead of him, he observed. Admiral Garret Donnelly's ample girth was embedded in the middle of the largest sofa in the room. Duke Walter and Hank McKinney sat on either side of the blazing fireplace. These men were all Zachary's direct reports. The Admiral headed the Navy, Duke Walter the Air Force and Hank McKinney was Commandant of the Marine Corps. Duke Walter got his nickname because he walked just like John Wayne, even though he resembled him in no other way.

'Don't let me put a damper on anything," said Zachary Walker. "This isn't a meeting of the Joint Chiefs."

"Oh, hell, Zachary. We were only discussing a matter of national security. Hank's golf game!" kidded Duke.

The senator entered into the light banter in the room and Zachary Walker suddenly realized he was on his second Scotch, when Sheila Gregory arrived. Tall and elegant, she greeted everyone with a reserve befitting a Justice of the Supreme Court. Many said that she felt that the President should have appointed her Chief Justice. She was eminently qualified. But the consensus was that her views and judgements were conservative in the extreme. Some said that she held a grudge against the President.

She accepted a soft drink. The light banter in the drawing room ended. The small talk became nothing but small talk.

Phil Mannion and Bob Maxwell arrived within ten minutes of each other. Still in time for dinner but too late for the seafood terrine that everyone had praised. The senator had escorted them into the diningroom promptly at six pm. Phil Mannion was deputy Director of the FBI. A career agent, he had worked his way up in the bureau and had served as Deputy Director during the past three administrations. The top job had eluded him. But no one, not even FBI Director Redington, knew the inner workings of the bureau better than Mannion. He was a born-again Christian and a 'general of the religious right'.

Bob Maxwell, the last of the invitees, took his seat at the table at exactly six-thirty. Chairman of the House Finance Committee and the most influential member of the House

The CIRCLE of SODOM
A Gripping New Thriller

Banking and Ways and Means Committees, Bob Maxwell controlled the purse strings of Congress. Many said that he was more powerful than the Speaker. A man whose philosophy was rigidly to the right of center he was another general of the religious right.

It was eight o'clock when the senator got down to the real business of the day. By this time everyone had dropped their defenses. Good food and good wine had sated their bodies and their minds.

"You all know why we're here. There's no point in delaying the agony any longer. Many of you believe as I do. Our President is mentally unbalanced. And there's no point in looking to the Vice President. He has no real authority. I seriously doubt that he could handle it, anyway. It's patently obvious that he was put on the ticket just to 'buy' the President's voters during the election campaign. He's just a rubber stamp. So, where does that leave us? The Speaker? I don't know about all of you but I do not trust the man. He's an opportunist, a truly shallow person. So, there's nobody there to succeed this President should anything happen to him."

"We're lucky he's in good health. We'd better hope he stays that way", said Admiral Donnelly.

"It's only till this year's election, Sam. We'll take him this time. Then you'll be in the oval office and we can set this country right again", Hank McKinney's voice tried to sound optimistic but didn't quite make it.

"We don't have until the election, Hank. We may not even have until next month", said the senator, his voice raised just enough to throw a hush over the table.

"Sam, what do you mean 'we may not have until next month'?" asked Zachary Walker.

"My intelligence tells me that the President is planning to take military action against us. Under the pretext that he's suppressing a coup!"

"But I'd know about it if anything like that was being planned," claimed Phil Mannion.

"No, you wouldn't, Phil. Tom Redington would. You wouldn't. It's no secret that you are on my Hardy for President committee. This President knows that. You'd be the last FBI man he'd consult," the senator pointed out.

"Well, if there was anything goin' on the Congress sure-as-hell would be kept in the dark. He hasn't consulted us on a goddamned thing in the last three years," bitched Bob Maxwell.

Looking over at Zachary Walker, Senator Hardy said, "Zachary, you will be one of the people he'll take into his confidence. He trusts you. You're an honest man, Zach. There's not too many of those left. And he'll need you. He can't mount an offensive like this without planning and support from people like you. Oh, he doesn't need the army, the airforce, the navy and the marines. Not for the kind of quick hit operations he plans. But he does need your forces to stand down. He'll want to be sure that no one moves against him."

Sheila Gregory had remained silent. Now she neatly summarized, just like a legal brief. "Senator, let me summarize what I think I've heard you say. The President is mentally incompetent. He's planning to engage in hostile actions against his political opponents. Against you, personally. These actions are imminent. You are saying that he must be removed from office. Now. You're also saying that there's no time to impeach. You further claim that the Vice President is an incompetent and the Speaker is a charlatan. Do I understand you correctly?"

"Sheila, I couldn't have summarized it better", answered Senator Hardy.

"You said 'your intelligence' told you that the President is planning these military actions. I would need to see some physical evidence of that," demanded Admiral Donnelly.

"That you will have, Garret. This is too serious a matter to proceed on my word alone," promised the senator.

The CIRCLE of SODOM
A Gripping New Thriller

"Sam, let's cut to the bottom line," Bob Maxwell said, reducing the entire matter to one of his financial proformas. "Are you suggesting that we 'remove' the President from office and install you in his place? If you are, that's a coup! Aren't you giving in to the President's paranoia?"

"Bob, it's a self-fulfilling prophesy. The President, by his intended actions, leaves us no other choice. And it will not be a coup. I will be a caretaker President. For a few months only. Until the elections. Then, assuming our support remains strong, I'll be elected for a four-year term. We're not planning to overthrow this democracy. Only to save it. I will explain that to the American people. You will help me do that. Don't underestimate the solidarity we have on the ground out there. The people will understand."

Zachary Walker woke up in a cold sweat. He could feel a tightness across his chest as though he was being pinned to the bed by a restraint. Dull aches extended down his left arm, and his fingers and toes sent pins and needles to his brain. He felt very weak. Waves of nausea swept over him. The clock at his bedside said it was three thirty in the morning. He wanted to vomit but feared getting out of bed. His heart was palpitating and it seemed as though the sound could be heard throughout the bedroom. His claustrophobia had started again. He closed his eyes and tried to control his breathing. He imagined a white dot in the far distance and lines extending from it to his arms and legs, just like a marionette. He tried to focus on that image and rid his mind of everything else. But it didn't work. The nausea got worse. He had to get to the bathroom, so he forced himself on to the floor and crawled to the bathroom door. Somehow he made the few feet to the toilet bowl and vomited. All the dinner that hadn't been digested. Then the dry retches commenced, racking his body and refusing to stop until he could hardly breathe. He lay there, in a fetal huddle, for at least fifteen minutes before raising himself up to the sink where he rinsed out his mouth and splashed water on his face. The vomiting had helped. He was still weak, but the nausea had disappeared and the claustrophobia had abated. He made it back to the bed and just lay there while his mind took over.

They were all spending the night at the Hardy mansion. It must have been close to one am when the evening ended. Too much cognac and coffee. Experience should have taught him that he would pay for it. But they had taken decisions that would alter the course of American history. If he didn't stop them. Last night he had no choice but to go along with it, and the cognac had dulled the pain inside. They had agreed to meet in four days time in the senator's Washington town house. The senator would bring his physical evidence to prove that the President was going to launch an offensive. They would plot the overthrow of the President of the United States. They would plot the details of execution. And that's exactly what it was. A plot. The enormity of what his dinner associates had contemplated scared him.

The Hardy Townhouse, Washington, DC
Thursday March 23, 2000.

Exactly four days later Senator Sumner Hardy presented his evidence. Tapes of conversations between the President and General Shields, between the President and FBI Director Redington, between General Shields and Owen MacDara. Enough evidence to hang the President. Enough to convict him in this 'court'. Even Zachary Walker had to admit that there was no doubt. The President intended to move against them. Zachary already knew that, of course. He considered himself fortunate that, on each of the last two occasions, he had met with the President in his living quarters, not the Oval Office. They must have a mole in the White House. He'd have to warn the President.

The CIRCLE of SODOM
A Gripping New Thriller

The decision was taken. They would immobilize the country, cripple the nation's nervous system, send the financial markets into a downward spiral, castrate the military, force the President to capitulate, and then take control. All media, TV, radio and newspapers would be marshalled to spread the gospel and explain the action to a bewildered American people. They would pledge less government, not more; promise to protect and restore individual freedoms; guarantee the right to bear arms; commit themselves to ending the godless direction of the nation and restoring the reign of the righteous. This would be an act of unselfish patriotism. And they were convinced that the American people would agree with them. It would be evangelistic, liberating. Another 1776, another American revolution!

The technical work to facilitate this action had commenced months ago. Several 'dry runs' had been undertaken recently. The teams and the organization were in place. All that remained was permission to execute. That permission had now been granted.

Zachary Walker played his part. Senator Sam never doubted his loyalty to the cause. The senator had a blind spot. He failed to comprehend that General Walker did not subscribe to the belief that the end justifies the means.

General Zachary Walker went directly to the President.

Pat Mullan

THIRTY-ONE

ASSIST, 0930 hours, Friday March 24, 2000

The phone rang incessantly on Aaronson's desk. Telephone answering machines were banned here. Central switchboard was just about to answer when Aaronson reached his desk and picked up the receiver.

"Roger Aaronson."

"Where the hell have you been?" It was his boss, Hank Hagan.

"Taking a shit! Is there a law against that?"

"Don't get wise with me, Aaronson. This is a Code 1. Get your ass in here right now. And don't take time to wipe it!"

Hagan was a tyrant. A big, beefy tyrant. But you had to give the big guy his due, thought Aaronson. There was no one, that's right, no one in the world who knew more about computers than Hagan. A Code 1 was the highest emergency. Something real bad must be going down. Aaronson grabbed a pad and pencil and headed for Hagan's office.

ASSIST stood for the military's Automated Systems Security Incident Support Team. They occupied the fourth floor of an old refurbished navy warehouse, just a stone's throw from

The CIRCLE of SODOM
A Gripping New Thriller

the Pentagon and directly across from Arlington National Cemetery. ASSIST responded to security breaches in the military's worldwide computer network. Their last MIS report showed that they had responded to over thirty thousand calls for help during the past year, an increase of fifty percent over the prior year. That statistic was giving the brass sleepless nights. They had isolated thousands of hacker programs and code, caged the critters and then taken them apart. It sometimes seemed to Aaronson that they were detectives in a field of haystacks looking for a needle.

Hagan simply grunted as Aaronson entered his office and took a seat. The other four members of the 'A-Team' were there already, plus one individual he'd never met before. Hagan took the opportunity to curtly brief Aaronson.

"We've got big trouble. At oh nine hundred hours our command and operational data centers in Denver, San Francisco, Baltimore, London, Brussels and Tokyo started to crash. Everything's gone haywire. Communications lines scrambled. Hard hits on banks of disk drives. Databases scratched. Bugs in update programs. Spurious messages issued to console operators. Backup and recovery systems sabotaged. Halon released for no reason. It's war, I tell you! War!"

Nodding towards the individual Aaronson had never met, he continued. "This is Owen MacDara. He's our direct liaison with the White House. The President wants answers and he wants them now."

Looking at the five assembled staff he said, "You're the A-Team. The best we've got. I'm going to tell MacDara to inform the President that we'll give him an update by noon. That gives you guys two hours. The 'morgue' is open. Critters are coming in by fax, tape, disk, download, you name it. I want you to start carving them up now. I'll join you myself in thirty minutes. Mr. MacDara, you want to add anything?"

"No, Mr. Hagan. You know how to reach me. I want a briefing every twenty minutes, even if you have nothing to tell me. OK?"

"You got it," said Hagan and, standing up, he addressed the A-Team. "Let's go. Move it. I want answers!"

MacDara's beeper went off as he was leaving Hagan's office. It was Shields. Owen grabbed the phone on Hagan's desk and dialled his private number.

"Owen, meet me in the Situation Room in the White House right away."

That was it. No further explanation. Shields was gone. Owen MacDara didn't need to know any more. The tone in Shields's voice was enough to light a fire under him. He was out of the building without even the courtesy of a goodbye to Hagan and his team.

The Situation Room had been turned into a Command Center. Banks of telephones, fax machines and television screens fronted maps of North America and the world. Three or four conversations were going on simultaneously, phones were ringing constantly, faxes were disgorging paper, CNN and NBC were competing for attention and someone was highlighting sites on the maps with information that seemed to change with every phone call. The President was standing, sleeves rolled up, tie pulled down, hair tousled and looking like he hadn't slept. Bart Shields, Tom Redington and Zach Walker stood by him. Shields beckoned Owen to join them. The President nodded. He was getting an update from a youngish major general.

"Mr. President, this is the situation as of eleven hundred hours. Automated teller systems at Citibank, Chembank and Nationsbank have been debiting and crediting thousands of dollars in and out of customers' accounts. The banks have shut down the ATM networks but we're afraid it's been too late to stop the panic. People across the country are lining up to withdraw their money."

The CIRCLE of SODOM
A Gripping New Thriller

"Bart, get me the Chairman of the Fed. And tell all the national television networks to standby. I'll need to talk to the American people real soon," cut in the President.

"That's not all, Mr.President," the major general continued. "Our telephone systems are also under attack. Southern Bell have already had three exchange shutdowns caused by viruses or bugs. Interconnect switches are down at two of our army bases, and the reservations networks at Kennedy, La Guardia and O'Hare are out. These crashes seem to have been caused by waves of mass-dialing bombardment coming in over the Internet."

The update was finished. For now. This was escalating rapidly.

"What about our Washington phones?" asked Bart Shields.

"OK at present. But I don't think we can rely on that for too long. We'd better make the most of it while we're still up," responded the major general.

"Zach, I want all the governors, all the mayors, all the Fortune 500 CEOs, all utility company heads, all the church leaders and every key person in this nation. Get them on a video conference link with me by one o'clock."

As Zach turned to pick up the phone, the President continued. "And, Zach. Alert the National Guard. I want public order maintained at all costs. We do not need rioting on our streets."

MacDara's beeper went off again. It was Hagan with an update. He called him on the nearest phone.

"We're still up to our asses in diagnostics. But we've had some luck. Aaronson traced a virus to a software release provided by a defense contractor in Cambridge, Mass. I know that software company and I know two of the directors personally. I'll cut this short. I called them. They gave me the names of the three programmers who worked on the release. I'll have them checked out.'

Pat Mullan

MacDara took the names, briefed the President and Shields and turned the names over to Tom Redington. The Bureau was on the case in a matter of minutes.

It was pizza for lunch, and the President was halfway into his second slice, smothered in everything but anchovies. He detested anchovies. *That's one thing we have in common*, Owen noted. He was just finishing his first slice of pepperoni when the phones started ringing off the hook again. Owen could see Tom Redington and the major general out of the corner of his eye. They were both intently making a beeline towards the President, each oblivious to the other. The major general got there first.

"Mr. President. More bad news. Wall Street's trading systems have gone crazy. They're executing irrational buys and sells and artificially inflating and deflating the value of stocks. Utilities and banks have lost fifty percent of their value in the first hour of trading. The Dow Jones has hit an all time low! There's panic in the markets. Overseas too. London and Paris reacted wildly. Lucky it happened toward the end of their trading day. But huge blocks of stocks are being dumped at great losses. And opportunists are buying in at the sharply discounted prices. The New York Stock Exchange has been shut down for the day."

"Get me Tony Blair and Jacques Chirac right away. And you might as well get me Gerhard Schroeder too. They need to know what's happening. Directly from me," said the President, "I'll be in the Oval Office to take the calls. I want a full update in forty-five minutes. I'll take the conference with the governors and the mayors and the others at one. Bart, you're in charge here."

Tom Redington had been impatiently waiting to speak. "Mr. President. Before you go. We found the programmer who bugged the military's software. We traced three large cash payments to him during the past year. From an account in Switzerland. He's been living well beyond his means. We have him in custody and he's started to talk. Guess what? His good buddy. The one he blames for getting him into this. He's a

The CIRCLE of SODOM
A Gripping New Thriller

programmer in Colonel George McNab's state-of-the-art facility in Tennessee."

That stopped the President dead in his tracks. He looked at all of them. "That's proof enough for me. We can't wait around here like sitting ducks any longer. If I had any reservations about hitting these people, this sure takes care of it. Bart and Zach, I am going to take the actions we talked about. Now! I can't wait any longer!.""

The President's face was set in grim determination as he strode from the Situation Room.

**The Situation Room, The White House,
1100 hours, Saturday March 25, 2000**

The President sat awkwardly at one corner of the table in the Situation Room. His jacket was off and his sleeves were rolled up. He was talking.

"Ward, your RAT Force will move out tonight?"

"Yes, Mr. President. They'll assemble at Fort Benning. I'll join them tomorrow and brief them on their mission," confirmed Captain Ward Dobson.

"I want Owen to go with you", said the President, as he looked across the table at Owen. "He's recently been a 'guest' of the colonel's and I'm sure he's anxious to return."

"Ward, that computer center must be taken out before they cripple the country. Owen knows exactly where it is. Right?" added General Shields, raising a questioning eyebrow at MacDara.

"That's right, General," agreed Owen.

"Bart, brief me again on Dania. I don't want a repeat of Waco," said the President.

Bart Shields spent the next fifteen minutes thoroughly detailing each move planned against The Circle, with special emphasis on what could go wrong and the actions they would take. Everyone knew what had happened in Waco, Texas in April of ninety-three when the Branch Davidian sect's compound had burned to the ground after US agents had launched an assault using tanks and tear gas. At least eighty-five members of the cult had died, including the founder, David Koresh, their self-styled 'Messiah'. The President had made it perfectly clear that he did not want to lose control of this one. And if the Chosen One was there, he wanted him taken alive.

"Tom, are you comfortable with this?" asked the President.

"Mr. President, Bart and I worked this out together. It's our best effort. Most of the team on the ground is mine. That concentrates the mind," answered Tom Redington.

"Dick, I know you're not directly involved in these actions but I need your best assessment at this time. What are your operatives in the field telling you?" asked the President, bringing in CIA Director Richard Smallwood.

"You're making the right decision, Mr. President. Strike them first! We've been keeping a close eye on Lord Haverford. He's had a secret meeting in London with five key directors of his Advisory Council. That group only meets when it's absolutely essential," Dick Smallwood responded.

"Why did they meet?" pursued the President.

"We don't know that. We weren't able to bug the place. Haverford sweeps his homes and offices every couple of days. Scrupulous fellow," said Smallwood. "But we do know one very important thing," he volunteered. "One of the people at that meeting is a household name in the world of finance. He attended your Washington conference on trade last year. His name is James Scott Tsu."

A low murmur rose in the room. Everyone knew of James Scott Tsu, architect of the new ACU, the Asian currency unit exchange mechanism. He had made the cover of *Time* magazine in recent months.

"There's more, Mr. President. The day after he returned to Hong Kong he left for Beijing."

The CIRCLE of SODOM
A Gripping New Thriller

Dick Smallwood didn't have to say any more. That information was sufficient proof that the Haverford meeting in London was important. Very important. A summit of the Advisory Council of the Thackeray Institute.

The business in the Situation Room had come to an end. The President was in somber mood. "These decisions are mine. Mine alone. I'll explain them to the American people. And I'll accept total responsibility for whatever casualties we suffer as a result."

Pat Mullan

THIRTY-TWO

**Fort Dix, New Jersey,
2200 Hours, Saturday March 25, 2000**

Walls was pissed off. He was supposed to be in the Bahamas with Angie this weekend. But all leave had been cancelled and they'd been on full alert for the past forty-eight hours. It was twenty-two hundred hours on a Saturday evening and they'd just received their orders. They'd been packed and ready to ship out since they went on full alert. Walls grabbed his duffle bag and piled into the waiting bus with the other nineteen men. For tactical deployment reasons the hundred-strong RAT Buster team was split into platoons of twenty, each commanded by a platoon leader. Two platoons were based on the west coast and three on the east coast.

Walls squeezed in beside Farley. "They just had to pick this fuckin' weekend, didn't they?"

"Shit happens, Walls. It goes with the territory!"

"Bullshit, Farley. I'll bet this is just some chicken-shit exercise, that's all!"

"Aw, relax, man! What's your beef anyway?" growled Pascarelli from the seat behind him.

The CIRCLE of SODOM
A Gripping New Thriller

"I was supposed to be in Paradise Island with Angie this weekend. That's my beef. This better be for real!"

"Where we goin', Lt. Johnson?" yelled Hedge from the rear of the bus as they moved out of Fort Dix.

"Hedge, you got the same news as me. What you see is what you get. We fly out of Philly at oh one hundred hours. We'll assemble in Atlanta," Lieutenant Johnson yelled back.

"Well, I'm still pissed off," griped Walls.

The Plaza Hotel, Manhattan, New York, Sunday March 26, 2000

In the months since Angelo's death Liz Russo had felt as though she was on parole. The NYPD was still investigating Angelo's murder. They had arrested no one, although Assistant DA Stern couldn't be blamed for that. He had hounded her. Interrogated her half a dozen times. He as much as told her that he believed she was guilty. In a way she was. She had wanted Angelo dead. Oh yes, she played the black-dressed, bereaved widow to the hilt at the wake and the funeral. But she hadn't fooled her close friends. They knew she was not in mourning.

Tonight Liz Russo didn't give a damn. This was the first time she'd seen Tony Thackeray since Angelo's death. There were things she needed to know. But that could wait. The taxi dropped her at Elaine's. Tony was already there, and he took her hand and kissed it, lingering just long enough to make it erotic. She noticed famous and familiar faces as they were escorted to their table, but all of that soon faded out of focus into the background. Dinner became a sensation of tastes, textures and touches.

They went straight to bed when they got back to Tony's suite at the Plaza. Much later, as they showered together and Tony massaged her back, Liz said, "It was you, wasn't it?"

"What do you mean?"

Pat Mullan

"Remember Miami. We were lying beside the pool at the Fontainbleau. I was wishing that Angelo were dead. And you said that you wished you could make my dreams come true. Well, did you Tony? Did you make my dreams come true?"

They were out of the shower and Liz was towelling Tony dry. He didn't answer. She let the towel drop to the floor and turned him around to face her.

"It was you. Wasn't it, Tony? Oh, I don't mean that you did it. But you arranged it, didn't you?"

"Liz, let's just say that I thought you were entitled to some happiness in your life. Shall we leave it at that?"

"It was you! I just knew it."

Somehow, the confirmation of her suspicion didn't put Liz's mind at rest. Wanting to know and knowing were two entirely different things.

Tony's breathing was deep and regular but Liz couln't get to sleep. She couldn't turn off her mind. It was three am when she last remembered looking at her watch. Sometime later she must have dozed off because she was now wide awake. It was five am. She turned over and the bed was empty. Tony was gone. She eased herself out of bed and went to the bathroom. He wasn't there. Just then she noticed the strip of faint light under the bedroom door. She walked to the door and stood listening. She could hear Tony's voice. Curiosity and a sense of foreboding compelled her to reach for the door handle. She turned it cautiously and opened the door a couple of inches. Tony was speaking in a low voice but his diction made everything perfectly clear. She didn't have to strain to hear what he was saying.

"I don't care about them. Eliminate them. It's the girl I want. No! No! Do not kill her! Kate Whiteside is the bait. I want MacDara dead this time!"

Liz didn't wait to hear any more. She tiptoed back and crept into bed, pretending to be asleep when he returned. But he knew she was awake. He had closed the bedroom door when he made the call and it was ajar when he returned. Tony Thackeray never

The CIRCLE of SODOM
A Gripping New Thriller

made mistakes about details like that. Now he knew that Liz Russo knew too much.

A breakfast of coffee and blueberry muffins was brief enough for each of them to keep up the pretense. Liz excused herself to go to the ladies' room. Instead she tried calling Owen MacDara. No response; just his answering machine. At the tone she left a warning. Maybe he'd get it in time. Tony had finished breakfast when she returned. They kissed and parted on the front steps of the Plaza. Liz declined the concierge's offer of a taxi, choosing to walk instead. She needed to think and walking always helped. She headed crosstown towards Madison and Park. She just needed to put distance between herself and Tony Thackeray. She didn't see him double back after they parted and follow her across the street.

Liz didn't know Kate Whiteside. And she didn't know why Tony Thackeray wanted Owen MacDara dead. She only knew that he was capable of killing. She had to stop it. She thought about going to the police. For just a moment. They already suspected her of Angelo's murder. There had to be another way. But she couldn't think of any. By this time she had crossed Madison and had reached Park. She turned south towards 53rd Street. She'd try phoning Owen at his office. Maybe she'd take the Lexington Avenue line to Grand Central. Take the next train home to Connecticut. Give herself more time to think. Maybe she'd come up with something. At least Tony was unaware that she knew anything. That knowledge helped her. There were two telephone booths at 54th Street and Lexington Avenue. One was unoccupied. She called Owen at his office and got a prerecorded message that he would be away for some time and that all business matters should be referred to Dick Massey. She called his home number again. Still no answer. She didn't leave a message this time. Once to a machine was quite enough.

She walked to the corner and took the stairs down to the subway. It was nine thirty am and the morning rush had not yet subsided. The platform was crowded. People were bunched together precariously. Twenty minutes later she was still standing there. Two trains had come and gone. There hadn't been enough room to absorb the throng. She had been standing back, not wanting to jostle for position. Now, fed up, she moved into the fray and elbowed her way into the middle of the people bunched together where they expected the train doors to open. Lights in the tunnel signalled an incoming train and the mass of people seemed to suck in their collective stomach. Moving back just that inch from the platform edge.

Liz felt the push in the small of her back that propelled her off balance. She teetered on the edge of the platform like a highwire artist, then lost her footing entirely and plunged to the tracks in front of the oncoming train. The driver applied the brakes at the last minute. But it was too late. The first two carriages passed over her. She was decapitated immediately.

**Fort Benning, Georgia,
1800 Hours, Sunday March 26, 2000**

"Attention!"

Conversation died and a hundred chairs clacked in unison as their occupants stood to attention. Captain Dobson entered from the rear and bounded the foot and a half on to the raised platform facing the troops. He was followed by Owen MacDara.

"At ease, Gentlemen. Be seated."

MacDara grabbed an empty chair in the front row, right beside Walls and Farley. Captain Dobson was speaking: "This is not an exercise. This is the real thing. And let me tell you some other things this is <u>not</u>. This is not a hostage situation. We are not going up against Middle East terrorists. Or any other kind of foreign terrorist for that matter!"

Stopping to let that all sink in, the captain nodded his head, the lights were dimmed and an aerial photograph was projected on to the screen at the rear of the platform.

The CIRCLE of SODOM
A Gripping New Thriller

"You are now looking at the target. Right in the hills of Tennessee. Yes, that's right, gentlemen. Right here, in our own country."

You could hear a pin drop in this place, thought MacDara. Silence, accompanied by disbelief, seemed to have transfixed everyone. Dobson continued to describe the imminent threat and then delivered the best intelligence available on the Millennium Covenant's strength and firepower. When he concluded he nodded to Owen MacDara who left his seat and joined him on the platform.

"Gentlemen, let me introduce Owen MacDara. He is on special assignment for the President. Owen will accompany us on this mission. He's been inside the Millennium's compound. He'll brief you on that and tell you what he knows about the target. When Owen is finished I will go over our plans for this operation."

Owen MacDara took over and described his incarceration by McNab and the subsequent manhunt he survived. As he did so, he pointed out specific buildings in the main complex and their suspected function, with particular emphasis on what he'd come to think of as 'building four', the computer center. He then went on to tell about the terrain in the area. When he finished, Captain Dobson detailed the plan of attack and ended by putting on the overhead lights.

"Gentlemen, there's someone else who wants to address you this evening." The captain walked over to the podium at the side of the platform and pressed a button. The voice was familiar: "This is the President. By now Captain Dobson and Owen MacDara have briefed you. Let me assure you that your mission is vital. Our democracy is in imminent danger. More so than at any time in our history. If you do not succeed in the coming days, your government will be overthrown and you will have a dictator sitting in the Oval Office. I know you do not want to see that happen. I am confident that you will prevail. Thank you. And may God bless you."

Pat Mullan

Captain Dobson bounded onto the platform again. "Gentlemen, that's it. We'll assemble at twenty-one hundred hours. Thank you."

Long Island, New York, Monday March 27, 2000

Kate Whiteside was sitting out on the deck at the rear of Owen MacDara's house on Dune Road, alone with her thoughts and a large mug of coffee. She didn't hear the doorbell ring at first but the persistence of it finally cut into her consciousness. She wasn't expecting anyone and decided that it must be one of the security men that Shields had assigned to look out for her.

It was a courier with a package for Ms. Kate Whiteside, c/o Mr. Owen MacDara. He stood at the door looking nervous. One of Shields's agents towered over him. The agent insisted on inspecting and opening the package. Satisfied that it was not an explosive, Kate signed the courier's document. When she was alone again she took the package inside and opened it with great curiosity. She read the brief letter enclosed and then opened the small box tucked inside. It cushioned a beautiful gold ring with the most magnificent amethyst she'd ever seen. The inside was engraved with the words '*from Z to J-S with love*' Her eyes were moist as she read the letter once more. The words were simple. She read the last lines over and over again:

> *Your mother was a beautiful lady and she died giving birth to you. I loved her very much. This was her ring. I think she would have wanted you to have it.*
> *All my love,*
> *Zachary*

The tears were flowing freely now, blurring her vision and giving her mouth a salty taste. She had loved Henry and Ruth.

The CIRCLE of SODOM
A Gripping New Thriller

But she had always wondered who she was. Now that she knew she felt both happy and sad. Sad at the loss. And happy that she finally knew. And frightened. And a sense of trepidation. About Zachary Walker. About Owen. She felt a sense of danger. She didn't want to lose any more of the people who loved her. She picked up a sweater, left the house without even locking the front door, and crossed Dune Road. She ploughed through the sand dunes and started walking across the beach towards the ocean.

David liked his work. He was a perfectionist and he liked the feeling of satisfaction he got from a job well done. Sometimes that feeling stayed with him for days. He enjoyed praise too. Especially when it came from someone that he idolized. And David idolized the Chosen One. As he rubbed the gold earring in the lobe of his right ear his mind wandered. The Chosen One had been most satisfied with the Canadian assignment. David had not felt the same way. He liked the danger and challenge of an assignment and he was always erotically aroused when the victim showed fear. There was no challenge in taking an old man in the dead of the night from his cabin and tossing him into the sea. But the words of praise from the Chosen One went a long way to compensate for his feeling of letdown.

David liked to work alone. He had a partner on this assignment and he didn't like it. Sal was not his favorite brother. Too timid, too fastidious. As they sat on the dunes, watching the scene below with a pair of binoculars, David tossed his empty coke can into the long grass. Sal got up and retrieved it. David gave him a 'drop dead' stare. Then he handed the binoculars to him and said, "Take a look. Now's as good a time as any."

The woman was walking alone about a mile down the beach. She was wearing a bright red sweater and her hair was blowing in the wind. It was a cool clear fall day and the sand glistened in the sun's rays. Two men stood together watching her. It was eleven am and there wasn't a thing moving elsewhere on the dunes. Summer was over and all the houses were empty in mid-week October.

"Yeah, I guess you're right."

"OK! Let's do it."

It was a turkey shoot. David fixed the silencer and adjusted the scope. Firing from the prone position, his first shot felled the man on the right and, as the other man turned around, the second shot caught him in the shoulder, spun him around and the third shot dropped him in a heap right across the body of his colleague. David put the weapon away and scrambled over the dunes. Sal spotted a garbage bin a few yards ahead on the boardwalk. He ran to it, deposited the coke can, then jumped back over the dunes to join David.

The woman was unaware that anything had taken place. She continued on her walk. It wasn't until David and Sal were almost on top of her that she sensed their presence and turned around. It wasn't anything they said. In fact, they didn't say a thing. She just knew. She ran but she didn't get very far. David caught her first. She fought back. He swung a right with full force hitting her in the temple and knocking her unconscious. She crumpled at his feet.

"Goddamn, we're supposed to take her alive," screamed Sal.

The first thing that Kate felt was the bumpy rolling motion and the hardness underneath her. The next thing she felt was the terrific pain in her head. She struggled to sit up but found it difficult to get leverage. Her hands had been handcuffed behind her back. Then she felt someone pull her into a sitting position. Her eyes adjusted to the light and she could see that she was inside some kind of commercial vehicle. There was an odor of decayed vegetables and rotten onions. She felt nausea but stifled it. There were no windows. The only light came from a wire-meshed square opening into the driver's cabin. She was sitting on a lumpy car-seat cushion and her back was supported by the side panel of the vehicle.

The CIRCLE of SODOM
A Gripping New Thriller

She could see him now. He was one of the two men from the beach. Not the one who hit her. The other one, the smaller one. He was sitting opposite her, his legs crossed in the lotus position as though he were about to attempt yogic flying. His face was dark, thin, ferret-like. She looked directly at him but he averted his eyes. He just sat there, silent. Kate tried to speak but found her throat too dry. She concentrated on making saliva and swallowing. After a while she looked across and spoke to him.

"Why are you doing this? Where are you taking me?"

He continued to avert his eyes, saying nothing. Kate tried again but the outcome was the same. She estimated that the vehicle must be travelling at about forty or fifty miles an hour over sideroads. Her legs had not been tied together, so she started to exercise them, bending and unbending her knees and flexing and tensing her calf and thigh muscles. About twenty minutes must have passed this way when the grill to the driver's cabin slid open and a voice yelled back, "Is the bitch awake yet?" And, when there was no response, repeated, "Sal, Goddamit, did you hear me?"

Sal rolled over on his knees then into a crouch and finally dragged himself on to his feet. He lurched the couple of steps to the open grill and said, sullenly, "Yeah, man, she's awake."

"We're gonna stop up ahead. Grab a bite to eat. And I need to take a piss. You can take the wheel for an hour."

About a mile further ahead the van slowed and made a sharp left turn. It proceeded slowly for a while longer and then stopped. Sal helped Kate to her feet as the rear doors swung open and the man who had punched her stood there grinning: "Have a nice ride, babe?"

"Lay off her, David", said Sal.

"OK, OK. Sandwiches and coke. You get a choice of ham and cheese. Or ham and cheese. That's what I got."

"I can't eat unless you free my hands", said Kate.

David thought about that for a moment and agreed. "Yeah, I don't think I want to sit here feeding you. Unless you do, Sal", he said derisively. Sal didn't respond, just went behind Kate and took off the handcuffs. Her arms were stiff and the muscles in her upper arms and shoulders hurt. Her wrists were chafed and angry looking. David returned with three cokes and three ham and cheese sandwiches on white bread. Kate hated white bread, but she was hungry. They seemed to be on an isolated lane, bordered on each side by bushes and hedgerows, effectively blocking any view of the surrounding area. They had parked beside an old reddish weatherbeaten barn. It looked like it hadn't been used in ages. Tufts of long grass skirted the front doors, and most of the wood had rotted at the bottom. Kate found a place to sit and ate her sandwich while David disappeared around the side of the barn. Sal only took a couple of bites, then threw his sandwich away and gulped down his coke. He seemed restless, nervous. He stood near the front door of the van, kicking the dirt with his right toe. Almost seemed anxious to get going again. Kate tried to take stock of her predicament. She convinced herself that they weren't going to kill her. They would have done that already. No, they were taking her somewhere, to someone. She thought about her chances of escape. Maybe she could get them to relax, get them off guard. They didn't like each other. That was obvious. She had already decided that David was the dangerous one. She wasn't sure about Sal.

David appeared again, zipping up his fly as he walked towards them.

"OK, let's move out", he ordered.

"I need to go first", said Kate.

David looked at her belligerently, and then ordered Sal to keep an eye on her. Kate went around the side of the barn. Sal followed and stood at the corner. There was no privacy but nature couldn't wait. Sal just stood there, kicking the ground and looking down at his feet. When they got back to the van David was ready to go. He grabbed Kate and pulled her arms behind her back to handcuff her again. But Kate pleaded with him. "Please don't handcuff me again. My wrists hurt real bad. Look

The CIRCLE of SODOM
A Gripping New Thriller

at them." And when she felt David hesitate, she continued, "I can't go anywhere. I can't get out of the van. Please don't handcuff me!"

David stopped and spun her around to face him, still holding her upper arms in a vice-like grip: "OK, babe. You win. But I'm warning you. Don't try anything. If you do, I'll truss you up real good. Just like a Christmas turkey." This idea seemed to tickle him. He started laughing loudly and tossed the keys to Sal as he pushed Kate ahead of him into the rear of the van. He had been looking at Kate; leering at her would be more accurate. Then he started taunting her. "It's a real shame. Untouched by human hand. That's our delivery instructions. What a waste!"

Kate said nothing. She was afraid. She had huddled into the corner of the van near the driver's cabin. She wanted to make sure that Sal could hear what was going on. A false sense of hope, she told herself. But she would reach for any straw at this point.

"Isn't that right, babe? Just a waste. You need to be comforted. You should try being nice to me for a change. This trip can be easy. Or it can be difficult. Do you know what I mean?"

He had moved closer to her now. Sitting only inches away, he had boxed her into the corner, like the final move in a game of checkers. She had nowhere to go. He leaned forward and grabbed her legs, pulling her towards him. She reacted like a cornered rat, and the point of her toe caught him right between the legs. He released her and buckled over in agony. She braced herself against the corner. He grabbed her again, yelling, "Bitch! You just bought yourself a bad trip!"

He was on top of her, pulling her sweat pants over her hips. Kate was screaming and flailing out with her arms. She caught the side of his neck with her fingernails and ripped. He yelled and slapped her hard across the face. She was stunned. Her strength was no match for his. Her sweats were around her ankles and he had ripped off her panties. He was on his knees,

Pat Mullan

pinning her to the floor with one hand while he loosened the belt on his pants with the other, still yelling, "Bitch! Bitch! Bitch!" Kate was powerless to stop him. She struggled under his grip, dazed by the blow to her face, crying and screaming at the same time.

It took a while for her to realize that the van was filled with daylight and the rear doors were open. Sal stood there holding a gun in both hands. David had loosened his grip on her and had turned to look at Sal, a look of incredulity. The gun was trembling in Sal's hands and he was talking: "Get away from her!"

David was now on his feet, buckling his belt, sneering at Sal and shouting, "Give me the gun, you little fuck!", as he held out his hands and began to move towards him.

"I warn you! Don't come any closer!" Sal's voice was almost at breaking point but he wouldn't lower the gun.

"Don't fuck with me, Sal! You're a wimp! Give me the gun", said David.

The gunshot reverberated like a cannon inside the van. The gun was still trembling in Sal's hands. David had stopped, a look of disbelief on his face. He sunk to the ground, both hands holding his midriff, as the red stain began to spread outwards around his fingers. Sal just stood there, repeating, "I warned you. I warned you."

Kate thought this might be her chance to escape and moved towards the back door. But Sal trained the gun on her: "I can't let you go. I have to deliver you. Safely. I gave my word." He stuck the gun in his belt, pulled her out of the van and handcuffed her again. They were parked at the side of a lonely country road. Nothing stirred for miles. Then he went inside the van and appeared moments later, dragging David. He let him fall from the rear of the van onto the road beside Kate. She could see that he was either dead or unconscious. He was soaked in blood from his midriff to his thighs. Sal jumped down from the van, grabbed David's ankles and dragged him off the road and into the ditch at the side. Then he put Kate back inside the van, telling her that he had a delivery to make and nothing was going to stop him.

THIRTY-THREE

The Millennium Covenant,
0100 hours, Monday March 27, 2000

Captain Dobson, the five lieutenants who commanded the RAT platoons, and Owen MacDara conferred before the assault.

"Give me a twenty minute head start before you move in", said MacDara.

"Lieutenant Johnson, you're going with Owen. Lieutenant Mullery will command his own platoon and yours. They're already in position for the main assault," said Captain Dobson. Then, just to confirm what they had already covered in their tactical planning, the captain looked at the other three lieutenants. "Jones and Garner, your platoons will flank the compound on the right and the left. Cossin, you and your platoon will move out when Owen does. I want you in position at the north end of the compound before Lieutenant Mullery moves out. And remember, gentlemen, nobody gets careless. I will be with Lieutenant Mullery. Synchronize your watches. At oh two hundred hours we will commence the assault on the main compound. Owen, you've got an hour to neutralize the computer center. Good luck!"

The CIRCLE of SODOM
A Gripping New Thriller

Two guards were still in position at the main gate of the compound. The first was sitting in the guardhouse reading and the second was walking back and forth about ten yards in front of the gate. Lieutenant Johnson waited till he turned, and then sneaked past and made the few yards to the guard box. At approximately the same time that Owen MacDara planted the hunting knife under the second guard's ribcage, Lieutenant Johnson broke the neck of the first guard.

Fifteen minutes later, Owen and Johnson had covered the mile to the main compound without encountering anyone. They waited. At least four guards were patrolling this part of the compound: two covering the perimeter to their left that circled the motor pool and passed the indoor firing range where MacDara had first met McNab; two covering the perimeter to their right that extended around the assembly area and the main entrance. MacDara decided to enter by the motor pool again; just as he did on his last 'visit'. They waited until the two guards met, exchanged greetings, and turned to cover the ground they'd just patrolled. MacDara and Johnson crouched and crawled till they reached the perimeter. The fence had been reinforced since last time. MacDara cut the two bottom rows of barbed wire and held it back until Johnson crawled through, then followed.

Lieutenant Cossin and his platoon moved fast. By the time that MacDara and Johnson had entered the motor pool, they were already beyond the compound, beyond the guarded perimeter fence and crossing the first rutted track that led into the densely forested terrain that MacDara had described so well. They continued north for another half-mile and stopped. Lieutenant Cossin split his platoon into teams of four men each, spread them two hundred yards apart, fanned out and turned back towards the compound. They halted two hundred yards north of the perimeter fence and held their position. Lieutenant Cossin checked his watch. It was 0140 hours.

At 0130 hours Captain Dobson and Lieutenant Mullery, with their two combined platoons, headed north through the main gate. The bodies of the two guards still lay where MacDara and Johnson had left them. At 0145 the platoons were deployed in an arc stretching from the extreme left to the extreme right of the compound and one hundred and fifty yards south of the perimeter. Captain Dobson and Lieutenant Mullery had set up a command post in a cluster of trees fifty yards from the main entrance.

MacDara and Johnson double-timed from vehicle to vehicle in the motorpool until they reached the southern wall of the firing range. Everything was still. The night was clear, not even a breeze, with just enough moonlight to silhouette the buildings and throw shadows behind trees and bushes. MacDara and Johnson hugged their way in shadow north along the wall of the firing range until they reached the gap that separated them from the next building. They crossed the gap and flattened themselves against the gable end of that building. They waited and listened. Silence. By MacDara's reckoning the next building should be the computer center. It was. A long, rectangular building with rows of windows on one side - opaque glass, screened by wire mesh and covered with steel grilles. It would be a futility to try to penetrate such a place. MacDara had been in too many high-security data centers to realize that. But they hadn't come here to steal. They had come to destroy. If they were right, this was the command center for the infowar that McNab had started. MacDara took the east side of the building and Johnson the west. They each took three semtex packs with timed detonators from their backpacks and planted them at both ends and the middle of the building. The timers were set for fifteen minutes. It was now 0145 hours.

Captain Dobson broke silence on his radio. He confirmed positions with Jones, Garner and Cossin. He hadn't expected to hear from MacDara and Johnson. It was 0155 hours.

The explosions ripped the night air and shook the bed under George McNab. He always slept combat-ready and only had to

The CIRCLE of SODOM
A Gripping New Thriller

pull on his boots. He grabbed his .45 and ran out the front door. Just in time to miss a mortar round that landed right in the center of the compound. He had enough time to see the flames leaping skyward from the computer center before he hit the ground. Pulling his radio from his belt, he started yelling orders.

"Black! Wainwright! Where the fuck are you? We're under attack! Get your men and move out. Black, take the armory and hold it! Wainwright, make every bullet count. I want the bastards dead! Do you hear me?"

His voice was drowned out by another mortar round hitting somewhere near the motor pool. Then the unmistakeable sound of automatic rifles seemed to be coming from everywhere, north, south, east and west. His people were piling out of buildings, some half-dressed. Most had been asleep. Some didn't make it far. They pitched face down into the gravel, stopped dead in their tracks. Others made it to cover. Firefights had broken out on all sides.

Pascarelli was gurgling in his throat. Bubbles of blood were forming at the corners of his lips. The platoon paramedic, 'Doc', had applied a pressure bandage to the wound in his chest but his lungs were filling with blood. Walls and Farley were providing fire cover. They looked at Doc again, who was now trying to get an airway into Pascarelli. Doc simply shook his head. Firing to their immediate front had slackened, only one rifle shooting sporadically. Walls and Farley moved out towards it. Walls to the left, Farley to the right. Mortars were still landing in the compound and fighting to their right sounded intense. Garner's platoon was bogged down. Mullery started to move Johnson's platoon to reinforce Garner. But Walls and Farley were bent on avenging Pascarelli. Farley took a position about forty yards from the lone rifleman and kept up a steady stream of fire, pinning him down. Walls moved in on his left, crawling the last thirty yards, then rising and storming the position. Just as he did, explosion after explosion rocked the entire compound, lighting the night sky and illuminating everything. The armory had been blown. Walls, at that moment, was naked and the bullet caught him in the throat, exiting and blowing away the back of his skull. Farley didn't see Walls die. Mullery had moved to a crouch beside him, ordering him to move out. Captain Dobson would mop up and then reinforce Jones.

MacDara had seen Colonel McNab hit the ground and take cover, just after the explosions had ripped apart the computer center. He crawled on his stomach, halving the sixty yards between himself and McNab. He wanted to take the colonel alive. A shot careened off the ground, kicking dust and gravel into his face. He rolled away, taking cover behind some large shrubbery at the edge of the parade ground. When he looked again, the colonel was gone. He reached the position where he had last seen McNab but there was nothing to indicate where he had gone. But Owen MacDara wanted the colonel badly. This was personal.

Crawling and running and dodging, MacDara reached the perimeter of the compound, adjacent to the armory, and sighted his quarry. McNab was huddled with one of his captains. He was barking orders like a maniac. Timing is everything. In this case, it certainly was on the side of McNab. Just as MacDara reached his position, a mortar round came in. McNab hit the ground, twisting to his left, giving him a clear view of MacDara. He came up firing, oblivious to the incoming rounds. MacDara's aim was deadly accurate. His bullet caught McNab somewhere on the upper right shoulder but he kept on coming. Another mortar round came in and McNab hit the ground, losing his weapon as he did. The shoulder injury was taking effect. MacDara was now within twenty yards and he could smell the kill but he wanted McNab to suffer. Taking aim he moved steadily towards him, watching the colonel, seeing only the image of a trapped animal. But McNab wasn't going away so easily. He suddenly rolled over and came to his knees, holding a hand grenade in his left hand. MacDara could see the agony as he held it to his chest and pulled the pin with his bad right arm.

The CIRCLE of SODOM
A Gripping New Thriller

MacDara fired again, hitting McNab and spinning him around. The grenade dropped at his feet but McNab summoned up enough energy to move like a man possessed by a demon. MacDara had immediately hit the ground when he saw McNab drop the hand grenade. He didn't see the end. He didn't see McNab reach the shelter of the armory just as it was hit again by another incoming round. McNab never had a chance. But he probably wouldn't have survived MacDara's bullets anyway. Colonel George McNab had fought a losing battle. But Owen MacDara still felt cheated.

Dawn was breaking through the trees and throwing dappled light on the gravel of the parade ground and on the huddle of men sitting in a circle. Other prisoners, in single files of twos and threes, hands in the air, arrived and joined the huddle. The battle was over. Only an occasional shot rang out as the RAT busters mopped up the last holdouts. Casualties were heavy. About one hundred of the Millennium Covenanters had died, over half their numbers. Many more were seriously wounded. Some of them would not survive the evacuation. Twenty-three RAT busters had died, the equivalent of a full platoon. They had paid a heavy price.

Owen MacDara was weary. He joined Captain Dobson in a call to the Situation Room at the White House. They were put through to the President immediately. His first concern were for the families of those who died: "Get me all the information on their families right away. I want to talk with each of them personally. I want them to know, from me, that their sons and husbands gave their lives for their country. I want them to know that the nation owes them."

Only then did his voice change, turning upbeat again, the old confident voice forcing its way through the tiredness. "And the nation owes you too. I am proud of you. I knew you had taken out that computer center the minute it happened. The hacking of our financial networks and phone systems stopped cold. We've

Pat Mullan

also been able to trace the bugs they put in the military software and we're debugging that now. Gentlemen, I want to see you when you get back here. I want to thank you for a job well done."

After the debriefing, MacDara watched Colonel George McNab's body being removed to a litter and placed on board a waiting field ambulance. Only then did he accept the hot mug of coffee proffered to him by Lieutenant Mullery. But he got no time to rest. Shields was looking for him. He'd left two urgent messages at Field Ops Command during the action. Fields Ops patched him through, on a secure line, to Shields. Shields's voice sounded gravelly, stressed. He didn't mince his words.

"Owen, better get a grip on yourself. Kate is missing."

"What do you mean she's missing?"

"Both of our agents are dead. Shot. On the beach at Dune Road. Kate's gone. We're assuming she's been kidnapped. Liz Russo is dead. New York subway. Under a train. They say she jumped. I don't believe it. Before she died she left a message on your answering machine. I think you'd better listen to it. I've got a plane waiting for you at Wilson Field. Get here as fast as you can."

Owen dialled into his answering machine and listened to his messages. There were five. The cleaners called twice reminding him that his suit was ready. Doc Levin's office called to set up another appointment. The fourth message was Liz. She sounded rushed, anxious; the words came in short salvos.

"Owen, this is Liz. Listen. They're going to kidnap Kate. This is not a joke They're planning to kill you...Owen, I don't know what this is all about...Tony Thackeray wants you dead. I overheard him. I've got to go."

Confirmation came in that last message.

"MacDara, we've got your lady. If you want to see her again you will follow our instructions. Exactly. We will contact you in twenty-four hours."

The CIRCLE of SODOM
A Gripping New Thriller

Owen was the only passenger on the Learjet as it took off from Wilson Field. Croissants and coffee awaited when he got on board. Daily papers and a selection of magazines had been provided. But he couldn't relax or concentrate enough to read. Kate was their captive. His mind ran through the full gamut of his fears and imaginings. His own recent captivity only enhanced those fears. Kate could be injured. Raped. Dead.

He told himself he had to regain control. He had to remain calm. Then the fear and imaginings ceased just as quickly as they had commenced. Now he didn't feel angry. Just cold and icy inside. He wanted Kate back safely, but he wanted to see Thackeray dead. He wanted to exterminate him, just like a bug. This was a side of himself that rarely appeared. Owen knew it was there. He'd experienced it before. Something genetic, ancestral. A cold, dead feeling, unemotional and unexcitable. He was ready to kill.

Pat Mullan

THIRTY-FOUR

**Alligator Alley, Florida,
1800 hours, Monday March 27, 2000**

Javier Uribe had been waiting at the layby on Alligator Alley for thirty minutes. He had been punctual as usual but there was still no sign of the Feds. Even though it was six o'clock in the evening the temperature was still in the nineties and the heat was oppressive.

Alligator Alley, appropriately named, bisected Florida, joining the West Coast with the East. The Feds had assembled at Fort Myers on the West Coast and would be travelling south until they reached Naples, where they'd make an almost right-angled turn to their left and head directly east across the Everglades. Uribe was sweating profusely. He had pulled his car into the layby, but he couldn't keep the engine running constantly just to maintain the flow of cool air. He had closed his windows to block out the mosquitoes. They were big and ferocious here and congregated around discarded waste on these laybys. They also attacked in dense clusters, like locusts. If they ever got inside his car he'd have an entirely different war on his hands. As he contemplated hordes of black mosquitoes sucking

The CIRCLE of SODOM
A Gripping New Thriller

his blood like leeches, an unmarked grey Ford Taurus pulled in beside him followed by two Greyhound tour buses. A stocky man in navy blue coveralls got out of the Taurus and walked over. Javier Uribe risked rolling down his window.

"I'm Special Agent Dan Bredin. Javier Uribe?"

"That's right. You got here in the nick of time!"

Preliminaries out of the way, Uribe joined Bredin and two other Feds in the Taurus to review the game plan for the assault on the Circle. Javier was a quick study. He'd been on many special assignments for General Shields. His target this time was the person who called himself the Chosen One. Take him alive, but take him, Shields had said. This should be a piece of cake, Javier thought.

An hour later, the combined force of eighty Feds, eighty-one counting Javier Uribe, had assembled a mile away from the El Habesh mosque in Dania. It was 1930 hours on Monday evening. Services at the mosque always commenced around 2000 hours on Mondays, Thursdays and Saturdays. They were sure to net ninety percent of the cult. And the President had said he didn't want a repeat of Waco. Special Agent Bredin had had that impressed upon him forcefully by Director Redington. Well, logistically they couldn't repeat Waco if they tried. The Feds at Waco had stormed that compound with tanks and pumped the place full of CS gas. Bredin had CS gas with him, but he certainly didn't have any tanks.

This was not going to be a 'megaphone' assault. Nobody would warn anyone in advance. There was no need for that. Redington and Bredin didn't want a media spectacle played out over the nation's networks. Quick and deadly, if necessary. That was Redington's directive.

Bredin had split his force; thirty surrounding the mosque would play a rearguard action and close the net on any brethren who tried to escape. The remainder were divided into two teams: one team headed by Dan Bredin would enter the south door at

Pat Mullan

the same time as the other team, accompanied by Javier Uribe, entered through the north door.

The place looked eerie from the outside. Amber lights, casting an almost phosphorescent glow, illuminated both entrances. Spotlights on the grounds cast halo-like beams around the dome, giving the entitre building a supernatural appearance.

Bredin and Uribe were unprepared for the sight that met their eyes. Two brothers, one on each side of the central chamber, were swinging incense burners just like automatons. White-robed brethren lay side by side in two circles covering the entire floor of the chamber, their feet pointed towards the central altar. At first Javier Uribe thought he was witnessing a solemn ceremony. Until he saw the blood. Splashes of red everywhere, on the white robes and the floor, almost as though it had been thrown there by some maniacal Jackson Pollock. Bredin and Uribe's teams converged, in total silence, and stepped over the bodies, almost in slow motion, moving towards the central altar and that coiled red snake that looked as though it were poised to strike.

The first four Federal Officers died instantly. Maybe they were the lucky ones. No one had noticed the two brothers exchange their incense burners for the Uzis secreted under their robes. The Feds returned fire, trying to seek cover behind the bodies on the floor as doors opened on the perimeter of the chamber and a dozen of the Inner Circle rushed them, firing as they ran. Javier Uribe, Dan Bredin and about twenty of their men sought shelter behind the altar. They didn't know that the altar had been booby trapped with enough high explosive to topple a ten-storey building.

The thirty Feds surrounding the mosque were blinded by the explosion and fire. The mosque seemed to disintegrate before their eyes, flames and smoke belching into the night air. Sparks and pieces of burning debris flew like shrapnel, setting fire to the hills of used tires stacked nearby.

Nobody survived the explosion.

The CIRCLE of SODOM
A Gripping New Thriller

THIRTY-FIVE

Monday March 27, 2000

Kate didn't know how much time had passed. Strangely enough, she had been dozing. The steady rumble of the engine combined with the rolling motion of the van had made her drowsy. The silence awoke her. The van had stopped and the rear doors were open. Sal jumped in and came towards her.

"We just passed a hick gas station. I'm goin' back to fill her up. You can't get outta here. Just in case you feel like yelling."

Then he moved behind her and told her to open her mouth. He put a rolled up cloth on her tongue. It tasted foul. He then tied a gag over her mouth. Kate's heart was pounding fast and she felt as though she was choking. Sal closed the van door and got behind the wheel again. She could feel the van sway as it turned around. Almost immediately it stopped and soon she heard the gas pumping. Self service. As soon as the pumping ended she heard Sal walk away. It was at least ten minutes before he returned. Then he started the engine and drove off. She was still gagged.

Kate knew they must have entered a major roadway. The van had stopped. She could hear the noise of other traffic. Then they turned right. It felt as though they were on a two-lane highway. They didn't remain on it for very long. Maybe three or four miles later the van slowed again and made another right turn. She could hear the traffic receding into the distance. Now there was only the rumble of the van's engine again. They had left the highway.

The road got bumpier and bumpier; then, suddenly, the van stopped. Sal turned off the engine, opened the doors and told Kate to climb out. It was dark, pitch black, no moon, no stars. He led her to a building, opened a creaking wooden door and guided her inside. It smelt musty and damp. He handcuffed her left wrist to what felt like a perpendicular iron bar. He dragged over a hard wooden chair and told her to sit. Then he removed her gags. Kate was too frightened to speak.

"I brought you some chow. Sandwiches and coke. I'll be gone for about an hour. I won't gag you again. There's no point in yelling. Not a soul would hear you out here".

Moments later Kate heard the engine start and the van leave. Now there was total silence. A silence that was deafening.

The Learjet had brought him to Washington before noon. He had been debriefed by Shields, checked into his hotel, soaked in the bathtub for the best part of an hour, caught a badly needed two-hour nap, then ordered a meal in his room while he contemplated his next move. He didn't have to wait long. When he heard the knock on his door he opened it, anticipating room service with his meal. Instead it was the bellboy delivering a letter. Finding a couple of dollars to tip him, he closed the door and examined the ordinary brown business envelope with his name typed on the outside. He tore it open. It contained one plain white typewritten page with the words *Your instructions* typed across the top of the page. It had been brief and unambiguous: *If you want to see Kate Whiteside again - go to McGinty's and wait.*

The CIRCLE of SODOM
A Gripping New Thriller

He could feel the adrenalin kicking in, his heart beating faster, unconnected thoughts crowding his mind: *Who sent this? How did they know where to find me? They knew I was meeting with Shields. The President was right: moles everywhere.* Well, they had kept the promise they had left on his answering machine. The words were still branded on his mind: "MacDara, we've got your lady. If you want to see her again you will follow our instructions. Exactly. We will contact you in twenty-four hours."

The note had told him how to get to McGinty's. He found it with ease. It was the only bar in its neighborhood. The lights were so low that only the outline of the wood on the long bar on his left was discernible. One disinterested patron sat slumped over a beer while the seedy looking bartender wiped a glass and watched some banal TV program blaring from a small black and white set mounted high over the bar.

Owen sat down at the bar until his eyes adjusted to the light. McGinty's was a long cavernous place with a very low ceiling. He could only see about one-third of the way inside. But the clack of balls hitting balls told him that there was a pool table somewhere in those inner reaches. And Glen Campbell singing '...by the time I get to Phoenix...' told him that someone was playing a jukebox.

The bartender finally looked at him and nodded. MacDara ordered a Bud. He took a slug, picked up the bottle and decided to reconnoiter. As he walked deeper into the bar he saw the jukebox in a smoke-filled alcove on the right. A sleazy blonde, old before her time, was sucking on a cigarette and punching the buttons for more selections. She never gave him a glance.

The ceiling in the poolroom seemed to be even lower and the ventilation poorer. Stale smoke clung to his nostrils and fresh smoke shrouded the interior in a haze alleviated only by two low hanging lamps in chipped green shades centered over the pool tables. The nearest table was idle. Two males were playing eight-ball at the other one. A young man hovered nearby, lighting a

Pat Mullan

cigarette from the butt of the one he had just smoked. A fourth male, wiry, dark, with a thin ferret-like face, sat on a barstool in the corner sipping a can of beer. Nobody spoke or even acknowledged his presence. The only sound came from the clacking of the balls and the muffled refrain of Glen Campbell. MacDara walked deeper into the room until he reached the table with the action.

The two players couldn't have been more different in appearance. One was wearing a dark business suit. The jacket hung over a nearby chair. The sleeves on his white shirt were rolled halfway up his forearm and his designer tie was loosened just a fraction at the neck. MacDara estimated his age between twenty-five and thirty. The other player wore jeans with the knees ripped out, a loose T-shirt, dirty sneakers worn down at the heels and long straggly hair tied in a pony tail with a rubber band. He was unshaven and unkempt. The young man who had been hovering close by had moved back into the smoke-filled shadows. MacDara felt uneasy. Nothing he could put his finger on; the kind of feeling that makes you look over your shoulder on a lonely street or turn all the lights on in an empty house.

He turned to leave. Just in time. The heavy end of the cue stick missed his skull and landed with a painful crack on his left shoulder. He fell to his knees, twisting around as he did so. Designer tie was standing there, feet wide apart, wielding the cue stick in an arc as he moved in for the kill. MacDara rolled sideways, hit the ground and came up under designer tie, kicking both heels into the man's testicles. He was back on his feet when ponytail rushed him with a blade. MacDara circled the table, keeping him at a distance and noticing, out of the corner of his eye, that ferret face was still sitting, unmoved, sipping his beer. The fourth guy was no longer in sight. Ponytail made his move. The blade came slicing through the air, missing MacDara as he ducked but catching the sleazy blonde in the throat as she wandered in to see what all the commotion was about. She staggered a couple of paces, a look of astonishment on her face, while her jugular began to spurt her life away.

MacDara had pulled from his shoulder holster the .45 Shields had given him. Taking dead aim, he put a bullet into ponytail's midriff, doubling him over. Flashes of gunfire erupted in front of him and splinters flew from the corner of the table. The fourth player had joined the action. MacDara hit the floor and started crawling. He'd heard the shots, seen the flashes, but couldn't get a fix on a target. Reaching the end of the table, he decided to make a run for it. He got to his knees and, still holding the .45 in his right hand, used the fingertips of his left to spring himself into a dash. A dash right into a bullet. It grazed his upper arm, slicing through the skin and drawing blood. He rolled again and came up firing in the direction of the gunfire. Accurate or lucky, it didn't matter to MacDara. Either way, the fourth man had just staggered out of the shadows, crumbling to his knees, his weapon clattering to the floor. Crouching there, holding his bleeding right arm, MacDara noticed that ferret face was no longer sitting on the bar stool sipping his beer. But he hadn't left. He was lying on the ground moaning and holding his left leg. MacDara knelt down beside him and put the gun to his head: "Where's Kate? Where is she? What have you done with her? I'll give you twenty seconds. Then I'm going to blow your brains out!"

"No, man, no! She's OK! I promise, man! I'll take you to her!" beseeched Sal, as he writhed in pain.

MacDara put the gun back in his shoulder holster, bandaged his upper arm with a strip from his own shirt, fixed a makeshift tourniquet on Sal's leg, then, supporting him on his good leg, stepped over the carnage, noting that the bartender was nowhere in sight as they left.

Moonlight shone a beam through a broken pane of glass in the small dirty window midway up the wall, illuminating the ground in front of Kate and reaching into the darkest corners.

Pat Mullan

She could see that she was being held in some disused commercial building. The walls were cinderblock and the floor looked like it was composed of hard packed dirt. Cobwebs and dust clung everywhere. Old wooden crates were stacked in a corner and bits of cardboard and other packing debris littered the floor. Apart from the chair she was sitting on, there wasn't another stick of furniture in the place. She was hoping there were no rats, and had reconciled herself to a night of lonely waiting when she heard the sound of a vehicle, growing louder as it approached, and the screech of brakes as it pulled up outside. She'd recognize that screech anywhere. Sal was back, and she steeled herself for what was to come. As the door was wrenched open, the sound of its rusted hinges sent a tingle down her spine. Someone approached from the dark reaches of the building and she knew it wasn't Sal. Sal dragged his feet as he walked.

She thought she must be dreaming as he walked into the moonlight. But he kept coming, knelt down beside her without saying a word and hugged her.

"Oh, Owen," she sobbed. All her stoicism vanished into tears of joy and tears of fear. Joy at being in Owen's arms. Fear as a delayed reaction to the terrible trauma she had suffered. Owen had the key to the handcuffs and he released her, took her in his arms and just held her - it seemed for ever.

It didn't take much to make Sal talk. MacDara didn't even have to threaten him. Sal was supposed to have contacted his boss as soon as MacDara had been disposed of. He would then have been told what to do with the girl. Sal gave him the phone number. It was a number that he easily recognized: Senator Sumner Hardy's home in Blacksburg. He assumed that Thackeray planned to be there tonight. Sal never mentioned Thackeray by name, but then he wouldn't have known his boss's real name anyway. Owen decided to surprise them with an unannounced visit.

The CIRCLE of SODOM
A Gripping New Thriller

General Zachary Walker seethed with anger. He had been there when Bart Shields had called Owen MacDara. Their euphoria at the success of the mission against McNab and his Covenanters was short-lived when they learned of the killing of their agents in the Hamptons and the kidnapping of Kate Whiteside.

It was a private agony, a private hell. He hadn't seen his daughter since she was a little girl. And even that had been pure chance. He had bumped into Henry, Ruth and Kate at Dulles International Airport. Ruth had said, 'Zachary, this is our daughter, Kate,' and he had smiled and said how pretty she was. He had not seen her since. He hadn't wanted to. It would have been too painful. She looked so much like Joy-San.

He had to try and find her. He didn't know this man Thackeray and he didn't know where to find him. But Senator Sam would know. He and Thackeray were partners in this madness. He only knew of one place to begin. The Hardy Mansion.

The Hardy Mansion, Blacksburg, Virginia, 2:00 am, Tuesday March 28, 2000

It was two in the morning. Senator Sam Hardy and Tony Thackeray were alone in the Hardy Mansion. The senator had alternated between here and his Washington townhouse as the 'war' had progressed. Finally, he had moved to Blacksburg two days ago, dismissed the servants and was spending his time trying to snatch victory from the jaws of defeat. He was losing the infowar and with it the leverage he needed to topple the President. A bloody coup had never been an option. His compatriots would never have countenanced that. Neither would the American people. So, he had spent the last few days trying to convince the others that they could still remove the President from the White House and get away with it. He tried to prove

Pat Mullan

that the country did not have to be on the verge of chaos to give them the imperative to act. But they had all got cold feet. In these waning hours the senator realized that they had lost. The death of George McNab and the destruction of his computer facility had effectively ended their capability to wage the infowar. Sure, there were still some viruses and 'time bombs' lying dormant in military and civilian systems. But they were just like landmines at the end of a war. They'd be sought out and destroyed and, if one did go off, the damage would always be limited.

"What will you do now, Sam?" asked Tony Thackeray.

"Nothing! There will be no inquisition. It would backfire on the President. If he ever permitted the events of these last weeks to be exposed to the intense scrutiny of a national investigation, he would lose more than we would. Remember this: I still have the allegiance of the American people. And I'll prove that at the next election. No, the President will tell the American people that these acts have been the insane work of right wing extremist militias. The same extremists that bombed Oklahoma. He'll take the glory for the destruction of McNab and his Millennium Covenant. And we'll stand back and let McNab take the blame for everything," said the senator.

"But the President knows the real story," said Thackeray.

"Yes. But he can't do a damn thing about it! I'll remind him of that." The senator was talking as though nothing had happened, as though the power he had held before he launched the infowar was undiminished. Looking at Tony Thackeray, he said, "And he can't do a damn thing about you, either. There's no proof that you were involved in any of this. Unless they take the word of that fellow, MacDara. By the way, what the hell happened to him?"

Tony Thackeray smiled for the first time that evening. "Owen MacDara won't be giving us any more trouble after tonight. I can assure you of that, senator."

The CIRCLE of SODOM
A Gripping New Thriller

Thackeray's sense of smugness was shaken at that moment by the ringing of the doorbell. After four or five rings it stopped and they both waited in suspense. No one was expected, the servants were gone and it was well after two am. Maybe if they waited whoever it was would go away. But the ringing started again, relentlessly this time. Whoever was out there was insistent. The senator decided he'd better see who it was. Both he and Tony Thackeray were armed so they didn't feel defenseless. Still, the senator was relieved when he discovered General Zachary Walker standing, impatiently, at the front door.

"Zachary, my God! What brings you here at this time of night?" greeted the senator.

Zachary Walker didn't respond. Grimly, he brushed past the senator into the entrance hall, where Tony Thackeray stood expectantly at the open door to the drawing room. Still silent, General Walker marched across the hall and into the drawing room without even a nod to Thackeray. The senator followed, exchanging a quizzical stare with Thackeray. All three of them were now standing there, face to face. General Walker looked terrifying. His usual solemn countenance was transformed into fierceness by whatever demon had him in its grasp.

"Sam, I want you to tell me where she is!" ordered the general.

"Zach, what the hell are you talking about? Are you all right?" asked the senator, completely baffled.

"Who are you?" Walker barked at Tony Thackeray.

"Tony Thackeray. I'm a guest of the senator's," responded Thackeray, in a conciliatory tone.

"So, I finally get to meet you. I have only one question for you and I want an answer. What have you done with Kate Whiteside? Where is she?"

Senator Sam Hardy now knew what Thackeray had meant when he said that MacDara wouldn't be giving them any more trouble. He knew that Owen MacDara and Kate Whiteside had become lovers. They were together in Palm Springs the last time

Pat Mullan

that Thackeray had blown it. *So he's taken the girl to get MacDara. So what! Why has that gotten Zach so riled up? There's something here I don't understand,* thought the senator.

"Why are you so riled about this Kate Whiteside?" asked Hardy, quite unprepared for the shock he was about to receive.

"She's my daughter, that's why!" screamed Walker.

At that very moment, Owen swung the van carrying himself, Kate and a badly wounded Sal on to the avenue of the Hardy Mansion. MacDara reckoned that if the senator and Thackeray were here they would not be expecting guests. Otherwise, they'd have posted guards at the gate. He parked the van near the front door, gave the .45 to Kate and asked her to keep it on Sal. Sal might be in poor shape but he still didn't trust him. He took Sal's Uzi and headed for the house.

He'd never been here before and he certainly didn't intend announcing his presence by ringing the doorbell. He could see one lighted window, at ground floor level, midway along the side of the house. He skirted the front and took the concrete pathway around the side. As he got closer he could see that the light was coming from french windows that led onto a small patio looking over the mansion's extensive gardens. Heavy drapes prevented him from seeing into the room. MacDara could hear voices, raised in anger it seemed. But he couldn't understand what was being said. To hell with it, he thought. If possession is nine-tenths of the law, then surprise has to be good for nine-tenths of the action.

Events had gone from bad to worse in the Hardy drawing room. General Zachary Walker was a man possessed. He had pulled a gun from his overcoat and, clasping it in both hands, was now pointing it at Tony Thackeray: "I can blow you away right here, Your Lordship," he mocked, "but you're not worth the cost of the ammunition. So I'll give you one last choice to save your ass. Take me to Kate. Now!"

The CIRCLE of SODOM
A Gripping New Thriller

The senator's hand held firmly to the gun in his pocket. For the last couple of minutes General Walker had devoted his attention to Tony Thackeray. But Senator Hardy knew that, if he had to make a choice, he'd shoot Zach Walker. In a way, he had no choice. But the senator never got to play his hand.

The breaking of the glass in the french windows startled them. Senator Hardy pulled the gun from his pocket and backed towards the hall door. General Walker froze in place with his head twisted towards the french windows and his weapon still levelled at Tony Thackeray. The drapes surrounding the window billowed out, as if pregnant, and just as quickly delivered their surprise. Owen MacDara stood there, holding the Uzi, equally surprised to see General Walker. He moved forward into the room, covering everyone with the Uzi: "General, I didn't expect to find you here," he said and then looking at the senator: "Move away, Senator Hardy. I came here for one reason only. To kill you, Thackeray. You killed Liz Russo. I can't prove that. I just know it. And you kidnapped Kate to get to me. What were you going to do with her after you took care of me? Kill her too? Give her to your mad dogs to play with? But your dogs fucked up again, Thackeray!"

"Where is Kate? Is she alright?" Zach Walker's voice was strained to breaking point. But before Owen had a chance to reply he was answered by more glass crashing from the french windows.

Kate was violently pushed into the room by Sal, hobbling behind her, holding the gun on her and screaming, "Here she is! I delivered her! I kept my word!"

Perfect timing for Thackeray, who leapt for the nearest cover and came up firing at Owen, who hit the ground, diving to get close to Kate to protect her. He would have been too late. Zachary Walker, jolted out of his fixation on Thackeray, jumped across the room and pushed Kate behind him. Thackeray's bullet caught him in the chest but he just stood there in front of her,

Pat Mullan

shielding her, as the second bullet severed his aorta. He crumbled to the floor at Kate's feet.

Sal had been caught in the crossfire. The socket of his left eye was missing and he lay there staring, quite dead, from that one open eye. Owen had stopped firing. Thackeray and the senator had made their escape from the room in the heat of battle but Owen didn't follow. Kate was his priority.

Kate just sat there, cradling Zachary Walker's head in her lap. Owen knew there was no hope. Zach seemed to be struggling to say something to Kate, but the words never came. Kate leant down and whispered in his ear. She told him that she loved him. And she called him Daddy. He died then, in her arms. Owen could swear that he saw the shadow of a smile on Zachary's face in those last seconds.

They were halfway to Thackeray's car when the senator stopped. Running from his own home was a panic reaction. He had no reason to run. The President could do nothing to him. All the mayhem back there had nothing to do with him. Nothing at all. Thackeray looked over his shoulder. Senator Hardy just stood there.

"I'm staying. I have no reason to leave my home."

"The Chairman of the Joint Chiefs is killed in your home! And you have no reason to leave?" said Thackeray, incredulously.

"That's exactly right. My judgement hasn't changed. The President will do nothing. We'll mop this mess up. I'm sure Walker's death will be given a heroic explanation. You'd better go," replied the senator, with a cold logic, as he turned his back on Thackeray and walked, unhurriedly, towards his front door. But he'd never reach it. He realized that too late when he heard the click. The bullet left a neat entry hole, framed in powder burns, behind his left ear. He didn't hear Tony Thackeray bid him a last farewell.

The CIRCLE of SODOM
A Gripping New Thriller

THIRTY-SIX

**The Doldergrand Hotel, Zurich,
4:00 pm, Thursday March 30, 2000**

James Joyce said that the weather in Zurich was like a baby's bottom, which meant that it could rain on you unexpectedly. That's exactly what it did when Claude Fymat stepped out of his car in front of the Doldergrand. He sprinted the last few yards into the hotel, suffering only a few damp spots, which didn't show up on his blue serge suit.

It was four pm and the restaurant at the Doldergrand was empty. Well, almost empty. One man occupied a table at the very rear of the restaurant. A pot of espresso and a bottle of sparkling San Pellegrino sat in the middle of the table. Claude Fymat strode directly there, and the man stood up to greet him. Claude Fymat noted that there was nothing in Tony Thackeray's demeanor to give even a hint of the crises he'd been through in recent days.

Tony Thackeray was talking. Claude Fymat was listening: "Hardy was premature. America wasn't ready. But they will be, Claude. Soon. And, when they're ready, they'll know themselves. Then they'll take charge of their own destiny again.

Dump the rot overboard. Just like they did with that tea in Boston Harbour. We didn't lose. We only postponed the inevitable."

Fymat could see the old familiar messianic look in Thackeray's eyes as he continued.

"We have work to do. We will meet Tsu three days from now in Beijing. You will return after that meeting. I will continue to Moscow and St. Petersburg."

They left the Doldergrand an hour later. No one saw them.

The CIRCLE of SODOM
A Gripping New Thriller

EPILOGUE

**Dune Road, The Hamptons,
Thursday March 30, 2000**

They were packed and ready. The Aer Lingus flight was scheduled to leave Kennedy in two hours time. MacDara had told Shields he didn't want to be around. It was over. The President would never acknowledge the role he had played in recent weeks. He knew that. And that's the way he wanted it. He had taken the call from the White House this morning and had graciously accepted the President's thanks. As well as the invitation for both himself and Kate to spend a week at Camp David upon their return.

**Ardree House, Connemara, Ireland,
Friday March 31, 2000**

It was a bright, clear evening. Owen and Kate stood close together at the edge of the boat jetty. The sky was a sheet of pale turquoise between blankets of orange. Slate-grey and purple clouds sat low on the hills beyond the lough. The water had tints of orange and red, and dappled grey waves shimmered on its surface.

Owen could feel dusk descending. It was almost five thirty. Time to go inside and turn on CNN. It would be 12:30 pm in Washington and the President would be talking to the American people and to the world.

The CIRCLE of SODOM
A Gripping New Thriller

**More
Pat Mullan!**

**Please turn this page
for an
excerpt from**

WHO KILLED HAMMARSKJOLD?

arriving very, very soon

Pat Mullan

WHO KILLED HAMMARSKJOLD?

by

Pat Mullan

PLOT TO KILL HAMMARSKJOLD

CAPE TOWN - South Africa's truth commission chairman, Archbishop Desmond Tutu, yesterday released documents that he said suggested a Western plot was behind the death of the head of the United Nations in 1961. Tutu said the Truth and Reconciliation Commission, which is investigating apartheid-era crimes, decided to release the documents although it could not verify their authenticity. "The commission has discovered…documents discussing the sabotage of the aircraft in which the UN secretary general, Dag Hammarskjold, died on the night of September 17 to 18, 1961", he said.

The letters, under the heading the South African Institute for Maritime Research, or SAIMR - said to be a front for the South African military - include reference to the US Central Intelligence Agency and the British MI5 security service. "In a meeting between MI5, special ops executive and the SAIMR, the following emerged," reads one document marked Top Secret, "it is felt that Hammarskjold should be removed." The document said, "I want his removal to be handled more efficiently than was Patrice." The CIA last year opened its files on Cold War assassinations and admitted it ordered the murder of Patrice Lumumba, Congolese independence hero and pro-Soviet prime minister. Another letter headed 'Operation Celeste' details orders to plant in the wheel bay of an aircraft explosives primed to go off as the wheels were retracted on takeoff. Hammarskjold and fifteen others were killed when their aircraft crashed entering what was then Northern Rhodesia, now Zambia, where the UN head was due to meet rebel leader Moise Tshombe to negotiate a truce in the Congolese civil war.

The UN sent a peacekeeping force to newly liberated Congo in 1960 when the new government asked for help in the face of mutiny in its army, secession in Tshombe's Katanga province, and the intervention of Belgian troops. Newspapers at the time alleged British involvement in a plot to kill Hammarskjold to prevent UN support for Tshombe and his diamond-rich Katanga province.

"We have it on good authority that UNO (the UN Organization) will want to get its greedy paws on the province," reads a letter dated July 12, 1960. The letters came to light as truth commission researchers were combing South African security documents in preparation for the commission's final report. Tutu said the commission mandate to investigate such matters expired at the end of July, and the commission therefore decided to publish the documents *with names of individuals deleted* and hand them to Justice Minister Dullah Omar. The archbishop said he hoped releasing the documents would help set an example for more openness in government.

REUTERS, August 24, 1998.

Extract from the novel
©*Who Killed Hammarskjold?*

Leopoldville
The Congo
Africa

1961

The two men waited uneasily in the shabby little office stuck to the side of the empty hangar. The airfield had been abandoned months before, its pockmarked runway testimony to the fierce fighting that had taken place. Silence descended between them. The American stretched his body awkwardly into the old swivel chair and used the open desk drawer to support his left foot. He lit another Chesterfield from the dying butt between his lips. The Russian paced relentlessly back and forth past the small, grimy window, peering out into the dusk and stopping frequently to listen.

It was the American who heard it first. He stubbed out his Chesterfield in the overflowing ashtray, pushed the chair out of his way and took two long strides to the window. The Russian stopped his pacing. They both stood there, side by side, ears straining.
"Yup! That's it. Listen", said Kearns.
"Da! Da! Now I hear", said Zhukov.
The faint rumble grew louder, very soon turning into the steady throb of a jeep's engine. Two dim lights in the distance became brighter until the jeep stopped about a hundred yards

from the hangar. A figure emerged, moving towards them in a loping gait. Zhukov held the door ajar for him. The light from the naked bulb in the ceiling struck him as he entered. He was a big man, over six feet, wiry and lean. His waterproof overcoat was open, revealing combat fatigues underneath and the insignia of a Major in the mercenary command of Colonel 'Mad Mike' Hoare.

"How did it go?", asked Kearns.

"Easy as pie, old boy", responded the Major in an accent more Anglo-Irish than English.

"You will be successful, yes?", Zhukov asked.

"Do you doubt me, Comrade?", asked the Major.

"Nyet! Nyet!", said Zhukov," we are anxious, that's all."

"There's a lot riding on your success, Major", said Kearns.

The Major strode further into the office, removed his overcoat and seated himself on the edge of the desk. He helped himself to one of the American's Chesterfields. Then he stood up again and took a pen from the pocket of his fatigue jacket. Telescoping it into a pointer, he walked over to the aging map of the Congo that hung from the office wall.

Taking a mouthful of smoke deep into his lungs, he began.

"He'll land here, at Kamina. Then he'll travel overland to his meeting with Mobutu. Three hours later he will return by a different route. This one. Precaution. For his safety. The plane will be refuelled and prepared for his flight to Ndola to meet Tshombe. But he will never reach Ndola!"

The Major returned the pointer to his pocket, stubbed out the remainder of the Chesterfield, picked up his overcoat, and said; "Gentlemen, I believe you owe me something."

Kearns already had the envelope in his hand.

"Major, a deposit to your account. As agreed. 50% now and 50% when the job is done...I know...You'll just have to trust us on that. Just as we trust you now."

"Thank you, Gentlemen", said the Major, turning at the door as he left, "we will not see each other again."

They stood together at the window, watching the Major's loping gait merge with the dark silhouette of the jeep, listening to the engine come alive, and seeing the red taillights recede into the dusk of early evening.

Three days later the plane carrying UN Secretary-General Dag Hammarskjold and his entourage crashed, killing all on board.

Khimki Woods, Moscow

Gathering ferns was an annual Spring ritual for Sasha and Irina. Their mother cooked the fern stems, added spices, and served them as a family delicacy. The forest is central in Russian folklore and is seen as a source of food and protection. In the fall it provides mushrooms, nuts and berries and always ferns in Springtime. But the forest can be a malevolent force too. Folktales talk of the evil witch, *Baba Yaga*, and the female hobgoblins, the *kikimoras*. They punish anyone who enters the forest to do bad things.

Sasha and Irina were so busy gathering ferns that they had lost all sense of time and direction. It was only when Sasha looked around and couldn't see Irina that she became worried. Turning back, she tried to retrace her steps but the sun was beginning to set and its dying rays were penetrating the treetops. Feeling panic, she called Irina's name louder and louder, but there was no answer. She started to run, but the forest floor was littered with obstacles. Her foot caught a root and she stumbled. Instead of trying to break her own fall she clung to her precious ferns, afraid of losing them. Pitched forward, her head hit a fallen tree, stunning her. Everything seemed to be getting darker and darker and she thought she might be losing consciousness. But she didn't.

She lay there for a while feeling the pain in her head begin to throb. Then she got up slowly and started looking for her sister again. She walked this time, calling Irina's name over and over again. Finally, she heard the screams. Terrifying screams. Her sister's screams. Ignoring her own safety, she dropped her precious ferns and ran towards the screams.

Minutes later she saw her. Irina was standing with her back firmly against a tree, her arms behind her holding the treetrunk, looking as though she had been impaled there. Her screams had been replaced by loud sobbing. Sasha ran towards her and tried to take her in her arms, asking her over and over again what was wrong, but Irina wouldn't budge. Sasha saw the terror in her sister's eyes and turned in the direction she was staring.

She saw the dim outline of a car but nothing else. Letting go of Irina, she approached the car slowly. It was an old car, a Lada. She was almost on top of the car before she saw them. Her hands automatically flew to her mouth to stifle her own screams. But she knew she had to remain in control. For her sister's sake. Slowly her mind began to comprehend what her eyes were telling her.

The woman was lying on her side with her face pressed against the window. Her eye was open and staring, left like that when rigor mortis set in. The other side of her face was missing entirely. Just a bloody pulp, with one eyeball dangling where her cheekbone should have been. Bits of flesh and clotted blood had pebbledashed the inside of the windscreen. The man was sitting upright, too upright, behind the steering wheel. A shotgun was braced between his knees, the muzzle in his mouth, and his finger wrapped around the trigger. His brains were sprayed all over the car.

The official news release, buried in small print in the Moscow Daily News, simply stated that Leonid Fomin and his wife had ended their life in a murder suicide pact brought on by the husband's gambling debts and their mutual descent into alcoholism and despair.

Shannon, Ireland.

'THE GREEN IRELAND OF YOUR ANCESTORS'
Dr. Ernesto 'Che' Guevara Lynch de la Serna

Aeroflot Flight 697 landed at 2:30 pm, just fifteeen minutes later than scheduled. Conor Brady grabbed his carryon bag and was one of the first off the plane. His Irish passport propelled him through and soon he was turning the keys in his rented car. Conor was no stranger to Ireland. This was his fourth visit since he had left Argentina. His trips to Ireland had been necessary. Necessary for his own soul, necessary for his own identity, necessary for his understanding of his grandfather, necessary to help him survive under a false name. It was the 'green Ireland of his ancestors'. Those words had branded his soul ever since the day he saw the postcard that Che Guevara had sent to his father from Dublin in 1964. His mind's eye still saw the words *'I am in the green Ireland of your ancestors. When the television found out they came to ask me about the genealogy of the Lynches'*.

But he wasn't thinking about any of this as he maneuvered the car through Shannon and headed for Ennis and Galway. He was thinking instead about Owen MacDara. He was troubled by his mission this time. Usually he never gave these assignments a second thought. Always the target was nothing more than a target. A cardboard cutout. Maybe it was MacDara's Irishness that bothered him. No, he thought about that for a minute. He had no compunction about taking out an Argentinian. Why should it be any different with an Irishman? Maybe it was curiosity? Maybe it was the need to know the victim? Maybe he was losing it? Whatever it was, something inside him made him want to meet MacDara, made him want to see what made MacDara tick. Maybe it was the need to find a victim worthy of his skills. Maybe he wanted to risk himself this time. Maybe it was boredom. He had briefed himself well on Owen MacDara: born in Ireland, paramedic in the US Army in Korea, black belt in Karate, founder of his own consulting company, self-made millionaire, special agent for the President of the United States, lost his pregnant Kate only a year ago, and now the biggest obstacle for Misha. Yes, he had to meet MacDara.

Conor was still trying to come to grips with this behavior of his when he realized that the city of Galway was behind him and he was squeezing his car through the crowded narrow streets of Oughterard, the village beside Lough Corrib. He pulled the car over, stopped and ran in to Keogh's, the little village supermarket, to satisfy his addiction for a Coke. His non-alcoholic beverage of choice. As he paid for it the mounted photo of Bob Hope taken on his last visit was proudly displayed over the cash register. To Conor's curious look, the lady at the register said, "Ah, sure he's just a darlin' man. Comes here all the time. To visit his daughter, you know. She's been livin' here for years."

As Conor slid the coke into the slot beside the ashtray and slipped the car into first gear he thought that the little scene involving Bob Hope's picture defined the Ireland that he'd come to know. A place where everybody knew everybody. Small enough for the famous and the notorious to rub shoulders in the nearest pub with the locals. A place where nobody was unduly impressed by celebrity. A place where people respected your privacy. A good place for a Conor Brady.

A few minutes later the landscape changed dramatically. The green fields were gone. Replaced by brown heather dotted with clumps of yellow gorse running down to shimmering water sparkling like diamonds. And bogland reaching the foothills on the horizon, with the hazy outline of the Maamturk Mountains tracing craggy lines in the sky. He was now in Connemara. Forty five minutes later he reached Clifden, the capital of Connemara, a small market town on the Atlantic shore. He was expected at the Abbeyglen Castle Hotel. He had stayed there before. They made a point of remembering.

Owen MacDara lay on his back about a half mile from Ardree House. His elbows dug into a bed of springy sphagnum moss and he watched a large black bird circle overhead. Soon it was joined by a smaller bird and they climbed higher, two black dots against the blue ceiling. Flying free. That's what Kate and my son are doing now. Their souls are flying free. But I'm not a believer. I don't believe in reincarnation. Still? He pondered deeply as he watched the two birds separate. Now only one remained. The little one. A tiny black speck in that vast expanse of blue. Suddenly, he was twelve years old again, lying out on his father's bog, resting from his morning's turf cutting, watching the lark in the sky above. I wrote a poem about that. I wonder if I can still remember the words. Let me see……

The barking dog brought him out of it. He pressed his hands deep into the moss till he felt firmer ground. Then he leveraged himself to his feet and looked across the hillside. A farmer was herding his sheep, his dog rounding up the strays. It was time to go. He'd flown in from Moscow two days ago and had spent the time tracking down Major Lacey. It hadn't really been very difficult. That's the advantage of Ireland. Small enough that everyone knows everyone else. Or have a sense that they do. One phone call to a friend, a member of the Military History Society of Ireland, and he soon discovered that the Major was in reality Richard de Lacey, the seventh Earl and head of the de Laceys. It was no secret that Lacey had been a mercenary with 'Mad Mike' Hoare in the Congo. Colonel O'Beirne of the Military History Society seemed to take a vicarious pleasure in that when he briefed MacDara. President Mobutu of Zaire employed Hoare in the Congo in the early sixties. Some of the actions of Lacey and his mercenary colleagues, such as rescuing nuns, made heroes of them. But they were totally ruthless. They took no prisoners, especially their Simba rebel captives.

O'Beirne was only too glad to relay stories of these events to MacDara. Especially if it included dinner and copious amounts of his favorite South African pinotage. They were on their second bottle. Actually the Colonel was on their second bottle and MacDara was still on his second glass when the stories started to flow.

"Y'know, Owen", said Colonel O'Beirne, using 'Owen' in that instant intimacy bestowed by alcohol, "this is confidential. Not classified. Not secret, mind you. But, still confidential. Right from the horse's mouth. In Jo'burg."

"Jo'burg?", quizzed MacDara.

"Johannesburg. I was attached to the UN in the seventies and eighties. Ireland, neutral nation and all that. Thought we could be honest brokers between the ANC and the Afrikaners. It was O'Brien's influence, y'know. The Cruiser."

"The Cruiser?", Owen repeated, although he already knew the reference.

"Sure. The Cruiser. Conor Cruise O'Brien. Another relic of the Congo. He was the UN Representative in the Congo in 1961. You knew that, didn't you?"

"Yes, yes. Of course," said MacDara, but the Colonel had moved on, not really waiting for an answer.

"Where was I? Jo'burg?", continued the Colonel, finishing his glass an refilling it. He offered to top up Owen's glass but Owen declined.

"Kruger. That's who told me. He had been there with Lacey. In the Congo. When Mike Hoare formed '4 Commando'. He was never sure of Lacey's standing in the chain of command. As a major Lacey was a rank higher than Hoare's rank of captain."

The Colonel stopped just long enough to gulp down more of the pinotage and then looked intimately at MacDara, "Did you know that about a third of '4 Commando' were South Africans?"

"No, I didn't. Why so many?", asked Owen.

"That's easy! South Africa were up to their ears in the Congo."

Major Lacey was still alive and living only a few miles away. Owen had called that morning and made an appointment. The Major was expecting him at three. He glanced at his watch. Just past noontime.

Conor Brady had also heard the dog barking. He adjusted the right eyepiece of his Nikons and watched the skill of the sheepdog for thirty seconds. For the past hour he'd lain on a rocky, heathery knoll that commanded a view of Ardree House and the surrounding countryside and watched Owen MacDara lying on his back staring at the sky. If only binoculars had the ability to read minds. He'd have given a lot to know what was going through MacDara's head as he lay there staring at the sky, occasionally flicking a hand across his face. A perfect target. I could easily fill my contract right here. Getting away couldn't be easier. There isn't a soul around except for that farmer and his sheepdog. But I'm in no hurry. MacDara has a flight booked to New York three days from now. New York will do fine. He swung the binoculars back in time to see MacDara rise to his feet and walk back towards Ardree House, picking his way through the hidden minefield of bogland swamp. He was beginning to enjoy his cat and mouse game with MacDara. Usually these contracts of Misha's were boring and predictable. Not this time. He was in no hurry to take out MacDara. He put the binoculars back in their case, slung them over his shoulder and began his trek back down to the main road.

MacDara was only six miles from Ardree House on a road that he had travelled numerous times. Yet he couldn't find the major's house. He turned back for the third time, traversing the same stretch of roadway. This time he saw it. The opening was barely visible between overgrown hedgerows and whin bushes. It had to be the entrance, he decided as the bushes brushed the side windows of his car. Once inside he could see that he was on a solid lane, much wider than he expected. It was covered with tufts of grass and weeds, testimony to its lack of use. A jungle of trees lined each side, blocking any vision of what lay beyond. So it was a surprise when he turned a corner to find himself in front of a house that had once been an elegant mansion. The architecture was mixed, part French chateau with Palladian style wings, but it had been allowed to deteriorate. An ornate fountain, now dry and surrounded by ferns and nettles, formed a centerpiece in the middle ground that used to be a circular driveway. As MacDara left his car and walked toward the front door he could imagine other days, days of dinner parties and carriages arriving with ladies and gentlemen in their finery.

MacDara was expected but not at the front door. A door in the right wing was ajar and Major Richard de Lacey, a tall thin, Patrician looking man in his early seventies, extended a bony hand with a remarkably firm grip.

"Mr. MacDara?"

"Please just call me Owen. And thank you for taking the time to see me."

"Do call me Richard. All the 'blow-ins' call me Major but the locals always refer to me as 'His Lordship' although I have never used that ridiculous title. And, Owen, don't thank me. Time is all I have these days. Now, just follow me. Mind your step here. The floor is a bit irregular at this corner."

They negotiated a narrow, dimly-lit corridor whose walls were covered with ancestral paintings, dark in pigment, many of them almost floor to ceiling, until they emerged into a flagstoned entrance hall squared between two enormous fireplaces. MacDara had a glimpse of pistols on the mantlepiece and crossed sabres on the wall as the Major's loping gait seemed to gather speed crossing the hall. Almost in a tour guide voice, without stopping or turning around, the Major said, over his shoulder.

"We haven't used this entrance in years. Not since our grandmother passed away."

Crossing into another corridor extending beyond the central entrance hall they soon reached a large dark green oak door. The major opened it and ushered MacDara inside. The contrast was stark. Comfortable chairs, booklined walls, collectables and art, all warmed by a blazing fire in the hearth made the room personal, lived-in, human.

"Please make yourself comfortable", said the major, directing Owen to a chair by the fire as he crossed the room to an array of drinks displayed on a corner table. "Cognac, Irish, Scotch?"

"A Paddy please, if you have it."

"Indeed I do. I like it myself. Smooth. I'll join you."

The major returned with two large Waterford tumblers generously filled with the amber glow of Paddy. They toasted in the Gaelic.

"Slainte!"

The major didn't sit down. Instead he wandered over to the bookshelves. He looked as though he intended to reach for a volume, then changed his mind and turned to face MacDara. "The original De Lacey came to Ireland in the twelfth century with Strongbow. The Norman Invasion! And you know that Strongbow was Richard de Clare, the Earl of Pembroke, a Norman himself. So when the Irish say that the English invaded Ireland, it was really the Normans, my ancestors. A century or two later we'd become 'more Irish than the Irish themselves'. But you know all that, don't you, Owen?"

"Yes, Richard," said Owen and quickly tried to keep the major from wandering, "the reason I came to see you…"

"I know the reason you came to see me," said the major and then proceeded as though that was unimportant. "How many of us own our ancestral lands today?" It was a rhetorical question. He didn't wait for an answer. "Very few. But we still do. It hasn't been easy. How much do you think it would cost to heat this whole place? The Colonial Service of the Crown. That's how we did it. That's how we kept our lands. We practiced the Art of War and the spoils of those foreign wars paid our servants and our debts. But the Empire ended and we weren't needed."

"And the Congo…?", MacDara tried again.

"What skills did I have. Only those of the warrior. It was either that or lose our lands. Can you see me in some one roomed cottage? Of course you can't. So I fought for the person who paid me the most. Colonel Mike Hoare was a fellow Irishman. He and I served together in the British army. So when he asked me to join him I couldn't refuse."

"But the CIA and MI5……And the KGB?," asked MacDara.

"Oh, don't be so naïve, Owen. I worked for all of them. Numerous times. War is a dirty business!"

"But why the Secretary General of the UN?", MacDara's tone got louder.

"The UN! Hah! They were not peacekeepers. They were up to their eyeballs in that mess in the Congo. The Secretary General was one of their Field Commanders. He was fair game and we weren't playing by the Marquis of Queensbury rules. Besides Colonel Mike could never have paid me what the Yanks and the Russians did. You see, Owen, I would have done anything to save our lands. I did not want to be remembered as the de Lacey who lost the ancestral home and sold off the family titles to some vulgar Texas oil millionaire."

He gulped down his Paddy, refilled his glass and offered Owen another. But Owen declined and went straight to the heart of the matter, his reason for being there.

"Richard, we know from the KGB documents that Zhukov was the Russian who contracted you for the Congo assignment but they didn't give the American's name. Zhukov is dead so he can't tell us. That's why I am here."

"You know, old boy, you really can't prove any of this and I've got little time left so it doesn't matter to me any more. Prostate cancer. Six months at best", said the major, matter of factly, as he finally conceded that his strength had ebbed and sank into the armchair opposite MacDara. Owen waited, sensing that he would get what he came for.

"I never liked the American. A bully, I'd say. It doesn't matter to me if you know his name or not. It was Kearns. Yes, that was it. I don't believe I ever knew his first name. We weren't really on a first name basis. But I don't see what good it will do you. It was obvious to me that they were just somebody's messenger boys. And you may not want to find out who that somebody was. For your own health, I mean."

The major was enjoying the company and would have been quite happy to entertain MacDara all evening. But Owen had got what he came for and, as graciously as he could, made his exit. As he turned at the green oak door to say goodbye, the major spoke again, his voice tinged with just the right sense of curiosity and bemusement.

"Owen, I do think you people should talk with each other. I told all of this to that young Russian lady from the UN who came to see me a couple of days ago. What was her name? Anna? Nina? Something like that."

Deep River, Connecticut, USA

General Bartley Shields was at his house in Deep River, Connecticut, when he got the call from CIA Director Richard Smallwood.

Smallwood was in New York on company business so it was easy to take the Amtrak train to Essex, a small sleepy town on the Connecticut river, about a twenty minute drive from Shields's house. As he descended from the train, dragging his carryon bag behind him, he didn't recognize the General standing on the other side of the railroad tracks, wearing jeans that were threadbare at the knees and a misshapen Aran sweater that had seen better days.

Bart Shields took his hands out of his pockets, waved a greeting and waited as Dick Smallwood crossed the tracks. A few minutes later they were headed out of Essex in Shields's ten year old Mercedes.

The General's house was deceptive. At first glance it appeared to be a single story ranch but that was only the 'tip of the iceberg'. Once inside the house revealed its secret: three stories clung to the hillside and a second story deck captured the panorama of the Connecticut river and the lush surrounding countryside. The evening was warm and the sky a clear blue, perfect for the table that awaited them out on the deck. Dick Smallwood was a vegetarian and Millie Shields, renowned among the Washington wives for her skill in the kitchen, had prepared a vegetarian goulash with wild rice followed by her special dessert of pears in red wine sauce. Bart already had a bottle of good chablis cooling on ice and proceeded to decant a bottle of Cousino Macoul, his favorite Chilean red.

Listening to Dick Smallwood's superlatives about the 'best vegetarian goulash he'd ever had' and watching her husband circumcise a fresh macanudo cigar, Millie knew it was time to make her exit.

Bart Shields reached for the tall black bottle of Otard VSOP and poured two generous glasses of cognac. They both sipped and savored in silence, lulled into a feeling of wellbeing by Millie's marvellous meal, the excellent cognac and the peaceful vista that stretched beneath them to the horizon. Bart Shields finally broke the silence.

"Dick, I gather you've got something important to tell me."

"That's right, Bart," replied Dick Smallwood as he reached into the inner pocket of his jacket and retrieved a small, black, scuffed and dog-eared notebook. Handing it across the table, he said. "Read the first three pages."

Bart Shields opened the notebook and, looking at the small dense writing, fished his reading glasses from his breast pocket.

It seemed obvious that the writer had wanted to cram as much as possible into the notebook. He read the first page.

This is my insurance policy, life insurance to be exact, and I hope that it never needs to be used. On the other hand, maybe this story can be told when I am dead - to set the record straight, to correct the falsehoods of history. I haven't decided that yet. For now, its only purpose is to keep me alive. This notebook will be made public if I meet an untimely end. Everything recorded here is true.
This I swear by Almighty God.

Signed this 5th day of October, 1969,
John Casey Wainwright.

The next two pages were written in the same dense style so it took Shields's full concentration. His cognac sat untouched and the ashes on his cigar had outgrown the ashtray and toppled onto the table. But he was oblivious to all of that. Snatches of Wainwright's 'insurance policy' seared themselves into his brain.

'I was there when Director Dulles ordered the assassination of Patrice Lumumba'...'we were protecting the billions we had invested in the Congo's mineral resources'......'Helms has detroyed all the documents'.........'my words written here will be all that survive'............'it was the decision to take out Dag Hammarskjold that has destroyed me'............' *Washington and Moscow are in collusion'............*

Shields read the last paragraph at the bottom of page three before closing the notebook and looking across at Dick Smallwood: *'on the following pages I have recorded the key events and decisions covering CIA involvement in Africa. The dates and locations of each event are accurate. I have identified the people who participated, including those who made the decisions and gave the orders. Where I was present I have admitted that. Where I was culpable I have said so. I am not using this to exonerate myself.'*

"Wainwright! Didn't he disappear from the face of the earth? Just like Judge Crater!," asked Shields, rhetorically.

"Yes! He disappeared alright. About a year after he wrote this. He left the company and just dropped out of sight. It was news for a couple of weeks until it was pushed off the page," replied Smallwood.

"Rumor had it that he was in the running for Director once upon a time," said Shields, seeking confirmation of his recollection.

"I believe if the timing had been right for the appointment of a Director from within the company, he'd have made it. Jack Wainwright had the inside track," confirmed Smallwood.

"How did you get this notebook? And what happened to him?" asked Bart Shields.

"I'll take your last question first, Bart," said Dick Smallwood, as Shields reached over and refilled his cognac glass, pushing aside a weak protest.

"Around the time Wainwright was writing this he was also getting ill. Severe allergic reactions. Heart palpitations. Rashes. Lupus."

"Lupus! I thought that was a woman's disease," interjected Shields.

"That's what I thought too, Bart. So I've educated myself on the subject. Apparently a small percentage of men also suffer from the disease. There's basically two forms of it, systemic and drug induced. Some people have gotten lupus from medication, especially drugs that are used to control heart arrhythmia. Nobody seems to know what causes systemic lupus. There was no agreement in Wainwright's case and he had not been on any heart medicine. Some people believed that his ailments were stress related. Others, less kind, said that it was all in his mind, that it was psychological, self-induced. At any rate, he got worse and worse until he couldn't work any more. This was all kept quiet by the company, of course."

"What happened to him?"

"Well, he was finally diagnosed with something called MCS, although most of the medical profession will not acknowledge that there is such a disease."

"What's MCS?"

"Multiple chemical sensitivities. Wainwright had developed severe allergic and immune system reaction to anything and everything that was remotely chemical. And, in our modern world, that means practically everything."

Smallwood was caught up in the drama of his story and Shields noted that he had barely touched the last cognac he'd given him. Getting up from the table he stretched himself, looked out over the Connecticut river in the far distance, and then turned towards Shields. "But we think he may still be alive although no one, not even his family, has heard from him in at least ten years. He quit the agency, left everything and everyone and went in search of a place that was free from the poisons that were killing him. He has one daughter and she last heard from him ten years ago. From Fort Davis, Texas."

"Fort Davis? That's as far west in Texas as you can get?"

"It sure is!," said Smallwood, sitting down again and taking a sip of his cognac.

"Now to answer your first question. I'm afraid we got his notebook by devious means. We discovered that he had instructed his daughter to turn it over to the Washington Post after his death. The rest was simple. We faked a death certificate and convinced her that he was dead. Then we waited. About a week later she called the Washington Post. She didn't know that we were intercepting her calls. So it was easy to set up a 'sting' operation and pose as the Washington Post. She had no reason to suspect anything so she turned over the notebook to us." There was the suggestion of a smile on Smallwood's face, more like the look of satisfaction on the face of a cat that had just swallowed a mouse.

"Jeez, Dick! You don't give a shit about the laws of the land, do you?" Shields exclaimed.

Smallwood didn't answer that. Shields picked up Wainwright's notebook again, opened it and said, softly, almost to himself. "There's one thing that I must know. Who ordered the assassination of Dag Hammarskjold?" He paged through the notebook, almost reluctant to find the answer. When he did he read it without breathing, then he sank deeper into his chair deflating like a large balloon that has just burst. Smallwood looked at him.

"Now you know why I had to see you here. Away from Washington."

"Who else knows this?" asked Shields.

"Only you and I. And Wainwright. If he's still alive," Smallwood replied.

"Well, if he is alive he may not stay alive much longer. We'd better find him fast. I suggest we get MacDara on this immediately."

"I agree. Where is he?"

"He and Leslie Scott are in New York. Nyack. They went to talk to Kearns.

You can find out when WHO KILLED HAMMARSKJOLD? will be published by visiting Pat Mullan's website at <u>www.patmullan.com</u>

Childhood Hills

Childhood Hills

By Pat Mullan

A reader from United States of America, 18 November, 2000
★★★★★ **(on Amazon.co.uk)**

I found this book of poetry to be beautiful, touching, and approachable. It had me in tears, and laughing, all within the space of a few lines. It covers childhood, early working years, family, social-consciousness, etc. all from a Northern Irish perspective - but highly applicable to any life, anywhere.
I highly recommend it!!

Konstantin Chopine from Kaliningrad, Russia, writes (on Amazon.com): ★★★★★

"I found most of your poems really interesting and capturing, some being moody, but colorful and vivid. You just revived my long lost interest in reading literature, poems in particular."

★★★★★ Childhood Hills, March 6, 2001
Reviewer: A reader from **Sag Harbor, NY USA**

As a painter, I found that Mr. Mullan can paint with words canvases that can compare to any paintings I've seen.

ABOUT THE AUTHOR

Pat Mullan was born in Ireland and has lived in England, Canada and the USA. He spent two years with the US Army in Japan and Korea. Formerly a banker, he is a graduate of Northwestern University and the State University of New York where he studied creative writing. He lives in Connemara, in the west of Ireland, with his Scottish wife Jean and their two young daughters. His book of poetry and prose, *CHILDHOOD HILLS,* is available on Amazon.com, Amazon.co.uk, Borders.com, Barnes&Noble.com and on order through *Barnes & Noble* bookstores nationwide. He is currently at work on a new novel, *WHO KILLED HAMMARSKJOLD?*

Printed in the United Kingdom
by Lightning Source UK Ltd.
1337